Also b

THE TATTERED & TORN SERIES

Tattered Stars
Falling Embers
Hidden Waters
Shattered Sea
Fractured Sky

SPARROW FALLS

Fragile Sanctuary
Delicate Escape
Broken Harbor
Beautiful Exile
Chasing Shelter
Secret Haven

THE LOST & FOUND SERIES

Whispers of You
Echoes of You
Glimmers of You
Shadows of You
Ashes of You

THE WRECKED SERIES

Reckless Memories
Perfect Wreckage
Wrecked Palace
Reckless Refuge
Beneath the Wreckage

THE SUTTER LAKE SERIES

Beautifully Broken Pieces
Beautifully Broken Life
Beautifully Broken Spirit
Beautifully Broken Control
Beautifully Broken Redemption

STANDALONE NOVELS

Further to Fall
All the Missing Pieces

all the Missing PIECES

CATHERINE COWLES

sourcebooks casablanca

Cover design by Stephanie Gafron/Sourcebooks
Cover images © Skylines/Shutterstock, underworld/Shutterstock, Nazarii_Neshcherenskyi/Shutterstock, HelenField/Shutterstock, YamabikaY/Shutterstock, Abbie/Shutterstock, fokke baarssen/Shutterstock, varuna/Shutterstock, Rileysmithphotography.com/Shutterstock, ioanna_alexa/Shutterstock

Published by Sourcebooks Casablanca, an imprint of Sourcebooks
P.O. Box 4410, Naperville, Illinois 60567-4410
(630) 961-3900
sourcebooks.com

Cataloging-in-Publication data is on file with the Library of Congress.

Printed and bound in the United States of America.
LSC 10 9 8 7 6 5 4 3 2 1

For all those who have lost someone they loved beyond measure.

Don't let the pain harden you.
Let it become your reminder that you experienced
the most beautiful thing this world has to offer.

And for my dad.
Who would've gotten such a thrill out
of seeing my words in bookstores.

You taught me all the best lessons.
I carry them, and you, with me always.

Prologue
Ridley

"You look like I'm dragging you to the gallows," I said, glancing over at my sister as I headed down the dirt path toward the crowd below.

She was my mirror image in every way yet somehow managed to be my complete opposite. While my blond hair was a wild tangle of waves, hers was tamed into sleek curls. I'd opted for a favorite sundress and flip-flops, and Avery was in khaki shorts and a white cap-sleeved blouse.

My twin sent me a droll look. "I think I'd take the gallows over the Greeks' bonfire."

I rolled my eyes. "You need to go to one party before you graduate."

Avery let out a huff of air, smoothing hair that was already perfectly in place. "I've been to plenty of parties. I'm just not into frat boys chanting, '*Chug*!'"

"They do look like overgrown Neanderthals half the time, but it's part of the quintessential college experience. Wouldn't want you to miss out on mocking their keg-stand form."

A laugh bubbled out of Avery's mouth. More like a giggle than anything. A sound that reminded me of childhood. Of countless nights spent in our room at home, whispering about anything and everything as we stared up at the glow-in-the-dark stars on the ceiling. The ones over my bed were a chaotic spray with no rhyme or reason, but Avery's were arranged to perfectly replicate the Orion constellation.

She knocked her shoulder lightly into mine, grinning. "I do love to critique a boy-man."

I couldn't help but snort. "We should've stolen those numbered cards from the gym that they use for gymnastics meets."

Avery shook her head. "I want to believe you're joking but I know you're not."

I shrugged. "Gotta use those team captain keys for something fun."

She stared at me as if I'd sprouted another head. Avery took responsibility seriously, from her classes to her role as captain of the women's lacrosse team. Her dedication had led to great things: graduating with honors, a scholarship to an incredible physical therapy graduate program that would start in the fall, and a state championship for her team.

But me? I was still waffling. Unsure of what I wanted to do, I'd ended up majoring in journalism with a minor in environmental studies. Neither were especially calling to me. But it wouldn't matter soon. I'd have to take whatever job I managed to land.

Avery shifted, her whole body turning toward mine as she instantly read the change in my mood. "What's wrong?"

I shook my head, forcing a smile. "Nothing. Just thinking about how tomorrow's the end of an era." We'd walk across that stage and nothing would ever be the same.

My sister's face softened as she looped her arm through mine and musical strains from the party below wafted up to us. "Come to Chicago with me. We can share the apartment, and you can get a job in the city."

There was a part of me that wanted that. To keep things just as they were. Avery and I had been together since the womb, and this was the first time we'd ever be separated. Just thinking about it made an ache take root in my chest. But I knew Chicago wasn't for me. "I'd feel like a rat in a maze," I admitted. I craved wide-open spaces, fresh air, and nature. Not smog and honking horns.

"There are a bunch of lake communities not far away from the city. Maybe one of those," Avery suggested.

"Maybe," I echoed. But she knew the word lacked any real commitment. Because I simply wasn't sure what my purpose was.

I tugged on her arm, quickening our pace. "Come on. No future-talk for one night. You know Mom and Dad will be on me the moment graduation ends."

Avery sighed. "Lead me down the plank, Captain Hook."

I laughed and picked up my pace. Nestled in the Arizona mountains with plenty of outdoor activities and on the outskirts of a picturesque town that had lots of restaurants and bars for us to frequent, the small private college a couple of hours outside Phoenix had been an idyllic setting to get an education.

I'd miss it. The comfortability of it. The beauty. But I itched to see new places too. Different landscapes and terrains.

Music and voices got louder as we rounded a curve in the path and the party came into view. There were a handful of houses a few frats rented and a large bonfire in the center. Beyond it all was only trees—that and the faint outline of a mountain in the moonlight. That called to me more than the party, but I knew before long the buzz of the people and the music would catch hold.

Just as we approached the crowd, a handful of guys began chanting, "Chug! Chug! Chug!" as they lifted someone I recognized from the men's lacrosse team in the air and someone else held the tap to his mouth.

Avery sent me a sidelong look. "Three at best. His arms are already shaking."

I barked out a laugh. "Hey, he's one of yours. A jock. A lacrosse player at that."

She shook her head. "Gonna have to talk to Coach Carter about upping their conditioning. This is just pathetic."

"You show no mercy."

Avery grinned back at me. "Damn straight."

An arm slid along my shoulders as lips grazed my temple. "Hey, baby."

I tilted my head back to take in the familiar face. Amber eyes framed with dark lashes. Light-brown hair kissed with lighter strands thanks to all his time in the sun playing tennis. I smiled up at Jared, leaning in to meet his mouth.

The kiss was all warmth and comfort. Easy and no pressure. I let it deepen, hoping for the spark of *more*. Hoping for fire to catch. It didn't come.

Jared pulled back, kissing the tip of my nose before glancing at my sister. "Hey, Avs. This is a surprise."

"Granting my sister her one final college wish."

Jared laughed. "Definite heaven points for that."

Avery's lips twitched. "I see Carly. I'm going to go say hi."

"Remember," I called as she walked away. "No drinks from random men, just say no to drugs, and no candy from strangers in vans."

She flipped me off and went right on walking toward her teammate.

Jared chuckled, the sound skating over me in a familiar vibration. But there was no pleasant shiver, no hint of *more*. "You really do work miracles getting her to one of these things," he said.

"I feel like we should probably follow her. Who knows what sort of trouble she could get into?"

He pulled me against his chest, arms wrapping around me. "Or you could stay here with me."

I tipped my head back to take in his beautiful face. "I could."

I let the buzz of people and music pull me in, the heat of the fire and the excitement of tomorrow. Jared led me toward a group of people—a few guys he roomed with from the tennis team and their girlfriends—I'd become friends with over the past year and a half.

We chatted about graduation plans and trips some of them had planned for after the ceremony. Easy, light, but with the undercurrent of possibility.

Jared's lips ghosted against my ear. "Have you thought about New York?"

My stomach bottomed out. Jared's life had been planned out for him since the moment his dad found out he was a boy, which meant majoring in finance and going to work for his father's hedge fund in the city. Even tennis was on a list of appropriate choices for hobbies, the others being golf and racquetball.

At school, Jared was a bit more free. Hiking with me or taking trips to the lake. But every time he was in his father's presence, that changed. He colored within the lines.

"New York isn't for me." I said the words softly, trying to ease into them, as if that would keep them from stinging.

Jared's jaw hardened, that narrow muscle along it fluttering. "You don't know unless you try."

"I know." The two words lost a bit of the softness. They weren't harsh, but they were firm.

His eyes flashed with a flicker of heat, temper. "Then you're sure about me too, aren't you?"

"Jer, don't do this tonight."

His back teeth ground together. "And when exactly am I supposed to have this conversation? As you're bailing out of town right after graduation? I've been trying to talk to you about this for months."

A tightness settled in my chest, squeezing my lungs. "I just wanted us to enjoy these past few weeks. Not get into anything too heavy."

Jared stared at me for a long moment, jaw working back and forth. "And *heavy* means you're done. Which you've probably known for months. But instead of growing the fuck up and telling me that, you just avoided it. Thanks for that."

"Jer—" I reached for him, but he ducked out of my grasp.

"At least you don't have to have the conversation now. We're done." He took off, moving away from the party and toward the path that would lead to the road where everyone parked. All I could do was stare after him.

An itch spread over me, my skin feeling too tight for my body. Because Jared was right. I had avoided it. Hadn't wanted to hurt him or see the betrayal in his eyes. And my avoidance of that had only caused more pain.

A hand landed on my shoulder, and I jumped, whirling.

Lana, the girlfriend of one of Jared's roommates, looked back at me with kind eyes. "You okay?"

Her gaze tracked down my cheeks, and it was only then I realized I was crying. I quickly wiped at my face. "I'm an asshole."

Lana's dark eyes hardened. "Don't talk about my friend like that."

I wanted to smile but couldn't quite get my mouth to obey. Instead the truth tumbled out. "I hurt him."

"Oh, babe." She pulled me into a hug. "He just couldn't see there was no way this was going to work."

I sniffed as she released me. "But you saw."

Lana gave me a gentle smile, the dark skin around her eyes crinkling with the action. "Two different worlds. And it wasn't like he was offering to meet you in the middle. I love Jared, but it's his way or the highway. He's never once thought about going against his dad's wishes."

Something about Lana's words eased the worst of the guilt. Because she was right. There was no asking what *I* wanted. There was only asking me to join him in what *he* wanted. "It was never going to work."

Lana gave my arm a squeeze. "I don't think either of you really wanted it to."

"It wasn't that light-your-soul-on-fire love. It was comfortable love," I admitted.

"You deserve that burn-everything-to-the-ground love." She sent me a sympathetic look. "But that doesn't mean saying goodbye to this love is any easier. So what's it going to be? Get shit-faced and dance to forget everything? Go home and stuff our faces with ice cream while cursing his name?"

My lips twitched at that. "I think the latter. But I need to find Avery."

Lana looked over her shoulder. "I saw her with the lax girls earlier. Let me just tell Connor I'm going with you two."

"You don't have to—"

Lana sent me a look that had me snapping my mouth closed. "Don't say stupid things. Of course I'm coming with you."

A fresh wave of tears hit my eyes but for an entirely different reason. "I'm so damned lucky to have you."

She grinned. "Damn straight. Now come on."

Lana hooked her arm through mine, leading us through the crowd. We paused for her to tell Connor she was heading out. He sent me a concerned look that had him heading for the path himself, but in search of his friend. That was good. Jared would have someone to talk it out with. And he deserved that.

I scanned the crowd, looking for that familiar head of blond hair, but I didn't see Avery anywhere. She wouldn't have bailed without telling me, even if she'd wanted to.

"I don't see her. Do you?" Lana asked.

I shook my head. "There's Carly."

We hurried over to Avery's teammate.

"Hey," I called over the music. "Have you seen Avs?"

"She's here. Went to get a drink a little while ago, maybe fifteen minutes?"

I frowned as I looked toward the makeshift bar. It was covered with liquor, soda, and bottles of water, but there was no Avery in sight.

"Maybe she went to get a jacket from the car? It's getting cold," Lana suggested.

"Maybe," I echoed. We shared the slightly beat-up sedan, and she had her own key.

"Come on," Lana said. "Let's go check."

I nodded absently, searching the crowd as she led me through it. The music grated on my ears now, making my head pound. Lana clicked on her phone's flashlight, illuminating our path. The same tree-lined trail that had seemed so innocent on my way in now cast ominous shadows.

We walked quickly up the hill and toward the road, but just as we were about to get out of the forest, something caught my eye. "Wait." I grabbed Lana's arm, my throat constricting as blood pounded in my ears.

It was the tiny silver lacrosse sticks formed in an X that had caught the light. My heart thudded, painfully slow and trippingly fast all at the same time.

I bent, grabbing the custom key ring I'd gotten Avs for Christmas two years ago. A sick feeling settled over me as I saw the *A* in the center of one of the lacrosse sticks.

When I turned it over, something else caught the light. A dark-red substance. Sticky almost.

"Oh God," Lana whispered. "Is that blood?"

And my whole world crumbled.

Chapter One
Ridley

Five years later

I LEANED INTO THE CURVE OF THE ROAD, MY RESTORED VW Kombi van hugging the bend perfectly. Bessie and I had been together for over three years, and I knew just the speed at which she could take turns like this one. I'd spent every cent of my savings to bring her back to life and customize her insides. From the kitchen and seating area to my office in the back to the pop-up bedroom in the roof. And who could forget the cat tower for Tater.

As if she could sense my thoughts drifting to her, she stretched in her bed on the dash, leaning over to lightly nip my fingers on the wheel.

"We're almost there. No need for tooth hugs," I chastised.

She meowed in answer. But it sounded more like a demand. And once she got started, there was no stopping her.

But Tater's *talking* only made me smile as the road curved again. The two-lane highway was blanketed by a wall of massive trees on either side, but they didn't make me feel claustrophobic. They made me feel free.

My work brought me to cities occasionally, but I did my best to pick locations off the beaten path. Ones where I had access to my drugs of choice: mountains, forests, deserts, or bodies of water of any kind. They were the only places I found comfort now. The only places I could find peace for a fleeting moment. In nature and in my work.

As if the thought summoned him, my phone rang out with the *Jaws* theme song. It was a good thing my boss didn't know this was his ringtone, because he wouldn't have been pleased.

I tapped *accept* on the screen, choosing speakerphone. "Hey, Baker."

"Where are you?" he clipped.

Never any pleasantries with my producer. Always in a rush. In his book, time was money and he wasn't going to waste a dime. "About five minutes out from Shady Cove."

I heard a chair squeak over the line as Baker sighed, and I could picture my boss in his office on Sunset Boulevard, looking out over Los Angeles and wondering how he ended up with such an obstinate podcaster under his umbrella. "You could keep going another few hours north and take that case of the missing mom of three."

My stomach twisted. That mother deserved her justice too. But I needed this case in Shady Cove. This woman. This set of circumstances. "I can look into that one next."

I'd have to give Baker a win after back-to-back passion projects. But I'd gotten used to that cadence. Two for me, one for him.

He sighed again, as if disappointed in me. "I don't get what's so interesting to you about this one. Bungled abduction. The girl got away."

That itch skated over my skin again, the need to move, to roll down my window and breathe the fresh mountain air. "Which means I'll have a victim to interview. How often do we get that?"

Baker made a humming noise in the back of his throat as he

mulled that over. I knew what called to him. Any angle that would push the numbers. Subscribers, downloads, listens. The hope of going viral on TikTok. Anything that would up what he could charge advertisers.

"You could have a point."

I went in for the kill. "They never found the perp. Maybe we get lucky and nab him."

I'd been doing this for over four years now. I'd covered over a dozen cases. I'd made headway in almost all of them, but I'd broken three wide-open. One had left a man doing twenty to life for murdering his wife, the other had a man on trial for the abduction and assault of eight women in Wyoming, and the final one had meant a life ended in a shootout when a man opened fire on the FBI instead of being brought in for questioning in the disappearance of a college student—they'd found her body in his basement.

"I want you to start posting tonight," Baker ordered.

I shook off the chilling memories and did a mock salute even though he couldn't see me. "You got it."

He hung up without a goodbye, just another waste of time for him. But I didn't mind. Anything to get off the call quicker. And I didn't mind the social posts either because that forward progress on a case came from getting the community on your side. Activating them to become a force of amateur sleuths.

That public involvement had its downsides for sure. False leads and people getting in my way. The occasional safety concern. But I took precautions. People didn't know who I was, not really. I used my middle name, Sawyer, as my last on the podcast. And I never spoke about what had spurred me into the world of true crime to begin with—knowing what it was like not to have the answers you needed and feeling like no one gave a damn.

I was careful about more than the links to my past. I was

cautious about the here and now too. I never posted around where I was staying. Never took photos or videos of my vehicle. Bessie was unique after all. Her teal-and-white paint job, the paddleboard fastened to her side, the cat almost always perched in the window.

Since taking care with those safety measures, I hadn't ever had someone find where I was staying. Probably because anyone interested enough to look checked hotels or short-term rentals. But I was always staying in Bessie.

It was necessary. Because with that first breakthrough case, there'd come attention. Just over a million followers on Instagram. One and a half on TikTok. And we averaged over two million monthly downloads of the show between all platforms. It was a community. There were some kooks for sure. There were some folks who thought they were the next Sherlock Holmes. But mostly there were people who wanted justice for those who had been forgotten.

They were my people.

It might have been because they too had lost someone. Or maybe they had been victims themselves, unable to speak up in the moment or even now. Or they could simply be empathetic humans who wanted the world to be better than it was.

No matter the reason, I was grateful for them.

As the road straightened out then dipped down a bit, I caught sight of a sign in the distance. I could see the white letters spelling out *Welcome to Shady Cove*. The paint was chipped in places, worn by weather and time.

I quickly tapped the camera app on my phone from where it was in the charging dock and hit record. People loved the rolling-into-town footage that meant I was on a new case. As I got closer to the sign, I could see more of its details. The waves that marked the large lake the Northern Californian community sat on, the trees carved into the wood and painted a dark green for the surrounding forests. All of it aged, raw, real. And followed by *Population 2,033*.

Small. Almost minuscule.

But I knew that the most horrific things could happen in the places you least expected.

Chapter Two
Ridley

I PULLED INTO THE DOWNTOWN OF SHADY COVE, MY camera app still rolling. My listeners loved getting a feel for the place I was working, and they would look for clues everywhere. I'd gotten used to small towns across America. They were different than the suburbs of Dayton, Ohio, where I'd been raised, where I'd returned for one torturous year after Avery had gone missing, where *Sounds Like Serial* had been born in that time when I so desperately needed purpose.

A true small town had a feel. People knew instantly when you were an outsider. They'd welcome you in but with caution just the same. They'd tell you where to eat and what sights to see, but they wouldn't open up about the underbelly of their community until they trusted you.

And I needed that underbelly.

That was where the secrets lay. Where revelations came from. Where the hidden truths needed to be exposed. But often those truths were ugly, and there were others who'd do anything to keep them buried.

You wouldn't guess that by the images greeting me as I drove down Old Miner Road, the main drag through town. It looked exactly like the name suggested, as if the town was straight out of gold-rush times. The building facades screamed *Old West*. A mixture of wood and stone but with the exaggerated fronts that looked more like the set of a Western than an actual town.

"We might need a Clint Eastwood movie marathon," I said to Tater as I reached over to scratch her ears. She purred and then bit me.

I scanned the row of buildings lining the main street. There was a quaint hotel, a bar, restaurants, and tourist shops. When I spotted a small grocery store, I flicked on my blinker. I pulled into an open parking spot and grinned. "This has to be a good sign," I said as I took in the coffee shop next to the grocery store.

The sign read *Cowboy Coffee & Café*. There was a cowboy boot painted below the script. I hoped Cowboy Coffee didn't mean that instant crap brewed over a campfire, but judging by how full the café was, I doubted it.

I put Bessie in park and switched on the battery-operated air-conditioning to keep Princess Tater comfortable. It was only in the seventies, but the sun was shining, which meant the van could be baking in a matter of minutes. "You going to behave while I'm gone?"

Tater sat up, exposing her three-legged status, and meowed at me. But the meow was more like a yell, and I knew exactly what she wanted.

"Oh fine." I opened the console and pulled out her toy mouse, stuffing it with a dash of catnip. She instantly swatted it out of my hand and onto her bed like a star batter for the Yankees. "This is why we should've said no to drugs. Makes you aggressive."

She just let out another yelling meow in my direction.

Chuckling, I reached behind my seat for the reusable grocery bags I had stowed there. I grabbed those, my phone, keys, and wallet, and hopped out of the van. Every inch of the vehicle had purpose. From my makeshift podcast studio in the back, to my paddleboard storage on the side, to the bike rack on the rear hatch that held my e-bike for getting around town in good weather. It might've been small, but it was home.

I snapped a couple of quick shots of the town, making sure I got some good ones of Cowboy Coffee. I'd be spending a decent amount of time there since it had been where Emerson Sinclair worked after school when she'd been abducted. But first, groceries. Nobody needed me getting hangry.

A bell jingled as I opened the door to The Hitching Post, the sound just a bit rusty as if the bell had been there for decades. A woman looked up from her newspaper, tanned skin crinkled with age and her hair more silver than black. "Afternoon."

I smiled at her, not too wide but not too hesitant either. Over the past four years, I'd learned that people didn't trust overly smiley, but they also didn't like rude. "Afternoon."

I took in the small grocery store. It was packed to the gills with shelves overflowing with items. But it looked like they had a good array. Plenty of the organic, healthier fare I favored. After my first six months on the road had been largely fueled by fast food and vending machines, and one too many sugar crashes and stomachaches, I'd made the switch.

My first stop in any town was a grocery store to get supplies that were easy to prepare. Bessie's fridge wasn't large, but I'd gotten good at the Tetris of putting items away.

I could feel the woman's eyes on me as I wandered the aisles, grabbing a seven-grain bread for sandwiches, some almonds, ingredients for my favorite spring vegetable pasta. When I reached the table of desserts, I let a true grin stretch across my face.

Devil's food cupcakes with vanilla filling. There was no way I was passing those by. Snatching them up, I carried everything to the counter.

There was amusement in the woman's deep-brown eyes now. "Cupcake fan?"

"Baked-goods-of-all-forms fan."

She chuckled as she began scanning my items and punching in codes for produce. I waited, not pushing the conversation. People got skittish when you pushed. Finally the woman spoke again. "Just passing through?"

I glanced out the windows at the front of the store. "I'm going to stay awhile actually. It's beautiful here. Heard there are some epic trails in the mountains."

The woman nodded. "Sure are." She studied me for a moment. "You're not hiking alone, are you?"

My lips twitched. "I've got a sat phone and bear spray."

Her mouth thinned as she muttered something under her breath I could barely make out. "Dead tourists. Just what we need." She punched in a final code and read off the total.

I tapped my card to the reader and took my bags as my head dipped to a name tag on her shirt. "Thanks, Mira."

She simply grunted. "See you around if you don't become bear kibble."

I couldn't help but laugh. "I'll be sure to let you know I'm still alive and kickin'."

Some people got too fixated on that. So obsessed with health and safety that they forgot to truly *live.*

A memory of my mom's pale face, stricken with panic, shot through my memory.

"You're leaving now? It's dark. Anything could happen." Her fingers twisted in her sweater. They'd become bony over the last several months because she barely ate enough to sustain herself.

The woman in front of me was barely recognizable now, but still my heart cracked for her. "Mom, it's an open-mic night at the coffee shop. I'll be home before ten."

She shook her head so fast she looked like a bobblehead doll whose head was moving in the wrong direction. "No. You have to stay. Anything could happen."

"Sheila," my dad began.

"I said no.*" Mom's voice cracked like a whip in the entryway of my childhood house.*

But it wasn't home. Not anymore. And I wasn't sure it ever would be again.

I shook off the memory, pushing open the door and letting the sunshine stream down on me, baking my already golden skin. I tipped my face up to it, soaking in even more. This was my comfort and my drug. The sun and the fresh air wrapping around me.

While my mom had turned inward, I'd done the opposite. My need to get out and experience everything could turn clawing at times, but there was no way around it. Because I wasn't just living for me anymore. I had to experience everything Avery would never get to.

I took in one last beat of the sunshine, dropped my bags in the van, and headed for the coffee shop. There was no bell over the door of this shop, but I understood why when I stepped inside. The place was two-thirds full, and it was after two. It was likely they did a steady stream of business all day long.

My gaze swept the café, taking in the vibe and trying to picture Emerson Sinclair here. The only photos I'd been able to find of her were those from when she was sixteen, around the time she'd been abducted, but that was almost ten years ago now. Within the year or so after, she'd become a ghost. No social media, no public job listing, not even an email I could find. The only confirmation I had of her still living in the area was a deed on a house just outside of town.

But the photos I'd seen of her painted a completely different picture than someone hiding away from the world. She looked carefree, her blond hair in a tumble atop her head as she dove for a shot on the tennis court or her hazel eyes shining as her head tipped back midlaugh with some friends. I could see her here, chatting with customers, weaving through antique-looking dark wood tables set amongst black-and-white photos that kept with the cowboy theme. Just like so many other teenagers with after-school jobs.

"Welcome to Cowboy Coffee," a voice boomed from behind the counter.

I turned to the source of it and found a middle-aged man with a ruddy complexion and reddish hair to match. "Thank you." Crossing to the counter, I took in the menu painted on the chalkboard above. One side held drinks and the other food.

"What are ya after today? Caffeine or calories?" the man asked, grinning wide and revealing chewing gum between his teeth.

I sent him an answering smile, reading that he wouldn't be put off by it. "How about both?"

"Gal after my own heart. Haven't seen you in here before; want some suggestions?"

"I'd love insight from an expert."

He chuckled, turning slightly so he could take in the board and me. "Since I own the joint, I'm about as expert as you can get."

Owner. Good to know. I needed to do a little research to see if the café had changed hands since Emerson had worked here.

"Hit me with it," I said.

"Can't go wrong with an iced hazelnut latte now that it's getting warmer. On the light side of grub, the Kale Krunch salad, or heavier, the prosciutto panini."

My smile only grew. "I do have a weakness for hazelnut. I'll take that and the Kale Krunch to go, but I'll be back for that panini."

"Staying in town?" the man asked as he rang me up.

"Camping." I didn't tell him where. I wasn't an idiot. The fewer people who had that information the better.

He groaned. "You're more hard-core than I am. I'm partial to hot showers and my own bed."

I didn't bother telling him that I had both thanks to Bessie. "Fair enough. But I get some beautiful sunrises."

"They aren't too shabby from right here in town."

"I bet." Shady Cove, while getting plenty of tree cover, had stunning mountain views. Since no one was behind me in line, I didn't hurry off. "You live here long?"

"All my life," the man said and then extended a hand. "Ezra."

I took the offered hand and shook. "Ridley. Nice to meet you."

"You too. Looking for local recs?"

"Always." That was one of my favorite perks of my job. The way I'd set up my podcast, *Sounds Like Serial*, not only did I deep-dive unsolved cases; I got to deep-dive a town. Finding the best restaurants and hiking spots, the insider secrets, meant I really got to experience each and every place I worked.

"Well, good news is you've already found the best coffee in town."

I laughed. "I can see by your crowd."

Ezra's chest puffed up with pride. "Damn straight. The Whiskey Barrel is your spot for harder drinks. Joe's Pizza for Italian. And surprisingly, we've got a decent Thai place down the block too."

I raised a brow at that. "I'll be testing out all of the above."

A teenage girl came out from the kitchen and smiled at me as she handed me an iced drink and a bag. "Here you go. Enjoy."

"Thanks," I said and then turned to Ezra. "And thank you for the tips." I took a sip of the coffee and grinned. "I'll be back for more of these."

Ezra tapped the counter twice. "See you soon."

Cowboy Coffee was my in. The town hub. There were always one or two in a community. A place where people gathered, where information flowed. And that was exactly where I needed to be.

As I stepped outside, a shrill, raised voice said, "Colter Brooks, I have known you since you were in diapers. Do not give me the runaround."

My brows lifted as I took in a woman who looked to be in her seventies. Her wiry gray hair hung around her shoulders in wild curls, and she wore a T-shirt emblazoned with a cow, and above it read, *Friends Not Food.*

I couldn't see the man, not his face anyway. But that didn't stop me from staring. He was tall, likely bordering on six foot five. But that height took a back seat to shoulders that were so broad they made the tan shirt he wore pull taut across them, something likely helped by the fact that his arms appeared to be crossed as he looked down at the woman.

"Celia—" The man's words were cut off by the woman's shrill tone, but I was still stuck on the single word he'd spoken. His voice. Deep with a rasp that spoke of whiskey and dark promises.

"That cat is going to die of heatstroke!" the woman screeched.

Her words had me snapping out of my lust-induced haze. Hell, I needed to get laid if broad shoulders and a single husky word was doing me in.

Save the Cows thrust a hand toward my van. "That poor creature is trapped inside."

I followed her hand toward my VW, where Tater was staring down at her with a look of complete disdain on her face.

"It's barely seventy degrees out," the man argued.

"Seventy degrees out here means that cat could be *cooking* in that van!"

Tater, clearly affronted by the idea, shifted her weight back so she was balanced on her hind legs. She snagged her nearly decapitated mouse with one paw and threw it at the window.

"See," Celia demanded. "He's trying to break free. Now get out one of those Jaws of Life things and break this baby out."

The man was silent for a long moment, and then he let out a sigh that sounded as if it carried the weight of the world with it. "We don't use the Jaws of Life for a cat rescue."

He shifted then, his body canting to the side slightly. The movement revealed two things. Thick scruff lining an angular jaw, with a muscle lining it that was currently fluttering wildly. And a shiny silver star pinned to his shirt.

The hot guy was a hot cop. Even more interesting.

But hot cop had said the wrong thing. Celia's entire form puffed up as her face turned a mottled shade of red. "This is a living, breathing being. He should be treated with respect. He is worth saving."

With that she stormed toward a trash can that looked as if it weighed twice as much as she did. Even though it was bolted to the ground, she started yanking on it with all her might.

"Celia," Hot Cop growled. "Do not make me arrest you."

"I've done my time before. I'm not afraid to pay for what's right."

"You chained yourself to a dead tree that was threatening to fall on the library," the man gritted out. "That's not exactly Nobel Prize–worthy."

I bit the inside of my cheek to keep from laughing. I would've let the show go on because it was an epic one, but I didn't want the woman to hurt herself. So I cleared my throat. "Excuse me."

Celia paused her trash can efforts, and the man turned slowly, his eyes narrowing on me. I just smiled in response, giving a little wave. "Hi. This is my van."

"You left your cat inside to *fry*?" Celia demanded.

"Tater has AC. She's just fine."

Celia released the trash can and straightened. "AC?"

I nodded.

The woman's entire demeanor shifted. "I've heard about this. You can get a separate system for your vehicle that doesn't run on gas."

"Mine runs on solar," I explained, gesturing to the panels on top of my van.

She beamed. "I'd love to get the name—"

"Celia," the man growled.

She huffed out a breath. "Just relax, Colt. The cat's fine. Take a chill pill."

Colt's jaw turned to granite. "A chill pill?"

I bit my bottom lip to keep from laughing.

"You call me out here, demanding I break into a vehicle. Something that could've cost the citizens of this county more than I want to think about. And you want me to…chill?"

Celia shrugged. "No harm, no foul."

A laugh did escape this time.

Colt's gaze cut to me. "You think this is funny?"

It wasn't a question but I answered anyway. "A little."

His eyes narrowed. Eyes that were a brown so dark they almost looked black. Storm eyes. And they should've warned me about the thunder incoming. "I could've bashed your window in. Your irresponsibility could've prevented me from being on a call out where there was an *actual* emergency. The least you could do is leave a note saying the damned cat was fine."

I stiffened, hackles rising. I had a healthy respect for law enforcement, when they were doing their job. I appreciated that they were often underpaid to do the impossible, just like teachers and nurses. What I didn't appreciate was this too-attractive-for-his-own-good jerk suggesting that I was an idiot.

I crossed to the front of my van and tapped on the window. "You mean a note like this one?"

I knew it was sitting on the dash since I'd made it myself. It had paw prints drawn along the border and said, *Tater has food, water, and AC. She is very happy to stare down at you in supreme judgment from her perch.*

Celia let out a cackling laugh. "She does have a good judgy face."

"Celia…"

The growl was back again and I hated the fact that it skated over my skin in a pleasant shiver.

"All right, all right," she said and then waved at my cat. "See you around, Tater."

"I fucking hope not," Colt muttered.

I choked on another laugh as Celia hurried down the sidewalk.

Colt turned slowly to me. Those dark eyes flashed, and I swore there was a hint of mischief in them. "You know, this van should be parked in oversized parking. It's not."

My eyes narrowed on him. "It's a van, not a monster truck."

He shrugged, making what I saw now was a sheriff's department uniform pull taut over a muscled chest. "Maybe so, but I'm guessing it meets the weight requirements to be ticketed and towed."

I gaped at him. "You wouldn't."

"ID please."

Chapter Three
Colt

GOD, I WAS AN ASSHOLE. BUT IT HAD BEEN THE DAY from hell, and this woman was trying my last ounce of patience. The only problem was that the moment the challenge slipped free, her blue eyes flashed in a way that had me sucking in a breath.

There was no denying she was beautiful. That had been clear as day the moment I'd turned around. Long, blond hair that hung to her waist and looked bleached by the sun. She wore shorts that exposed long, tanned legs, and flip-flops revealing toes painted in an array of sparkly colors. Rainbow fucking toes and even they were cute.

Her face had the kind of symmetry that meant she could've just as easily graced the cover of a magazine as this cement sidewalk. But it was those eyes flashing that nearly did me in. Because there was fire in those eyes. A kind of fire that spoke of vitality and an absence of fear. That fearlessness grabbed me by the throat and wanted to pull me right in.

She tugged something out of her back pocket. A tiny wallet that looked more like a coin purse. A second later she was handing me a card. "Here you go, Officer."

"Sheriff," I corrected. Those blue eyes flashed again. They

were a deep blue, the tones you'd find deep in the ocean, but when they flashed, it was as if they turned liquid.

"Sheriff," she ground out.

The annoyance had me fighting a laugh as I took the offered piece of plastic. Her driver's license, I realized. My gaze dipped. Ridley Sawyer Bennett. Twenty-seven. From Ohio. "Far from home."

"Is that a crime?" she challenged.

And damn, I liked the way her voice transformed with it, taking on an almost sultry air. "That depends. If I run you, am I going to find any warrants I need to arrest you for?"

Her eyes didn't flash this time; they danced. "Only one way to find out."

Hell. The dancing was worse. I cleared my throat and handed the license back to her. "I'll let you off with a warning. This time. Try to keep from inciting any future riots, would you?"

She snatched the license and shoved it and her wallet into her back pocket. "Can't make any promises, Law Man."

And with that she climbed into her van.

I couldn't help but watch as she expertly backed out, navigating the van in a way that said she was perfectly comfortable with the vehicle, which matched the aura of the woman completely. A light, sunshiny teal, flowers laid along the dashboard, and some sort of pendant hanging from the rearview mirror.

I stayed standing there until the van completely disappeared from sight. Something about it, about *her,* held me to the spot until the connection was completely broken. The moment it was, my back teeth ground together. *Goddamned moronic.*

For all I knew, Ridley Bennett was a con woman making her way across the US by swindling grannies. I should run the license just in case. Time had given me a good memory for those combinations of letters and numbers.

Pulling out my cell, I typed the license number into my notes app. I'd look it up back at the station. Then I switched to my text app.

Me: You need anything from town? I'll swing by your place on the way home.

Shortcake: I wouldn't hate some coconut curry… My treat?

I stared down at the screen. She had the menu memorized by now even though she'd never once seen it in person.

Me: You got it. Banana fritters?

Shortcake: I never say no to dessert.

I checked the time and then shoved my cell back into my pocket. I had two and a half hours before the end of my shift and a mountain of paperwork I needed to catch up on, but still, I found myself wandering in the opposite direction of the station.

In a matter of minutes, I was pushing open the door of The Whiskey Barrel. It took a second for my eyes to adjust to the low light of the bar. At half past two, only the diehards were present, a couple at tables and a few more at the bar.

I clapped a man on the shoulder as he stared up at a silent game on the screen in one corner of the bar. "Hey, Hal."

He didn't look away. "Colt. Any good trouble today?"

"Celia tried to rip a trash can out of the ground."

Hal chuckled. "Protecting baby geese crossing the street or raging at someone for not recycling?"

"Trying to break a cat out of a car."

That had Hal glancing my way, eyebrows raised. "That cat recover from the ordeal?"

"Thankfully she didn't succeed."

Hal shook his head and turned back to the game as I headed toward a man on the other side of the bar. His dark-blond hair was in its usual disarray, facial hair halfway between scruff and a beard. His gray eyes in their usual fixed position, on a worn paperback.

"What is it today?" I asked.

Trey lifted the book as he kept on reading. The title had an epic string of words that involved cults and bioterrorism. I grunted. "Real cheery reading."

He folded the corner of the page as he finished whatever paragraph he was on. "The human mind is a fascinating place."

"Or a terrifying one," I said as I slid onto a stool.

"Ransom?" Trey asked, readying himself to reach for my favorite whiskey.

"Still on duty."

He reached for a tall glass instead, filling it with ice and then reaching for a soda gun. "Who pissed in your lemonade?"

The question only made me scowl. "I didn't say a damned thing."

Trey slid the Coke across the bar. "Known you practically since the womb."

That was true enough, and a couple of decades as a bartender gave him plenty of insight into people. But he'd always had that. Could take someone's pulse in two seconds flat. It had saved both our necks more times than I could count. Just like I was sure it saved Trey's when he took off on his bike every couple of months for parts unknown.

"Long day."

Trey leaned against the bar, hands gripping the wood as he waited. Never in any hurry. The man had the patience of a saint.

"Mayor called. Wants me to downplay the rise in oxy arrests."

Trey let out a low whistle.

"Carl called, demanding I arrest Joe because Joe added an Italian sandwich to his menu that is too similar to his own."

Trey's lips twitched. "It's hard being a crotchety deli owner."

"Celia called the station five times in twenty-five minutes wanting us to break a cat out of a van and nearly took the job on herself."

The twitching turned into a full-out grin. "Would've liked to see that one. She's what? One hundred pounds soaking wet?"

"She was making a go of ripping a trash can out of the ground," I muttered.

"What happened to the cat?"

"Tater."

"Huh?" Trey asked, confused.

"Cat's name is Tater."

He barked out a laugh at that. "I'm going to take it that Tater is just fine."

"Owner came back in the nick of time. Apparently the van has an AC unit that runs independent of the engine."

"Fancy."

"Something like that." Ridley's face flashed in my mind. The way those blue eyes sparked and swirled.

"What's that about?"

I blinked a few times, refocusing on Trey. "What?"

He drew a circle in the air around my face. "That look."

"Nothing. Just want to look into the owner."

Trey groaned. "Colt, not every person that passes through town is a serial killer or a terrorist."

"I was actually leaning toward con woman if you wanted to know."

He stilled and then a smile stretched across his face. "Woman, huh? The pieces are coming together."

"Piss off," I muttered.

That only made Trey grin wider. "For the love of all that's holy, I hope she's staying in town. You need someone to keep you on your toes."

That was the last thing I needed. No surprises, nothing unexpected. I needed steady, predictable. And my gut told me Ridley Bennett was anything but.

Chapter Four
Ridley

"Home sweet home," I cooed to Tater as I sat back on the small couch in the heart of the van. It faced the picture window in the van's door that currently had an absolutely epic view. That was the thing about moving around; it was like hanging a new painting in your living room every couple of months, sometimes even more frequently than that.

The latest work of art was breathtaking. A view of the mountains and a small lake flanked by a mix of redwoods and other pine trees. As the sun dipped lower in the sky, it painted that landscape in an array of colors, a rainbow but not in any sort of predictable order, and it was more beautiful that way.

Tater rolled onto her back, exposing her belly. I knew an order when I saw one. Bending over, I lightly scratched her exposed fur. She purred for a few moments. And then as if a switch had been flipped, she jackrabbit-kicked my arm as her teeth sank into my hand.

"Shit! Ow." I snatched my hand back. "Your love is a little violent for my taste."

The telltale ring of an incoming video call sounded from my phone, and I braced. The satellite on top of my van gave me access to the internet anywhere I was, just as long as I didn't have too much tree cover. It was necessary for my job, but there were times I wished I could throw it all away and disappear into the silence.

Relief swept through me as I swiped up the device and saw *Sully* flash across the screen paired with a ridiculous photo I'd snapped of him last year when we were on a video call. He was wearing a Santa hat and a Rudolph nose. The look only complemented the growing gray in his blond hair and the paunch around his middle.

I hit *accept*, and the familiar face, minus the Santa hat and light-up nose, filled my screen. He sat at his desk, the New York skyline barely visible through his blurry apartment windows. "You made it okay?"

I bit back my chuckle. He could see I had, but I answered him anyway. "This spot might make my top ten."

I flipped the camera around as I pushed off the couch and opened the van door. I slid out quickly so Tater wouldn't also make her escape. "What do you think?"

Panning the camera, I gave Sully a view of the small campground and the landscape beyond. He let out a low whistle. "She's a beaut."

"There are only five sites, and they're all super spread out. It's going to make for the perfect home for the next month or so."

"Just make sure you're being careful," Sully ordered gruffly.

I flipped the camera back to me. "You know I always am."

Sully had come on board as my editor right before *Sounds Like Serial* had blown up. He'd seen the good, the bad, and the ugly. And he always had my back.

"Baker called a few minutes ago. Wanted to know why you hadn't posted yet."

I let out a groan. "I haven't even been settled an hour."

Sully grimaced. "You know that prick's impatient."

Did I ever. And Sully got it too. Baker always wanted faster turnaround times and the miracle of zero background noise. "I'm about to post the town intro. Just picking the right music."

"That should appease him for…" Sully checked his watch. "Six hours, give or take."

I couldn't help but laugh. "But we'll take all the peace we can get." I glanced at the clock in the corner of my screen. "I'm gonna get into town. See if I can get a little more of that nighttime flavor."

What a community looked like during the day, who you met then, was completely different than the vibe after dark. I needed the feel of both. Needed to know the characters and players.

"Be careful," Sully commanded.

"Always, boss."

He scoffed. "We both know you're the one who runs this ship."

"Just don't tell Baker that," I muttered.

Sully chuckled. "Never. I'll have that edit to you for first listen tomorrow."

"Thanks, Sul. Enjoy your evening."

"You too." I hit *end* on the call and took a second to really take in the beauty in front of me. The way the small lake peeked out through the trees. How the mountains looked a deep pink in the setting sun.

Sliding my hand into my pocket, my fingers closed around the familiar metal charm. I'd memorized the feel of it over the past five years. Every divot and ding. A tiny chip had been taken out of one of the lacrosse sticks somewhere along the way. But that didn't change the memories they held.

I could still see Avery swinging them around her finger as she walked, a soft smile on her face. The smile was a punch to the sternum every single time it filled my mind. But I only grabbed on to the pain.

Some days it felt like that pain was the only thing still connecting me to her. That and this damned key ring.

I gripped it tighter, staring down at the water below. "It's beautiful, Avs. Soaking it in extra for you. But it would be so much better if you were here with me."

The pressure built behind my eyes, a burn lighting there from my effort to keep the tears at bay. I didn't let them take hold. Not ever. Because there was part of me that feared if I started, I'd never stop.

The light on the front of my e-bike cut through the night and I was glad that I'd switched out the one the bike had come with for a brighter headlight. It was complemented by the lights on the back, which told cars exactly where I was. Having the bike meant being able to leave my van at the campsite, a dose of fresh air, and the option to move after sitting for long periods on the road.

I made the turn onto Old Miner Road and downtown Shady Cove came into view. It somehow managed to look quaintly cozy and like a ghost town all at once. It was only eight o'clock, and every shop and restaurant I passed looked as if they'd been closed for hours. I just hoped like hell the same couldn't be said for the bar.

Easing my pace, I searched for any signs of life, but didn't see a single one until I reached the block The Whiskey Barrel was on. A grin tugged at my lips as I took in a row of motorcycles, mostly Harleys and a few Triumphs, but there was even a Ducati that didn't match the Old West feel of the place one bit. There were also more than a few vehicles. Mostly pickups, but several SUVs and sedans as well.

I slowed my bike and hopped off. Lifting it over the curb, I guided it toward a nearby lamppost. In a matter of seconds, I'd shut off the battery and locked it up along with my helmet. Grabbing my phone from the basket, I headed for the bar.

Even before I opened the door, I could hear strains of Lynyrd Skynyrd from inside. I grabbed the worn wooden door handle and tugged. The music hit me in a wave. Not obscenely loud but enough that it would hide low conversations of people who didn't want to be overheard.

I felt eyes land on me as I stepped inside. As much as I was used to that, so often being the new face in established communities, I had to fight the urge to pull my worn leather jacket tighter around me. I forced my legs to just keep moving with the bar as my destination.

But as I crossed the uneven wood floor, I scanned the space, taking in the different crowds. I could see two groups of bikers. A rougher crowd and the weekend warriors. I glimpsed a couple of tables I guessed were tourists, given their attire and a hiking pack or two. A few dates or folks who had already paired up for the night. I spotted Mira, the woman from the grocery store, with a group of friends. And then I picked out the barflies.

That last group were the ones I wanted to befriend first. They overheard it all from their never-wavering stations on stools or at tables. And even though they were varying levels of inebriated, they often had surprisingly good memories.

The bar itself wasn't crowded, just a handful of patrons scattered along it. My boots clipped across the floor as I approached. I chose my seat with purpose, picking a stool two down from a man who wore a grin and a slightly glassy-eyed look.

As I slid onto the leather seat, I met astute gray eyes on the other side of the bar. The man was handsome, there was no denying it, but he didn't have my nerve endings standing at attention the way Law Man had earlier today.

The bartender slid a napkin across the well-cared-for wood. "What can I get ya?"

I slid my gaze away from his rugged face and toward the back of the bar. "Whiskey. You don't happen to have any Ransom, do you? The Emerald?"

The man was already moving. Without even looking, he plucked up a familiar bottle. "Rocks or neat?"

"Now why would I want to dilute that beautiful flavor?"

He chuckled, the action making the thick, dark-blond scruff around his mouth twitch. "A woman who knows what she likes."

I slid off my leather jacket, letting it fall to the back of the stool, and set my phone on the bar. "That a good thing?"

"Always." The bartender grabbed a glass and gave me a healthy pour. "Tab or cash?"

I shifted to the side, grabbing my card from my pocket. "As much as I'd love to do some serious damage to that bottle, I need to get myself home tonight."

"Safety first," the man said, giving a salute with my card.

As he ran the bill, I lifted the glass to my lips. I let the wave of flavors hit my tongue. It was always those hints of caramel that were my favorite. That and the feel of being warmed from the inside out.

The bartender slid my check and card back across the bar top. "Good?"

"The best."

His lips twitched. "Tourist?"

"Kind of," I hedged.

He studied me for a long moment. "You got a cat named Tater?"

My entire body turned to granite. I hadn't gotten the superfan vibe when I'd walked up, but maybe this guy was a true-crime junkie. I didn't like to put my face on camera much, but I did so occasionally to avoid people getting *too* curious about me.

He barked out a laugh. "Shit. You should see your face.

Small town. Heard about a run-in over a pretty tourist's cat. That's all."

My shoulders relaxed a fraction. "Careful. You could read stalker real quick."

He leaned on the back bar, arms crossed comfortably over his chest. "In small towns, everyone's a stalker."

It was my turn to laugh. "Fair enough." I took another sip of whiskey. "Well, stalker, I'm Ridley."

He reached across the distance and offered me a hand. "Trey. Nice to meet you."

"You too. Especially if you stock the good stuff."

Trey grinned as he pulled his phone out of his back pocket, fingers flying across the screen. "Got a friend who's partial to it."

"Well, that friend has excellent taste."

Trey's smile only grew at that and he shoved his phone back into his pocket. "I think so."

The sound of heavy footsteps lifted just above the music and Trey's gaze shifted to my left.

"Get a bottle of Jack?" a deep voice asked.

I looked up to see a man with a long, gray beard. The leathers he wore told me he was a biker, and the patch over his heart read *Ace*.

"That depends," Trey said coolly. "You gonna destroy half my bar again?"

So he was the owner, not just the bartender. That meant Trey would likely be my best source of information in this place.

The biker's cheeks reddened a fraction. "One time, man."

Trey raised a brow. "Once is enough for me."

"Not gonna happen again," Ace muttered like a petulant child.

I bit the inside of my cheek to keep from laughing as Trey crouched, going in search of a fresh bottle.

Ace tilted his head toward me. "You wanna join, darlin'? We got plenty to go around."

I was sure he meant that in more ways than one. I simply lifted my glass. "I'm good. Thanks for the tempting offer though."

"Open invitation," he answered with a wink.

Trey broke the seal on a bottle of Jack and handed it to Ace. "Remember, I got your card. This bottle and any damages go straight on it."

Ace grabbed the bottle. "Piss off."

Trey just grinned, shaking his head. "I swear this job is more daycare attendant than drink slinger sometimes."

"I have no doubt." I took another sip of my drink and leaned back on my stool. I chose my first question carefully. Something to ease us into conversation, nothing that would trip any triggers. Even though what I really wanted to know was how long Trey had lived here and if he knew Emerson Sinclair. "So what are the do-not-misses around Shady Cove?"

"Depends on what you're after."

"Hikes, lakes, anything unique."

Trey mulled it over for a moment. "If you're in real shape, there's a hike that takes you through a waterfall. Wouldn't go alone though. The rocks can be slippery."

I tried not to bristle at that but mostly failed. "I know how to handle myself."

"Doesn't matter if you're a third-degree black belt; you can still get dead if you slip."

That was true enough, but I still ignored it. "Anything else?"

"Got a skydive outfit outta the private airstrip next town over. Get you an up-close-and-personal view of those mountains."

That familiar buzz lit in my muscles. I'd been skydiving a few times before but with this backdrop? I couldn't pass that up. "I'll call tomorrow."

Trey nodded, moving slightly to fill two pint glasses and slide them over to waiting patrons. As he moved back to his original spot I tried to ease into a new approach.

"Anything I need to be aware of?"

Those gray eyes sharpened. "Aware of?"

"You know, single woman traveling alone. What's the crime like in the area?" That was always my excuse. Before long, word would get around *why* I was asking and I could be more direct. But for now, I liked going in broad.

Trey nodded. "Pretty safe on the whole, but that's not a reason to be stupid."

"Never is."

"The worst we usually have are drunk-driving accidents and opiate overdoses."

Made sense. Opiates had made a home everywhere, even in these smaller, rural communities, and it was an invasive beast. "I'll be avoiding both those arenas."

"Glad to hear it. Still wouldn't hurt to take a buddy when you hit those trails."

A prickle of annoyance skated over my skin. "I told you, I know how to handle myself."

"Do you now?"

That voice. Deep, raspy, and a tone that had my whole body jerking to attention. It was just too bad it belonged to a giant dick. And not in a good way, no matter how much my body seemed to disagree.

Chapter Five
Colt

It didn't matter that Trey had sent a text telling me my con woman was at the bar. My eyes would have gone to her instantly in a crowd. Those acres of blond hair tumbling down her back and over the back of the stool. The way her sun-kissed shoulders peeked out from some sort of tank top with too many colors to count. She oozed an effortless sort of beauty. But more than that, a light. From her golden hair to the fire in those blue eyes.

And that fire was currently pointed straight at me. And because I was a masochist, I liked it right there.

"Law Man," Ridley greeted.

"Chaos," I returned.

Those eyes sparked. "Chaos?"

"Can't say you don't bring that in your wake."

Ridley lifted her glass, preparing to take a sip. "Or maybe you're just boring as hell."

Trey burst out laughing, and I leveled him with a glare. He held up both hands. "I didn't say a damned thing."

I pulled out the stool next to Ridley, sliding onto it. But the moment I did, I realized my mistake. A scent washed over me. One that was so goddamned *her*. Bright waves of orange but smoky somehow, as if the fruit had been singed.

Ridley pressed the glass to her lips, tipping back a sip. "You following me, Law Man?"

"Just having a drink at my friend's bar at the end of a long day."

Trey grabbed my favorite bottle of Ransom and poured it straight into a glass, sliding it across the bar. Ridley watched him with a fascination that had a niggle of jealousy settling in. And if that wasn't fucking ridiculous, I didn't know what was.

"Well," she said with a sigh. "At least you're not boring when it comes to beverages."

Trey grinned like a hyena with rabies. "Ridley here's partial to The Emerald as well."

Fuck.

I did not need to know that this woman who smelled like smoky sunshine and looked like a walking temptation had a taste for *my* whiskey. So I just grunted.

"He's a real winning conversationalist," Ridley muttered.

Trey chuckled and leaned against the back bar. "I was just trying to convince Ridley to take a buddy when she hikes that waterfall trail. You know that trail pretty well, don't you, Colt?"

My eyes narrowed on my friend since birth. What the hell was he playing at? But then the first part of his statement hit me. My head whipped in Ridley's direction. "You're thinking about doing that trail alone?"

She shrugged, the action making all that blond hair slide over her skin the way my fingers itched to do. "I'm a big girl. Done plenty of hikes by myself."

My back teeth ground together. "Doing any of that shit alone is fucking stupid. But doing this one? It's a death wish. There are too many places you could fall."

Ridley's gaze shifted back to Trey. "He's a real charmer. I've spent a total of fifteen minutes in his presence today, and he's threatened to tow my van, and write me a ticket, and now he's calling me a moron."

Trey's jaw went slack. "You threatened to tow her car?"

I shifted on my stool. "I wasn't serious."

"Dude. Your prickishness is getting out of control."

Trey's tone was light, but it still stung. Because I knew he was right. I'd been a bear lately. It wasn't like I was warm and fuzzy on a good day, but recently it was…more. I knew in my gut it was because the anniversary was approaching.

Every year, I checked in on the case. Went over every piece of evidence in lockup. Forced myself to read Emerson's statements at least three times. It didn't matter that going through it all ripped open that wound and made it so it would never heal. I owed it to her. It was the least I could do after failing her like I had.

But some part of me had always thought I'd figure it out by year ten. That I'd find the bastard and put him away so Em would finally feel safe again. That hadn't happened.

The feel of eyes on me pulled me out of my spiraling thoughts. The stare burned, as if it was peeling back the layers I used as a shield. Seeking out the source of it, I found those blue eyes peering back at me. Eyes with countless questions.

Ridley didn't fill the silence between us. She simply let those questions hang in the air. But I didn't give her an answer either.

"If you two are done with your weird-ass staring contest, Ridley, do you need a refill?"

Trey's voice was an unwelcome intruder, and I nearly growled at him for it.

Ridley slid off the stool at that. "I think one is all I'm good for if I'm going to get myself home."

"Hope you parked that van in an oversized spot this time, Chaos."

She sent me a droll look. "Rode my bike into town, so Bessie is safely stowed."

My fingers tightened around my glass. "You. Rode. Your. Bike?"

"Aw, hell," Trey muttered.

Ridley looked between the two of us. "Don't tell me bike riding is illegal in Shady Cove or something."

"You could get hit by a car or snatched by a goddamned biker," I growled.

"Or abducted by aliens. Or clobbered on the head by Bigfoot," she singsonged as she slid a worn brown leather jacket over her shoulders.

"Don't be an idiot," I gritted out.

Ridley's eyes narrowed. "I'm not. I've taken plenty of precautions. But I'm also not going to live my life scared of every single thing that could go bump in the night. Now, unless you're going to arrest me, I'll be going."

She started for the door, her jeans hugging her sinewy curves as she went. She threw up two fingers in a wave. "Thanks for the booze, Trey."

I watched her until she disappeared, the same way I'd watched her van. It was as if she'd cast a spell on me and there wasn't a damned thing I could do to stop it.

"There's a story there."

Trey's softly spoken words had me turning back around. "What do you mean?"

He glanced over my shoulder to where Ridley had disappeared out the front door. "She asked about crime in the area."

My skin prickled, a combination of awareness and worry.

"Could be her usual MO," Trey went on. "Single woman used to traveling alone, wants to get a lay of the land."

"Or something happened to her before, and she's trying to make sure that never happens again." The thought had a sick feeling roiling in my gut. Because I knew that it only took one moment for someone's life to shatter into something unrecognizable.

Chapter Six
Ridley

I DIPPED MY PADDLE INTO THE GLASSY LAKE, SENDING ripples across the surface. The sun had barely surfaced, sending beams of that pink, reddish light across the landscape, but I'd been up for hours. I'd had the nightmare again.

The same as always. It started out beautiful, a lake not unlike this one, if a little less mountainous. But this specific body of water was the one Avery and I had grown up visiting. We'd be swimming and playing until all of a sudden, Avery was drowning, screaming for my help. But I was stuck in the quicksand of the shallows, never able to get to her. Never able to save her.

It came less often these days, but it made sense as to why it had sprung to life in my subconscious last night. At least it meant I got to see this sunrise. It was my favorite time of day. A time when everything was so still you could fool yourself into thinking nothing bad could ever happen.

Even Tater appreciated the sanctity of sunrise. She perched toward the front of my paddleboard, clad in her life vest, taking in the view. And likely looking for fish.

I switched my paddle, from side to side, in a practiced rhythm, soaking in the gift of it all. The fact that my muscles were strong enough to propel me through the water. That I had a job I loved that afforded me this paddleboard and campsite fee. That I was breathing.

A familiar stabbing pain hit my sternum. But I just grabbed on, holding it close.

"You're with me, Avs."

For the first few years after she went missing, I held out hope. That she was out there, still breathing too. But then I started to wonder what exactly I was hoping for. That she was chained up by some madman? Trafficked overseas for drugs or worse?

Some part of me knew she was gone and that the best I could hope for was that she'd found peace. My mom didn't share that opinion, and I didn't blame her for it. How could you let go of a daughter without hard proof that she had left this earth? Mom dove headfirst into every rabbit hole. It wasn't until she nearly drained my parents' savings account paying for psychics and people who had so-called tips on Avery's whereabouts that my dad finally put his foot down.

He took Mom off the investment accounts and everything financial but their joint checking. If he hadn't, I wasn't sure they'd even have a house to live in anymore. Now, Dad was living with two ghosts, his daughter's and his wife's. But then again, I wasn't sure he was truly living either.

We traded the occasional email, checking in, but he was distant. That distance had come on slowly, so slowly I hadn't noticed it until one day I realized that talking to him was more like conversing with a coworker than my dad. Maybe it was a self-protection mechanism. A desperate effort so that if anything ever happened to me, he wouldn't be leveled again.

That was the thing these monsters didn't realize. They thought they were only ending one life, but it was so many more. The ripple effect of cruel violence that would live on for generations to come, all of us still breathing branded by it.

I turned the paddleboard in a wide circle, pointing us back toward shore. I could've stayed out here for hours more, but I'd woken to half a dozen emails from Baker wanting to know if I'd found anything worth covering in this case. The urge to block his email address had been strong.

Covering missing persons cases wasn't anything new for me. It was just that usually the victims were still gone. More than six hundred thousand people went missing every year in the United States, and while many were found, there were others who stayed gone. Ones who became forgotten by all but their nearest and dearest.

I gave those people a voice. Making sure the world didn't have any choice but to hear their stories. Each case I covered had a tip line funded by the show. Those tips came to me but then got dispersed to the law enforcement in charge of the case, forcing them to pay attention. Sometimes those offices were grateful for the help. Sometimes they didn't want to lift a finger they didn't have to. It didn't matter, I would keep fighting regardless of their attitudes.

It made sense why Baker was confused about my need to cover this case. While it was still unsolved, the victim was safe, home, whole. But my gut was screaming that this was where a reign of terror had begun. And I had a string of cases to prove it. I just wasn't ready to let Baker or anyone else in on that yet, not until I had more. I just hoped Emerson would be the one to give it to me.

I leaned my bike against the lamppost next to Cowboy Coffee and locked my chain around it. Pulling off my helmet, I deposited it in my basket and shook out my hair. It was still damp from my post-paddleboarding shower. But I was damn glad I'd installed the shower last year.

It wasn't exactly a five-star hotel, but the fact that it hooked off the side of my van meant I got a view of the sky while I got clean. But whenever I did spring for a hotel or a short-term rental for a time, I took every bathtub soak I could get.

Grabbing my small bag, I slid it over my shoulder and headed inside. The scent of freshly roasted beans was almost as good as sunrise mountain air. The café was only about one-third full, which meant I'd missed the breakfast rush. There were a couple of teenagers, which told me school was out for the year, a group of women with babies and toddlers, and two men who looked to be in their eighties playing chess at a corner table.

"Back already?" a voice called from behind the register.

I grinned at Ezra as I walked toward him. "I need another hazelnut latte. That thing was downright dangerous."

"Coffee addiction is my goal."

"Well, you've succeeded. But I'm going to get some breakfast too."

Ezra nodded. "Want a rec?"

"Always."

"Breakfast burrito or the cowboy hash. I rotate between the two daily."

I chuckled. "I'll do the burrito today and hash tomorrow."

"You got it. For here or to go?"

"I'll do here today. Need to get a little work done."

"I'll get that in right now. Total is sixteen-fifty."

I tapped my card to the reader and waited for the beep. "Thanks so much."

"Anytime," Ezra said and moved to hand my order to the cook.

Sliding my card back into my wallet, I surveyed my table options. It didn't take me long to decide. There was one against the window that would allow me to overhear both the group of moms and the two men playing chess. Both had interview potential.

I studied the women as I approached my chosen table. They looked to be anywhere from midtwenties to early thirties, so in the range where they would know Emerson if they were lifelong Shady Cove residents.

The town intro I'd posted to TikTok and Instagram was getting enough attention that my days going under the radar were limited anyway. People had already begun digging into cold cases in the area wondering which one I might pick up. There weren't many, but my followers had found all the options.

A woman in her midfifties who'd been murdered during a home invasion eight years ago. A hit-and-run that left a man dead five years ago. A string of robberies eleven years ago that resulted in a deputy's death. A few even thought I might be taking on the opiates ring that was rumored to be running in the area. And, of course, Emerson's case.

She'd been kidnapped from a local park after tennis practice. A star athlete, she'd always stayed after for an hour or two to hit balls on her own. While waiting for her ride, someone had hit her from behind, knocking her unconscious.

She'd woken up in the back of a covered pickup truck, wrapped in a burlap sack, limbs bound. It wasn't clear if her abductor thought he'd killed her or if he simply thought she'd be unconscious for longer. Regardless, she managed to get free of her bindings and jump from the moving vehicle.

Emerson had fractured her hip and dislocated her shoulder in the fall but still managed to walk until she found someone from the search party out looking for her. But she never played tennis again. In fact, as far as I could tell from the records I'd found, she'd dropped out of high school altogether.

I didn't blame her. I couldn't imagine the kind of fear you lived with having to walk around never knowing when you might come face-to-face with your abductor.

Lowering myself into the chair that gave me the best vantage point of both groups of patrons and the street outside, I dropped my bag onto the seat next to me. It only took a matter of seconds for me to get my notebook and laptop set up.

I'd read any article I could get my hands on. The case had been covered by every news outlet in the area, everyone wondering how this could've happened in such a small, safe community. As I'd dug deeper into the troves of Facebook, I'd been able to find out about a handful of people the police had brought in for questioning.

Emerson's tennis coach, a teacher, a member of the parks and rec maintenance staff. I didn't have every person's name, but I was working on putting together the pieces. And I knew with time I could find them all.

My fingers flew across the keyboard, putting the finishing touches on my Open Records request. It likely wouldn't get me much since the case was still open. But they'd have to give me the basics. Sending it in would mean blowing any sort of cover I had. But I wouldn't get anywhere without asking the questions I needed to. I couldn't picture the broody sheriff being thrilled with my nosiness, but he'd just have to get used to it. My fingers hovered over the trackpad mouse for a moment, and then I hit send.

Here we go.

"Breakfast burrito and nectar of the gods," Ezra said as he slid the plate and coffee onto the table.

"Thank you so much." I took a small sip of the coffee. "Damn, *nectar of the gods* is right."

He chuckled. "Decades of slinging coffee, and I've finally got it down."

It was the perfect opening. That faint buzz lit in my muscles. The kind that always took root when I was starting a case. The type of buzz that reminded me anything could happen. That I might be the one to break a case wide-open. Only this time it was more.

"How long have you owned Cowboy Coffee?" I asked, leaning back in my chair.

Ezra scrubbed a hand over his cheek, the barest hints of reddish scruff there. "Over fifteen years now. Worked here for a decade before I bought it."

I let out a low whistle. "Coffee's in your blood by now."

"It's definitely baked into me. I still smell it every night when I get home."

I grinned. "There are a lot worse smells you could carry with you."

His mouth curved in answer. "True."

"Can I ask you a question?" That buzz intensified, making my muscles almost vibrate. It was like that feeling of being at the top of a roller coaster, knowing you were about to fall.

Ezra's expression grew puzzled. "Sure."

"Did you know Emerson Sinclair?"

I watched as his body language changed, could see as the wave of tension washed over him. Ezra's jaw tightened and his eyes went hard. The jolly coffee enthusiast was gone, and I knew I'd made a miscalculation on whom to approach first.

Shit.

Chapter Seven
Ridley

Ezra stared at me for a long moment before saying a word, and all I could do was wait. Wait and see just how bad his reaction might be. He could ban me from the establishment, which would be a blow on multiple fronts. He could cuss me out right here. I didn't read violence in him, but I could be wrong there too.

But I'd seen it all before. Faced it all. I could handle myself whatever came my way.

"What do you want with Em?" Ezra's voice pitched low, not aggressive exactly, but it held a hint of warning.

I looked him dead in the eyes, hoping he would see the honesty in mine. "I want to find the bastard who kidnapped her."

Those brown irises flashed in surprise. "You a PI or something?"

"Or something."

"She's the host of one of the biggest true-crime podcasts out there," a voice said as the chair opposite me was scraped back. A gangly teen boy with raven-dark hair and a lip ring sat without invitation, his black clothing completing his goth demeanor. "She's solved three cases completely on her own and found new leads on almost a dozen others."

Ezra's gaze moved back and forth between the teen and me. "He right?"

I fought the urge to squirm in my chair. "Not the *on my own* part. I'm only successful with the help of the communities I come into."

That gaze narrowed. "I don't talk about anything without Em's permission."

Curiosity sparked to life. His response seemed too vehement for casual work colleagues. It was possible he was simply protective due to all the media attention on Emerson in the wake of the abduction. Small communities could be insular and their inhabitants bulldogs in the way they tried to protect each other.

"I'd never force someone to talk to me. Victim or otherwise." That was true. If a family or the victim didn't want to speak to me, I gave them a wide berth. I understood the pain that came with digging up trauma. How the rehashing of it could be like carving open a wound that had scabbed over.

But I also knew that sometimes reopening that wound was exactly what was needed to bring complete healing. I just hoped one day I could find it for myself too.

Ezra stared at me for one long, hard moment. "Won't be saying a damn thing until I hear from Em." And with that he strode away, a pissed-off look on his face.

The boy across from me let out a low whistle. "Takes a lot for Ezra to get pissed like that."

My focus moved to him, trying to assess his age and get a read. The clothes, hint of eyeliner, and lip ring were a mask. I needed to see beneath it all. But only time would give me that. "It's fair. I'm nosing into something that's more than painful."

I'd take the pissed off, even the rage, over the tears. The tears gutted me every time.

"But you're trying to help. You always do," the boy argued.

A small smile tugged at my lips. "So you listen to the show?"

His blue eyes sparked, showing a little more of his age. "Every freaking week. It's fire. I'm in your forums and on your socials too. When you posted the intro to Shady Cove, I flipped. I've been trolling town ever since, hoping I'd see you."

I couldn't help but laugh now. "Well, you've got me. You going to tell me your name?"

"Shit, yeah. I'm Dean."

"Nice to meet you, Dean."

"This is so freaking wild. *Sounds Like Serial* in my bumfuck town," Dean muttered. My brows raised at that, and his cheeks flushed. "Sorry. It's just *nothing* ever happens here. It's so boring."

Except that wasn't true. Something had happened, and it had marked the town and its residents.

"I can show you around," Dean went on. "Introduce you to people. But I'm not sure they'll talk. People are real protective of Emerson. I heard *Dateline* wanted to do something on the case back in the day, and the town basically locked them out. I get it. I mean she never even leaves her house. Like ever."

I guess I'd been right about the residents of Shady Cove looking out for Emerson. I was glad she had that, even if it meant my job was harder. But something else Dean had said caught my attention. "You mean she doesn't come into town very often?"

"No, I mean she never comes into town," Dean said. "I haven't seen her since I was like six. My parents were friends with her mom, so they used to come over for dinner sometimes."

"Were friends?" I asked.

"Her mom died a couple of years after Emerson was kidnapped. Heart attack."

Hell. I already knew that Emerson's father had split when she was young. She was all alone in the world.

"Her brother brings her groceries and stuff from town. I heard even her packages and stuff go to him first. She never leaves her place."

That feeling low in my gut shifted slightly. The unease was still there, but anger was overtaking it now. Rage at the person who had turned Emerson's life upside down with one careless action, not giving a damn about the agony they'd wrought.

I did my best to keep the fury from my voice. "I didn't know she had a brother."

That hadn't been mentioned in the articles I'd read, but their sparse details made more sense now that I knew Shady Cove had rallied around Emerson. To get them to open up, I'd need to convince Emerson I might be able to give her the closure that could bring healing.

Dean nodded. "Different dads but the same mom. He's like ten years older, but they're tight."

Apparently there was a lot I didn't know about this case, and that was a feeling I hated. I wanted to be as prepared as possible when coming into something. But in this instance, I wasn't going to find the information I needed on the internet, that much was clear. I grabbed my laptop, shoving it into my bag.

"What are you doing?" Dean asked, his brows pulling together.

"I need to go see Emerson before someone talks her out of speaking with me." As protective as this town was and with the fact that I'd sent in my records request, the clock was already ticking.

"I could help you," Dean offered, so much hope in his eyes. "Be like your intern or something."

I grinned as I pushed up from my chair and shoved the rest of my belongings into my bag. "I'll be sure to let you know if I have more questions."

He slumped against his chair. "That's a blow-off."

"For now," I admitted. I couldn't have a kid getting mixed up in my investigation. "But you can have my breakfast burrito as consolation."

He brightened slightly at that. "I could smash one of these. They're fire."

I chuckled. "It's all yours." Dean grabbed the plate, and I grabbed my coffee. "See you around."

"See ya," Dean called, his mouth already full of burrito goodness.

I hurried toward the door but didn't miss the cool stare Ezra sent me as I went. Somehow I didn't think I'd be getting any more menu recommendations when I came in.

Unlocking my bike, I hopped on and secured my helmet. I'd already memorized the town's map and knew exactly where Emerson's house was. It would be a bit of a ride since she lived just outside of town, but I'd likely be less intimidating showing up on a bike versus in a van. And I wasn't sure I had time to go back and get my vehicle anyway. I was racing against the clock.

Flipping on the electric power, I started out. Even though I was in a hurry, I couldn't help but take in the streets I traveled down. Once I was out of downtown, there was a mix of neighborhoods, everything from small older homes to newer builds with more flash. I passed through an area that seemed to be struggling a bit more with overgrown grass and trailers that had seen better days.

But the moment I got outside the town limits, the properties grew in size. The houses here looked like they sat on multiple acres, with sprawling yards and some with accompanying barns. The road became lined with tall pine trees, casting eerie shadows over the pavement.

I caught sight of the sign that read *Spruce Lane* and guided my bike onto it, the trees growing thicker as I did. The road went from cement to dirt, and I thanked my lucky stars that I'd upgraded the bike with all-terrain tires. A sign on one tree read *Dead End—Property Owners Only*. It wasn't an official street sign, but the warning could land me in handcuffs if there was an overzealous cop involved.

The thought had an image of Colt's face popping into my mind. The grumpy scowl and then that hint of humor as he threatened to write me a ticket. I hoped like hell he wouldn't be the responding officer if Emerson did call the sheriff's department.

Just when it felt like the trees were going to swallow me whole, the road opened up into a clearing. The sun poured in through the opening in the trees, shining down on a house that was meant for sunbeams. The exterior paint was a bright yellow, not neon, but like the sun itself. It had a wraparound porch painted white, and every available surface was brimming with flowers. So many I didn't know how one person could tend them all.

As I stopped my bike, all I could do was stare for a moment. The house didn't fit its setting deep in the forest, and yet it was perfectly at home here. Slowly, I got off my bike and lowered the kickstand.

I knew I had all the gear I'd need in my pack. I traveled light when it came to necessities. My phone could pair with two wireless lavalier mics I always kept on hand just in case an impromptu interview presented itself. But I'd never go in sticking a mic in someone's face. Especially someone who'd been through what Emerson had.

Images filled my brain, ones my imagination had painted in vivid horror about what she'd endured. The panic as she was struck, darkness closing in around her. The terror as she woke bound in the back of a vehicle. Only it wasn't Emerson's face I saw as she escaped the burlap sack and threw herself from a speeding truck. It was Avery's.

I squeezed my eyes closed for a moment, trying to force the

pictures from my mind. When I opened them again, I focused on the flowers. The beautiful rainbow of them all, no two blooms alike.

Taking a deep breath, I headed for the steps. It took me only a matter of seconds to spot the cameras. The ones tucked just under the eaves and the one positioned above the door. They weren't a bad thing. Hopefully Emerson wouldn't see any threat when she looked at me.

Still, I didn't move quickly. I took my time with each step, hoping I gave Emerson a chance to prepare, to do whatever she needed to feel safe. The doormat had *I Hope You Like Dogs* scrawled onto it. Before I could knock, I heard a deep woof from the other side, followed by yappier barks and even a howl.

Expert early-warning system.

I lifted my hand and knocked on the door. The barking intensified and then muffled as if the dogs had been put in another room. Then I heard one lock turn, another, and finally a third. Each sound drove invisible ice picks into my sternum, but I did my best to keep my reaction relaxed.

Slowly the door inched open. It was less than a foot of space, but it allowed me to get my first glimpse of Emerson Sinclair in the flesh. My first thought was that she was stunningly beautiful. Her golden-blond hair hung in loose waves around her shoulders, and her eyes were a hypnotic shade of hazel, the gold and green swirling together. My second thought was that she had a very large dog.

Emerson's fingers gripped the dog's collar as he stood between her and me. A Bernese mountain dog, if I wasn't mistaken. And while massive, he wasn't exactly menacing. But I had a feeling that could change if I made any sort of move against his owner.

Emerson's gaze swept over me, a mix of wariness and confusion. "Can I help you?"

"Hi. I'm Ridley Sawyer." I'd gone over and over in my head

what I wanted to say to her, but suddenly it all flew from my brain, my tongue growing heavy in my mouth as if I'd just been to the dentist and gotten shot up with Novocain.

"Hello?" She said it like a question, and I didn't blame her.

"Sorry—I—I have a podcast. I work on cold cases, and yours came across my desk."

A blank mask slipped over Emerson's features, as if she suddenly turned the world from color to grayscale. "I don't talk about it."

Even the words themselves sounded numb. Devoid of any emotion. I understood it. Felt for her. Felt more than she would ever know. But still, I took a deep breath and went on.

"I get that. I just want to tell you one thing, and then if you want me to leave and never come back, I will. Promise."

A little life flickered back into Emerson's face, a hint of color. "Okay..."

"I think your abduction was the first in a string of abductions, assaults, and murders. I think the man who took you went on to kidnap twenty-three others. And he's never been found, the cases never linked."

Emerson's jaw went slack. "Twenty-three?"

I nodded. "I want to find him. I want to make him pay for what he's done. But more than that, I want to bring the families closure, justice. It won't bring their loved ones back, but it might help them begin to truly heal."

It was more than a want. It was a need so desperate, it had almost turned me feral in my single-minded focus. But I didn't care. I would do whatever it took to find answers. Anything except force survivors like Emerson to talk. It didn't matter how deep the need to solve this particular case went. I'd never steal someone's free will, never become a monster like *him*.

Emerson opened the door a little more. I could just make out the entryway, lined with paintings and sketches of every size, shape, and medium. Her fingers gripped the doorknob tighter. "Why?"

My brows pulled together.

"Why do you want to find him?" she asked. Her voice didn't tremble, and while everything about her situation here, from the cameras to the fact that she didn't leave her fortress, suggested she lived in fear, nothing about that voice was weak. "You want more streams on your show? Want to be the one to solve it and get that reward?"

"I want *justice*." The word vibrated in the air between us, the force of it linking us together. "And I don't want him to hurt another soul. Don't want him to destroy another family. And if he started with you, you're the one who can help me find him."

Emerson's eyes widened in shock, but then a steeliness slid into them. The kind of strength I knew this woman must have had to get free from a monster and launch herself out of the back of a truck, to walk miles on a broken hip to find help, to, no matter what, survive.

She opened her mouth to speak, but it wasn't her voice that rang out. It was a masculine one, a familiar one. And it was full of fury.

"Get the hell off my sister's property."

Chapter Eight
Colt

The moment a deputy dropped that Open Records request on my desk, dread had pooled in my gut. But fast on its heels had come anger—no, rage. People like Ridley didn't have the first clue the kind of damage she could do with her bullshit questions and nosiness. They had never known what it was like to have a single moment rip your world apart.

It had done the most damage to Em, no question, but the rest of us hadn't exactly made it out unscathed. Mom had held us so close after that, the fear creating fractures in her heart that had finally broken it altogether. My whole worldview had changed that day; everything seemed darker. I'd ditched my plan to open a bar with Trey and went to the academy instead. And that didn't exactly help my perspective. Instead of seeing the best in humanity, I started to see the worst.

It didn't matter how many people I helped, even the handful of lives I'd saved. Nothing could erase the guilt I felt. The knowledge that everything would've been different if I just would've been there when Emerson needed me, been there when I was *supposed* to be.

Twenty minutes past when I'd said I would be there to pick

Em up from her obsessive tennis practice, I'd finally arrived. And when I got there, she'd simply been gone.

At first, I'd been pissed. Beyond annoyed she hadn't texted to let me know that she'd gotten a ride with a friend and didn't need me going out of my way to get her. And then I saw her duffel. The pink one with the sports company's logo on the side and her name written in purple Sharpie on the strap. A panic unlike anything I'd ever known had set in.

My little sister, the one who'd come along from my mom's second marriage, the surprise who'd taken to me instantly as if she believed I was the one who could keep her safe in this world, had vanished. No, *vanished* was the wrong word. She'd been taken. And it was my fucking fault.

"Your sister?" Ridley parroted as she gaped up at me as if I were some sort of alien who'd crash-landed on my sister's front porch.

I was sure she was confused by the fact that we had different last names, but I didn't give a damn. It only pissed me off more. As though the fact that we were half-siblings would make me care less somehow.

"My. *Sister*. Now get the hell off her property before I arrest you."

"Colt," Emerson said softly. "That's not necessary."

My gaze swung to her, and she snapped her mouth closed.

I turned back to Ridley, who still hadn't moved. "What? You get some sort of sick charge out of harassing victims? Bringing up the worst moment in their lives and forcing them to relive it? You're scum."

Pain streaked across Ridley's face. It was so vicious, I swore I could feel the fiery claws of it rake at my chest. But just as quickly as it appeared, it was gone, tucked away under a mask of nothingness.

I'd seen Emerson do something similar. Lock away the pain by tuning out the whole world around her. The masks were different, but a sudden twisted fear punched through me as I wondered if she'd been through something similar.

"Ridley—"

But then the fire was back, sparking through those blue eyes. "You don't know a damn thing about me." Her gaze jerked away as she tugged something from her pocket and handed it to my sister. "If you want to talk, you can reach me here. But no pressure. Only you know if you're ready to go down that road. I'll keep looking for the truth no matter what. Promise."

That rage came flooding back, drowning out any worry for Ridley. I opened my mouth to tear into her yet again, but she was already jogging down the steps and toward that goddamned bike I couldn't believe she'd ridden all the way out here. As furious as I was, I still couldn't take my eyes off her as she climbed on and took off.

"Think you could've been any more of an ass?"

Emerson's exasperated question tugged my gaze back to her. I could see a slight tremor in her hand as she gripped Bear's collar. That kept the anger burning bright. "She doesn't have any right to come up here, to shove all this back in your face."

Em opened the door wider, finally releasing Bear, who ran to press up against me in search of pets. "Maybe, maybe not, but I can ask someone to leave if I want them to go. And if they don't, I have pepper spray and the sheriff's department on speed dial."

I gaped at my sister. "You didn't ask her to leave?"

Emerson nibbled on the corner of her lip. "I was going to, but there was something about her."

"Yeah, probably that she's a fucking con woman." Ridley might not be stealing money out of grannies' checking accounts, but that didn't make her any less of a swindler. Instead, she made that money off others' pain and suffering.

My sister was quiet for a moment, and the hairs on the back of my arms stood at attention.

"What?" I pressed.

Emerson swallowed as she looked down the road where Ridley had disappeared. "She said she thought I was the first in a string of twenty-three abductions. That I could help her find him."

An invisible fist twisted in my stomach. *Him.* The bastard who had nearly torn my sister from me.

I knew from every law enforcement training I'd done that the chances of Emerson's abduction being a one-off were slim to none. But in the months and years following, there hadn't been a single abduction in the area that fit the profile. So I'd always figured that the unsub had changed his MO. But Emerson's words had a niggle of doubt settling in.

"She was bluffing. Trying to get you to talk to her. I had a deputy look her up while I was on my way over here. She has one of those true-crime podcasts." People obsessed with that sort of stuff only made law enforcement's job harder. Sticking their noses in where they didn't belong and mucking up cases.

"I don't know. There was something about her. Something that said she cared. She was desperate almost."

"Desperate for a big payday probably," I muttered.

Emerson stared at me for a long moment, as if she was trying to recognize the person in front of her.

"Come on," I said, ushering her inside. "I'll make you some tea and check the security system, make sure the alerts on that camera out by the road ping my phone along with yours. I'll know if she comes back. I don't want you opening the door for her again."

Emerson stopped in the entryway crowded with her various works of art, Bear weaving circles around us. "If you keep dealing with everything for me, I'll never get stronger."

A fresh wave of guilt swept through me, a more complex one. The kind that meant trip wires and land mines. Because I hadn't realized until it was too late how Em's world had gotten smaller and smaller, until she was terrified to leave the property at all. She wouldn't even go outside unless Trey or I was here with her.

The therapist in town called it agoraphobia. Said it could be triggered by a traumatic event. Em had tried to keep up with seeing her, but it finally became too much, and she stopped going altogether. Em had finished all her high school credits online, even gotten a college degree in graphic design that way. Now she worked in the same field, one where all her work could be completed over the internet. I delivered her groceries and mail. Our local doctor even made house calls for her.

"I'm not dealing with everything," I argued. "I'm dealing with people who could cause you harm."

Emerson's jaw hardened. "I'm not weak."

I reared back. "I didn't say you were."

"Maybe not with your words. But your actions say it time and time again."

Acid burned at her accusation. Just more pain I was dumping at my sister's feet. More guilt making its home inside me. So deep I knew I'd never get it out. I hated that I'd hurt her. I'd never wanted to cause Emerson any more pain than she'd already endured. But I couldn't seem to stop stepping in to protect her. Because her safety mattered more than anything. So I'd take that guilt and let it drown me just a little more. It was the least I could do to atone for not being there when she needed me most.

Chapter Nine
Ridley

Pressure built behind my eyes as the wind whipped against my cheeks. But there were no tracks of wetness for the wind to find, no evidence of my grief for them to grab hold of in a stinging slap. My thighs burned as I climbed the hill on my bike, but I relished the pain, the proof I was alive.

I'd opted not to use the bike's electric aid, simply tearing out of Emerson's drive and heading for my temporary home. I knew I'd need the bite of discomfort to reel in my rioting emotions.

Colt's words echoed in my head. *You're scum.*

Maybe I was. Maybe I was worse than that. The lowest of the low. And not just for reminding Emerson of the worst moments of her life but for abandoning my sister when she'd needed me most.

My lungs burned as I pulled up to my campsite and slowed my bike to a stop. I simply stood there for a moment, just breathing. Breathing for her and for me—just like always.

I fished in my pack, pulling out my keys. The silver key ring glinted in the sunlight. I traced the lacrosse sticks with my fingertip as they rested in my palm. "I'm so sorry, Avs. You'll never know how much."

My phone dinged in my bag, and I tugged it free of its pocket. A new text flashed on the screen.

Marsha: On to a new one, I see. Hope they know how lucky they are to have you working it. Be careful but get it done.

That pressure behind my eyes intensified, the tornado of emotions dying to break free. That single kindness in the wake of all the ugly swirling was the thing that nearly broke me. But I didn't let it.

Me: Not the warmest welcome I've ever had.

Three dots appeared for a few seconds.

Marsha: If I remember correctly, I wasn't too pleased when John brought you home that day.

A laugh bubbled out of me as the memory of her creative cursing floated to the surface of my mind, along with her promise to make her husband sleep in the literal doghouse for promising to do an interview with me.

But when I'd told Marsha Ross a little of my story, she'd softened, tears filling her eyes at my loss. And when I was done sharing, done telling her how much I wanted her to find justice for her daughter, who'd gone missing from a local college campus, she'd agreed to an interview.

It was the first case I broke. The first where I'd helped put a monster away. One that gave me hope I could make a difference.

A new text filled the chat, pulling me out of the swirl of memory.

Marsha: If you let them know that beautiful heart of yours, that warrior spirit, there's no way they won't be on your side. And they are so damn lucky to have you as their champion.

The pressure was back, digging in, demanding release. I shoved back just as hard, trying to bury it deep. I didn't typically share my own story with the people I interviewed, only if I sensed they needed it. To know that they were in the hands of someone who had walked the path too. But there was always a cost to it. A price. But I'd pay it every time if it helped someone else.

Only, I wasn't sure Colter Brooks was open to hearing it. He'd painted me in his mind already. Looking only for the ugly and evil, not any possible good.

That was fine. He could think what he wanted to. I was going to find him closure all the same.

Not for him. For Emerson. And for so many more.

Me: Thanks for the reminder. Grateful for you. Hug Lucy and John for me.

Marsha: Will do. Send me a snail mail address if you can. I'll stick a dozen mint chip cookies in the post for you.

I smiled down at my phone. Of course she would. She'd become a second mom along the way. Following my every move and cheering me on. In the face of my own mother never acknowledging what I did, it was a balm. She'd never know just how much.

Grabbing my bag, I shifted off the bike and headed for my van. As I approached, a prickle skated over my skin, the kind I'd learned not to ignore. My gaze swept the surrounding campground. Nothing out of place. The only other sign of life was a tent set up at least two hundred yards away, but there was no car present with it.

I slid a hand into my pack and pulled out my Taser. My fingers curled around it, holding tight as I flipped up the safety. I crossed to my van and froze. There were scratch marks on the door, right around the lock.

Someone had tried to get in.

I didn't think they'd succeeded. They likely would've left the van door open if they had. For a fleeting moment, I thought about calling the sheriff's department. But somehow I didn't think Colt and his team would be too keen on riding out to a call from me.

Taking a deep breath, I slid my key into the lock, thankful I'd upgraded the system when I'd had it customized. I twisted the key and gripped my Taser tighter. Sliding the door open, I held my breath.

Nothing moved.

But the door to my narrow closet was slightly ajar. I let my bag fall to the ground so I was ready to fight. Stepping into the van, my pulse thrummed in my neck. I held my breath and counted to three.

One.

Two.

Three.

I jerked open the closet. A figure flashed in my vision, and then something hit me full force, and I was falling.

Chapter Ten
Ridley

I HIT THE FLOOR OF THE VAN WITH AN *OOMPH*, AND MY head slammed back against it. The force had pain flaring bright as light danced in my vision. Then a loud and panicked *meow* sounded in my ear.

My eyelids fluttered, my surroundings coming into focus again. The van. The open closet. And lots of fur. I hadn't been taken out by an intruder. I'd been taken out by my three-legged cat.

"Tater," I muttered.

She meowed again, settling into pissed-off chatter. I stayed lying on the floor of my van for a moment, my head aching. My hand sifted through Tater's fur, trying to calm her. The chattering eased, and she started to purr, but it only took a few seconds before she bit my hand.

The bites were never hard, exactly. It was her way of showing affection. But her *tooth hugs* could still draw blood on occasion.

I let her bite away as I nuzzled her to me. "I love you too."

The purring was back.

Slowly, I pushed to my feet, setting Tater down and surveying the van. It hadn't been ransacked. All my valuables were still in place. No one had made it inside.

But someone had tried.

That had a chill running through me. It must have been someone simply passing through the campsite, seeing what valuables they could find within easy reach. Because no one knew where I was staying. And the locals had just found out I was here. There wasn't time for sabotage.

I still hated the idea of someone trying to break into my haven. Pushing to my feet, my head thrummed. I needed some Tylenol stat.

Tater made a sound of protest as I moved.

"It's okay. You can come with me."

There was an excited meow this time as she bounded out of the van after me. I'd had Tater since she was a kitten. When her leg had been damaged in the birthing process, her owner had dumped her at a local shelter. Something about the determined, little, three-legged creature had called to me, and we'd been together ever since.

Because I'd had her since she was so young, taking her wherever I went, Tater was used to following me in the outdoors. The only issues arose when she spotted a dog. She was not a fan and would climb me like a tree until she was perched on my shoulder like a parrot, leaving claw marks in her wake.

But as the sun dipped toward the horizon, Tater stayed close. I made quick work of locking up my bike and let my gaze scan my surroundings as I went. Nothing out of place. But that didn't mean someone wasn't there.

A video call alert came from inside the van, and I whistled for Tater to follow me. She easily jumped up into the vehicle, and I shut the door behind her, locking it. As I hurried toward my computer, I saw the incoming video alert. I groaned as I took in Baker's name. Not exactly something that would help my headache.

Sliding quickly onto the chair at my desk, I hit *accept*. I'd expected just Baker, but instead it was a group call with him and

Sully. They appeared onscreen, Baker with LA behind him, and Sully with New York as his backdrop, so in opposition to my current setting. I forced a smile, trying to shake off the events of the afternoon. "Hey. What's up?"

Baker frowned at me. "What's going on with your hair?"

My gaze flew to the rectangle on the screen that showed my face. My long blond locks had formed a sort of rat's nest. I felt atop my head, wincing as I hit the tender spot where I'd clocked myself. "Was just out on my bike. That's all."

Tater jumped up onto my desk, meowing at Baker in an accusatory tone.

Sully leaned toward the camera, squinting. "You okay, Ridley?"

"Just dandy," I lied and had a feeling Sully could read it.

"The first episode is going up tomorrow," Baker cut in. "I need assurances that you actually have something here."

I wanted to growl at him but bit it back. "I have something." In reality, all I had so far was the background I'd managed to gather on Emerson's case. Recording it between paddleboarding and my trip into town had taken hardly any time at all. And I knew that wasn't a good sign. If I didn't get some firsthand accounts and quick, I was going to be in trouble.

"And that something is?" Baker pressed.

I hadn't wanted to lay my cards out just yet. I was still putting the pieces together. And I wanted the listeners to go on the journey with me, to care about Emerson's story so the others' would hit them even harder. Because if they cared, they'd rally around me. They'd turn over every rock until we had answers.

Answers I needed more than anything.

"I'm talking to locals. Getting a feel for the town and finding out more about Emerson."

"You've got people willing to go on the record?" he pressed.

I fought not to wince. "Not yet, but I will."

I knew Dean would go on the record, but he'd need parental permission, and I doubted they'd give it. Not to mention the fact that he didn't really know Emerson and would barely remember what had happened a decade ago.

Baker sighed as if so damned disappointed in me. "Ridley. Pull the plug on this. Come to LA and do the spin-off I pitched you for a couple of weeks."

I couldn't help the way my nose wrinkled, as if I smelled something bad. Baker had wanted me to help launch his newest true-crime venture. A podcast hosted by a bunch of reality TV stars who had made names for themselves by being total douchebags on a variety of dating shows. He was calling it *Reality Rampage*.

"No thanks. I'm good here."

"Ridley," Baker gritted out.

"Give her a few weeks," Sully interjected. "You know Rids always finds what she needs to."

A muscle fluttered wildly along Baker's jaw. "Fine. You've got two weeks. You fuck this up and the leash gets shorter. These advertising dollars pay your salary too."

And with that, he hit *end* on the call. But Sully remained.

I slumped in my chair. "Thanks for having my back."

"Always." He studied me for a long moment, a grandfatherly concern radiating through his blue-gray eyes. "There a reason why this one is calling you?"

I usually shared with Sully. Told him my thought process. But I hadn't with Emerson's case. Couldn't get myself to say it out loud quite yet. So I gave him a half-truth. "She might be alive, but he still stole her life."

Sully's mouth pulled down in a frown. "How so?"

"She's still so traumatized she never leaves the house. I don't blame her. She has no idea who took her. She would have to walk around not knowing if the man who'd just held the door open for her is the same one who kidnapped her. She has no idea what he'd planned to do with her. All those unknowns, they've taken everything from her."

Sully scrubbed a hand over his stubbled cheek. "Can't imagine."

"Me either." I sighed, toying with a pen on my desk. "There's more. I think there's a chance this was the first in a series of abduction murders."

"Well, why the hell didn't you tell the suit that? You know he would've laid off you if you connected it to something serial."

I winced, knowing he was right. "I also know that he would've pushed me to lay it all out right at the beginning. But I have to follow the trail. Start where he did. And that's with Emerson."

Sully squeezed the back of his neck. "All right. What do you need from me?"

"Right now I gotta prep some stuff for tomorrow. You good to get the episode submitted? I didn't have any tweaks."

He straightened, jerking his chin in a nod. "I'll get it uploaded and ready to go."

"Thanks, Sul. Don't work too hard."

His lips twitched. "That's you we're talking about."

I grinned. "Don't worry. I'm hitting the lake with my paddleboard again tomorrow morning."

"Glad to hear it. Be safe," Sully called, reaching for the end button.

"You too."

The video call ended, and I was left to look at the background of my desktop. It was a photo of Avery and me. We were thirteen and in our backyard in Ohio. We'd been having a summer picnic, and my mom had taken the photo without us knowing it. Our heads were tipped back, and we were laughing full-out.

Avery had always been shyer than me. She didn't laugh like that with just anyone. Only the people she trusted most. And that laughter was a gift, a gift I got because I was in that inner circle.

I couldn't remember what we'd been talking about at the picnic. What had spawned that sort of cackle. And that killed. It felt like I lost more and more pieces as time passed. I'd replay old voicemails and videos just to remember what Avery's voice sounded like. But I didn't have her laugh. Didn't have that full-out, uninhibited cackle that she only shared with me and a couple of others.

Pain—the kind that made it hard to breathe—washed through me, digging in and pressing against my chest. It wasn't constant anymore, the way it had been in the beginning. But that just meant, when it sidelined me out of nowhere, it stole my breath.

Only it wasn't out of nowhere. Not really.

I tugged the keys from my pocket and found the tiniest one, the one that resembled a mailbox key. It wasn't as if I had visitors to my van, but still I kept one drawer on my desk locked. It wasn't the one that held my recording equipment, even though that would've fetched more than a decent price if sold. This drawer housed something much more important.

Sliding the key into the lock on the bottom-left drawer, I twisted it, feeling the lock give way. Countless file folders peeked out. Names and locations. All the details I could find. But I went for the first file, the one where I housed my overview.

Sometimes, I'd deep-dive into one specific case; for others, I needed the big picture. Today it was the overview. I needed to see how all those pieces connected and remind myself why what lay in front of me was so important. It wasn't just Emerson's story. It was twenty-three other women's too.

I laid the file on my desk, making Tater jump down and move to her cat tree in the corner, and steeled myself before opening it. I always did. Because what lay inside suggested that the monster who'd taken Emerson was still out there and he'd only grown crueler.

Flipping open the file, I stared down at the first sheet of paper. As I'd pulled the strands together, I'd put them in chronological order. And as I'd done that, I'd seen how the monster had developed. How he'd twisted further and further.

It started with Emerson. A thwarted abduction. I hadn't found a single case that fit the parameters before her.

And after her, he'd gotten smarter, learned from his mistakes. The next girl he'd taken, he'd used chloroform, knocking her out for longer, so when she woke on the side of a road, everything had been hazy. That may have been his only gift, that she didn't remember the assault that had occurred.

The next five victims he'd left alive, but with growing expressions of violence. Until number seven hadn't survived at all.

That was his turning point. When evil truly took hold.

No one survived after that as far as I could tell. And as time passed, the bodies that were found showed increasing evidence of torture from their time in captivity.

The pressure was back in my chest, the burning pain. I just kept breathing. I focused on the ties between the women. The ties that no law enforcement thought were enough to pursue, not even the FBI when I'd brought the new information to their attention.

All blonds ages sixteen to twenty-four. Athletes who excelled at their chosen sport. It wasn't always the same one, everything from tennis to soccer to gymnastics. They were state champions, medal winners, scholarship recipients. All were high-achieving students as well, and when I'd done a deeper dive there, I'd found out they had all been members of the National Honor Society.

I'd gone down a rabbit hole with that, searching every employee of the organization I could find. But there wasn't a single one I could prove had been away from home all the times girls had gone missing.

Because not all the women I'd identified as his victims had

been found. In fact, only about two-thirds had. Survivors or bodies that families had been forced to lay to rest across the country. But I knew the torture of not having bones to put in the ground, a framework to say last goodbyes within as I hoped they'd find peace. It was a special kind of torture, the type that occasionally slid the tiniest flicker of hope into that black night. The taunting voice that said, *Maybe she's still alive*.

I flipped to the next page, my finger following down the list of names. Some missing persons cases. Some open murder cases. That finger stopped on the name that burned.

Avery Bennett.

Victim number ten. Lacrosse player. Arizona State Champion. National Honor Society. National Merit Scholar. Recipient of the Hayes Fellowship for sports medicine. Daughter. Sister.

Gone.

As if she'd disappeared into thin air, never to be seen again.

"I'm going to find you, Avs. I promise."

No matter how many interfering sheriffs got in my way. No matter what accusations they threw at me. I would find my sister, my twin.

Whatever it took.

Chapter Eleven
Colt

"Don't give me that look," I muttered as Bowser looked up at me from where his head rested on his paws. The mix of lab, cattle dog, and basset hound had given him eyes that were especially good for begging. "Oh all right." I tossed him a piece of bacon.

Even though Bowser was approaching twelve, he was surprisingly spry when meat of any kind was involved. He caught the piece on the fly, practically swallowing it straight down.

I shoved the final piece into my mouth and chugged the rest of my coffee. I'd need it. Sleep had been fitful at best, Ridley's pain-streaked eyes haunting my mind in waking and sleep. The deep blue calling out with unspoken accusations and a woundedness that was somehow still beautiful.

The legs of my chair scraped against the floor as I pushed back from the kitchen table. I didn't need to think about Ridley's pain. I needed to think about my sister's, the one who needed protecting in all of this. Not to mention the rest of Shady Cove, who didn't need the pain of the incident dredged up or the eyes of the world turned on us once again.

It wasn't a time any of us wanted to revisit. One where people had begun to look at one another with suspicion instead of kindness. It didn't help that the sheriff's department and the state police had called in everyone under the sun for questioning. All of Emerson's teachers, her tennis coach, the support staff at the high school and park where she practiced, the people she worked with after school. It had cast a shadow on all of them.

We didn't need to return to that. I wouldn't let it happen.

Grabbing a thermos from my cabinet, I filled it with the rest of the pot of coffee. "You want to hang on the porch today?" I asked Bowser.

He ambled to his feet in answer. Trey and I had made him a doghouse that lived on the back deck, and he had plenty of water out there. He knew not to leave the cabin's property, not even to jump in the lake.

And it was tempting, since my cabin almost became one with it, the deck hovering over the water. But Bowser knew better than to go there without me present.

I pressed a hand to the biometric lock on my gun locker by the door. It housed my service weapon, a rifle, and a shotgun. We hadn't had trouble with bears at my place, but it was always better to be safe than sorry. Donning my weapon, I headed for my SUV with only one destination in mind.

It hadn't taken long for me to find her. Not when I had access to all the local databases and her driver's license number in my phone. Ridley Sawyer Bennett had reserved a campsite out at Lonepine Lake for an entire month. She'd have to eat the cost of that reservation because there was no way she was seeing it through.

I knew the trek to the lake like the back of my hand. As I crested the hill, I slowed, taking in the one other campsite that was taken. I couldn't stop the way my gut twisted. Ridley was so damned exposed up here. Alone except for that damned cat.

I told myself the concern was simply a natural byproduct of

my job. I was used to looking out for others. Warning them of things that could compromise their safety.

But I knew I was a goddamned liar.

I shoved that down and parked my SUV by Ridley's ridiculous teal van. The entire back was covered in stickers. They mostly had to do with places I assumed she'd been. The colors and shapes were vast, but there was one thing they all had in common. An absurd whimsy.

There was a unicorn with a sparkly rainbow overhead. An alien with *Beam Me Up* and *Roswell, NM* beneath it. What looked like Bigfoot with *Bend, Oregon* above it. A tie-dyed *Keep Austin Weird*. And countless more.

Together they formed a chaotic beauty that mirrored the woman herself.

I forced myself to think about everything that was at stake here. To think about Emerson and everything she'd been through.

Rounding the van, I took in the pulled curtains. Probably still sleeping. She'd just have to get up.

I knocked on the door. No answer. I waited for a moment, listening for any signs of life. There were none. I knocked again. Still nothing.

A prickle of unease shifted through me. Not even the curtains rustled from the cat hearing me. I stepped back, taking in the campsite with new eyes. Everything was in place. Bike locked up. Picnic table cleared.

What Emerson had shared circled in my mind. Twenty-three other victims Ridley thought were linked to Emerson. Something that felt a lot like dread settled in my gut.

I walked around the van, a memory tickling the back of my brain. Her paddleboard. It was missing.

Relief rushed through me. A relief I didn't want to look too closely at. Instead, I headed toward the lake below.

As I approached, I caught sight of movement. My steps faltered as I took her in. Blond hair piled high atop her head. Clad in only tiny spandex shorts and one of those workout tops. Her arms flexed as she drove a paddle into the water, golden skin glowing in the early morning light.

Then she simply stopped all movement, letting the board coast through the water. She tipped her face up to the sun, letting the rays soak into her skin. She stayed that way for a long moment.

I wanted to know what was passing through her mind. What thoughts swirled there. And as her board got closer to shore, I saw more. The dark shadows that rimmed her eyes. The way she gripped the paddle for dear life. It was in such opposition to the image I thought I'd seen. A woman at peace on the water. Maybe it was peace that she was searching for, she just hadn't found it yet.

Fuck.

I didn't need to be worried about Ridley and her peace. I cleared my throat.

The sound made Ridley's eyes fly open and that startling blue settled on me. Her board wobbled slightly, making the creature at the front of it hiss.

I watched in shocked fascination as her three-legged cat, clad in a life jacket, leapt from the board and into the water, easily swimming to shore. The moment it reached the lake's bank it shook out its fur and simply waited.

"What the hell?" I mumbled.

The cat just stared back at me, eyes full of judgment.

"Can I help you, Sheriff?" Ridley stepped off the board and into water that went to her knees. I knew it had to be freezing given that it was only late May and the lake was fed by snowmelt. But it had nothing on the frigid tone of her voice.

My gaze moved over her face in an attempt not to settle on any one thing. If I couldn't take in her beauty, her pain, then maybe I could keep myself in line. "You haven't left yet."

Ridley lifted the paddleboard out of the water with ease even though I knew it wasn't light. Her shoulders flexed with the movement, the golden skin pulling taut over lean muscle. My fingers itched to trace the divots and curves. I bit the inside of my cheek until the coppery taste of blood filled my mouth.

"Doesn't sound like a question, Law Man," Ridley said as she slid her feet into sandals and headed for the trail, the damned cat bounding after her.

Annoyance flared as I followed her and the animal. "I'm wondering why you haven't. Emerson isn't going to talk to you. This town won't talk to you. And I'm sure as hell not talking to you."

She flicked a look over her shoulder, those blue depths pinning me to the spot. "Sure looks like you're talking now."

I snapped my mouth closed, my back teeth grinding together. "You know what I mean."

Ridley shrugged, navigating the final stretch of trail with ease. She seemed at home here even though it had only been a couple of days according to her campsite reservation. Maybe it was that she was at home in nature as a whole.

It fit. Hair bleached by the sun. Skin kissed gold by the same. A body toned by traversing mountains and water.

Fucking hell.

"I haven't forced a single soul to talk to me. Never have, never will. I'll give people the opportunity, for sure. I'll plead my case and hope they're willing to help. But if it's too painful, I'll accept their need to stay silent."

"Help?" I scoffed. "That's what you think you're doing? Helping?"

Ridley's body tensed but she kept on moving, leaning her board against the van. She turned to face me, not slow, not fast, but as if she were in complete control. "Yes. I'm helping to find the truth. To bring closure. To stop someone from hurting *more* innocent people."

My gut churned. I wanted to know about that *more*, but I wasn't about to ask her. "All you're doing is ripping open old wounds. And for what? A few thousand more followers on TikTok? More money in your pocket from whatever fucking sponsorships you have?"

Fire blazed in those blue eyes. So hot I swore there were hints of silver flecking her irises. A white-hot flame that turned me to ash on the spot.

"You don't know the first thing about me. If you did, you'd know that's the furthest thing from the truth. But you haven't taken a damned second to get to know me. It's been snap judgments and bitter assumptions from the second you first saw me. Maybe that's why this case has been unsolved for as long as it has. You won't open your eyes and actually *see*."

With that she unlocked the van's door and climbed inside, slamming it in her and the cat's wake.

I stared at the van for a long moment. The way the curtains rippled with the echoes of that slam, the same way the sound echoed in my ears. The sound of the slam and her words.

Because she'd gotten one thing right, I hadn't solved Emerson's case. Not in the nine years I'd been on the job. And that just made me hate myself a little more.

Chapter Twelve
Ridley

The words Colt had hurled in my direction clung to me like smoke from a campfire. It was as if they'd been baked into my flesh. After he'd left, I'd tried yoga, meditation, even going for a quick run. None of it had helped.

Because there was a tiny voice inside my head that wondered if I was hurting others in my quest for the truth. I sure as hell was hurting Colt. Because that's what was fueling his verbal lashings—pain. The agony that came from losing a sister. I knew that pain well. It was just that he'd found his again. I never had.

I guided my bike around a curve in the road, letting the wind try to wash away his accusations. Or at least help me push through them so I could take the next steps I had to for the podcast—for the investigation. I wasn't going back to Cowboy Coffee, at least not yet. I wanted to give Ezra time to cool down, to consider that I might have something to offer.

So instead, I headed for The Whiskey Barrel. It was lunchtime now, and I hoped I might find a few day drinkers who'd be willing to give me background on the story. Maybe they'd remember players at the time who had been overlooked by law enforcement. Anything that might give me a lead. Because if this was the perpetrator's first crime, a bungled one at that, there was a good chance they'd left more clues behind here than anywhere else. There was even a possibility the unsub had lived in Shady Cove at the time. Maybe they still did.

I parked my bike outside the bar and locked it, heading for the thick wooden door. The moment I stepped inside, I had to blink. The sun outside was bright, but in here, it might as well have been midnight. The low glow of bar lighting made people forget they were drinking their days away.

As my eyes grew accustomed to the low light, I took in the crowd, or lack thereof. A woman and man sat at the bar a few stools apart, while another guy sat at one of the tables with a burger and fries in front of him. My stomach rumbled. All I'd had for breakfast was an energy bar, and I'd been too pissed off to eat anything after Colt's visit.

Gray eyes lifted from a worn paperback and locked on me as I approached the bar. They were assessing eyes. They didn't have the anger Colt's had carried, but they weren't exactly welcoming either.

I didn't let that stop me. I headed straight for the bartender. "I take it you've gotten a warning message about me."

Trey stood there, his form at ease but somehow still appearing ready to strike as he set the book down. "Small town. News travels."

"You want me to leave?" I asked. It was better to know now.

He studied me for another long moment. I had no idea what he was searching for, but he seemed to find it. "Lunch, booze, or both?"

Relief swept through me as I pulled out the stool and sat. "Food please, and I wouldn't hate a Shirley Temple."

Trey's lips twitched, making the dark-blond scruff there move in a comical sort of way. "Shirley Temple?"

I shrugged, resting my bag on the stool next to me. "Don't

judge. It's a happy drink, and I think we could all use some happy now and then."

"Fair enough." He slid a single-paged menu across the bar and got to work on my drink.

"Plus, who doesn't have a weakness for maraschino cherries?"

Trey chuckled. "I'd say the majority of the population. Most pluck 'em out of their drinks and leave them behind."

"They're missing out," I mumbled as my gaze scanned the menu. "Any recommendations?"

"I'm partial to the barbeque chicken wrap and you can never go wrong with the fries."

"Sign me up," I said, setting the menu down.

"You got it, boss." Trey placed a tall Shirley Temple complete with cherries and an umbrella on a napkin. Then he set a small dish full of more cherries next to it.

I stared at them for a long moment as I heard Trey holler my order back into the kitchen. When he turned back to me, I was still staring at the two items.

"Something wrong?" he asked.

I blinked a few times, trying to clear the burn in my eyes. "Why are you being nice to me? Pretty sure your bestie is googling ways to have me evicted from town limits or how to dissolve a body in acid."

Trey barked out a laugh and leaned against the back bar. "Colt takes the weight of the world on his shoulders. And he'll do anything to keep his sister or anyone else he cares about from harm. It's the kind of duty that's burned into a person."

All of that read true. I'd seen it flare to life at Emerson's house. But also in his concern for every person that crossed his path. Even me.

"All right. But shouldn't you have his back and be giving me the boot?" I lifted the drink and put the straw to my lips, the sweet combination of Sprite and grenadine playing on my tongue.

Trey was quiet for a moment. Even in the short interactions I'd had with the man, I could tell he wasn't afraid of silence, and he wouldn't be rushed. This time it was as if he was deciding whether I was worthy of the truth. "Emmie says you linked her case to others."

My brows pulled together for a split second before the confusion cleared. "Emerson?"

He lifted his chin in assent. "You've found other similar incidents?"

That buzz was back. Trey was one of the last people I'd expected to be my in. The fact that he was close with Colt being high on the reasons why not. But it also made sense that he'd know Emerson for that very reason. "Twenty-three of them."

Trey's fingers tightened on the bar behind him, knuckles bleaching white. "Holy hell."

"I want to follow the trail, but I have to start where I think it all began, and that's with Emerson's case."

Trey's gray eyes flashed. "You don't know what you're asking. Digging up that sort of pain."

"I do know."

The spark of anger in those eyes shifted to curiosity.

I knew what I had to do. There was no way the people of this town would trust me enough to talk unless they knew my own scars, understood that I was one of their own, that we were members of a club no one wanted to be a part of.

Taking a deep breath, I steeled myself. I pulled that layer of numbness over me so I could say what I had to without losing it. "My twin sister went missing the night before our college graduation. One moment we were at a party, the next she was simply gone. Nothing left but her key chain smeared with blood. Police never had any leads."

Trey didn't move or speak, that silence he was comfortable with wrapping around us both for a few long moments. "You never found her."

It wasn't exactly a question, but I answered it anyway. "No. And trust me, I've tried. I'm still trying. But in the meantime, I'm also trying to help others. I'm not always successful. Life doesn't guarantee grand movie endings. But every once in a while we get one. We put the bad guys away so they can't hurt anyone else. *That's* what I'm trying to do."

Trey let my speech wash over him, taking in each revelation. I thought he'd say something about that loss, about my mission, but he didn't. He gave me something else entirely. "I was the one who found her. Emmie, I mean."

My jaw went slack. That hadn't been in a single article I'd read. All they'd shared was the road she'd been discovered on. "How?"

Trey's throat worked as he swallowed. "I'd been camping. Spotty service. So I didn't get the text from Colt that Emmie was gone until an hour or so after he'd sent it. But the moment I did, I packed up and got back in my truck. Everyone was out searching, and I told them I'd do the same. Pure dumb luck I hit the road she was walking down."

He let out a shuddering breath, and suddenly it was like he wasn't looking at me at all. "I'll never forget it as long as I live, my headlights hitting her. She was limping, blood staining one side of her clothes, holding her arm close to her body the best she could. Terrified out of her mind."

He worked his jaw back and forth as the memory played out in his mind. "People think she's weak, even Colt sometimes, no matter how much he doesn't mean to. But they're all dead fucking wrong. She's the strongest person I've ever known."

"You're right. Because she got out. Got free."

Trey blinked a few times, clearing his vision. "Yeah." His

voice was more of a rasp now, laced with the pain the memory brought on.

Colt's accusations filled my mind. I was causing pain. There was no way around it. So in some ways he'd been right. But I also knew that sometimes pain in the here and now was your only chance for true healing. I'd seen it in Marsha and John. Seen it in countless others.

And more than that, wasn't some pain worth it if there was a chance we could keep innocent lives from being lost in the future? A chance that we could stop others from having to mourn their loved ones?

"Can you tell me where exactly you found her?" I asked. "I want to retrace Emerson's steps from that night."

Trey stiffened. "Not sure she's ready to share that with you."

I met his stare dead-on. "I'm not asking her to. I've got enough information to piece it together. I just didn't know the exact final spot. I won't press Emerson. She'll talk to me if and when she's ready. If she never wants to, that's okay too. It's whatever she needs."

Some of the tension left Trey's muscles. "It was on Country Road 33. Between Pine Butte and Cattle Run Road."

I pulled out my phone and plugged in the information. "Thanks, Trey."

He nodded, mulling something over. "Go easy on Colt."

My brows lifted at that. I'd expected a warning to stay away from Emerson, not Colt.

Trey met my gaze, not looking away. "Colt was the one who was supposed to pick her up that night. He was late."

A heaviness settled in my stomach, as though it was suddenly filled with liquid metal. I'd felt for Colt before. Understood what it was like to watch someone you loved disappear. But we had even more in common than I'd realized. The noxious monster that was guilt, eating everything around it alive.

Trey swallowed hard as he pushed off the bar. "If he comes off as an ass, it's just because he thinks he already failed Emmie and doesn't want to do it again."

And wouldn't I do the same damn thing if I found Avery now? I'd be a bulldog keeping away anyone who might cause her any sort of harm or discomfort.

Only I knew deep down that I wasn't going to find Avery breathing. I just wanted to find her at all.

Chapter Thirteen
Ridley

I SPREAD THE MAP OUT OVER THE PICNIC TABLE, TAKING in Shady Cove and its surrounding areas. It had cost me ten dollars and fifty cents at the local gas station and was well worth the price. The paper version would've annoyed Baker, but there were times tech just didn't give you the same perspective.

Grabbing a yellow highlighter, I popped the top and leaned over the map. It didn't take me long to find the local park where Emerson had been taken—it was where I now stood. I placed an *X* there and circled it. Then I found all the other points of interest—her house, Cowboy Coffee, the school—and placed *X*'s there as well. I was sure there were other places she frequented, but I wasn't certain how I'd find out what they were.

Next I went in search of the area Trey had told me he'd found Emerson in. It took me a couple of minutes to locate County Road 33. Once I did, I traced it with my finger until I came across Cattle Run Road. I placed another *X* in the section between there and Pine Butte, then circled it.

I covered the yellow highlighter and went back to the box. There was orange, pink, blue, purple, and green left. I went for orange first. Taking my time, I mapped out every possible route the unsub could've taken. There were seven.

It would've taken me a hell of a lot less time to drive them all, but driving them wouldn't give me time to take in the details. Plus filming a route or two would give me good content to post on my social media accounts. The videos would really let people feel like they were in Emerson's shoes. And if they felt that connection to her, they would do more to help. Maybe the locals would feel the same if they saw them too.

Glancing at my watch, I realized that I wouldn't have time to ride one before my first meeting. My first interview. My first puzzle piece. I'd spent hours after my video call with Baker and Sully going over the files and sending countless emails for interview requests. I'd had exactly two bites. But they were two I didn't have before.

Folding the map, I placed it back in my bag along with the highlighters. Then I swung the bag over my shoulder. I left my bike locked to the rack at the park and headed toward the tennis courts. I wanted to get a feel for it. To see what Emerson would've seen that night.

A yipped bark sounded, making me turn. A pack of three dogs strained against their leashes. There was a tiny fluffball whose eyes you couldn't see, a midsize beagle mix, and a larger dog of indeterminant origin. And the woman gripping their tethers with all her might was familiar.

I grinned as I crouched down to greet them. "Hi, Celia."

"Hello," she said with a smile. "How's Tater?"

I scratched the fluffball's chin while the largest pup licked my face. "Living the dream and judging everyone who crosses her path."

Celia chuckled. "As she should." She studied me for a long moment, curiosity in her gaze. "Visiting the crime scene?"

News in small towns was no joke, but I straightened and nodded. "I've got an interview in a few minutes."

Her mouth thinned into a hard line. "It was a dark period for us."

"Would you want to tell me what it was like to live through?" I asked gently.

Celia's brows flew up. "On your radio show?"

I fought the grin that wanted to surface. "It's not actually on the radio."

"You know what I mean. I can't be bothered to keep up with what they call all this stuff. From the Ticker Tocker to the graham cracker. It's all too much for these old bones."

My lips twitched. "I don't know. You don't look too old to me, wrangling those three beasts."

Celia cackled and bent to pet her dogs. "That they are. We've got to work on leash training before they can be adopted, but we're having minimal success there."

"You're getting them used to new sights and sounds. I think that's a victory."

"You're danged right," she agreed, chest swelling with pride.

I pulled a card from my back pocket and handed it to her. "If you do ever feel up to sitting down, on the record or off, I'd love to get your take on everything."

Celia frowned down at the rectangle of cardstock as if it held some sort of secret. "Don't want to hurt anyone by flapping my gums."

"I don't think speaking the truth is ever a bad thing, especially not if it's done with kindness and goodwill."

She stared at the card for a moment before her gaze lifted to mine. "Grew up with Julie Sinclair's mama. Would've broken her heart to see what happened to her family."

Julie Sinclair was Emerson's mother and I guessed Colt's too. After finding out she'd died of a heart attack, I'd done as much research as I could on her, but there hadn't been much to find.

She married young to her high school boyfriend, who went into the army not long after they wed. He had been killed in a training exercise while serving.

What I hadn't found in that research was the son they'd apparently had. Four years after her husband's death, she remarried to a Shady Cove local, Franklin Sinclair. But Franklin had split when Emerson was six, leaving Julie a single parent.

"Julie never recovered from what happened to her little girl," Celia whispered. "Even though she got her back, she saw monsters everywhere."

"It's easy to do when you've seen the evil out there," I told Celia. "It just means we have to hold onto the good that much more. The only thing that can cast out darkness is light."

Celia studied me for a long moment. "That's a profound thing to have realized for someone so young."

I shrugged. "Sometimes life teaches you lessons early."

"Sometimes it does."

Movement caught my eye as a sleek sedan pulled into the parking lot by the tennis courts. I hadn't expected my interview subject to arrive in what looked like a top-of-the-line Mercedes, but maybe he had family money.

I glanced back at Celia. "I think that's my interview. If you want to talk at any time, you've got my information."

She nodded but her mouth had formed that tense line again. "I'll think about it."

"All I can ask," I said, starting toward the sedan.

"Give Tater a snuggle for me," Celia called.

I shot a grin back at her. "Will do."

A door slammed, and I watched as my interview subject climbed out of his sedan. It seemed like the coach had kept up with his tennis practices or some other routine. He looked fit in his expensive-looking joggers and a polo shirt. But his smile was warm, accentuating the lines around his eyes. They were the kind of lines that told me he made the action often and that set my nerves at ease.

"Ridley Sawyer?" he asked as he crossed the parking lot toward me.

"Hi, Coach Kerr. Thanks for meeting me."

"Not a problem." He extended a hand. "And call me Bryan."

I took his palm in a shake, appreciating the honesty of the calluses there, ones I was sure were courtesy of the hours he spent with a racket in his hand. "Nice to meet you. Would you like to sit?"

I gestured to the picnic table. It would give us a view of the courts for our conversation, points of reference for a better feel of that night.

Bryan shifted from one foot to the other, casting a quick glance over his shoulder. "Sure."

I read his movements as nervousness but knew that a conversation like this would put anyone on edge. Lowering myself to the table, I reached into my backpack.

"I'd rather this not be on the record," Bryan said quickly as he sat.

My eyes flared. He'd agreed to an interview, though I hadn't specified whether that interview would be recorded. I slowly pulled my hand out of my pack. "Want to tell me why?"

His throat worked as he swallowed, his gaze pulling to the park and courts to his left. "There's not a day that goes by I don't kick myself for not staying around longer. For not waiting until Colt got here. But I'd had a long day, and all I was thinking about was myself."

There was no denying the true guilt in Bryan's voice and expression. It scraped at my skin, a reminder of all the lives that were affected by things like this, all the people who still bore the scars.

Bryan looked back to me. "I would love to help. Would love for the monster that took Emerson to finally be brought to justice. But I can't put my family through all that attention being on us again. It nearly broke us the first time."

It was my turn to feel the sucker punch of guilt. I knew that Bryan Kerr had been questioned twice before police retrieved footage from a local gas station that corroborated his alibi. But a lifetime could pass in the few days where people thought you might be capable of the worst.

"Off the record," I promised. "Is it all right if I take notes?"

Bryan nodded. "That's fine."

I grabbed a notebook and pen from my pack. It would be better than tapping them out on my phone, because if I held the device, part of Bryan would always wonder if I was recording him somehow. Low tech or no tech was better.

"How long have you known Emerson?" I asked, starting us off easy.

A soft smile played at the coach's mouth. "Around here you know just about everyone from birth. I went to school with Emerson's mom, Julie. Remember when Julie brought her home from the hospital."

"It must be nice, being a part of a community like that."

"It is. Most of the time anyway." Bryan took a deep breath. "Her being taken, it rocked us all. The kind of thing that makes you look at everyone with suspicion. But nothing like that has happened since, so I figure it must have been an outsider. Don't you think?"

That was a reasonable assumption to make, but I couldn't give him my certainty, no matter how badly he wanted it. "It's definitely possible. I'm hoping I can find something that will point us in the right direction."

Bryan nodded, scrubbing a hand over his clean-shaven jaw. "I don't know how. Colt's been circling back on this case every year since he joined the force."

My fingers tightened around my pen at the mention of Colt's name. I didn't need a reminder of the sheriff and his razor-sharp tongue. "Sometimes an outside perspective helps."

"Fair enough. How can I help?"

I appreciated the openness and willingness to aid however he could. "Think back to that time. Was there anyone who paid Emerson extra attention? Anyone who seemed to get too close?"

Bryan frowned, drumming his fingers on the picnic table. "Not that I can think of. Everyone liked to watch Emerson shine. She was one of those that even though she was shy, she radiated light. Kind and hardworking, and the best damn tennis player I coached in all my years."

"And that skill meant people paid attention to her?" I pressed.

The coach nodded. "Couldn't be helped. I had to pair her with the boys in practice because no one else on the girls' team was even good enough to practice with her."

I scrawled that little bit of information down. "Were the boys welcoming of her?"

Bryan's lips twitched. "Some laughed when she kicked their butts. A few were salty about it."

"Can you give me those names?"

"Oh, they wouldn't—"

"I just want to talk to them."

Bryan's mouth pressed into a firm line before he spoke. "Matt Anderson and Oren Mills come to mind. They both still live in town. Matt's got a wife and three kids now. Oren works at the local mechanic shop."

I quickly jotted the names down. "Do you—"

The sound of an engine had me glancing up to see an older-model truck pull into the parking lot by the tennis courts. Even though it had some years on it, it was still in good condition.

Bryan's eyes flashed with heat. "Are you interviewing Grady Smith?"

"Yes, but not for another thirty minutes," I said, glancing down at my watch.

A muscle fluttered in Bryan's cheek. "I'd rethink that if I were you. That man is a menace."

"I can handle myself," I assured him.

"I need to go," Bryan said, swinging his legs around the bench.

"We barely talked—"

The coach cut me off with a shake of his head. "It was a mistake. I shouldn't have said I'd meet you. Good luck, Miss Sawyer, but don't contact me again."

My jaw dropped. I'd had interviews end abruptly before, but it was usually because I'd touched on a sore spot. I watched as Bryan crossed to his sleek sedan just as Grady Smith climbed out of his truck. And the glare Grady leveled at Bryan was one that would've had me swallowing my tongue.

Chapter Fourteen
Ridley

Grady Smith was older than the last photo I could find online. His hair was more silver than light brown now, and he had more lines around his eyes and mouth. But they didn't seem to be the lines that came from smiling and laughing, at least as far as I could tell.

He'd worked for Shady Cove Parks and Rec as a groundskeeper when Emerson was taken. He was one of the few that law enforcement had circled around before finally giving up due to lack of evidence. But that attention had led to Grady leaving his job. As far as my online research could tell, he'd taken another on a road construction crew a couple of towns over.

"Hello, Mr. Smith," I greeted him, crossing toward him and extending a hand as Bryan peeled out of the parking lot. "Thank you for meeting me."

His gaze swept over me before coming to rest on my outstretched palm. "Grady," he said before taking it.

"Thank you, Grady."

He held my hand for a beat longer than was necessary. "You look too young to be doing investigative reporting."

The hold and the statement didn't read *creepy* to me, more like a display of dominance. I'd give it to him. Whatever he needed to do to feel okay about giving me this interview. I'd gotten good at feigning deference to alpha-male personalities. It didn't matter to me if they wanted to be known as the apex predator, just as long as they gave me the information I needed.

I gave Grady an easy smile. "Twenty-seven, and been doing this for more than four years now."

He ran a finger across the scruff below his bottom lip. "Practically still a baby. Your parents okay with your career path?"

A hint of annoyance flickered, but I shoved it down. "You'd have to ask them."

Grady chuckled. "Fair enough." He scanned our surroundings. "Where do you want to do this?"

Relief swept through me that he wasn't asking to be off the record like the coach. Because if I didn't come back with some interviews soon, Baker was going to cut this season short. "I thought we could walk and talk. You could show me where you were when you last saw Emerson and anything you observed."

His fingers tapped against the outside of his thigh. "Yeah. Whatever."

It was a bizarre statement for someone in his midfifties. It felt like the phrase of someone younger.

Swinging my bag around, I pulled out two wireless lav mics. "I'll have you attach one of these to your shirt so we can get good quality sound. It'll connect with my phone, which will be recording."

I'd found that it was better to explain how each step worked so no one felt like I was trying to pull something over on them. But Grady's eyes still narrowed on the mic, though he didn't say a word as he took it from me and clipped it to his tee.

I turned my own on and fastened it to my shirt. Pulling out my phone, I quickly attached the receiver to my lightning port and opened the recording app. "Testing, testing." My levels were in the acceptable range. I'd become an expert in where to place my mic to get that on the first try or two. I glanced at Grady. "Can you say something for me?"

"Something," he muttered.

The level was a bit high. "Can you move the mic a little farther away from your mouth."

Grady's amber eyes hardened but he moved to adjust the lavalier.

"Try it again."

"How's this?" he asked.

I watched the screen. "We're good." I hit the *record* button and carefully slid the phone into my pocket.

Grady started toward the tennis courts without waiting for me. There were four in total, and it looked like two were now being used for pickleball. Just one thing that I knew had to have changed in the past ten years.

The moment of distraction meant I had to pick up my pace to catch up with my interview subject. "What all has changed in the park in the past ten years?"

Grady sent me a sidelong look, surprise lacing it. He probably thought I'd dive straight into the heavy, but that wasn't how I liked to work. He took a moment to really take in his surroundings. "Fucking pickleball," he groused.

I couldn't help but chuckle. "A little louder than tennis."

He shook his head. "Thank God I got out of here before all the yuppies and millennials started playing that shit."

"Definitely a headache starter."

Grady's gaze moved on from the courts. "New playground equipment. Regraded walking trails into the woods there. And more lights. The lights went in right after the girl went missing."

It was interesting that he'd said *the girl*. Not using Emerson's name depersonalized her. But there could be a million different reasons he'd do that. "Can you walk me through the day she went missing?"

Grady's jaw worked back and forth as his molars ground together. "Just like any other day. Wife made me breakfast, and I headed to work. Boss wanted me to prune all the shrubs around the park. They were starting to creep into the lawn."

I followed his line of sight as he led me out onto the grass. I could see how the forest around the park on three sides could easily encroach. "That's a big task."

Grady simply grunted in agreement. "And it wasn't like his ass was going to help me. Worked all day with only a short break for lunch. But the boss wanted me to finish it in two days. Was still working when the tennis team started practicing."

"You had to see them practicing often, right?"

His eyes narrowed on me. "So what?"

The short answer was understandable. As far as I could tell from my research, Grady had been questioned at least half a dozen times by the sheriff's department and state police. That made a person defensive.

My hope was that he would lose the defensiveness around me. I didn't carry a badge or have the ability to lock him up, and maybe with time, he would tell me some detail he hadn't shared with the cops. Because sometimes a detail, no matter how tiny, could break a case wide-open.

I kept my posture easy, relaxed. "I just meant that you likely saw things others might have missed. Saw things the players and coaches might've missed because they were on the inside. A bird's-eye view is often the most powerful."

Grady kept on walking but didn't speak right away. He led me to a place where the woods met the park's grass. "Was working this section while they practiced that day. The girl was the star. That was easy to see. No one on that team held a candle to her. There were a few who were bitter about it."

"Do you know the names of the kids who might've been jealous?" I asked, wondering if Grady would list the same two names Coach Kerr had.

He shook his head. "Brunette girl with glasses. Another blond with a skirt so short I sure as hell wouldn't have let my daughter out in it."

So, not the same names. I needed a team photo, maybe a yearbook. Schools had gotten tighter about what they put online, and I hadn't found much through the Shady Cove High School website or local papers. But there might've been a feature on the team that would give me something.

"But I don't blame 'em for being jealous," Grady went on. "That coach did a piss-poor job of pretending she wasn't his number-one focus."

"What kind of focus?" I asked, trying to keep any opinion out of my tone.

Grady scoffed. "Greedy. Could've been he thought she was headed to Wimbledon, and he was gonna ride those coattails. Could've been something else…"

He let that *something else* hang in the air. We both knew what that *something else* could be. Something darker.

I didn't go there. Not when the coach had been cleared by camera footage, and there were plenty of other persons of interest. "When you left that evening, was the team still practicing?"

"Yeah. They weren't gonna call it quits for at least another half hour."

"And did you know that Emerson often kept practicing after her teammates left?"

Grady's hands fisted at his sides. "I seen her a time or two on my way home after a beer at The Barrel."

"And did you go get a beer that night?" I prodded.

"Yeah. Had a beer with a bud and then headed home."

Except there was an hour window between when his friend said he left The Whiskey Barrel and when Grady's wife said he arrived home.

"It took you a while to get there." It wasn't a question, but I still let it hang.

Grady's amber eyes melted into a gold color, hot with anger. "I told the cops. Sometimes I need a drive to clear my head after a long day."

"Did anyone see you on that drive?" I asked, keeping my voice calm.

"If I'd known the pigs had it out for me, I'd have installed a goddamned dashcam. But I didn't know, did I?" he snapped.

"Your wife said it was typical for you to get home late, but your friend, Wallace, said you usually hung at the bar longer. Why was that night different?"

Grady's hands fisted and flexed over and over. "What're you getting at? Thought this was a chance to clear my name."

I'd never once said that. I didn't have the facts to know if Grady's name needed to be cleared. "I said this was a chance to tell your story."

"You wanna know my story, bitch? This is my fuckin' story. I worked minimum wage for half my life. Bleeding for this town. And how do they repay me? Cops puttin' me in the back of a goddamned squad car in front of my kids."

He spat on the ground. "And they just kept on comin'. Time after time. My boss tells me he thinks it would be best if I quit so he didn't have to fire my ass. Didn't have a choice because I couldn't risk one more black mark on my record."

My heart hammered against my ribs as my free hand dropped, preparing to reach for my Taser if I needed to. That delicate balance of how long I could wait to find out if Grady was simply furious or if there was violence in him too.

Grady prowled toward me one step and then another, like a panther poised to attack. “Now I see you. You think you’re gonna come in here and pin this all on me? Not gonna happen.” His hand lashed out. “You don’t wanna know what happens to nosy little bitches—”

A figure stepped between us. The way the sun was angled in the sky, he was pure shadow to me. But somehow I still recognized him. The broad shoulders and dark hair. But more, the aura that radiated around him. That aura had turned to pissed-the-hell-off as he glared down at Grady.

“Don’t even think of laying hands on her.”

Chapter Fifteen
Colt

I COULD FEEL THE FURY COMING OFF GRADY IN WAVES. But that rage only stoked the anger reaching a boiling point in me. I'd seen his fuse catch from across the park, watched as he stalked toward Ridley, looming over her. It flipped something inside me, igniting a protectiveness that made no damn sense.

"She's interviewing me," Grady spat. "What? Now I'm not allowed to speak my mind? That's protected under the First Amendment."

"Not when those words are threats," I ground out.

He grabbed at the small microphone clipped to his T-shirt and tossed it on the ground. "I don't need this shit." His gaze snapped to Ridley. "You try to bury me, and I'll come for you. That's a promise," he said, stalking away.

Fucking hell.

I turned slowly, trying to keep my temper in check but struggling.

Ridley stared after him, no fear in her expression, only curiosity. As if she were trying to put the pieces of a puzzle together.

"What were you thinking?" I ground out.

Ridley's gaze flew to me, eyes widening. "You're blaming that on me?"

"You were the one asking the questions. Stirring up trouble."

Her jaw hardened, chin tipping up. "Searching for the truth isn't stirring up trouble."

That's where she was wrong. "What would've happened if I hadn't been here, huh?" I pressed.

"He would've tried to touch me, and I would've tased his ass before he could blink." Ridley pulled a small pink Taser out of her pocket. It looked more like a flashlight than a device that could bring a man to his knees.

"What you're doing is reckless. You think there aren't consequences to this sort of thing. And it's more than just you who's affected. Grady might be an ass, but his life got turned upside down just as much as the next guy. You think that suggesting he could be guilty on a podcast won't do him a tremendous amount of harm?"

Ridley blinked up at me, something shifting in those blue eyes. "You don't think he did it."

I didn't want to give her a damned thing. Not now. I sent a pointed look to the microphone pinned to her shirt.

Ridley sighed and pulled out her phone. She made a grand gesture of unlocking the device and stopping the recording.

"No. I've looked at him hard," I began. "But there's no sign of him doing anything other than working, drinking, and sleeping with any woman dumb enough to take him on."

Her shoulders slumped. "Knew he was too obvious."

I frowned down at her, brows pulled together.

Ridley glanced back at the tennis courts, as if she saw people playing there now even though there was no one. "Whoever this is, they've stayed under the radar for a decade. That means they blend in."

The wind picked up, lifting those strands of blond and carrying with them that burnt-orange scent. I hated to admit, even to myself, that she had good instincts. The kind that came from years on the job in law enforcement.

And I guessed she had been, in a way, working her own sort of cases. I'd spent hours that day looking into that damned podcast of hers and all the social media accounts that went with it.

She'd had some successes for sure, but when I'd called a detective in Iowa to get his take on her since she'd covered a case he'd led, he hadn't had good things to say. He'd used words like *interfering*, *bulldog*, and *nothing but trouble*.

"Maybe, maybe not," I said, voice going rough. "But you could start a chain of dominos you're not ready to tip. And more than that, you could get yourself hurt or killed. What if Grady *was* the guy? You think he wouldn't do everything in his power to stop you from making that public?"

Anger flashed in those blue depths. "I know how to be careful. How to take care of myself."

"Sittin' up at that campsite all alone in a goddamned van? That's not safe on a good day." I hated the way my gut churned at the thought. How I could suddenly picture a million and one ways for that to go wrong.

"News flash, Law Man. *Life* isn't safe. Someone could hurt you crossing a busy street in broad daylight. We can't protect ourselves from everything."

There was something there. An underlying reason to those words that had my eyes narrowing. "Someone hurt you?" The flash of rage that bubbled up at the thought took me completely by surprise, and I struggled to swallow it down.

Ridley bent, picking up the mic that Grady had thrown and shoving it into her backpack along with her own. "It wouldn't be any of your business if they had."

And with that, she stalked off toward the parking lot and that damned bike of hers. I squinted as she approached it. Even that was pure sunshine. Glittery teal paint and a fucking unicorn bell. *Jesus.*

I swung open the door to The Barrel, and the music wafted out into the cool evening air. It wasn't horribly loud, but it wasn't soft either. That perfect midrange for a bar. The space was about half-full, a decent turnout for earlyish on a weeknight. I greeted familiar faces with chin lifts and hellos but didn't stop to welcome any conversation. Instead, I went straight for the bar.

The moment my ass was on a stool, Trey was in front of me and reaching for my favorite bottle of Ransom. "I'm taking it it's a whiskey night."

I simply grunted in response.

"You want some food with that?"

"Burger," I returned.

Trey poured the Ransom whiskey into a rocks glass. "Your piss-poor mood is worse than usual. I'm guessing that has something to do with a five-foot-seven stunner who's getting in your way at every turn?"

I scowled at my lifelong friend. "She's going to get herself killed."

That had Trey pulling up short, concern washing over his features. "What are you talking about?"

I scrubbed a hand over my face. "Found her interviewing Grady. Pushing all his buttons until he looked ready to throttle her."

"Hell," Trey muttered. "There's a reason I eighty-sixed his ass. She needs to be careful who she's messing with."

My eyes narrowed as something that felt a whole lot like jealousy settled low in my gut. "What do you care?"

Trey's brows lifted. "Have you seriously become that much of an ass that you'd want that girl to end up getting hurt or worse?"

I struggled not to shift on my stool. No, I didn't want Ridley hurt. Just the idea of it had me wanting to ride out to her campsite to check on her, even though she wasn't the one I needed to be concerned about.

That thought had me pulling up short and glancing back at Trey. Usually he was just as protective of Emerson as I was. The images of her hurt and terrified were burned into him, leaving scars in their wake. But here he was taking up for Ridley.

"What happened?" I demanded.

Trey's jaw tensed. "She's not what you think she is."

"And what do I think she is?" I gritted out.

Trey pinned me with a hard stare. "I'm pretty sure the words you used were *a fame-hungry money grubber*."

I winced. I'd been pissed after Ridley had shown at Emerson's house. The house we'd grown up in. The one place she should've been safe. "Still might be true." But even as I said the words, I knew they weren't. The one episode of *Sounds Like Serial* I'd listened to had been more than careful. Ridley had interviewed the parents of a twenty-four-year-old woman who'd been murdered, and the tenderness she'd had in her approach told me she cared.

Trey was silent, still staring at me. But now it was as if he didn't know me at all. "You need to pull your head out of your ass."

I blinked back at him. "Excuse me?"

"I've given you a pass the last few years because I know that what happened to Emmie marked you. But you're going to push everyone in your life away if you keep pulling this shit."

Each word was like a carefully placed blow designed to inflict maximum damage. "And what shit is that?"

"You know exactly what I'm talking about. Looking at everyone with suspicion. Assuming their intentions are the worst instead of wondering if they're simply human. Guess what, Colt. No one's perfect. Not even you."

I reared back at that. "I sure as hell know I'm not perfect."

Trey gripped the edge of the bar, his knuckles bleaching white. "Then maybe you need to give yourself some grace too. Because if you stay on this track, you're going to end up completely alone."

I stared back at him for a long moment, not saying a word.

"And just so you know," Trey went on. "Ridley has her reasons for doing this. If you would've taken a breath and asked, I bet she would've told you. Her twin sister disappeared the night before their college graduation."

I'd thought Trey's earlier words had packed a punch, but they had nothing on this. Ridley had a sister. A twin. And she'd gone missing.

"Took me a while to find the case since she doesn't go by that last name publicly, but I finally did," Trey said. "They know it was foul play. Her sister's blood was found at the scene—a scene Ridley found. Police looked for months. No leads. Ridley's living every single day wondering where her sister is. But she didn't let that make her bitter. She channeled that hurt into helping others. And if you had pulled your head out, you might've seen that she's actually trying to help you and Emmie both."

Blood roared in my ears. The pounding beat of my pulse in my throat held accusation. But I didn't try to shove any of it down.

She didn't let that make her bitter. Trey's words circled my brain over and over because I heard what was beneath them. I had let what happened to Em make me bitter. I'd let it harden me. And I'd hurt people because of it. Not just Ridley, but Trey and Emerson too.

I let out a long breath, the air hissing between my teeth. "How long you been wanting to say that?"

Trey let out a huff that was almost a laugh. "Just the last five years or so."

I met his gaze dead-on. "Next time don't wait so long."

"You were messed up—"

"Doesn't matter. I need my best fucking friend to call me on my shit." I stood, shoving my stool back.

"Noted. I'll ream your ass next time."

"Good. Give my drink to Barney."

"Where are you going?" Trey called as I headed for the door.

"Where do you think?"

Trey chuckled. "I hope she doesn't knee you in the balls."

I'd deserve it if she did. I wouldn't even try to block the hit. The moment I stepped outside, I sucked in the fresh air. Even downtown, the pine scent still clung to the air. It had always been one of my favorite things about living in Shady Cove.

The sun still peeked out over the mountains as I headed for my SUV. Beeping the locks, I climbed behind the wheel and started the engine. The drive to Ridley's campsite wasn't long, but my brain played back every cruel thing I'd said to her on repeat.

Fuck, I was a bastard.

I didn't have the first clue how to make this right, but I was sure as hell going to try. My SUV took the mountain road curves with ease. Three of the five campsites were filled now. One with a nicer RV, another with that same tent and now a Subaru that had seen better days, and finally that ridiculous teal camper van.

I looked at the vehicle with new eyes now though. The bumper stickers on the back marking a life lived without her sister. The bright colors a search for light in a world that could be as dark as pitch.

Parking my SUV, I shut off the engine and climbed out. And that's when I heard the singing. The notes hit me square in the chest. It wasn't that her voice was perfect; in fact, part of the charm was that it wasn't. Those imperfections didn't stop Ridley from singing full-out.

I didn't recognize the tune, but that didn't dull its impact.

Her voice was sultry and smoky. With a rasp that had every nerve ending in my body standing at attention.

There wasn't a damned thing I could've done to hold back from the pull of it. Like a siren's song, it had me rounding the van in search of the source. If I'd been at sea, I would've easily crashed my ship on the rocks to get to it.

But I'd been so distracted by Ridley's singing, I hadn't picked up on the sound of water. Like falling rain. Only it wasn't coming from the sky.

As I reached the other side of the van, it took me a second to figure out what I was seeing. There was some sort of contraption sticking off the side of the vehicle. It held up a curtain covered in some sort of rainbow design and a showerhead. A breeze picked up and the curtain parted just a few inches.

But those inches would be burned into my brain for the rest of time. The curve of Ridley's waist, leading to her hip. Smooth golden skin I wanted to trace with my tongue. She turned slightly, exposing the hint of the underswell of her breast.

A single flickering glimpse and I was sunk. Everything in me responded. Wanted nothing more than to yank that curtain back and step in with her. There was just one problem.

Ridley hated me. And with good reason.

I was so fucked.

Chapter Sixteen
Ridley

I DIPPED MY HEAD BENEATH THE SPRAY, RINSING OUT MY biodegradable conditioner. The run had helped burn out the worst of my anger, but tendrils of it still clung. I'd been hoping the shower and singing my favorite Fleetwood Mac song would help clear the dregs of it, but so far, no luck.

A sound carried above the water and the soft strains of my voice. A throat clearing.

I froze. *Crap on a cracker.*

There was something about the sound, the deep timbre of it, that had me instantly knowing the owner. And he was just about the last person I wanted to see.

I quickly shut off the water, grabbing my towel and wrapping it around my body. I pulled my rainbow shower curtain back and met the ornery sheriff's stare. "Here to threaten me again?"

Colt's cheeks reddened slightly, and he gripped the back of his neck, squeezing as he averted his eyes. "No. I, uh, wanted to… talk."

In the handful of run-ins I'd had with the sheriff, he'd never once seemed uncertain. Brash and asshole-ish, sure, but tentative? Never.

"So talk," I said, gripping my towel tighter.

Colt's gaze moved back to me, roaming over my face and trailing down my neck to hitch on the spot where my fingers latched onto terry cloth. Those deep-brown eyes darkened, but not with malice. There was shadowy heat fueling them now.

Shit. Shit. Shit.

My nipples pebbled, pressing against the rough fabric. My body was an idiot. This man had been a dick of epic proportions. Rude and cruel. A grumpy-assed prick. My nipples should not be reacting to him. It was a betrayal of the highest order.

Colt's gaze dipped lower, tracking over my bare legs. I fought the urge to clench my thighs. Damn them too.

It was my turn to clear my throat. "Give me a second to get changed, since you obviously have a problem with nudity."

Colt choked on a laugh as I stalked past him. I hauled open the van door and then quickly shut it behind me, greeted by Tater's meows. It was as if she had a full opinion on Colter Brooks.

"Trust me, I know," I said as I pulled on joggers and a workout top. On second thought, I hauled a T-shirt over the bra top. My nipples couldn't be trusted around that man.

Wringing out my hair with the towel, I piled it into a messy bun. Tater let out another deafening meow, and I sent her a stern look. "You don't have to yell at me. You could just ask nicely."

As if she could completely understand me, Tater let out a softer sound. I picked her up and cradled her against my chest. I reached out to the van's door handle but stilled. "Now or never, right?"

Sucking in a breath, I slid the door open. When I did, it was to find Colt facing away from me. He stared down at the water below, his hands shoved into his pockets and broad shoulders on display.

I was a sucker for broad shoulders. They made me weak. But before my nipples could react, I noticed something else about those shoulders. Something different than the times I'd made a study of them before. Previously, they'd had a tension running through them. Something that wound the muscles tight, as if Colt were always poised to defend a strike.

Now, they had a slight tilt to them. Almost as if the muscles were defeated in some way. It didn't fit the man. Everything about it seemed all sorts of wrong.

As I walked toward Colt, he turned, taking me in. His gaze roamed over me again, stilling in several spots: my bun, my tee, the cat in my arms.

"What happened to his leg?" he asked.

"Her leg," I corrected. "It was injured during birth and had to be amputated. The owner didn't want to cover the cost of surgery or deal with a three-legged cat."

Colt's mouth pulled down in a frown. "People are the worst."

"Sometimes," I admitted, scratching behind Tater's ears. "But they can also be the best."

He stared at me in question.

"The volunteers at the shelter took good care of her. A rescue organization took her in and covered the cost of her surgery."

"And you. You gave her a home," Colt said softly.

God, I'd thought his rasp had my body doing stupid things. But the rasp had nothing on Colt's soft tenderness. I swallowed hard, as if that would clear away the buzz of attraction humming beneath my skin.

Stupid, stupid, stupid.

He reached out, scratching underneath Tater's chin. "You landed on your feet, huh? Three of them anyway."

Tater purred for a moment and then bit into Colt's hand.

"Shit. Ow." He snatched his hand back, glaring at my cat.

"Don't be a baby," I said, grinning. "It's just one of her tooth hugs."

Colt stared at me, jaw going slack. "Tooth…hugs?"

I nodded. "It's how she shows affection."

"That seems unhealthy to me."

My lips twitched as I fought to hold my laughter in check. I lifted my gaze to Colt's face. Dark shadows rimmed his eyes, and I hated the part of myself that wanted to know what had caused them. Colt didn't deserve my concern, and he sure as hell didn't want it. "What did you want, Law Man?"

He took a step back, those dark eyes swimming with something unreadable. "Your sister went missing."

My body stiffened, the only reaction in the past fifteen minutes that made any sense. "You know, bartenders are supposed to be like priests or shrinks or something. There's a confidentiality that's supposed to be sacrosanct."

"Don't be pissed at Trey. He was trying to stop me from being such an asshole."

One corner of my mouth tugged up. "An asshole, huh?"

Colt kicked at a rock, sending it flying. "I was trying to look out for Emerson."

I made a sound in the back of my throat.

"Okay, I was looking out for myself too. I hate going back there. Remembering what it stole from her."

"And what it stole from you," I added. Because it had stolen from Colt. It had changed him. There was no way it couldn't have.

Colt's gaze lifted to mine. "And you know what that's like."

"I do. Your whole view of the world shifts, like the twist of a kaleidoscope. You can't look at things the same way because you aren't the same person."

Colt was quiet for a long moment, but he didn't look away. It was as if he was trying to read beneath my words. "Not sure I realized just how much it changed me."

An ache settled in my chest. Because the moment you woke up and realized that you'd changed was the same one when you realized nothing would ever be the same. "It's your choice how it changes you."

Those dark brows pulled together. "Not sure that's true."

"It is," I challenged. "I won't say it's easy. I battle it every single day. Gratitude is a choice. Just like looking for the sun."

"Looking for the sun…" he parroted.

I shrugged, letting my fingers sift through Tater's fur. "Sometimes it's finding those actual rays. Just looking up, closing my eyes, and remembering it's still there. Every day it rises. Sometimes it's looking for those glimmers of light elsewhere. The amazing hazelnut latte I got from Ezra. The kindness Trey showed to me when I needed it. The run that reminded me I'm still here and breathing. Those glimmers are all around us; you just have to open your eyes and truly see."

A muscle along Colt's jaw fluttered. "Think I've been looking for the opposite lately. The shadows. Feels like it's all I see."

"Time to rewire your brain. Challenge yourself to see the good. Pick three things every day and see what happens."

One corner of his mouth kicked up. "You some sort of new-age life coach?"

I couldn't help but chuckle. "I bet I could get you and Celia on a meditation retreat."

"Dear God, please no. I know I've been a dick, but do I honestly deserve that?"

I arched a brow.

"Okay, I do." Colt sighed, scrubbing a hand over his jaw. "I'm sorry. I said things I had no right to." He paused, seeming to struggle for the next words. "I shouldn't have questioned your motives."

My lips twitched. "Ouch. That seemed painful to get out."

He glared at me. "It was."

"Thank you," I whispered. "I appreciate it." I searched for a way to say what I needed to without causing Colt more pain. "I can't stop looking into this case."

His jaw hardened again. "Had a feeling you'd say that."

"I've linked other cases to Emerson's. Similar victim profiles. I need to find out if I'm right. Because if I am, this monster isn't just kidnapping. He's killing." I wasn't ready to give Colt the Avery piece. Because I hadn't given it to anyone. Not a single soul other than the filing cabinet in my van.

Colt's throat worked as he swallowed. "Okay. Just—leave Emerson out of it. She's been through too much. Won't leave the house now because the fear and anxiety are too much. She won't even go outside unless Trey or I are there."

Pain washed through me for a young life cut short. Emerson might still be breathing but she wasn't truly living. At least not as fully as she should've been able to.

"I'm so sorry. For her and for you. I know that has to be hard to watch, and to want to help but not know how."

Colt dragged a hand through his hair, leaving it mussed. "I've tried everything I can think of, but nothing seems to help."

"Therapy?" I asked.

He nodded. "Saw a therapist for years, and it did nothing. Even tried a few experts online, but it didn't make a difference. Either that or she just wasn't ready."

"Maybe if we can find this monster, the real healing can start. She won't be afraid because he'll be behind bars."

"You don't think I've tried? I worked that case for years. Still pull it out every single year and go through all the evidence two or three times over, talk to witnesses. It's like whoever did this just disappeared." Colt gripped the back of his neck, squeezing hard. "And maybe they did. Maybe it was a random person passing through town. Crime of opportunity."

"Maybe," I said, trying to ease a little of Colt's pain.

"You don't think that," he pressed.

"No, I don't." If I was right about the link between victims, that couldn't be true. The unsub would've had to watch the girls. Research them. Be close enough to know they were just what he was looking for.

Shadows swirled in Colt's eyes. "Just be careful. If this is what you think it is, whoever's doing this isn't going to be happy with you going digging."

And more than that, I knew that I fit at least a piece of the monster's victim profile. How could I not? I was Avery's mirror image.

Chapter Seventeen
Colt

I LEANED BACK IN MY CHAIR, KICKING MY FEET UP ON the porch railing and watching the sun sink lower in the sky. It hovered now at that point where it almost seemed like the globe of light would slip beneath the forests and then pop back up again to give us one last light show. The movement painted the small lake below in a riot of colors.

Taking it all in had Ridley's words about searching for the sun playing in my mind. She wasn't wrong; each way you turned, there was a new unique beauty to be found. It was one of the reasons I'd bought the place. The single slice of private land in the midst of a national forest. The beauty and the solitude. I just occasionally forgot to appreciate it all.

I took a sip of my whiskey. That first taste slid down my throat, warming me from the inside out. I'd need it in a minute. Because the sun finally slipped beneath the horizon for good, which meant cold could come on quick, even as we headed into summer.

Bowser's head lifted from his paws, ears twitching. He might've been into his senior years, but his hearing was still just as good as when he was a pup. I followed his gaze, wondering if he'd heard a critter, but then I heard it: the crunch of wheels on gravel.

I couldn't help the scowl that twisted my mouth. The people who could find their way up here were few and far between, and I wasn't in the mood to see any of them. I was stewing. Maybe even pouting, if I was honest.

It had been a week since I'd tried to make things right with Ridley. I'd see her around town, talking to locals, doing interviews. If we were ever in close proximity, she'd give me a polite hello that I'd return.

I fucking hated it.

I missed her sass and fire. I missed her giving me shit and seeing those blue eyes alight with silver flames. And then guilt would sweep in for feeling that at all. Because she was digging up things that meant possible pain for my sister.

Lifting the glass, I took another pull of the whiskey. The heat didn't hit quite the same this time.

A door slammed, and moments later, I heard footsteps. It wasn't long before they hit the steps to my back deck.

"Jesus. Sitting out here in the dark, drinking?" Trey asked.

Bowser struggled to his feet and crossed over to him in search of pets.

"It's peaceful," I defended.

"It's sulking," he shot back, giving Bowser a scratch behind the ears.

I didn't answer because he wasn't wrong. I just stared out at the darkening lake. It wouldn't take long for the stars to come out, to see what Constellation Lake was named for.

Trey crossed to the chair on my right, lowering himself into it. Bowser simply dropped his head onto Trey's knee so that he could resume the scratches. "You pissed I laid it out for you?" Trey asked, looking out at the darkening horizon.

My gaze flicked to him. "Don't be an idiot."

He glanced in my direction. "What the hell am I supposed to

think? You basically disappeared this week. Haven't come into the bar, haven't seen you around town."

I shifted in my chair, that familiar shadow of guilt sliding over me. "It's not you."

"It's not you; it's me? That's what we're doing?" Trey asked, amusement lacing his tone as he studied me. Out of the corner of my eye, I saw when the grin hit his face. "You're avoiding Ridley."

I stiffened, my fingers tightening around my glass. "I'm not avoiding anyone."

Jesus, I was a shit liar.

"The apology went that badly, huh?"

"It went fine," I gritted out.

Trey chuckled. "Sure sounds like it."

"It did." I couldn't help the defensiveness that slid into my tone. "I just—I don't know what to do about her now."

"You could always ask her to dinner. That's what I usually do when there's a woman I'm interested in."

"I'm not interested in her," I spat.

This time Trey roared with laughter. "I've seen you two together exactly once and that I-hate-you-so-bad-I-want-to-tear-your-clothes-off vibe was so strong I'm pretty sure the whole bar could see it."

Just Trey's words had images flying through my head that I had no business thinking. My fingers locking on a strap of one of Ridley's damned workout tanks and tugging it down. My hand slipping beneath the band of those tiny spandex shorts.

Fuck.

I shifted, kicking my legs off their post. "Doesn't matter. That's one place I can't go."

I felt Trey's gaze burning a hole in the side of my face. "Why the hell not?"

"Conflict of interest," I muttered.

"Just because she's looking into Emmie's case doesn't make her the enemy."

"Doesn't it?" I asked.

Trey glared at me. "You look into it every year. In fact, now's about the time you start. I know because you get extra surly. And I understand it. But what I don't understand is what makes you two different."

"She's putting it out there for the whole world to consume. Em's pain, her story."

"She's putting it out there so that we can hopefully find new information." Trey leaned forward, dislodging Bowser from his knee. "Can you honestly tell me that your yearly rehash is helping?"

His words sliced, but I knew Trey didn't mean for them to. It was just that he was right. I hadn't made a single bit of progress. I'd started over on the search parameters after Ridley shared with Emerson that she'd found twenty-three similar crimes. But I'd only found one in a three-hundred-mile radius that had enough similarities to link it. I wanted to see her notes, how she'd made the connections.

Instead of asking, I listened to the two episodes that had gone up on her podcast channel. The first one had been solely background information, the kind you could gather from reading the news coverage at the time. The second had outlined the suspects the police had circled. She had clips from Grady, Coach Kerr's wife, and Emerson's math teacher.

And I had to give it to her. She handled them all with care, not pointing the finger at a single one. She had this sort of justice scale to her coverage. For every point leading to the suspect's guilt, she countered with one of innocence. And she also talked about how the crime had marked them all. There was an empathy to her episodes that was surprising. She didn't sensationalize the way I'd expected would be necessary for the kind of following she had.

Even through the speaker on my damn phone, I could feel how much Ridley cared. And that just made me more of a bastard for what I'd put her through.

"I need her notes," I admitted.

Trey stared at me for a long moment. "Have you tried, oh, I don't know...*asking*?"

I scowled at the water below.

"That's what I thought."

A ring cut through the night air, saving me from more of Trey's accusations. I reached for my cell, groaning as I saw the station's number on my screen. We didn't have a huge roster of officers and support staff, just enough to keep the small county humming along. But when there was an issue, I was always the one who got the call. Didn't matter that I'd just worked a full shift; it was what I'd signed up for.

I hit the *accept* button and put the phone to my ear. "Brooks."

"Evening, Sheriff," Dina, one of our night shift dispatchers, greeted. "Sorry to interrupt your evening, but we had a little incident at the station."

I pushed up out of my chair. "What kind of incident?" I was already moving for the back door.

"Someone broke into the secondary evidence locker. The one for cold storage. Deputy Dawson interrupted them, but they clocked him good. EMTs are with him now."

I let out a stream of curses as I grabbed my badge and service weapon. "I'm on my way."

"What's going on?" Trey asked, on his feet by the time I made it back outside.

"Break-in at the station. Can you get Bowser inside and settled?" I asked.

Trey had keys to my place, and if Bowser would listen to anyone, it was him.

"You got it," he agreed quickly. "Hope everything's okay."

I jerked my head in a nod and headed for my SUV. Beeping the locks, I climbed in and started for town. The only downside of where I lived was how long it took me to get anywhere. A good twenty minutes on a normal day, thirty-plus when there was snow. But tonight, I made it in fifteen.

The lights from the ambulance illuminated the station's parking lot in a staccato swirl. I pulled into my parking spot and jumped out of my vehicle, heading straight for the gurney. The back was raised, and I could see Dawson arguing with Gene, an EMT in his midfifties.

"I don't need to go to the hospital," Dawson protested.

Gene simply pinned him with a stare. "You were unconscious for at least thirty minutes. That means hospital and an MRI."

Dawson scowled at him. "I've got a bump on the head. That's all."

"We don't take chances with bullet wounds or head injuries," I said as I strode over.

"Sheriff," Dawson said, his cheeks reddening. "I'm so sorry. I didn't even see the guy coming."

"No apologies needed. Just tell me what happened."

Dawson nodded then winced, clear evidence he did, in fact, need to go to the hospital. "I'd just gotten on shift. It was slow, so I wanted to pull the files for the Martinez case. That's the cold one I'm on."

I nodded. Each deputy was assigned a cold case to go over and investigate. It helped teach them investigative skills, and there were times when they turned up new evidence that helped bring the perpetrators to justice.

"I went back there, and everything looked normal," Dawson went on.

"The door was closed and locked?" I asked.

He frowned. "I think so. I mean, I know it was shut, but I didn't test the lock. I just input my code like normal and then opened it."

I'd need to have our evidence techs test for tampering. "Then what happened?"

Dawson swallowed, his throat working with the action. "I went back into the stacks, and I heard someone. I didn't think anything of it. Just called out that I was in there, so I didn't freak anyone out. That place can be creepy as hell."

I wanted to smile because I agreed. It wasn't frequented by officers, and it could be a dusty, cavernous space. "Did they answer?" I asked.

Dawson shook his head. "Not a word. Everything went quiet. Seemed off, so I started searching row by row. When I rounded one of the shelving units, someone clocked me. I didn't even see them."

Gene moved in, gesturing to the side of Dawson's head. "He's got a decent gash here that'll probably need stitches. I'd guess he got hit with something substantial. Maybe a Maglite or something similar."

"Go get that injury checked out," I ordered.

"Sheriff—" Dawson started.

"No arguments," I said, pinning him with a hard stare. "You're not back on the job without medical clearance."

Dawson slumped against the gurney.

"Thanks, Colt," Gene said, lips twitching. "He sure as hell wasn't going to listen to me."

I gave them both a wave as I started into the station. That was youth for you. Thinking they were invincible until the world proved otherwise. An officer at the front desk was on the phone but pointed me toward the back hall.

The station had been added on to over the years, so it had a mazelike feel. The two doors that led off the reception area didn't have locks, but there was always someone manning the desk. If they went on break, they had to get a replacement. So in theory no one should've gotten past this area.

I pushed open the door to the right of the desk and headed toward the sound of voices. The hallway had a few windows, but they didn't open. The only other point of entry was a fire door that would've set off a deafening alarm.

As I reached the door to the cold storage area, I found our two evidence techs already at work. I shouldn't have been surprised since my second-in-command was already at the helm. She glanced up at me from where she was crouched next to our tech expert. "Colt."

"What do we have?"

She pushed to her feet, stretching up to her full height, which was all of five foot two. But if there was one thing Sophie Ryan didn't let get in her way, it was her height. I'd seen her put men three times her size down before I could blink.

"As far as Hamm can tell, the break-in happened here." Ryan gestured to the fire door. "They had some sort of tech that took the fire alarm offline. Then they used an alarm breaker to access the evidence locker."

"What about the cameras outside?" I knew we had at least two angles on this back door just in case.

Ryan shook her head, frustration making a home in her expression. "Spray paint. Whoever broke in approached each camera from the side and covered the lens with black paint."

I cursed. None of this fit. High-tech crimes weren't a staple in Shady Cove. I couldn't think of a single incident where things like alarm breakers had been used. And for what?

"Can you tell what cases were accessed?" I asked.

Ryan was quiet for a moment, her green eyes going blank. "I'll show you."

Her lack of reaction had me on high alert as I followed her into the evidence locker. We were careful to avoid areas where techs were working, but it didn't take long to find the spot that had been targeted. Files had been upended and tagged evidence bags spilled out onto the floor.

My gut twisted. All of these cases would be impacted now. Possibly every case in this lockup. Because a defense attorney would argue that an intruder had had access to the area. And they'd be right.

My back teeth ground together as I took in the items sprawled out over the linoleum. Then I froze. There were files from a suspicious overdose. More from a hit-and-run. But in the center of it all were the files from Emerson's case.

All the details about her abduction were spilled out over the floor like trash. Fury lit in my veins. I knew one person who desperately wanted access to those files. I also knew that two days ago, a deputy had given her a heavily redacted copy of them.

But maybe that wasn't enough for Ridley. She was like a dog with a bone when it came to the truth. So maybe she'd decided to find a way to get those original files, whatever it took.

But now she'd hurt someone in the process.

Chapter Eighteen
Ridley

"NEITHER THE SHERIFF'S DEPARTMENT NOR THE CALIFORNIA State Police ever gathered enough evidence to make an arrest in Emerson's case, which begs the question: What were they missing?"

I hit the stop-recording button on my computer and slumped back in my chair. It was a good ending. The kind of cliff-hanger that got people tuning in the next week, but more than that, it got them motivated to begin putting the pieces together themselves.

The only problem was, we didn't have enough pieces to begin with. I needed more interviews, leads. I'd burned through the easy yeses, the people who were happy to talk. It was time to start winning over the hesitant ones. I needed to get Ezra on the record for sure. Maybe some more of Emerson's classmates and teachers.

I reached for my mug and took a sip of tea as I hit upload on the files I'd recorded. They'd go to an online folder where Sully could access them for editing. I glanced at my watch. It was after eight here, eleven in New York, but Sully was a night owl, often working until two or three in the morning.

I opened my video chat app on my computer and selected his name. It rang four times before he answered, and when his face filled the screen, his gray-streaked hair was in disarray. I winced. "I didn't wake you, did I?"

"Naw," Sully mumbled as he sat in his chair. "Was just watching the tail end of the *Real Housewives of Salt Lake City* reunion."

I chuckled. "I've covered a lot of gruesome cases, but no one terrifies me more than those women."

"That's because you're smart," he said with a grin, his eyes moving over the computer screen. "These new recordings ready to roll?"

I nodded, taking another sip of tea to try to soothe my vocal cords. "I sent you an email earlier with the time codes for the interview clips."

"I'll get on those tonight," he assured me.

"We've got a few days, so there's no rush."

Sully peered at me through the screen. "You okay? Baker being a dick again?"

I scoffed. "Baker's always a dick."

Sully grunted in agreement. "More so than usual?"

I shrugged, shifting in my chair. Baker had sent me more than a few texts telling me the episodes didn't have the "wow" factor we needed, and pressuring me to wrap this up early and head to LA to help out with *Reality Rampage*. I shuddered at the idea. But the truth was, his doubts were getting to me because they were only compounding my own.

"Not enough people are willing to talk to me on the record," I admitted.

Sully leaned back in his chair. "Ah, the small-town curse."

"Usually once I get one or two on the show, more want to open up. But that hasn't been the case here. And I need people to talk. I need them to find a new lead."

Sully tapped his fingers along his desk, his curtains covering the New York City skyline fluttering in a breeze. "You feeling certain that the suspects the police had are in the clear?"

I mulled that one over. I still wasn't sure about Grady; he definitely had a darker streak. And there was something about Coach Kerr that didn't completely sit right with me the more I thought about our chat. But neither of them pinged my radar for Emerson. "My gut says it's not them," I admitted.

My gut wasn't scientific in any way. But over the past four years, it had been fine-tuned by case after case. By interviews with criminals and suspects, I'd begun to get a feel for who was capable of what.

Sully was quiet for a long moment. "Kid, if your gut says it's not them, then it's not. On to the next."

"I just don't know who the next is."

"Maybe—" Sully's statement was cut off by a swift knock on my van door.

I stiffened at the sound. No one should be out here this late.

"Mason County Sheriff's Department."

The familiar voice still had that rasp to it, but there was something beneath it, a tightly held anger just trying to break free.

Hell.

Sully's eyes widened on the screen. "Do you want me to call Baker? He can call the lawyer."

I gave my head a quick shake. "No. Just give me a second." The last thing I wanted was Baker overreacting and blowing this sky-high.

I pushed out of my chair and crossed to the door, Tater letting out a meow of protest at her nighttime nap being interrupted. Sliding the door open, I was greeted by Colt's glowering expression, a deputy standing behind him.

Shit. Shit. Shit.

Colt on his own was trouble in more ways than one, but Colt

with backup said this was official trouble. I swallowed hard and forced a smile. "Evening, officers, how can I help you?"

"You can give us your whereabouts for the past three hours," Colt clipped.

I frowned. So much for apologies and making nice. "I've been here, working on the next podcast episode."

Colt's jaw worked back and forth. "Can anyone corroborate that?"

Annoyance bubbled as I struggled to keep my cool. "Will you take the testimony of Tater?"

"No, I won't take the word of a damned cat."

My eyes narrowed on him. "Why do you want to know?"

The familiar energy began to buzz beneath my skin. Something had happened. Something that had to do with Emerson's case. There was no other reason for Colt to be up here demanding my alibi.

Colt opened his mouth, and I knew it would be to blow me off, but then he paused, and it was almost as if he were playing out his options in his mind. He changed tack. "There was a break-in at the station tonight. Someone got into the room where cold case files and evidence are held."

My jaw went slack. "And you think it was *me*?"

Colt glared at me. "Who else would have an interest in getting access to those records?"

"How about the goddamned kidnapper?" I spat. Anger surged, pressing against my skin. Colt had made such a show of apologizing, but that was all it was, a show. Moments where I thought I'd gotten true vulnerability from him had just been bullshit.

"They've been in that storage locker for years," Colt accused. "If a rogue kidnapper was wanting to cover his tracks, don't you think he would've broken in there before now?"

"He knows that I'm working the case now. Looking for leads.

He's worried that there's something in those files that points to him. We just have to find it."

Something passed over Colt's expression, a hint of doubt possibly. But he covered it just as quickly. "There is no *we*. You are a suspect in an assault case, not to mention breaking and entering."

"Assault?" I asked, shock bleeding into my voice.

"A deputy was injured when he surprised the intruder. He's at the county hospital now getting stitched up and undergoing tests."

Empathy for the officer swamped me, but fast on its heels was something that felt a lot like hope. Hope that I was on to something here. And there was someone who wasn't happy about that. Someone who was still here in Shady Cove.

"Now," Colt went on. "I'd like you to come down to the station for some questioning."

I gaped at him. "Are you arresting me?"

"No, but—"

"Excuse me." Sully's voice rose from the computer in the back of my van.

Colt's hand went to the butt of his gun. "Is someone in there with you?"

"Jesus," I muttered. "It's my editor. I was on a video call with him."

Colt eased up a bit, and Sully went on. "I've got an alibi for Ridley. The audio files she just uploaded are time-stamped. We can get them over to your techs to verify."

Colt frowned. "Time-stamped…"

"Yeah. Because I've been here for the past five hours working and recording just like I said. Now unless you really are going to arrest me, get the hell out and don't come back without a warrant."

Colt's deep-brown eyes darkened to black. "Ridley—"

"Don't," I snapped. "I forgave you once. Forgave you for being a dick of epic proportions at least three times. But now I'm done. Just stay the hell away from me."

And with that I slammed the door right in his face.

Chapter Nineteen
Colt

It was nearing midnight when I left the station, but I couldn't find it in myself to go home. Not yet. All that waited for me there were hours to mull over what a prick I was and Bowser's deep snores. So instead I walked toward The Barrel. If I killed another hour or two, maybe sleep would find me when I finally made it home.

Shady Cove was locked up tight, every shop and restaurant still. There was nothing that indicated someone in my town could do the things I knew they'd done: break into a police station, give Dawson a concussion that was severe enough the hospital was keeping him for observation...abduct Emerson.

Because it was looking like Ridley hadn't done it. The files her editor submitted had been verified by our tech. She'd been recording off and on during the entire window of the crime. There was no way she could've been the one to break in.

And worse than that, I'd hurt her. I could see it in those deep blues. I'd cut her to the quick.

Fucking hell.

I hauled open the door to The Barrel, and let the music and voices wash over me. It wasn't the balm it normally was. Neither was seeing familiar faces, like Ezra on a stool, or Celia and Mira chatting it up at a table, or even Trey at his usual station behind the bar. Still, I made my way over to him.

"Whiskey or Coke?" he asked, the most important question for now.

"Better make it a Coke." With everything going on, I needed my faculties.

Trey dumped ice into a tall glass and shot soda into it. "Start talking."

There was no sense in keeping the details close. They would make the rounds by morning regardless. "Break-in at the station. Our cold case room. Dawson got clocked good, and he's in the hospital for the night as a precaution."

"Hell," Trey muttered, then those gray eyes went flinty. "This is about Emerson."

It wasn't a question, but I answered it anyway. "There were three cases that were disturbed, and hers was one of them."

"That's not a coincidence," Trey growled.

"No, it's not." I pinched the bridge of my nose, trying to alleviate the tension headache that was brewing there. It didn't help. "You got any painkillers back there?"

Trey crouched, opening a cabinet and pulling out a bottle of Tylenol. He handed it over. "You need food? Kitchen's closed, but I could probably scrounge something up."

"Just need the drugs and a Coke," I muttered.

Trey's lips twitched. "Only the hard stuff for you."

I washed down the two pills with a swig of Coke. Somehow I didn't think they'd touch the ice pick jabbing the backs of my eyes.

I felt Trey's eyes on me more than saw them. That probing energy trying to figure me out. "There's something else," he said.

Again it wasn't a question. But that was the way Trey operated. Putting together the pieces without asking a single query.

My throat worked as I swallowed. "Had to ask Ridley where she was."

Trey was silent, letting the sounds of the bar swirl around us. Finally I was forced to look up. He leaned against the back bar, hands gripping the wood, a tattered copy of *To Kill a Mockingbird* resting there. He reread it every year. The pages were yellowed and bent, the spine cracked in a million ways.

I focused on that instead of him. I'd take the book's judgment over Trey's any day. But it was just as accusing. And it had every right to be. A different sort of prejudice lived inside me, but it was prejudice all the same.

Finally Trey spoke. "Why do I get the feeling it wasn't a polite inquiry?"

I forced my focus to my friend, taking in the disappointment on his face. "I thought it was her. She's the only newcomer I know of who's got an interest in Em's case."

Trey just shook his head. "You don't think her looking into this could stir things up for whoever took Emmie? Jesus, Colt. I know you're a better cop than that."

My hackles rose, irritation digging in. "I looked into Ridley. Detective in Iowa told me she bends the rules."

"Bending the rules is a hell of a lot different than breaking and entering and assault," Trey snapped.

He had a damn point. And I knew it wasn't Ridley, but that didn't change the fact that it could've been.

"What happened?" A voice cut into the tense silence between Trey and me.

I glanced over at Ezra, who was nursing a beer, and sighed. "Break-in at the precinct. Dawson was injured."

Ezra's eyes went wide, and his red cheeks paled slightly. "He gonna be okay?"

"He's fine. Just has to stay overnight as a concussion precaution."

Ezra gripped his beer bottle tighter. "You think it was that reporter? She doesn't look like she could pack a punch, but looks can be deceiving."

Yes, they could. And that was the thing I hated most about the aftermath of Em's kidnapping, how it changed the way we both looked at everyone around us.

"It wasn't her," Trey clipped from behind the bar.

Ezra's brows lifted. "You sure about that?"

"I am," I cut in. "She's got an alibi."

Ezra let out a huff of air. "I watch *Criminal Minds*; alibis can be faked."

"Jesus," Trey muttered.

And I didn't blame him. The last thing we needed was Ezra turning vigilante on us.

"This is airtight, Ez. So just hold off before you make a citizen's arrest," I told him.

He scowled down at his beer. "You two aren't the only ones who care about Em. Last thing I want is her getting hurt because this woman is digging where she doesn't have any right to."

"Emmie wants her here," Trey snapped.

My eyes flared as I shifted to take in Trey.

He shoved off the back of the bar. "She supports what Ridley's doing. Wants her to find the truth. So maybe both of you should ask her what she wants before assuming."

And with that, Trey stalked down the bar to check on the other patrons.

"Shit," Ezra muttered.

Shit was right. Emerson hadn't said a word to me about wanting Ridley here. But I also hadn't asked her how she felt about it. I'd simply avoided the subject altogether, thinking that was the best route to take.

Shoving my stool back, I stood and pulled out my wallet.

I tossed a ten-dollar bill on the bar. It didn't cover me being an asshole, but it was better than nothing.

I clapped Ezra on the shoulder. "Thanks for caring about my sister."

He glanced up at me, his ruddy complexion back to normal. "Of course. We take care of our own, right?"

I nodded but didn't say a thing as I headed for the door. Because I couldn't get my vocal cords to make the sound of agreement. Not when there was someone walking around who was capable of hurting the innocent and possibly so much worse.

Chapter Twenty
Ridley

My eyes burned as the wind hit them, but it wasn't the wind's fault. It was Colt's. After he'd left, I'd run things through with Sully, who was pushing for me to get Baker involved. I understood why. As much as Baker could be an ass, he was protective of his talent. He'd sic lawyers on Colt so fast his head would spin.

But I didn't want Baker meddling. And I didn't want any additional pressure to leave this case behind. It was too important.

And that importance was also why I'd struggled to find sleep last night. My mind spun round and round, trying to put the pieces together, to see how everything was connected.

I knew one thing: someone didn't want me getting access to those case files. Or they at least wanted to see what the sheriff's department had. To me that said whoever had abducted Emerson was still here. I was close. And I wasn't giving up.

I slowed my bike as I approached the sign for Cowboy Coffee. It was time to brave the café again, to test Ezra's waters about talking. Hopping off my bike, I locked it up and headed inside.

The sounds of a coffee machine and the scent of freshly roasted beans greeted me. The shop wasn't overly crowded this morning, but it was still early, just past six. That was before the normal work crowd likely hit and certainly before teens on summer vacation were out and about.

I headed in the direction of the counter just as Ezra looked up from his phone. His eyes widened for the briefest second, and then he schooled his features. Shoving his cell into his back pocket, he gave me a tentative smile. "Iced hazelnut latte?"

"That and the cowboy hash, please," I said, fishing my tiny wallet out of my bag as relief swept through me.

Ezra tapped a few buttons on the tablet register. "That'll be sixteen-fifty."

I tapped my card to the reader, then selected a twenty-five-percent tip. I wasn't above bribery. As I slid my card back into my wallet, I looked up at him. "Not barring me from service?"

Ezra sighed. "I thought about it."

"What changed your mind?"

"A friend reminded me that it should be Emerson's choice if she wants you here or not."

That buzz was back. "And what did she say?"

Ezra tapped his fingers along the counter in a slow beat. "That she's glad you're looking into things." His eyes moved to mine. "She's not sure if she's going to talk to you, but she doesn't want you to stop."

My heart squeezed. God, she was brave. Selfless.

"Does that mean you'd be willing to talk to me?" I asked Ezra.

He was quiet for a long moment and then finally nodded. "I'll talk to you. I don't know what help I'll be though."

"Just giving me an idea of Emerson's life at that time would help. Who she was friends with, what she loved doing."

"Tennis," Ezra muttered with a soft smile. "That girl lived and breathed tennis. There were times I'd catch her daydreaming, and she'd apologize and say she was playing a match in her head."

"That's exactly the sort of thing I'd love to hear about. Listeners need to connect with the victim. It's what makes them care. What makes them want to help. Someone out there saw something that will help. They had to."

Ezra shook his head. "Don't you think they would've come forward by now?"

I slid my wallet back into my bag and hoisted it over my shoulder. "People don't always know that what they saw had meaning. That's why it's important for me to talk to as many people as possible."

"I guess," he muttered. "I'll get your coffee and breakfast out to you as soon as possible."

I knew a brush-off when I heard one, and I didn't blame Ezra. People didn't want to think that it was possible they lived beside a kidnapper, someone who could terrorize a young girl and not give a damn. And when I came out with all of it, they'd know it was worse. That this person had raped and killed.

Nausea swept through me as Avery's face flashed in my mind. I didn't want it to be true, not for her or Emerson or any of the others. But just because I wanted it one way didn't mean I got it. And I couldn't be afraid to face the truth.

I wound my way through the tables to grab the empty one I'd sat at before. The one that had the perfect view of both the sidewalk and the restaurant. As I passed the two older men playing chess, one looked up. "You're that reporter, aren't you?"

I did my best to give him a warm smile, even though I didn't feel it. "The podcaster." I didn't always like the term *reporter*. It felt stuffy and removed.

The man shook his head. "You need to keep on moving. No one wants you here. Let sleeping dogs lie."

His words hit. They wouldn't normally, but I was already feeling raw from the night before.

"Aw, Norm, quit it. You need your daily dose of prune juice because your bullshit's backing up," the second man said.

My gaze moved to him as a hint of my earlier smile returned. He wore a button-down shirt and suspenders that were decorated with chess piece doodles. He extended a hand. "I'm Sam, and this ornery bastard is Norman, but you can call him Norm."

"Hi, Sam. I'm Ridley."

"You keep talking to her, and she's probably going to name you the kidnapper," Norm snapped.

"I got nothing to hide, you idiot," Sam shot back.

Norm let out a huff. "That's what you think. Just wait till your name is all over everyone's genius phones and those TV pads."

Sam stared at his friend for a long moment. "You mean smartphones and tablets?"

"I can't keep up with the terms," Norm groused.

"Get with the times or be left behind, you Neanderthal."

They kept up their bickering as I backed away to my table. But I put Sam on my list of folks to approach for an interview. I'd just have to do it when his buddy Norm wasn't around. I had a feeling Norm would tackle me to the ground before letting me pull out my microphones.

I got settled at the small table, setting up my laptop and notebook. While I kept all my files and notes digitally, I loved the feel of paper and pen. Something about it was satisfying.

"Here you go," Ezra said, sliding my plate and coffee onto the table.

The scent was heavenly, and my stomach growled. I realized I'd skipped dinner last night, never a smart move for me. Maybe that's part of what had caused me to slam the door in Colt's face.

Just thinking his name conjured an image of the man in my mind. Those fathomless eyes darkening to black. The anger pulsing off him in waves.

"You okay?"

My gaze snapped up to Ezra. "Sorry. I think this hash put me in a trance. It smells amazing."

He chuckled. "I'll be sure to tell the chef."

As Ezra walked away, I dug in and nearly moaned. The hash had bacon, cheddar, peppers, onions, potatoes, and eggs over easy. And as much as I'd learned to master the kitchen over the past few years, this dish gave me a run for my money.

A shadow fell over my table. One large enough that I resisted looking up. Or maybe it was the tiniest scent of bergamot and cloves. It cut through the air and the more overwhelming smells of coffee and breakfast foods. And it was one that my subconscious recognized before I did.

"Ridley."

The deep rasp skated over my skin in a way that had all my nerve endings standing at attention. Even the ones in my traitorous nipples.

Shit. Shit. Shit.

I swallowed my bite of cowboy hash and looked up. Colt looked like shit but somehow still managed to be gorgeous. The dark circles under his eyes only made the deep brown look more alluring and hypnotic. The thicker scruff covering his jaw only made him look more rugged. And the sheriff's uniform he wore clung to those damned broad shoulders like usual.

And worse? I missed him calling me Chaos. Missed that sort of shit-talking banter we'd developed. I was an idiot.

"Sheriff," I greeted.

Colt's jaw clenched, making a dimple pop in his cheek, as if he were annoyed by the formal moniker. "I wanted to apologize—"

"Don't," I snapped.

His eyes flared, a little amber flashing amidst the brown. "Don't apologize?"

"No," I clipped. "Because words don't mean a damned thing if they aren't followed up by actions. And you've proven that your words are pure bullshit. So just save us both the time, and don't bother."

I shoved another bite of hash into my mouth and turned back to my computer. But Colt didn't move. His shadow stayed cast over my table, and his damned scent kept finding its way to my nose.

"I shouldn't have jumped to conclusions," he gritted out.

"No shit, Sherlock," I mumbled without looking up.

"You have to admit that you were the most likely suspect," Colt said, defending himself.

I slammed my laptop closed and stood, making quick work of shoving my belongings into my bag. "No. I don't. And even if I were, there's a polite way to ask for someone's whereabouts, and then there's *you*." It shouldn't have gotten to me this much. I'd had countless other law enforcement officials question my motives and shut me out of a case. I hadn't ever been accused of assault before, but something told me it wasn't so much the accusation but the man making it that bothered me.

A strangled laugh-slash-cough sounded from the chess table, and Norm thumped Sam on the back.

Colt sent a glare in their direction before turning back to me. "I went about it the wrong way. I'm sor—"

"Don't you dare, Colter Brooks," I snapped, pulling my bag over my shoulder and grabbing my coffee.

"She full-named you, Colt. I'd watch out," Sam said. "When my wife does that, it means Couch City."

"You're not helping," Colt ground out and then turned back to me. "Ridley—"

"No. *N. O.* Seems like you haven't heard that word a lot in your life, but I'll be happy to educate you. It means this is an anti-Colt zone. You don't get in my space, and I won't get in yours. You don't stream bullshit at me, and I won't make you scowl on a daily basis. And right now, it means get the hell out of my way."

Chapter Twenty-One
Colt

I STARED AT THE DOOR FOR A LONG TIME AFTER RIDLEY sailed through it, the glass vibrating right along with her fury.

Fuck.

"I thought I had a bad track record with women," Norm muttered.

"You do," Celia shot back from her spot next to Mira at the counter as they waited for drinks.

Hell. I hadn't realized they'd come in. News of this would spread in no time flat. Not that I didn't deserve that little hit to my pride. I did. I just didn't want more people in Ridley's business, and mine.

"Woman," Norm hollered, "don't you fuss at me."

Celia arched a brow in his direction. "Careful there, Norm. I might not make you *dinner* anymore if you don't watch your tone."

Mira's lips twitched. "And by *dinner* she means—"

"Sweet baby Jesus," Sam cut her off. "I do not need to hear about what those two are up to in their love-hate relationship."

Neither did I. Where the hell was the brain bleach when you needed it?

Sam's eyes narrowed on me. "You going to fix that?"

I shuddered. "I don't think there's any *fixing* knowing that Norm and Celia are together."

"Colter Brooks, don't make me box your ears," Celia shouted.

Sam shook his head. "Two full names in five minutes has to be a record."

"Even I haven't gotten that," Norm mumbled.

I pinched the bridge of my nose. "I don't need your help with Ridley."

Mira's eyes danced with amusement. "Sure looks like you do from where I'm standing."

"Damn straight," Sam echoed. "That's a good woman you sent running out the door. Now you need to go make it right."

My back teeth ground together. I knew he was right. I just didn't have the first clue how to get Ridley to forgive me, not this time. "I gotta go," I muttered, heading for the door.

"Chicken!" Sam called after me.

"Now don't use that word as an insult; it's not fair to our feathered friends," Celia scolded.

God help me, this town was going to kill me.

I pulled up to my familiar childhood home, now painted that sunny yellow my sister loved. I stared at it for a long moment before finally shutting off the engine and climbing out of my SUV. I didn't know why I'd found my way here instead of the office, where I should be, but I headed up the front steps anyway.

Before I could lift my hand to knock, the door was opening and Emerson was greeting me with a scowl.

I sighed. "Who told you?"

She let out a huff, her exasperation clear. "Celia called. What were you thinking, Colt? Accusing Ridley of assault?"

I winced. I guessed word really had made the rounds and not

just the bits and pieces. Bear broke away from Em and made his way over to me in solidarity, leaning against me for some pets. "I fucked up," I admitted.

"No kidding," Emerson said, waving me in and back toward the kitchen as her two smaller dogs barked in the backyard. She moved to the fridge, pulling out some lemonade and pouring two tall glasses. "Sit."

"Why do I feel like I just got sent to the principal's office?"

"Because you did." Emerson set the glass in front of me with a thump against the worn wood. "What is going on with you?"

I stared at my sister as she sat. In moments like this one, she seemed like any other twenty-six-year-old with her whole life ahead of her. Normal. But I still saw the moments her hands shook when she stepped outside or how a panic attack could grab hold when a memory triggered her. Emerson's life had been stolen from her in so many ways. And that had messed with my head more than I wanted to admit.

I forced my gaze down to the lemonade, sunshine in a glass, so different from the storm clouds I felt brewing. "I don't know what's wrong with me," I finally admitted.

Emerson let out a long breath. "What happened to me isn't on your shoulders."

"I know that," I lied.

"And neither is it single-handedly your responsibility to find out who did it."

My jaw worked back and forth. "I know that too."

"You're such a shit liar."

I grimaced. "It could've been her, Shortcake. She could've been the one who broke in, who hurt Dawson."

Emerson was quiet for a long moment. "It would be easier if it was her. I get that much."

My gaze lifted to Em's. "You haven't seen how determined

she is. I just—I know that sort of single-minded focus can turn. I thought it might've."

"As determined as Ridley is, I don't see her breaking into a police station, let alone assaulting an officer." Emerson paused for a moment, really taking me in. And the focus had me fighting not to squirm. "She's trying to help, Colt."

"I know that," I ground out, the guilt only settling in further.

"So let her. Maybe offer some help, some information. I know you've got files upon files on my case."

I didn't miss the slight tremor in Em's hand as she reached for her glass. Bear instantly moved to put his head in her lap. This was just another example of why I didn't want Ridley digging—the ramifications it had.

"Colt," Emerson whispered, drawing my gaze back to her face. "I can handle this. Trust me to know what I can do and what I can't."

"It's my job to look out for you. I'm your big brother," I croaked.

A soft smile spread across Emerson's face. "I appreciate that. But don't take it too far, all right? Ridley isn't a danger to me."

"She might be to me," I muttered.

Emerson chuckled. "I like that she keeps you on your toes."

"You would."

That only made Em laugh more. "You need to apologize."

"I tried. She wasn't interested."

Emerson's mouth pursed. "That doesn't seem like her." I traced the rim of my glass, and Em's eyes narrowed. "What aren't you telling me, Colter Brooks?"

Three full names in thirty minutes? Sam would have a field day with that.

"I might've apologized already. I think my accusing her of assault afterward might've dulled the effects of my apologies."

Emerson groaned, leaning back in her chair. “You could use a good shake.”

“I know,” I sulked.

Em drummed her fingers on the table as she studied me. “You need to *show* her you mean the apology. Change the behavior.”

“I can’t change my behavior around her if she runs out of a room the second I enter it.”

Emerson waved me off. “Doesn’t matter. Actions speak louder than words, and since your words have been seriously lacking—”

“Hey!”

She arched a brow. “Where’s the lie?”

I slumped back in my chair. “Fine. She needs me to speak with my actions.”

Emerson grinned. “She does. And I know exactly how you’re going to start.”

Chapter Twenty-Two
Ridley

An hour of walking the streets of Shady Cove hadn't lessened my anger, not one single bit. Normally I was good at keeping my cool. Good at not letting people rattle me. I'd come across assholes of every variety in the last four years. Everything from harmless to murderous. None of them had rattled me the way Colt had. Not a single one.

I didn't want to think about what that could mean.

Or what my storming out of Cowboy Coffee could've told the world about how bothered I was by Colt's presence. But there was nothing I could do about that except practice my meditation breathing as I finally headed in the direction of the Shady Cove library.

"Ridley!"

The shout didn't have Colt's signature rasp, so I turned. Dean jogged down the block, his dark hair flying. He was clad in black again, and I could see he'd painted his fingernails a dark purple since the last time I'd seen him.

"Geez, you walk fast," he muttered as he reached me.

That was what happened when someone tripped your fuse. But I didn't share that tidbit with my teenage superfan. "Hey, Dean."

"Are you on your way to an interview?" he asked hopefully.

I shook my head. "Library actually. I wanted to pull some yearbooks."

"They don't have the yearbooks at the public library."

My shoulders slumped. "Great," I mumbled.

Dean just grinned. "They have them at the high school. Only students and faculty have access. But I could get you in."

Even with the frustrations of the past twenty-four hours, I laughed. "I admire your determination."

That grin just widened, making his lip ring glint in the morning sunshine. "I think it'll make me a pretty damn good podcaster when the time comes, don't you?"

"I do. Lead on, future true-crime king."

The walk to Shady Cove High School only took us about fifteen minutes. A fifteen minutes where Dean peppered me with every podcasting question under the sun. But they were good ones, not the basic stuff any Google search could give you the answers to, so I didn't mind.

When we reached the parking lot, I took in the dozen or so vehicles. "The school stays open during the summer?"

Dean nodded. "Summer school for the delinquents."

"And you're obviously not one of them."

He opened one of the double doors to the school and held it for me. "Naw. My parents are pretty cool, but they would not be chill with me getting anything below a B-minus."

"Seems like a good trade for cool parents," I said, stepping inside.

"Yeah. And I don't mind most of my classes."

The moment the door shut, I was taken back in time. There was a lot that felt universal when it came to high school—the school spirit posters, the notices littering a bulletin board, the artwork of various students covering the walls.

The memory hit me like a physical blow. Suddenly I wasn't looking at the maroon lockers in front of me. I was cast back in time to a navy-blue one.

I put the finishing touch on by gluing a pom-pom to Avery's wrapping-paper-covered locker. I'd had to special order the lacrosse-themed wrapping paper but had shared it with the rest of our friends who were decorating the team's lockers. For Avery, I had gone over and above.

It looked like silver and light-blue glitter had thrown up on Avery's locker. I'd done her number, seventy-eight, in the sparkly stuff and even drawn lacrosse sticks to the best of my ability. In her locker were cupcakes and brownies with more lacrosse paraphernalia as decorations.

"Ridley Sawyer Bennett, what did you do?" Amusement laced Avery's voice from behind me, and I spun.

"You weren't supposed to be here for another hour," I groused.

She just grinned at me. "You know I always need to get to school early on game days."

"Well, TA-DA!" I made a sort of Vanna White gesture at her decorated locker.

Avery moved in closer, taking in each and every detail, her eyes taking on a shiny quality. "Rids, I can't believe you did this."

"It's not every day my badass twin leads her team to the state championship."

She glanced at me as she ran a finger over one of the pom-poms. "But usually it's just the football team that gets this sort of treatment."

"Screw that," I huffed. "They're like one and five this year. If anyone deserves locker decorating, it's you guys. There are some treats in your locker, and I have the rest of the girls covered too. I thought it would be nice—"

My words were cut off as Avery tackle-hugged me, squeezing me so hard I could barely breathe. "I'm so lucky you're my sister."

"Love you, Avs."

"Love you, Rids."

"Ridley?" Dean's voice cut through the memory, bringing me back to the here and now.

"Sorry," I croaked. "Just going back to my glory days."

He chuckled. "Well, if you're done reliving those, the library's this way."

I followed him down the hall toward two doors that were propped open. In my research on the town, I'd found that while the population within city limits was small, their school system served a much larger population. So it wasn't surprising that the library was impressive.

From the entryway, I could see rows and rows of shelves along with corridors that I assumed led to even more books. "Whoa," I muttered.

"Yeah, it's pretty massive," Dean agreed.

"Mr. Mather," a voice greeted. "To what do I owe the pleasure of your presence during your summer break?"

I glanced at the woman, who looked to be in her midfifties. She was dressed on the formal side, wearing a linen skirt and a white blouse with a decorative necklace.

"Hey, Ms. Perkins. I'm here to check out some yearbooks."

The librarian's gaze cut to me. "And you are?"

I extended a hand. "Ridley Sawyer."

Her eyes flared. "The podcaster?"

I nodded and waited. I couldn't read her feelings about me in that initial greeting, but she didn't make me wait long.

Her face broke out into a big smile. "I love your show. I listen every week."

Relief swept through me. "Thank you. That means a lot."

"Let me know how I can help. Dean knows where the yearbooks are, but you might also take a peek at the school papers from back then if you're looking for background. They aren't available to the public."

That relief transformed into a bubble of excitement. "That would be great. Were you the librarian then?"

Ms. Perkins nodded, her excitement fading. "A horrible time. Emerson was such a hard worker. National Honor Society, varsity tennis even when she was a freshman, but more than that, she was incredibly kind."

I could feel the sorrow in her words. "Would you be willing to sit down for an interview later this week?"

The librarian's jaw went slack. "Me?"

I nodded. "It's helpful to get to know the victim through the people who saw her day in and day out. Get a feel for Shady Cove at that time."

"I don't know," Ms. Perkins began.

"Run it by Emerson if you'd like. She's been supportive of the coverage so far." I just hoped that continued.

"I'll think about it."

"Thanks. Here's my card so you can get in touch and let me know." I fished a business card out of my pocket and handed it to her.

Ms. Perkins just stared down at it for a long moment. "I hope you find the bastard."

"Me too," I whispered, leaving Ms. Perkins to her memories.

"They're over here," Dean said, leading me to a shelving unit in the corner.

"Thanks. I think we want the years Emerson was enrolled and then maybe two on either side." I crouched, scanning the years on the spines. *Bingo.* I grabbed the yearbook from exactly ten years ago.

That buzz of possibility was back. I didn't want to wait to get to a table or my van. I opened it right there, flipping through the pages. There was the usual fare, class pictures and individual portraits, team shots and clubs. Emerson's face shone up at me what felt like every few pages, she was so involved. Sophomore class government, tennis team, student council, school paper.

Then I reached the events section. The two-page spread on Community Service Day had Emerson grinning at the camera while wearing one of those horrid neon vests and holding a trash bag. There was so much life in her expression, so much openness and trust.

I flipped the page and found another too-common staple of a high school yearbook. *In Loving Memory of Jason Kipp*. There were a few candids and a shot of him playing baseball.

"What happened to him?" I asked, that journalistic urge never too far.

"It was super sad. He got high at an overlook outside of town and fell off the cliff," Dean said quietly.

My stomach twisted. The poor kid and his family. None of us made the best choices as teenagers, but some paid way too high a price.

I flipped the page again and was greeted by Emerson's smiling face again as she held up a trophy. The caption read, *Sinclair Leads Team to District Finals*. As I studied the shot, I picked out the two girls Grady had mentioned. Everyone else was smiling but they were looking at Emerson with envy, the curve of their mouths forced.

I made note of their names, Tara Gibson and Anna Swanson. "Do either of these two still live in Shady Cove?" I asked, pointing to the brunette and the blond.

Dean frowned at the picture, then pointed to Tara. "She does. I don't think the other one does. At least I don't recognize her."

It was worth me trying to hunt down both. It wasn't that I thought they were involved in Emerson's attack, but if there was jealousy fueling both of them, they likely paid more attention to her than others.

Scanning the rest of the shots, Emerson really did take center stage. There was one of her, expression serious as she served. Another of her getting instructed by a coach I didn't recognize. Or it might've been another student. "Do you know who this is?"

Dean shook his head and sent me a sheepish smile. "Sorry. Not much of an assistant, am I?"

I chuckled. "You got me the yearbooks, didn't you?"

"Damn straight I did."

I flipped the book closed, glancing at the stack Dean had assembled for me. There were six in total, just like I'd instructed. "You really are an excellent student."

He grinned, a slightly cocky yet adorable bent to it this time. "Gotta learn from the master if I'm going to start my own podcast in the fall."

I lifted a brow as I pushed to my feet. "Your own, huh?"

Dean nodded, his dark locks slipping over his eyes with the action. "Gonna call it *Mayhem and Murder*."

I chuckled. "It certainly has a ring to it."

"I thought so." He looked at the stack in my arms. "I think Ms. Perkins will let me check these out. Lemme ask."

"Thanks," I said as he hurried over to the librarian's office. Dean was coming through in all sorts of ways.

I was getting twitchy to get back to my campsite so I could really dive into the yearbooks. I wanted to make a list of everyone Emerson was in photos with. And a list of those she was in clubs or on teams with. I'd love to get a list of everyone who had classes with her, but getting that sort of information would be a stretch. Maybe if I befriended one of her classmates, they'd be able to remember.

"All good," Dean called as he headed out of the librarian's office.

"Thank you. How long do I have?" I asked.

"Two weeks."

That would be no problem. I'd be done in a matter of days.

Dean sent me a sidelong look. "So what's next?"

"Now, I head home and dive into research."

His shoulders slumped. "Sounds boring."

I laughed as we headed out into the sunshine and back toward Cowboy Coffee and my waiting bike. "I hate to break it to you, but there's a lot about this gig that's boring."

"Why is that always the way?"

"It's all worth it when you get a breakthrough. There's no high like that."

"Shit," Dean muttered. "I want that."

I glanced over at him. "You have a case you want to cover for your first podcast episode?"

"There's a few I've been circling. Not sure which one would be best," he admitted.

I nodded. "Choosing is hard. And it can paralyze you. At some point you just have to jump."

Dean toyed with his lip ring as he mulled that over. "That makes sense." But he didn't sound completely convinced.

"I'll tell you what: you record that first episode this summer, and I'll take a listen whenever you're done. Give you notes."

Dean's eyes widened. "Seriously?"

"Yup. But you gotta jump."

He grinned, looking more like an excited little boy than an emo teen. "That's sick. Thanks, Ridley." And then he took off at a jog in the opposite direction.

I couldn't help but laugh. Sometimes a little purpose was all we needed.

When I reached my bike, I loaded the yearbooks and my bag into the basket and headed back toward my campsite. The ride felt longer than it actually was because I was so anxious to get to work. But I made a plan as I navigated the dirt road. I'd make myself lunch and work outside at the picnic table. The weather was perfect, warm but not too hot.

Finally, my van came into view. I was getting used to this spot, with the incredible views and other sites not too close. It really was perfect.

Slowing my bike, I hopped off and turned the electric component off. But as I went to pull the items out of my basket, a silver container on my picnic table caught my attention. My skin prickled as I scanned my surroundings. No sign of a single soul. Crossing to the table, I saw a piece of paper taped to it. Scrawled in half-legible letters, it read, *Open me.*

I took a step back warily, eyeing the massive container and wondering if someone could fit a dead body inside. Taking a deep breath, I unlatched the container and flipped up the top. But there wasn't anything quite so morbid as my imagination suggested inside the bear-proof container. Instead, I saw a large wicker basket.

Reaching in, I tried to lift it. It took some doing because the sucker was heavy, but I managed to hoist it out and set it on the picnic table. When I set it down, I surveyed it as if the basket could be a bomb.

It was huge and fancy, not likely the sort of thing a bomber would waste money on. I caught sight of a tag tied to one of the handles with a piece of ribbon.

CHAOS,

I'M SO SORRY FOR BEING AN EVEN BIGGER ASS. IT SEEMS I CAN'T HELP MYSELF. BUT I'LL WORK ON IT.

—LAW MAN

The use of the nicknames had me simultaneously scowling and warming. *Damn him.* I didn't need to be softening toward the douche.

I flipped up one side of the picnic basket. Another note lay inside.

MIRA AT THE HITCHING POST SAID YOU WERE INTO THE HEALTHY, ORGANIC STUFF. SOUNDS AWFUL BUT HERE YOU GO.

I couldn't help but laugh at that and began pulling items out. There were some ice packs around the outside, keeping things cool, but even with those, I knew he'd gone overboard. There was an array of prepared foods, everything from grain salads to veggie medleys to stir-frys. There were four different kinds of cheese, high-end whole-grain crackers, and a variety of dried meats. There was even some local honey and jam and a loaf of fresh bread.

And when I'd gotten every food item out of the basket, I felt something else at the bottom. At first I thought it was another ice pack, but as I tugged it free, I realized that wasn't the case.

The file was protected by a Ziploc bag, and there was a note inside.

Don't make me regret giving this to you.

My heart beat faster, and I opened the bag and pulled out the file. Flipping it open, I saw Emerson's name at the top. I recognized the pages I'd been given previously, only this time there were no blacked-out sections. It was a completely unredacted copy of the case file.

That hum of excitement and possibility was back, but stronger than anything I'd felt before. I laid the file on the table and quickly began gathering up the food. I'd get everything stored and then get to work because I had new ground to cover.

It didn't take me long to get settled at the picnic table with one of the grain salads and a small cheese plate. Tater lounged in the sun on the top of the table as I ate and read. The interview transcripts were the most interesting. I didn't disagree with Grady that Coach Kerr had a bit of a creep vibe. Even though his alibi had checked out, I was going to look harder at him. Nothing so far had suggested partners committing these crimes, but I couldn't know for sure.

But when I reached the end of the pages, I sighed. I felt the weight of frustration Colt must have. There wasn't a clear-cut answer. And no one pinged my radar in the way a true suspect usually did.

Tater let out a meow, bringing me back to the present. I looked up and shivered. I'd been so caught up in the file that I hadn't realized how much time had passed. At some point the solar lantern decorating my picnic table had turned on because the sun had completely disappeared.

"Sorry, Princess Tater, I know it's past your dinnertime."

She squawked back at me as if to say, *Damn straight.*

I pulled the last of my papers together and closed the file. Gathering up my food remnants, I crossed to the van and slid open the door. The trash inside was almost full, so I pulled the liner and tugged it closed.

"Want to make a trash run with me?" I asked Tater.

She meowed in response and bounded after me.

The campsite had a few bear-proof receptacles for trash and recycling about a hundred yards from my site. It was a hell of a lot better than having to take my trash into town.

Tater and I made the trek quickly even in the dark. The full moon gave us enough light to illuminate our path. When we reached the cans, I quickly unlocked one and placed the bag inside, moving to relock it.

Tater let out an angry meow, and I turned, but it was too late. Someone grabbed me by my hair and jerked me back. Shock hit my system, panic quick on its heels as a hand closed around my throat, cutting off my air supply.

I thrashed and kicked, trying to get at my attacker, but nothing seemed to land. They just squeezed my throat harder as they leveled a brutal blow to my ribs. Spots danced in front of my vision as darkness closed in.

A deep voice cut through my gurgled attempts to scream. "Go home, or I won't let you off this easy next time."

Chapter Twenty-Three
Colt

I LEANED BACK IN ONE OF THE CONFERENCE ROOM chairs, its metal groaning with the movement. It felt like my bones were giving the same damn protest. But I reached for my coffee because I knew we weren't close to done.

"I don't like this," Ryan muttered as she pulled her hair up into a knot on the top of her head.

I scowled down at the array of photos and files. "There's nothing to like."

I knew most precincts were fully digital now, but I liked holding the paper in my hands. The tactile experience of being able to see all the pieces at once like we were now. Ryan and I had been locked in this room since lunch, after a quick trip to talk to Dawson.

He hadn't provided any new information, but the footage from the cameras had. It wasn't like we had a lot of them, but we had enough. And every single lens that pointed at the route from the woods to the side door had been blacked out. Someone had approached each device from the side and spray-painted the lenses black.

Fucker.

But whoever it was, they were a bastard who knew their way around the station. And that told me it was a Shady Cove local, not someone who'd merely been passing through town now and then.

My gut twisted at the thought that whoever had taken Em was still living among us. All of a sudden, her fear of going out in public seemed less like an illness and more like a perfectly logical decision.

"Colt," Ryan said, cutting into my spiraling thoughts.

I sat upright again. "Sorry."

She studied me for a long moment. Even though she was a few years my junior, she had a wisdom in her green eyes. "I know this has to be a lot."

I appreciated that her voice hadn't gone gentle with her words. There was no pity in them, just simple facts. "I hate thinking that whoever took Em has just been living free and easy ever since. Watching us walk around with our thumbs up our asses."

Ryan's mouth thinned into a hard line. "I go over the case every year too. The casework is solid. They talked to everyone in Emerson's orbit."

"So maybe it wasn't someone close. Maybe it was someone watching from afar." My gut roiled at the thought of some creep watching my sister for days or even weeks, just waiting for the perfect moment to strike. And he had because I'd given him the opportunity.

"If it is the same person, they're getting desperate. And desperate people make mistakes."

I grunted in agreement. But it wasn't enough. Not with this much at stake.

"Gotta thank the Sawyer woman for that," Ryan muttered. "She's obviously pushing buttons."

I shifted in my seat, my mind drifting to Ridley, wondering if she'd gotten the basket I'd left her. I knew she must have. I wasn't sure what reaction I expected. For her to show up at the station and throw herself at me in thanks? It was more likely she'd dumped all the food out for the bears. And I wouldn't have blamed her.

I scrubbed a hand over my face. The scruff there had officially tipped over from stubble into a beard. I needed a shave.

"Still not a fan?" Ryan pushed.

I sent a scowl in her direction. "I think that what she's doing is risky."

"Never said it wasn't. But sometimes risky is needed to break through."

"Or all hell is going to break loose," I argued. Because if there was one thing that Ridley was good at, it was chaos.

Ryan shrugged. "That's what we're here for, to make sure it doesn't get out of hand."

I wanted to believe it could be that simple. That we could rein it all in when things got out of hand. But unless Ridley was letting us in at every step, that wasn't possible. And it had dread stirring somewhere deep. Worry for Emerson and for Ridley.

I shoved it all down and turned back to the files. "I want to get an alibi for everyone who was a suspect in Emerson's case. See where they were last night."

Ryan's brows lifted. "Going hard, no tiptoeing."

It wasn't a question, but I answered it anyway. "There's no point. I think the shock of a head-on approach might actually tell us more."

She nodded and ripped a piece of paper off the notepad in front of her, then picked up a pen. "You want to go with the core three or talk to everyone who was questioned at all?"

"Everyone," I answered immediately. The three main suspects the sheriff's department and state police had circled were Grady, Coach Kerr, and Emerson's math teacher. The math teacher was in his early seventies now and had Alzheimer's, so I doubted he could've managed a break-in like this one. Grady and Kerr needed to be talked to for sure, but we needed to cast a wider net.

"That's over thirty people," Ryan reminded me.

"I know. And they're not going to be happy."

"Understatement of the century. It pissed people off back then. It'll be worse revisiting it."

I knew she was right, but there was no way around it. We had to start somewhere, and this was the best shot we had. "We can start tomorrow. I want you or me in on every interview. No sending deputies alone."

Ryan nodded. "You got it."

A knock sounded on the door and then it opened, Dina stepping inside. Her halo of frizzy, gray hair always made her look a little frazzled, but the fact that her gaze jumped all over the room added to it tonight.

My gut hollowed out. "What's wrong?"

Dina swallowed. "It's that woman. The podcaster. Someone found her beat to hell at the campground."

Chapter Twenty-Four
Ridley

A LIGHT FLASHED ACROSS MY EYES, MAKING ME WINCE.

"Does that hurt?" the doctor asked, concern radiating through her voice.

"Doesn't feel like kittens and rainbows," I rasped. My voice sounded like I'd been a chain-smoker from the age of two and followed it up with whiskey on the regular. But I guessed that was what happened when someone tried to strangle you.

I shivered at the reminder. The memory of that voice in my ear. Of slipping into the darkness.

That darkness was punctuated by shouts. A twentysomething and his girlfriend who were camped nearby had found me. The EMTs asked me all sorts of questions.

And the pain. So much pain.

That hadn't left me. Not yet. And Dr. Sapra hadn't wanted to give me drugs yet. Not until the MRI results came back.

She hadn't messed around when I arrived. After getting my vitals, it had been straight to get X-rays and an MRI. Thankfully the X-rays had shown that nothing was broken, but the MRI took longer to read.

"Are you cold?" Dr. Sapra asked.

I shook my head but immediately realized my mistake. My vision swam, and a wave of dizziness swept over me. The combination had nausea rising on its heels as I gripped the blanket tighter.

"Let me get some antinausea meds into that IV," she said, moving to a corner of the small ER room, where a syringe was already prepared. In a matter of seconds, she was sliding the needle into the tubing connected to my arm. "This should take effect almost immediately."

"Praise all the angel kittens," I muttered.

As if she knew what I was talking about, Tater let out an angry meow from the carrier she was in. But I would take the indignant anger. I was just glad she was safe and that one of the reporting deputies had a cage in the back of their SUV.

Dr. Sapra made a cooing noise at the carrier. "Poor little thing isn't used to being in a crate."

"Definitely not. Princess Tater usually runs the show."

The doctor chuckled. "Well, you need to be quiet, Miss Tater, or our hospital will get in trouble if anyone reports your presence."

"Thanks for looking the other way." It wasn't like I had any friends or family close who could come get her, and if I had to stay the night, I knew Tater would be forced into a shelter.

"Cat? What cat?" Dr. Sapra asked with a smile.

There was a knock on the door, and she crossed to it, opening it quickly. A young man was there. "Ridley Bennett's MRI results are in her file, and there's someone here who says he's family—"

The nurse was cut off by Baker shoving past him and Dr. Sapra. "Ridley. Jesus. What the hell happened?" He strode across the room to my bedside. "Are you okay?"

I gaped at him in confusion. "What are you doing here?"

"You were giving me the runaround, so I decided to come check on you in person, but when I got to the campsite, it was crawling with cops. They wouldn't tell me a damn thing, but you weren't there, and you hadn't called our lawyer, so I started calling hospitals." His gaze dropped to my throat, and I knew there had to be marks there.

"I'm okay, really," I assured him, but my voice was so raw it didn't exactly sound convincing.

"I'll be the judge of that," Dr. Sapra said as she strode to the computer in the corner. "Do you want this gentleman here? I can call security if not."

Baker let out an indignant huff, his gray eyes flashing. "Do you know who I am?"

I wanted to crawl under the covers. Who actually said that? "Bake, you sound like a badly written Bond villain. Please just be chill."

Dr. Sapra chuckled. "I'm taking that as a reluctant yes."

"He can stay," I muttered.

"All right." Her fingers flew across the computer's keyboard as she brought up a chart and images, humming as she looked at everything.

"I told you this case was a bad idea," Baker said, pitching his voice low.

I scowled at him. "You thought there was nothing here. But there obviously is if someone's trying to strangle me over the trash cans."

"It's not funny," he snapped.

"I didn't say that it was. Just that there's something here, and I'm not being scared off." Especially when it meant I might finally have the answers I so desperately needed—answers that possibly meant Avery could rest once and for all.

"There are no signs of a traumatic brain injury on the MRI," Dr. Sapra interrupted.

"See?" I pressed.

The doctor shook her head. "That doesn't necessarily mean

anything. Eighty percent of TBIs don't show up on MRIs or CAT scans."

"What's the point in doing one then?" I groused.

Dr. Sapra sent me a patient smile. "We'd want to know if you had a brain bleed of any sort."

"Brain bleeds?" Baker exclaimed. "This is what you're willing to put up with?"

"Baker—"

"No," he snapped. "We're packing you up, and I'm taking you back to LA. If this case is so important to you, I'll send the *Reality Rampage* boys out here to cover it. There are four of them. It won't be as risky."

"The hell you will," I growled. "This is my case. And you don't own me."

Baker's eyes narrowed in my direction. "Don't I?"

My jaw went slack as I stared back at him. Was that honestly what he thought? That he could snap his fingers, and I'd do whatever he wanted? Baker didn't give a damn about my well-being. I was just an investment to him. His podcast with the most subscribers and downloads. He couldn't risk losing that because the host got murdered.

Dr. Sapra cleared her throat, but I could see heated annoyance in her eyes. "I don't feel comfortable with you staying alone tonight. I can keep you for observation—"

"She's staying with me," Baker snapped.

"The hell I am. I'd rather swallow shards of glass followed by ghost pepper juice."

Tater hissed as if to punctuate the point.

"You can stay at my place, Chaos."

The rasp cut through the hospital room with ease, and my eyes instantly sought out the sound. I'd been so caught up with Baker's delusions, I hadn't noticed the figure standing in the open doorway. I should've, because Colt's broad frame filled the entirety of it, casting a shadow over the linoleum.

Those dark eyes pinned me to the spot but somehow managed to be comforting at the same time. They shouldn't have been. This was the same man who'd accused me of breaking and entering, of assault. But yet here he was. Showing up when I needed him most.

"What did you say?" I squeaked.

Colt didn't look away for a single moment. "You can stay with me."

Chapter Twenty-Five
Colt

I WAS A GODDAMNED IDIOT.

The last thing I needed was Ridley in my space. Her nosy nature and burnt orange scent. Her blinding smile and ridiculous cat. But I wasn't about to leave her to this asshole, especially after she'd been attacked.

The asshole puffed up his chest, trying to make himself look taller, more intimidating. It failed. "Who the hell are you?"

I grinned at him, but knew it was sharkish. I tapped the star on the left side of my chest. "Sheriff Brooks."

The douche scrunched up his nose as if he smelled something bad. "Ridley doesn't want to stay with you."

"Ridley can speak for herself. I've found she's real good at that."

Ridley's lips twitched. "When people are willing to listen."

The woman had a damned good point. And it was time I took it to heart. "What do you say, Chaos?"

She glanced between the two of us.

"Ridley," the douche hissed.

She looked at me. "Can I bring Tater?"

I sighed. "Yeah, you can bring the weird water cat."

"You do *not* want to do this," the man next to the bed warned.

"That sounds a hell of a lot like a threat," I growled, starting toward him.

Ridley held up a hand and sent me a pleading look that had me stopping in my tracks. She turned her focus to the douche. "Baker, you need to back off. You know our contract. I get final say on all cases. You can decide not to run the rest of this case if you want, but I'll just publish it under my own umbrella. I'm not letting some gutless asswipe scare me away. All the attack told me is that I'm getting close."

An invisible fist ground against my sternum. She was so damn brave. But it was the kind of bravery that could get you killed. And I wouldn't be able to live with that. No way in hell.

Baker stiffened. "I made you."

Ridley just scoffed. "The hell you did."

"We'll just have to see what happens when I put all my resources behind *Reality Rampage* instead of you."

She shrugged. "Have at it. My approach has always been grass-roots. And that's not something you control."

Baker spat a curse, turned on his heel, and stormed past me like a toddler having a tantrum.

"Jesus," I muttered.

"My thoughts exactly," Dr. Sapra echoed.

Ridley slumped against the gurney's mattress, suddenly looking exhausted. "I'm sorry. He's a douchebag on a good day."

"Your producer or something?" I asked. I didn't like that he was conveniently in town the night Ridley was attacked.

She nodded. "I've been with him for almost three years now."

Three years. I didn't even want to think about the bullshit she'd had to deal with in that time. "Might be time to rethink that arrangement."

Ridley sighed. "You're probably right. I just haven't wanted to deal with the nightmare of leaving him."

I bet the little shit would throw a hissy fit. But at least the relationship would be severed. I'd get his full name from the podcast's website and run him. Just to cover my bases. I turned to Dr. Sapra. It wasn't the first time I'd been in her ER for a case. This one just felt a hell of a lot more personal.

"Ridley good to go?" I asked.

Dr. Sapra immediately turned to her patient. "Do you feel safe going with Colt? I am happy to admit you for the night, and I can find a temporary home for Tater."

An angry meow sounded from the corner. My gaze locked on the carrier in the corner and the very pissed-off cat inside. "Might want to be careful there," I warned. "That thing is liable to take out your jugular."

Ridley glared at me. "Tater isn't a *thing*. She's a cat. And she wouldn't hurt a soul."

"Tell that to my hand," I shot back.

"Oh please. She didn't even break the skin." Then a smile stretched across her face. "You know, Dr. Sapra, just to be safe, we should probably give Colt a round of rabies shots. I hear they're extremely painful."

Dr. Sapra choked on a laugh. "That they are."

I turned to Ridley and scowled, but relief swept through me. If she was giving me shit, things couldn't be that bad. "What do we need to get out of here, Doc?"

She glanced at Ridley. "You're good to go with Colt?"

Ridley nodded. "He's better than the alternative."

"Gee, thanks," I muttered. But another dose of relief hit me.

"And are you okay if I share medical information with him?" Dr. Sapra asked.

"That's fine," Ridley said, but the words held a strain.

She was so damn strong. Didn't want me to see the slightest evidence of weakness. But this wasn't her weakness. It was someone else's—someone I was going to find and make sorry they'd ever touched her.

"All right." Dr. Sapra turned to me. "We don't see any signs of TBI in the tests, but that doesn't mean there isn't one. If Ridley shows any signs of confusion, vomiting, blurred vision, or difficulty standing and walking, I want you to bring her back immediately."

I swallowed hard. *Fuck.* How badly had she been hurt? I didn't miss the way the doctor skirted that issue. But Ridley would have to share at some point.

Dr. Sapra crossed to Ridley's bed with a syringe. "This is a painkiller. It'll make you sleepy but should also ease the pain in your neck and throat, and along your ribs. I'll want Colt to wake you up every three hours for the next twenty-four, just as a precaution."

"Thanks," Ridley whispered as the doctor slid the needle into her IV.

Ridley's voice always pulled you in, the musical bent to it, but with groundedness you couldn't fake. Now it was raspy, as if her vocal cords had been shredded. The difference and Dr. Sapra's statement had me seeking out Ridley's throat.

As my gaze settled on the usually golden skin, rage blasted through me, so intense it burned me from the inside out. There were fingerprints ringing her throat in an angry array. They hadn't darkened to purplish blue yet, but I knew they would. Right now they were red, broken blood vessels dotting her skin.

It should've been the first thing I'd noticed when I walked through the door, but I'd been too damned distracted by the asshole producer. But as my gaze settled on the abused skin again, the violence of the attack became all too clear.

Someone had strangled Ridley. Maybe even tried to kill her.

As if Ridley had a radar for my emotions, her gaze cut to me. "Law Man," she started cautiously. "You okay?"

"Who. The. Hell. Did. This. To. You?"

Chapter Twenty-Six
Ridley

I COULD FEEL THE FURY COMING OFF COLT IN WAVES almost as if it were a living, breathing thing. After everything I'd been through tonight, it should've scared me. It didn't. It was somehow comforting. Because he cared.

Colt's chest heaved with his ragged breaths. "Who?" he demanded.

"Oh no you don't," Dr. Sapra said, stepping between my bed and the furious sheriff. "Any and all questions wait for tomorrow."

"I need to—"

Dr. Sapra cut him off instantly. "Whatever you need isn't as important as Ridley's well-being. Her *healing*."

That had a little of Colt's defiance slipping away. He scrubbed a hand over his face, suddenly looking defeated. "Yeah. You're right."

"I didn't see him anyway," I mumbled. My words were slightly slurred, the pain medicine taking hold.

Dr. Sapra crossed to my bed. "I'm going to take out your IV now. We'll get you in a wheelchair so you can get home to sleep."

"I don't have a home," I murmured.

Dr. Sapra's pitying expression swam in my vision.

Then a hand slid into mine. It was large, the skin rough. A hand that belonged to a man who had lived life and not shied away from it. "You've got one for now, Chaos."

"Okay, Law Man," I agreed, my voice taking on a dreamy quality.

And I almost believed him.

A hand ghosted over my cheek, sweeping the hair back from my face. "We're here."

I blinked a few times, coming to in the dark of Colt's SUV. I struggled to remember the events that had landed me here, and it all came back in flashes. The attack. The hospital. Baker. Colt. The loopy wheelchair ride to the SUV as Tater squawked.

"Hi," I croaked.

"Hi, Chaos," Colt said, a small smile tugging at his lips. But it quickly fell away. "How are you feeling?"

He was close. So close that scent of bergamot and cloves swirled around me, teasing and tempting. I found myself wanting to lean in, to close that distance between us and finally know what it felt like to have his lips pressed to mine. To know what he tasted like.

I swallowed hard, my throat sticking on the action. It was the drugs. I was high out of my mind, and that's why I was thinking about kissing the grumpy bastard. That was the only plausible answer. It had nothing to do with those broad shoulders and fathomless eyes.

Colt's brows pulled together in concern. "Chaos?"

"I'm good," I said, the statement more rasp than actual words.

"You sure?" he pressed.

"Promise," I whispered. "Just trying to get a little more with it. They gave me the good stuff."

Colt chuckled and lifted the small pharmacy bag. "There's more where that came from. But not until tomorrow."

"Pretty sure if I had more tonight, I'd be comatose."

"Can't have that," he said. "I'm going to come around and help you out."

"I can—"

Colt cut me off with a pointed look.

"I can wait for you to help me out," I amended.

"That's better."

Colt slid out of the SUV, tucking my meds into his pocket. I waited in silence, my nerves ratcheting up with each moment that passed. Then the back door opened, and Tater let out an accusing meow.

"Don't worry, Tripod. I got you too," Colt said.

"I wouldn't—"

"Ow!" Colt yelped. "She bit me through the damn cage."

"I told you we should've started you on rabies shots."

The back door slammed and a second later, my door opened. I was greeted with that familiar scowl that somehow made Colt hotter. Something was seriously wrong with me.

"This cat needs one of those behavioral specialists or something."

"Good luck with that," I said, grinning.

Tater hissed but it sounded more like a viper spitting.

Colt's scowl only deepened. "Maybe she needs to be on medication. A nice sedative."

Tater lunged for the bars and nipped Colt's pinky.

"Goddamn it!" he cursed.

I couldn't help the laugh that bubbled out of me, but the moment it left my lips I regretted it. The pain along my ribs flared to life. My laugh cut off, and I sucked in a breath.

"Chaos," Colt said softly. "He get your ribs?"

I nodded. "Got off a punch or two. Nothing's broken."

He glared at my side as if he could see the injury. "Probably bruised though."

"Maybe," I hedged. "But I'm sure it'll feel better tomorrow."

"Yeah," Colt said, but it didn't sound as if he believed me. "Come on. Let's get you inside."

He leaned across me, unfastening my seat belt. His arm brushed against my chest as he straightened, and my nipples instantly pebbled. Those damn traitorous nipples.

I bit the inside of my cheek, trying to steel my body's reaction to Colt's closeness. But apparently no amount of pain could stop my attraction to this man. And I was the genius who had said I was okay with staying with him.

"Here," Colt said. "Take my hand and slide out easy. Or I can lift you."

I didn't want his damn hand. My nipples would probably react to that too. But I *really* didn't want to know what would happen if I let him carry me. I'd probably end up dry-humping him.

"Okay," I rasped.

I slid my hand into his, shivering at the calluses, the feel of that rough skin. He closed his fingers around mine, bracing me.

As carefully as possible, I slid out of the SUV. Everything hurt—my ribs, my head, my throat. And there was an ache in every muscle, probably from hitting the ground when I went lights out.

When I was standing and steady, Colt's gaze swept over me. "You okay?"

I nodded and shut the door. "Good."

Then I looked up to see where we were going and gasped. I hadn't noticed the cabin when we'd pulled up. I'd been too lost in wooziness and pain and Colt. But now I couldn't look away.

Cabin wasn't exactly the right term. It was too nice for that. It was large but not massive. Beautiful but not ostentatious. The craftsmanship was expert. I could tell that even from where I was standing. The attention to detail was next-level.

The house was a mixture of wood, stone, and glass. The wood had a reddish hue, and I wondered if it was built from the redwoods surrounding us. That detail made the cabin feel like it sank into the forest, like it was somehow still a part of it. The stone of the walkway matched the rock the chimney was built out of, and I knew there had to be one hell of a fireplace inside. And the glass. So much glass I knew you could take in every inch of every possible view.

And thanks to the full moon, I could see that the whole structure almost hovered over the lake it was set on. If I could've built the house of my dreams, it would've been this one.

"It's beautiful," I whispered.

I felt Colt's gaze move to me, but I couldn't look away from his home.

He was silent for a moment before he spoke. "I'm glad you like it. Let's get you inside."

He kept hold of my hand as we approached the house, navigating the stone path with care. When we reached the front stoop, he set Tater's cage down so he could unlock the door, but he still didn't let go of my hand.

Once the door was open, he first set Tater inside and then led me in. "Here we go."

I moved into the entryway, forcing myself to let go of the hand that was giving me so much comfort in the moment. Too much. Instead, I focused on his house. I'd been right about the windows. The whole back of the house was glass. And it felt like we were on top of the water.

"Amazing," I breathed.

Movement caught my eye. A large dog struggled to his feet from a pillowy bed in the corner of the living room and ambled over to greet me.

"Well, hey there, handsome." My hand went to his head, giving him a scratch. The dog pressed into the attention.

"This is Bowser, and he'll love you for life for doing that," Colt said.

"He's perfect."

Tater let out an angry sound that was a cross between a snarl, a hiss, and spitting. She swiped at the cage as if she'd do battle with Bowser if given half a chance. Bowser simply sent her a look of confusion as he sniffed the air.

"She's not the biggest fan of dogs," I warned.

Colt lifted a brow. "What gave that away?"

I grinned.

"I've got you in a guest room with its own bath, so we can sequester the attack cat in there. I had Trey pick up a litter box and the same food that was in your van."

The backs of my eyes burned. "You got me a litter box?" Why was that the thing that had me almost breaking? Something about the thoughtfulness of it, the foresight. Colt doing whatever he could to make this as easy on Tater and me as possible.

"It's no big thing."

"It is," I argued.

He simply shrugged.

Then the second part of his statement about Tater's supplies hit. "Wait. What happened to my van?"

Colt winced and I knew whatever he was about to say wouldn't be good. "I'm sorry, Ridley. But whoever attacked you did a number on it. The inside is completely wrecked."

Chapter Twenty-Seven
Colt

Hell. The last thing I wanted to tell Ridley was that her van had been trashed. I'd gotten photos from my techs, and the inside would need to be completely rebuilt. I didn't even want to think about the time and money that would take. Hopefully her insurance would handle the money part, at least.

Ridley blinked rapidly, and I knew she was fighting to keep her tears at bay. Her hands fisted, fingernails pressing into her palms. The fact that she was battling so hard to stop the sobs from hitting only wrecked me more.

Her eyes closed for a moment, and I watched as she slowed her breathing, fighting back everything she was feeling. Back into some vault inside herself that she wasn't about to let me into. Something about that grated. I wanted to know what she hid in there. What she was feeling now and then. I wanted to know…everything.

Ridley's eyes opened, that startling deep blue locking on me. "My laptop?"

My back teeth ground together. "Gone."

She cursed, and Tater let out a sound of agreement from her carrier that made Bowser's ears twitch. "My desk. There's a locked drawer. Did the bastard get in there?"

My brows pulled together, and I shifted, pulling out my phone. I hit our lead evidence tech's contact. It rang twice before she answered. "Sheriff," she greeted.

"Hey, Tricia. How's it going?"

"It's going. I'd say we're about halfway done. No prints other than the ones I'm assuming are our vic's."

Something about Tricia referring to Ridley as a victim didn't sit right. It was the kind of thing that was said day after day, but when it was Ridley, it just felt *wrong*. I swallowed down the urge to bite my lead evidence tech's head off. "Ridley said there's a locked drawer in her desk. The unsub get into that one?"

"Not unless he's Houdini. It's still locked up tight."

My gaze moved to Ridley, her own was locked on me, looking for any sort of sign. I shook my head, and she let out a long breath. It was as if I could see the relief sweeping through her in a wave.

I forced my focus back to Tricia and the task at hand. "Think you'll finish tonight?"

Voices sounded in the background, the familiar chatter of the techs as they worked. "Should wrap it up in about four hours."

"Can you have someone drop the van by my place when you're done?" I asked.

Tricia was quiet for a moment. "You want to do a once-over?"

"No," I said quickly. The last thing I needed was Tricia thinking I was second-guessing her work. "Ridley's staying here."

The beat of silence was longer this time, and I started to wonder if the second-guessing would've been better. Tricia cleared her throat. "Sure thing. Max and I can drop it off when we're finished."

"Thank you. Send any reports to my email, and make sure you file the paper copies too." I wanted to be certain we had backups in at least three places from now on, because whoever this was didn't want us to have all the pieces.

"You got it. Anything else?" Tricia asked.

"Nope. Good luck."

"Thanks, Colt." And with that, she hung up.

I pulled the phone away from my ear, locking it and sliding it into my pocket. "What's in the drawer, Chaos?"

She swallowed hard, her gaze dropping to Bowser as she scratched behind his ears. "My research for the case."

Interesting. I itched to see what she had, to know if there was some piece that we'd missed. "They'll bring the van out here when they're done processing everything."

Ridley's shoulders slumped, and she suddenly looked so damned tired. "Thanks."

"Come on, I'll show you to your room." I picked up Tater's carrier and headed down the hall.

"Your house is stunning," Ridley said.

Her voice was neither soft nor loud but the sound of it still hit. And I liked the words a little too much. "Took way too long to build," I admitted. Largely because I'd been an obsessive asshole when it came to construction, making sure everything was just right. Sometimes it felt like the house was a piece of my soul.

"Worth it," she murmured. "Feels like you're floating on water."

Which was exactly what I'd wanted. I led Ridley toward the end of the hall, picking the guest room closest to mine. I told myself it was just a precaution, but I knew I was a liar.

Opening the door, I stepped inside. The bed faced a wall of windows so Ridley would be able to see the sun reflecting off the lake each morning. There was a chair in one corner that was more decorative than practical and a dresser on the opposite wall.

"There's a bathroom through there." I gestured to another open door.

But Ridley stood stock-still in the open doorway. "It's gorgeous. I—thank you."

"It's no big thing." I set the cat carrier on the bed so Bowser wouldn't have easy access to it. "Let me get the litter box. We can put it in the bathroom and close the room off from Bowser. Do you, uh, need something to sleep in?"

The barest hint of pink stained Ridley's cheeks. For a woman who'd given me shit when I walked up on her taking a shower, the fact that she was now blushing was adorable.

She nodded. "That'd be good."

"Coming right up. Bathroom is stocked with toiletries, but let me know if there's anything else you need."

"Okay," Ridley whispered.

I hated the softness in her tone, the lack of fire. It made me want to wrap her in my arms and tell her everything would be okay, which was goddamned ridiculous. So instead, I strode out of the room and toward my own.

Heading for my dresser, I pulled out a worn tee and some sweats. I went for the smallest stuff I had even though Ridley would still be swimming in them. But it was the best I could do. Hopefully, the asshole who'd hurt her hadn't ruined her clothes too.

Dipping out of my room and back to the guest room, I saw that the bathroom door was now closed. I crossed to the bed, Tater glaring at me the entire time. "I'm trying to help," I muttered to the cat as I set the clothes on the bed.

Tater hissed in response, swiping at the carrier's metal grate.

"Yeah, yeah. I've got some stuff for you too."

I turned back and headed for the kitchen, snapping my fingers for Bowser to follow. He didn't come right away. He was too busy gazing at the bathroom door longingly. My damned dog was already half in love with Ridley.

"Bowser," I hissed.

He glanced my way but didn't move.

I sent him my best I-mean-business stare. My dog wasn't moved.

I gave in and asked, "Want a treat?"

Those ears twitched, and he lumbered to his feet. I rolled my eyes and headed for the kitchen. Bowser ambled in behind me, and I found him a rawhide to keep him busy and out of Ridley's room. A pile of cat stuff lay on the kitchen table with a note from Trey.

Got all the essentials and took the Bow-Man out around eight-thirty. Hope Ridley's okay.—T

I pawed through the bags and scowled. The essentials apparently included half a dozen toys, a scratching post, five kinds of treats, and a catnip plant. Trey was making too much money on the side playing poker if he'd bought all this.

Still, I grabbed the cat box, litter, and a couple of the toys, and headed back to the guest room. The door to the bathroom was still closed, and I could hear water running inside, but the pile of clothes was gone.

I shifted uncomfortably, unsure if I should stay or go. I glanced at my watch. It was almost two in the morning. Dr. Sapra said Ridley needed to be woken up every three hours and asked simple questions. If there was any confusion, I needed to bring her back.

The thought of that had my gut churning, so I distracted myself by setting up the litter box in the corner and pulling the tags off a couple of toys. Tater simply watched like I was her damn servant.

The water shut off, and I straightened, bracing as the door opened. Ridley stepped out, her sun-streaked blond hair piled on top of her head. I'd been right about the clothes; they dwarfed her. But I hadn't been prepared for the sight of her wearing something that was mine.

The way my chest tightened and some sort of demented male pride surged. It was fucked, the way it felt *right*. Because I barely knew the woman opposite me.

"Hi," she squeaked.

"Hey." I cleared my throat. "How are you feeling?"

"Not bad, all things considered. A little jumpy maybe," Ridley admitted.

That had any thoughts of how good she looked wearing my clothes fleeing. Of course she was jumpy. She'd been attacked. And the marks on her throat, which were beginning to darken, were just more proof of that. "It's normal. Your body's going to be hypervigilant for a while."

Ridley nodded. "Makes sense." She crossed to the door, shutting it and letting Tater out to sniff around. I thought for sure the cat would jump off the bed and explore, but instead, she went and curled up on one of the pillows.

"I guess she's tired too," Ridley mumbled.

"Why don't you get some rest?" I suggested. "I'll be back in three hours to check on you." I started for the door, but she stopped me.

"Law Man?"

I turned.

"Could you stay? Just until I fall asleep?" Ridley suddenly looked like she wanted to take back those words. "Sorry. That was stupid—"

"Not stupid," I ground out, crossing to the chair and lowering myself into it. "Sleep, Chaos. No one's going to hurt you here."

I'd make damned sure of it.

Chapter Twenty-Eight
Ridley

THE SOUNDS OF BIRDS CHIRPING INFILTRATED MY slumber, a sleep I wanted nothing but to sink deeper into. But I let my eyelids flutter open, taking in my surroundings. I expected to see the sides of my pop-up tent on the van, but instead I was greeted by nothing but water, trees, and sunlight.

Everything came back to me in flashes. The attack. The hospital. Colt.

As if just thinking his name conjured him, my gaze locked on the man in the chair. His broad frame was far too large for the seat, which looked like it would be more appropriate for dropping your jacket and purse. He curled slightly to the side, using his arm for a pillow. His face was completely relaxed in sleep, and I couldn't help but stare.

At the way each exhale made his dark lashes flutter. How his thick scruff was now more of a beard. The haphazard array his nearly raven hair made.

He was beautiful. But it was more than something physical. Colter Brooks was beautiful because of his actions. Stepping in for someone he wasn't all that fond of just because she needed it. Giving that person a place to sleep. And staying just because she was a little jumpy.

Something shifted inside me, forgiveness breaking away at those final pieces of anger I was holding on to. Colt wasn't perfect, but he was kind. His words might not always be the best, but his actions always were. And I'd take actions over pretty lies any day.

Tater stood, stretching out her spine and then leaping from the bed. She crossed slowly to Colt, sniffing the air as she went. Then her eyes locked on the hand that dangled by Colt's side.

Panic washed through me. "Tater, don't," I whisper-hissed.

But it was too late. Her little teeth came down hard on those too-tempting fingers.

Colt jolted awake on a curse, wrenching his hand free as he jerked upright. "What the hell?" His gaze went from Tater to me. "Just a tooth hug, right?"

I winced. "Sorry about that."

He shook his head and rubbed at his hand. "How do you feel?"

Memories swept through my mind of Colt waking me up during the night and asking me simple questions like my name and birthday. "Better than I should," I said honestly. My neck and side were tender, but my throat felt a million times better.

"Your voice is back to normal," Colt said, his gaze roaming over me. And I had the sudden urge to right my hair, which I was sure looked like a rat's nest. "How's your head feel?"

I did a mental sweep. "Not bad. Low-grade headache."

"You can take your pain meds after breakfast."

"Bossy much?"

Colt just scowled at me. "You need to stay ahead of the pain, and if you take them on an empty stomach, you'll probably barf them up."

I threw back the covers and slowly sat, making sure my world didn't spin. I felt like I'd taken a spill on my bike but not like I had a brain injury. That was good. I pushed to my feet. "I think I'll be okay with Tylenol. And how about I make breakfast as a thank-you for letting Tater and me stay?"

That scowl only deepened to a glare. "You need to rest."

"I need to move. If I don't, my muscles will just lock up, and I'll feel worse. Trust me, I know."

Those deep-brown eyes flashed and then darkened to almost black. "You've been attacked before?" Colt growled.

Shit. Abort mission.

"No," I hurried to say. "But I've fallen while mountain biking, been bucked off a surly horse, and taken a spill while white-water rafting. I know how to recover from mild to moderate injuries."

A little of the rage in Colt's expression eased, but not for long. "I wouldn't exactly call being almost strangled to death mild or moderate."

Memories flashed in my mind. The feel of the man's hand around my throat, squeezing. Trying to fight him off with zero success.

"Shit," Colt muttered, pushing to his feet. "I'm sorry. I didn't mean—"

"It's okay." I took a few steps, relieved when the room still didn't spin. "Let me brush my teeth, and then I'll make breakfast. Do you have food in this place?"

Colt eyed me carefully. "The basics. You going to poison me?"

I laughed, ignoring the pain along my ribs. "I solemnly swear not to poison you, Law Man. Even if you sometimes deserve it."

It was his turn to chuckle. "All right. I'm going to jump in the shower. Help yourself to anything in the kitchen."

"Okay." I waited while Colt strode out of the room, images of him in the shower dancing in my head. Images I had zero right to but couldn't seem to control. Letting out a long breath, I moved to the bathroom and made quick work of washing my face and brushing my teeth, trying to avoid glimpsing the angry bruises ringing my neck.

I couldn't help but wonder who usually stayed in this guest room. Because it was, indeed, stocked. It had little travel bottles of face wash, lotion, toothpaste, and everything else you could dream up. I bet Colt had been a Boy Scout in his youth. Always prepared.

Looking for Tater, I found her scarfing down a bowl of dry food that Colt must've set up during the night. For not being the biggest fan of my cat, he was certainly taking good care of her. But I shouldn't have been surprised. He was doing the same for me.

I slipped out the door and listened. The faint sounds of a shower came through the door next to mine. I swallowed hard as images of the man in that shower filled my mind. His tall, broad body filling the space. Water tracking over his defined chest and down to—*nope*, I wasn't going there. I turned in the opposite direction, seeking out the kitchen. But the view kept stealing my focus. Every wall along the back of the house was dominated by windows, and as the sun glittered on the lake, I found myself getting lost in the art it created.

A large furry body pressed against my side, and I looked down, grinning. "Morning, Bowser."

He simply gazed up at me adoringly.

I gave his head a scratch. "All right. Let's go make some breakfast."

I found the kitchen and began searching the cupboards, pantry, and fridge. Colt's kitchen wasn't what you'd call *stocked*, but there were enough things to put together a decent breakfast. I lost myself in the prep work. The chopping and sautéing, cleaning as I went. You got used to that sort of routine in the van.

It wasn't long before I slid my creation into a preheated oven and poured myself a second cup of coffee.

"Smells amazing in here," Colt said.

I turned and froze. I couldn't help it. Colt rumpled from sleep was bad enough, but Colt freshly showered and shaved was devastating. The scruff wasn't completely gone, thank goodness, just shorn back. But his hair looked almost black since it was still damp. And those brown eyes seemed to glow in the early morning light.

I tried to force my focus to stay on his face, not to dip to those shoulders and chest, but I couldn't help it. That damn tan uniform shirt strained slightly over the curve of his shoulders. And that star glinted over planes of muscle.

Shit. Shit. Shit.

"Ridley?" he asked, that perfect brow furrowing.

"Sorry," I croaked. "Coffee hasn't kicked in yet apparently. Breakfast should be ready in five."

"Thank you. You feeling okay being on your feet?"

My grip tightened on my mug as I took another sip. "I feel pretty good. Just a little sore."

Colt studied me for another long moment, as if trying to tell if I was lying to him. "Okay. But don't push it today. You need to take it easy."

I made a humming noise that wasn't exactly a yes. What I needed was to borrow a computer until I could get a new one, and log into my files saved in the cloud. Then go through all the paper files from the van and try to put together who the hell was doing this.

Colt crossed to the coffee maker. Pulling out a mug, he poured himself a cup, black of course. "Don't think I missed how you didn't exactly agree to that."

A small chuckle slipped free. "I promise to rest if I feel I need it. How's that?"

"You'd say you didn't need it after hiking Everest," he muttered.

That had me fighting a grin. Maybe the grumpy sheriff knew me better than I thought.

"So," Colt went on. "What has my kitchen smelling better than it has in years?"

"It doesn't really have a name, but it's a greens and egg casserole."

Colt's face scrunched like he smelled something bad. "Greens?"

I turned to face him. "You had them in your freezer; you can't tell me you don't eat them."

He shook his head. "I put them in a chocolate protein shake so I don't have to taste them."

It was my turn to be disgusted, which I demonstrated by gagging. "Chocolate and greens?"

"You don't taste the slimy green stuff," Colt defended.

"Well, try it this way. I think you'll like it better."

He didn't look convinced. "Are you some sort of health nut? One of those vegans who eats nut cheese?"

I choked on a laugh. "Since I said it's an *egg* casserole, I think you're safe from nut cheese. But there are a few good kinds."

Colt gave an exaggerated shiver. "No, thank you."

"After you live on fast food and vending machines for six months, it loses its appeal."

He leaned against the counter, studying me. "So you were forced into the health-nut life."

One corner of my mouth kicked up. "I guess. Taught myself to cook with limited ingredients because my fridge is super small. But it forced me to get creative, and I found I liked it."

The timer dinged as if to punctuate my point. I grabbed the oven mitts and slid the casserole dish out of the oven. The egg, cheese, and veggie concoction was lined with crescent roll dough I'd found in the fridge, and it smelled incredible.

Colt leaned over my shoulder. "It looks really green."

I rolled my eyes and moved to grab plates. "I promise the scary vegetables won't get you. Now grab us some orange juice and sit."

He glared at me but did as I instructed while I plated the casserole. I was pretty damn proud of my creation, but the true test would be Colt's reaction. We sat and I waited as he studied his plate. He cut off the smallest bite he could manage and waited for it to cool. Finally he slid it into his mouth.

He chewed once. Twice. Then his brows just about hit his hairline. "This is really good."

I grinned. "No death by veggies on my watch."

Colt took a bigger bite this time, letting out a groan. "Damn, Chaos. You can cook."

Why did that feel like the best praise in the world? Maybe because it had been a long time since I'd gotten any sort of praise at all beyond comments on the internet. I'd forgotten what it felt like.

"What's wrong?"

I jolted, my gaze snapping back to Colt, who was staring at me intently. "Nothing."

"Don't lie," he ground out. "Tell me to mind my own business, but don't lie."

That was fair. Colt deserved way more than my lies. I sliced off a bite of the casserole. "I was just thinking it was nice to cook for someone who appreciates it."

Colt studied me as I chewed. "It's hard to build a community when you're constantly moving from place to place."

I nodded. "My community is online mostly. Other than the occasional in-person meeting."

"What about your parents?" He asked the question gently, as if approaching a possible land mine.

"I don't see them much. Maybe once a year. They didn't handle Avery's disappearance well."

I felt Colt's gaze on me as I ate another bite of casserole. But he didn't ask another question, simply waited for me to fill the silence.

I appreciated the gentle pressure that was far from forceful. It was more like a quiet invitation to share more.

"My mom tightened the reins to the point of unhealthy," I went on.

"In what way?" he asked softly.

"Didn't want me to leave the house after dark, even with friends. Wanted me to text her every thirty minutes. Didn't want me to move out."

"That's rough. On both of you."

I toyed with another bite of food, not lifting it to my mouth. "I tried to get her into therapy, but she refused."

"What about your dad?" Colt asked.

"He just sort of stopped living at all. Goes to work. Comes home. Eats dinner. Makes sure Mom eats something. Watches TV. Does the same thing the next day. I don't blame him. But I also couldn't do that. Do what my mom wanted just to ease her anxiety. So I left."

I lifted my gaze to Colt, expecting to see judgment there. Expecting that he would think I was an asshole or worse. But instead I found understanding.

Those deep-brown eyes searched mine. "You needed to go out and live."

It was the first time someone had really understood it. That need. That desperation. "I feel like I have to live for her and me. Experience everything I can because Avery will never get to."

Pain streaked across Colt's face. "That's a lot on your shoulders."

"And there's not the same sort of weight on yours?" I asked. Emerson was still here but marked by what had happened to her, changed.

"I need to make sure it doesn't happen to other people," he rasped. "Help when the horrible happens. But you know that pull too."

I did. And it was easy for it to become a compulsion. It was interesting, the way we all dealt with trauma, some of it so similar, and other parts as different as night and day. "I want to make sure they all get a voice. All the ones who lost theirs."

Colt's throat worked as he swallowed. "I'm sorry I didn't see that at first."

I lifted a brow. "At first?"

He chuckled, scrubbing a hand over his face. "Okay, at all. Until recently. Been listening to more episodes over the past few weeks. You do good work."

I tipped my chin down so that I looked him dead in the eyes. Those dark, fathomless depths. "Law Man…is that a compliment?"

His lips twitched, and I wanted to feel the movement of that stubble beneath my palm. "Don't be greedy, Chaos."

"I love being greedy," I said, eyes dancing. "It's how you get what you want."

Those dark eyes flashed with a smoky heat, reminding me of my favorite whiskey. *Our* favorite whiskey. And then he ruined it. "Walk me through what happened last night."

Chapter Twenty-Nine
Colt

I WATCHED THE LIGHT BLEED FROM HER EYES. THAT glimmer of lighter blue disappearing like a sparkler burning out against a night sky. I hated myself for being the cause of it.

I told myself it was necessary. A requirement. A duty. But I knew the truth. I was putting distance between us, a distance that was needed. Because it would be as easy as breathing to give in to Ridley. To let that energy swirling around her pull me in and never let go.

She took a long drink of orange juice, composing herself, creating her own distance. Then she set the glass down and met my gaze. "All right."

"Start at the beginning," I instructed. "Where you were before you went down to the trash cans."

Ridley took her time, eating another bite of that amazing-as-sin egg casserole thing. "I'd been working all afternoon and into the evening. Eating some of the goodies from that picnic basket you left. Thanks for that by the way."

Putting that apology gift together felt like a lifetime ago. But I got a surge of pleasure knowing she'd enjoyed it. "Least I could do."

Her mouth quirked, and I realized that Ridley's smiles were

rarely the common symmetrical ones that most people had. Hers were always a little off-kilter, unique. So like the woman herself. "It really was."

I chuckled but quickly reined it in, trying to stay focused on the task at hand. "So you were working. Did you see anyone hanging around?"

Ridley swallowed another bite and shook her head. "There's only been one or two other sites filled, and I hadn't met any of the campers until that couple found me."

I'd interviewed the couple myself, and they hadn't seen anything suspicious until they found Ridley unconscious by the trash cans, Tater standing guard over her owner. "Then what?" I pressed.

"I put my stuff away in the van and took the trash down to the dump site. Just as I was unlocking one of the cans, someone grabbed me from behind. He got my hair, and then his other hand went to my throat. I didn't see his face, not even when he punched me in the ribs."

She spoke with zero emotion, as if explaining the steps of a chemical reaction instead of an attack that could've left her dead. I understood the need for it, separating herself from the crime, but I hated that lack of emotion. It didn't fit the woman at all.

"Did you get a sense of his size?" I asked.

Ridley was quiet for a moment, shuffling back through memories. "Definitely taller than me. I got the sense he was big. Not massive, but definitely not a beanpole." She swallowed hard. "I tried to fight back, but he overpowered me pretty easily, so he had to have some muscle."

My back teeth ground together. I wanted this asshole to know what it felt like to be powerless, to be at the mercy of someone else. And he'd get that when I locked him up for good. He'd know that his life was no longer his own.

I worked to keep the anger from my voice—it was the last thing Ridley needed. "What about his hands? Was he wearing gloves?" Tricia hadn't found any prints other than Ridley's in the van, so we knew he'd worn gloves in there, but I wasn't sure about during the attack.

Ridley's lips pursed as she thought, her eyes glazing over. Then she jolted. "Yes. It felt like, I don't know, latex but stronger? Maybe some sort of rubber? Not loose like the ones you clean with, but tighter."

I'd need to do some research. We might be able to find this asshole through a specialty glove if it was specific enough. "That's good. Helpful. What about scent? Anything distinctive?"

"We were near the trash," Ridley began. "I don't think I got a whiff of his cologne." But then she paused, seeming to tug at a thought just out of reach.

I leaned forward, forearms pressing against the table. "What?"

Her nose scrunched, making little wrinkles appear there and accentuating the dusting of freckles. "I'm not sure." She shook her head. "When he spoke at the end—I smelled something…sweet?"

My hands fisted so tightly, it would be a miracle if I didn't dislocate a knuckle. "He. Spoke. To. You?"

Ridley nodded the barest amount. "He told me to go home, or he wouldn't let me off easy next time."

Rage pulsed through me in hot waves, lava taking out everything in its path. I'd known it was unlikely that this attack was random. But still, I'd hoped. Hoped that maybe it had been an addict passing through looking for money. But now I knew it wasn't.

"We're going to find him," I promised.

"I know," Ridley said, voice going quiet. "And he's going to pay for *everything* he's done."

That *everything* carried weight. The weight of Emerson. Of the other victims.

Ridley pushed her chair back and took her plate to the sink. "You have the keys to my van?"

Shit. I didn't want her in that vehicle right now. It was all but destroyed on the inside. One more assault to add to the list.

"Don't you think you should lie down now? Rest a little?"

She sent me a pointed glare as she grabbed my plate and rinsed it too. "I know what I can handle and what I can't. Keys please."

Hell. I pushed up, crossing to a key rack by the back door. There was one of those Magic 8 balls as the key ring. I tossed them Ridley's way, and she caught them easily, heading for the front door.

Bowser followed after her, abandoning his breakfast. If he was neglecting his food for the woman, he was more than half in love—he was sunk. The poor bastard.

But I followed them both, just falling in line with that fool's path. Bowser sniffed the morning air and found a spot to do his business. Ridley was already at her brightly colored vehicle. She stood there a moment before unlocking the door, bracing herself. Then in one swift move, she slid the door open.

The breath she sucked in was audible. Her gaze passed over the entire space. Papers strewn about, desktop monitor cracked, chair upended, dishes smashed, couch cushions sliced, and stuffing everywhere.

I couldn't help but move closer as if there were something I could do to ease the agony of Ridley's safe space being decimated. I knew there wasn't, but still I spoke. "I'm sorry, Chaos."

She let out a shaky breath. "Me too. Me. Fucking. Too."

Then she stepped up and into the van. I didn't miss the wince or the way her hand went to her side.

"Ridley. There'll be time to fix this later."

She sent me a look that had my mouth snapping shut. "I don't need another parent trying to control me. I know what I can handle."

Guilt swept through me. Her independent streak made a hell of a lot more sense now that I knew about her parents. Her mother's need for control had nearly strangled her in a whole different way.

"All right," I acquiesced. "What can I do?"

"Can you get me some garbage bags?" Ridley looked around the trashed van. "A lot of them?"

"Be right back." I turned and strode back to the house but gave Bowser a motion to stay with Ridley. He might have been old, but he was a good early-warning system.

I grabbed an unopened box of trash bags from the pantry and hurried back outside. Bowser lay in the grass, watching Ridley intently as she pawed through things.

"Here you go," I said, setting the bags just inside the van.

Ridley kept right on moving, searching. "Did your techs take the yearbooks?"

"Yearbooks?" My brows pulled together. "No. They didn't keep any items, just fingerprinted."

Ridley cursed, then slowly turned to me. "He didn't just take my laptop. He took the yearbooks and Emerson's case file too."

Chapter Thirty
Ridley

"OVERPROTECTIVE GRUMPY PANTS," I MUTTERED AS I tossed a shard of one of my favorite dishes into a trash can I'd lined with my thirteenth trash bag.

Bowser's ears twitched in response.

"Not you," I assured the pup. "You're perfect."

He laid his head back down on his paws.

"Your owner, on the other hand…" I mumbled as I picked up two more pieces of broken ceramic and tossed them into the trash.

After Colt had made sure I wasn't going to collapse into a pile of tears and snot at the sight of my destroyed van, he said he was going to head into work. I asked if I could hitch a ride into town, and he'd quickly squashed the idea, ordering me to stay here where I'd be safe.

Ordering me.

That wasn't something I enjoyed, especially when it was clear I was on to something. Why else would someone try to stop me from doing my job? Little did that asswipe know, it only made me more determined.

So I was rage cleaning and mulling over the list of suspects in my head. The only problem was that, without interviewing said suspects on their whereabouts, I had no ability to shorten that list. I gathered up all the bits of couch fluff I could manage and stepped out of the van to dump it into the trash without it going flying.

Turning back to my beloved Bessie, I gave her a once-over. It wasn't as bad as I'd originally thought. The couch cushions would have to be replaced along with my computers and some gear, but I could record with my lavalier mic and phone until those things came. I'd already ordered what I needed thanks to Colt's Wi-Fi. It would be here in two to four days. I just hoped insurance would cover at least some of it; otherwise I'd be taking a dip into my savings.

But in the meantime, Bessie was drivable now that I'd cleaned up the worst of the damage. I turned to Bowser. "I'd take you with me, but I think your dad would have me arrested for dognapping."

Anything to keep me locked up tight and out of trouble. The thought had a new flood of annoyance rushing to the surface. "Come on, B-man." I clapped my hand against my thigh, and the dog followed me inside. I checked that he had water, knowing Tater was set with her new scratching post and toys. Then I went in search of spare keys.

Like a true Boy Scout, Colt had two sets hanging on the key rack. I took one and headed out, making sure to lock up. I did not need a break-in on my conscience too.

In a matter of minutes, I was on my way into town. The pulsing headache behind my eyes told me it was time for another dose of Tylenol, but I wanted some food in my stomach first. So I headed for Cowboy Coffee and their Kale Krunch salad. I was hoping I'd run into Dean too. I hadn't gotten the kid's email address or cell number, but I thought he might be able to help me track down another set of those yearbooks.

Because that was where I needed to start. There was something in those books and Emerson's case file that someone didn't want me to see. I'd already gotten Colt to agree to bring another copy of the file home with him, but he didn't have easy access to six years' worth of yearbooks. And I was sure the school wouldn't be thrilled that I'd gotten theirs stolen.

I snagged a parking spot a couple down from the coffee shop and slid out of the van. My muscles protested the movement, my side flaring in pain. Apparently even sitting for the twenty-minute drive into town had been enough time for my body to tighten up. Tonight I'd do some gentle yoga and take a bath in that dreamy tub I'd eyed in Colt's guest room. That was if he didn't kick me out for disobeying his orders.

Heading toward Cowboy Coffee, I pulled up short as a man exited the shop. His gaze cut to me and then dipped to my neck. Trey's easygoing expression morphed into a scowl as he stared.

I fought the urge to cover the skin there somehow. Maybe I needed to find a scarf. I knew the marks had begun to darken to bruises, but they were obviously worse than the last time I'd looked in a mirror.

"Shouldn't you be resting?" Trey clipped.

"You sound like your bestie," I muttered.

He simply arched a brow.

I sighed. "I'm fine. A little banged up but not on death's door by any stretch."

The scowl was back at my *death's door* comment. "I really don't think you should be out alone."

I fought the urge to snap back at Trey. He didn't deserve that. But that slight flex of control flipped my trigger. "I appreciate the concern, but I doubt anyone is going to try anything in broad daylight in the middle of downtown."

Trey scanned our surroundings. People were out wandering the town and poking in shops. Cowboy Coffee was about two-thirds full. And there were no obviously nefarious characters around. "You'll head back to Colt's before dark?"

I held up my hand like I was being sworn in by a judge. "I solemnly swear."

Trey's lips twitched. "All right. Feel better and be safe."

"Thanks," I said, slipping around him and heading into the coffee shop.

I placed my order for lunch with a teenage girl who reminded me a lot of Emerson and found an empty table to hole up at. I felt naked without my laptop to work on, but I pulled my phone out of my bag, knowing I could do most of my work on it. The device dinged just as I set it down.

Sully: What the hell happened last night? Baker's in a rage.

Shit. I'd completely forgotten to bring Sully up to speed and give him my version of events before Baker got to him.

Me: I'm fine. Swear. Had a little run-in with an asshole but I'm good.

Sully: Baker said you were in the hospital.

Me: The ER. Not admitted. And just to be safe. All my tests came back good. Bessie, on the other hand, has seen better days.

Sully: What happened to Bessie?!

I knew that bringing up my beloved van would get Sully off the topic of my own injuries. We were both a sucker for cool vehicles and he'd listened to me talk about every set of upgrades I'd given the ole girl.

Me: Someone did a number on her guts. But I'll get her fixed up. Might be an excuse to do a few more projects.

Sully: That pullout couch so you don't have to winter
in the south anymore.
Me: Bingo.

Right now my bedroom in the van didn't have insulation, so I had to spend my winters places where snow was never in the forecast. It would be nice to have an alternative.

I watched three little dots appear, disappear, and then appear again.

Sully: I'm glad you're okay. But watch your back.
Baker's on the warpath, and I wouldn't put it past
him to try to oust you from the network.
Me: Thanks for the heads-up.

I knew Baker would be pissed about our fight last night, but actually trying to kick me out of his production company? That was too far. Even for him.

He had a board to answer to now, so it wasn't as easy as him simply giving me the boot. But he could screw me in other ways, and I knew it.

I pinched the bridge of my nose, the headache growing there. It was time to go out on my own. I knew it in my gut. But that was a process. One I wasn't sure I was ready for. I knew Sully would go with me. But who would deal with the advertisers? That wasn't something I wanted to tackle. It seemed like a giant waste of time other than the fact that they were the ones who kept food in my fridge and gas in my tank.

There had to be someone I could hire to take that on. Maybe a company or agent or something. But I didn't want to waste time researching that either.

"Ridley?"

Ezra's familiar voice had me lifting my head and forcing a smile. "Hey. How are you?"

He held my kale salad and hazelnut latte but stared at my throat, his jaw slack. "Shit, Ridley. I heard something happened. But damn, that looks bad. Are you okay?"

I winced, wishing for a scarf yet again. "I'm fine, really. Looks worse than it is."

Ezra shook his head as he set down my salad and drink. "I hope so. This is seriously messed up. Did you get a look at who did it?"

I shook my head. "No. But I'm not going to let it stop me."

His eyes widened. "You're going to stay on the case?"

"Of course she is," a younger voice cut in. I looked up to find Dean grinning at me. But that smile died when he caught sight of the bruises around my neck. "Damn."

"I'm okay. Promise. But I could use my trusty sidekick's help with something."

He instantly brightened at that. "Anything."

"Do you know if there's any other way to get ahold of another copy of those yearbooks?" I asked hopefully.

"Not for you," a new voice growled.

Chapter Thirty-One
Colt

Annoyance pulsed through me as I took in Ridley and her ragtag group of helpers, none of whom needed to get caught up in this. Especially Dean. The kid was barely sixteen. And this investigation had gone from cold case to open and potentially lethal last night.

Ridley beamed up at me, that smile tilting to the side slightly and making me want to trace it with my tongue. "Law Man. How's it going?"

Ezra choked on a laugh, and I sent him a glare. "It was good until I got a call about a certain podcaster back in the throes of her investigation."

She slumped back against her chair. "Who narced?"

"Trey."

"That bartender needs to learn a little about confidentiality," Ridley muttered.

"He was *worried* about you. Because, oh, I don't know…you almost got *dead* last night." A fresh wave of rage coursed through me at the reminder. And a healthy dose of anger on its heels at Ridley for being so careless. I knew she'd keep investigating, but she could've flown a little more under the radar.

My accusation had her straightening and leveling me with a glare of her own. "I know. I was there. But now is exactly when I should be pushing. And I can't do that if I'm locked up in your cabin in the woods."

Ezra started coughing again, and Dean grinned, extending his knuckles for a fist bump. "Nice move, dude. Real protective-like." I just stared in return, and Dean slowly lowered his hand. "Or not."

I turned back to Ridley. "Go back to the cabin. Please." The last word was an add-on, but I knew it was my only prayer of getting Ridley to go along with the request.

She faltered for a moment, and I thought I had her, but then she shook her head. "I'm sorry. I can't. I have things I need to do. But I'll make you the same promise I made Trey, even though he's a little traitor."

I battled between laughter and frustration, finally going with a sigh. "And what was that?"

"I'll be home before dark. Hell, before sunset, because I want to see the sun go down over that beautiful lake of yours. Might even grab a bottle of Ransom to share."

Damn it. I was a sucker for a woman who appreciated a good sunset. Even more for a woman who had a taste for *my* whiskey. I stared at Ridley for a long moment, knowing there wasn't a damn thing I could do to stop her unless I put her in a jail cell. Even then I wasn't sure the bars would hold her. So I did the only thing I could.

"Be safe, Chaos. It's going to piss me the hell off if you end up dead."

She grinned up at me. "You say the sweetest things, Law Man."

My feet rested against the railing of my back deck as the sun sank lower in the sky. Each millimeter it moved, my annoyance and worry ratcheted up a notch. Because Ridley still wasn't back.

In the midst of my worry, I'd realized that I didn't even have her damned phone number. But what I really needed was a tracker. One on that van and maybe one surgically implanted on her person.

As the logistics of that circled in my mind, Bowser's head lifted and his ears twitched. Then I swore the damn dog grinned.

"It's her, isn't it?"

He lumbered to his feet and headed off the back deck without waiting for permission like he normally did.

I scowled after my dog. "Well, I'm not going to be quite that pathetic." So I stayed right where I was. But my ears were trained for every little sound as I stared out at the lake's glassy surface.

"Who's a good boy?" Ridley's voice wove through the air. "I missed you too. I might have an extra-special bone in here just for you."

She was going to ruin my dog with her spoiling.

Then I heard feet crunching gravel and footsteps on the deck steps.

"Back by curfew and everything," Ridley called.

I didn't say a word. Still too damn annoyed that I cared so much.

She lowered herself to the chair next to mine, setting down a few bags. "I got whiskey, some Thai takeout, and a bone for B-man."

I simply grunted.

"Oh, come on," Ridley chided as she pulled out a massive bone and handed it to my dog. "You know I can't stop working this case."

"I know," I said, still not looking at her.

"But that pisses you off," she said, cutting to the chase.

I mulled that over for a moment before finally turning toward her. "It pisses me off that I care."

Ridley's blue eyes went wide as her jaw slackened. "I—you know, Law Man, you use the most insulting compliments I've ever heard."

I couldn't help the chuckle that slipped free. It released a little of the tension that had been thrumming through me. But not the source. Because that source was sitting next to me, her burnt-orange scent filtering through the air and invading my senses. "I hope you got some curry at least."

She arched a brow in challenge. "Do I look like an idiot?"

"Chaos, you look like a lot of things, but an idiot isn't one of them."

A hint of pink stained her cheeks, and hell if I didn't love knowing I affected her. She bent and went fishing in the bag, pulling out a carton and handing it to me. As I took it, our fingers brushed, and a zing of *something* shot through me. Not electricity, nothing as simple as that for a woman as unique as Ridley.

This was more. Like sparks detonating in a chain reaction through my bloodstream. Or a million and one nerve endings waking up after a century of sleep. Whatever the reaction, I was monumentally screwed.

I jerked the carton toward me. "Thanks." My voice had a rougher edge than it normally did, and I forced my gaze to the food. Coconut curry. My favorite. "How'd you know?"

"Asked the girl who took my order. Figured, small town, you've likely been there before. So I asked if you had a favorite."

I swallowed hard as I grabbed a carton of rice to go with the curry. "Em and I order from there a lot."

Ridley stilled for a moment, likely taking in the fact that I'd mentioned my sister for the first time without her prodding. She pulled out her own carton of noodles and a plastic fork. "I'm really not an idiot—"

"I know that—"

"Just listen," Ridley said, cutting me off. "I don't have a death wish."

That was good, but it didn't seem like it from where I was sitting.

She spun her fork in the pad Thai, which looked like it was full of tofu. "I've been looking for cold cases similar to my sister's for almost four years now."

My hand froze, fingers tightening around the spoon. I shouldn't have been surprised. Of course Ridley would be investigating her sister's case.

"I've found twenty-three of them."

My spoon dropped into my curry.

Ridley's deep-blue eyes swam with pain. "And I think your sister was the first."

Chapter Thirty-Two
Ridley

I WATCHED THE THOUGHTS AND EMOTIONS PLAY ACROSS Colt's face like a movie on one of those drive-in screens. He didn't hide a thing, not this time. He let me see as he put the pieces together in his mind, as he realized what *could have* happened to his sister. In some dark part of his mind, he already knew. But this made it more real.

"Twenty-three? You're sure?" The questions didn't feel like a challenge, but rather that Colt didn't want them to be true.

I nodded. "That's what I've been able to find anyway. I don't have access to any of those handy databases you law enforcement types have, so it takes me longer to research—"

"How?" Colt cut in before I could nervously ramble anymore.

"How did I research?"

"How do you know they're connected?"

I finally released my hold on the plastic fork. Little lines were carved into my fingers and palm from how tightly I'd been holding the thing. This was it. Where I laid out my case and told him everything. Where I hoped like hell he'd believe me, unlike the law enforcement I'd tried to convince before.

Taking a deep breath, I did the only thing I could. I began. "All of the victims were blond. Ages sixteen to twenty-four."

Colt's dark eyes cut to me. He didn't voice his doubts or tell me that wasn't enough, but I could feel them. So I pressed on. "All athletes, but not just any athletes—the stars. Ones who won state championships or received awards."

Colt leaned forward, setting his takeout containers on the edge of the deck railing. The hook had caught hold. He was really listening now.

"They were all incredibly good students, recipients of scholarships, on every kind of honor roll."

"All high achievers," Colt said, pulling the strands together.

I nodded. "Every single one was a member of the National Honor Society."

That had him jerking straight. "Have you—"

"Looked at every person at that organization who might have access to those kinds of records?"

Colt's brows twitched. Not in amusement exactly but maybe surprised admiration.

"Yes," I went on. "I can't be one hundred percent sure, but as far as I can tell from deep-diving their social media and getting a little help from a hacker friend—"

My words cut off as Colt scowled. "You know anything that hacker gives you is fruit from the poisonous tree."

I scowled right back. "My contact is a good dude. A white hat. He's just trying to help."

"It doesn't matter if he's a *good dude*. It's not anything we can use."

"Well, we don't have to, because what he found cleared all three of the people still on my list."

Colt sighed, sitting back in his chair and staring out at the water.

I'd already laid a heavy load on his shoulders, but I knew I had to keep going. Colt needed to know everything. "Every victim was taken from somewhere near a school campus or practice facilities. I've watched him evolve. He started with kidnapping and sexual assault, leaving his victims with fuzzy memories in places they didn't recognize."

Colt's jaw went so hard I could see the bone pressing against his skin, just trying to break free.

"Then he started to hurt them even more."

Colt's fingers latched on to the arms of his chair, knuckles bleaching white.

"He discovered he had a taste for it. The pain and torture." My stomach roiled, and I tried to detach myself from the words I was saying. But I couldn't quite get there. "Then he started ending their lives altogether."

Colt turned to face me, and his dark eyes would be burned into my mind forever. So much pain in those fathomless depths. So much need to make things right. "They never found your sister."

"No," I croaked. "There are victims on my list they never found. But there are more they have. Survivors and bodies. Enough to put the pieces together. But no one would listen."

Colt frowned, little lines bracketing his mouth amidst the scruff. "You took this to law enforcement?"

I couldn't help but scoff. "I've taken it to six local PDs, three state police forces, and even pled my case to the FBI. They all thought I was some little girl grasping at straws."

His jaw worked back and forth as if he were trying to loosen it, to force the tension to release. "You have files on all of these cases?"

"What do you think?"

"That you're not an idiot," Colt muttered.

My lips twitched. "So he can learn."

I was hoping for a chuckle, one of the ones that felt like warm grit skating over me. But Colt wasn't there. Not now. "Get the files, Chaos. We'll work in the dining room."

A buzz lit beneath my skin, hope that just maybe he believed me. I was moving before I could stop myself, heading back to Bessie and unlocking the drawer that held all my secrets. The stack of files barely fit in my arms, but I managed it.

As I headed back to the house, I found the front door open. An invitation. I just hoped like hell it was one I would be glad I'd accepted.

I moved inside, shutting the door behind me. I wound my way to the dining room, where a long gleaming table sat in front of floor-to-ceiling windows. But not even the gorgeous view could distract me now.

Colt was there, and he'd brought our food inside. There were plates now. Sodas to go with the meal. And there was a stack of office supplies—highlighters, legal pads, pens in an array of colors.

He looked up, hair looking just a bit unkempt, as if he'd been running his fingers through it repeatedly. "Tell me where you want to start."

"With Avery," I whispered. "You should start where I did, so you can follow the points I connected."

"All right." Colt pulled out a chair for me, and we began.

Everything came in fits and starts. Colt asked countless questions, ones I had answers to and ones I'd never even thought of. We approached things from different angles. Colt's was precise and measured. Mine was a little wilder, running on instinct. But the processes complemented each other somehow, each one filling in blanks that the other had left open, finding a few more of those missing pieces.

We talked for hours, long after the sun had sunk beneath the horizon. Papers and files had started to be organized in a timeline across the dining table. And when we finally finished, Colt sat back in his chair and stared at it all.

I didn't say a word. Simply let him process everything.

But the wait killed. I couldn't read Colt's face now. He'd turned inward, that impassive mask slipping over his features.

"Will you stay here?" he finally asked.

My brow furrowed. It was the last thing I'd expected to come out of his mouth. Maybe I'd hoped for him to shout *Genius!* or worried he'd tell me to take a long walk off a short pier. "What do you mean?"

Colt's gaze lifted from the papers, and he turned to me. "Tell me you'll stay here. I've got an alarm system and a dog that, while old, will definitely tell you if someone's here who shouldn't be."

Something shifted, some slight rearranging in the cavity of my chest. Colt was worried. About me. It didn't feel like the controlling machinations of my parents. Or even his interfering from the past few weeks. It felt like warm honey spreading over me. Someone wanting to know if I was okay.

"If I stay, will you help?" It was a barter, and I knew it. But I wasn't above striking a deal.

Those dark eyes of his swirled with different shades of shadow. "I'll help, Chaos. But you are going to stay safe. No more putting your ass on the line."

I opened my mouth to argue, but Colt shut me down with a single look.

"We aren't taking chances. Not with you. Not ever."

Chapter Thirty-Three
Colt

I slammed the door to my SUV a little harder than necessary. Okay, maybe more than a little, based on the way the vehicle rocked with the force of it. But I had to get the tension out somehow.

Runs weren't doing it. Hitting the heavy bag at the station gym wasn't helping. Not even ice-cold showers every night.

Ridley had been living with me for two weeks now. Two weeks of that burnt-orange scent bleeding into my space. Two weeks of her tilted smiles and amazing meals. Two weeks of seeing her put her all into this case.

A case that should've had my full attention but didn't. Because I was too distracted by tracing those damned tank tops she wore with my eyes. The countless straps that crisscrossed in designs I could never figure out but sure as hell lost hours trying to. The same way I lost hours trying to figure out how she twisted those tanned legs into a pretzel as she perched on a chair at my dining table.

My thoughts were so full of Ridley and her beautiful chaos that I couldn't get my head where it needed to be. So today, I'd walked away. Taken a break from hours at that dining room table just breathing Ridley in. I'd gone to the one place that would remind me where my focus should be.

I headed up the porch steps, taking in all the new flowers in bloom. I didn't know their names, but I could appreciate their color and beauty just the same. Before I could knock, the door to the house opened and Emerson filled the entryway. She beamed at me. "Where the heck have you been hiding?"

Guilt swept through me like a flash flood. I was one of two people Emerson let into her space with ease, and I hadn't seen her in over a week. I was a dick. "Sorry, Em. Things have been…" My words trailed off, but my sister stepped in.

"Interesting?"

My lips twitched. "That's one word for it."

Bear pushed past his owner to greet me. I gave him a good scratch and then moved toward the door, Emerson welcoming me in. There was a new art piece decorating a hallway wall. Oil paint, if I wasn't mistaken. A sunset over the mountains. Something Em hadn't seen in person in years. But she'd painted it as if she'd just laid eyes on it yesterday.

"Impressive," I said, nodding my head toward the work of art.

Emerson just shrugged and kept walking toward the kitchen as two smaller dogs ran out of the living room to follow her. Cheddar was a pug-chihuahua mix that looked like he needed his daily food intake cut in half. Saber was the tiniest Yorkie I'd ever seen. He had a single snaggletooth, which Em said reminded her of a saber-toothed tiger.

The moment we reached the kitchen, Emerson opened the fridge. "I've got lemonade, soda, sparkling water. I'd offer something harder, but it seems a little early for that."

"I'm good," I said, settling into a chair at her kitchen table. The same table we'd grown up around. It'd made all the sense in the world for Em to get the house after Mom died. It was the only place in the world she'd ever felt safe. But some small piece of me wondered if her staying here was part of what hindered her.

Emerson grabbed a sparkling water and sat opposite me. She looked like she was fighting a smile, her eyes glittering with amusement.

"What?" I asked. "Why do you look so weird?"

Em rolled her eyes. "Gee, thanks."

"You know what I mean. You're all smiley."

She laughed, twisting the top off her water. "I'm just wondering how things are going with your houseguest."

I stiffened. "Fucking Trey."

I hadn't told Emerson that Ridley was staying with me because I hadn't wanted her to feel pressured to talk to Ridley. Hadn't wanted her to know just how deep I'd gotten into the cases Ridley had pulled together.

Em only laughed harder. "I need to be up-to-date on town gossip somehow."

I cursed. "Thanks to Trey the town crier."

She leaned back in her chair and took me in. "So? How is it? What's she like?"

I worried the inside of my cheek with my molars, trying to think of the best way to describe all that Ridley was. "She's not what I thought she was," I admitted.

"Shocking," Em said playfully. "You mean she's not a con artist out to ruin everyone in Shady Cove?"

My eyes narrowed on my sister. "Don't be a dick."

She only grinned. "I think this is good for you. An exercise in learning and growing. My big brother finally admitting he was wrong."

I shifted in my chair. I had been wrong. So incredibly wrong. And I'd hurt a good woman in the process. A woman I was coming to respect more than anyone I'd ever met.

The smile slipped from Emerson's face. "What is it?"

I swallowed, my throat sticking on the action. "She's been through a lot. I didn't see that at first."

Em's form stiffened, her hand tightening around the glass bottle. "What happened to her?"

I mulled over whether it was my place to tell Emerson or not, but finally decided Ridley wouldn't mind. Because Emerson was a part of it all. A thread in the woven fabric. "Her sister went missing the night before their college graduation." My mouth went dry, and I wished I'd asked Em for something to drink when she'd offered. "Ridley thinks the man who took her is the same one who abducted you."

Emerson gripped her bottle as if it was the only thing keeping her in the here and now. And maybe it was. Because she stared across the table, but it wasn't like she was seeing what was actually in front of her. She was somewhere else entirely.

"She thinks I was the first attempt," Emerson said, her voice almost robotic.

"Yeah. She does."

"Ridley's sister. Did they find her?"

I swallowed acid climbing up my throat, all those *could've beens*. "No. They haven't."

Emerson kept staring at nothing, her gaze unfocused. "You think he's killed people."

I wanted to lie to her, to shield her from this, but I knew I couldn't. "We do."

"I was the lucky one," Emerson whispered. "I got away. Nothing really bad even happened."

"Em—"

Her gaze cut to me. "So why can't I just get over it?"

Pain swept through me, waves of icy shards. "Because it was a trauma. It takes time to process."

"It's been ten years!" Emerson shoved her chair back, releasing the bottle to rattle against the table. "Ten years, and my life just gets smaller and smaller. And here Ridley is, having gone through something horrible, and she's turned it into a mission. Why can't I be like that?"

I pushed to my feet. "Hey, now. Don't you talk about my sister like that. She's one of the strongest people I know."

"Colt…"

"It's true." I dipped my head so she was forced to meet my eyes. "Everyone's path is different. Takes different routes. You'll get to where you're meant to go."

Emerson's shoulders slumped. "I'd like to get there before I'm eighty."

I pulled my sister into a hug. "You will. I promise."

But my heart broke for all she'd already lost. All she'd missed out on. And I was going to make the bastard who'd stolen it all from her pay.

I pulled to a stop in front of my cabin but didn't turn off the engine. I simply stared at the structure. I'd been so damned proud of it when I'd had it built, but Emerson had never seen it outside of pictures. Never felt safe enough to come visit, even if Trey and I were both with her. That ache in my chest only intensified as my brain made a laundry list of all the things she'd missed.

I couldn't fix that for her. Couldn't erase it. But maybe if we found the monster from her nightmares, she'd be able to start living again.

Shutting off the engine, I climbed out of my SUV and headed for the house. I needed to go for a run. Burn off some of the anger coursing through me. Or maybe I should've gone to the station to work out the aggression on the bag.

But I hadn't. I'd come home. Because some part of me *needed* to see Ridley. Just lay eyes on her to make sure she was okay.

I unlocked the door and stepped inside, slipping off my boots as I quickly keyed in the code on the alarm panel. I'd insisted we both start using it from the moment Ridley had laid out those twenty-three cases. And the more I learned about each one, the more I didn't think an alarm was nearly enough.

As I walked deeper into the house, all thoughts of alarms and cases fled from my brain. My steps slowed and then stopped altogether. There was Ridley, her palms on the floor, one leg in the air, resembling some sort of weird-ass triangle.

She wore another of those damn tank tops, and it was worse because it was paired with those tiny shorts she always wore when she went paddleboarding. The outfit was golden peach, the sort of hue that melded with her tan skin. It made it almost feel like she wasn't wearing anything at all.

My gaze skimmed over her limbs, tracing the lines and curves, memorizing every detail, details I would torture myself with later in those nightly cold showers. Her perfect ass and hips dipped into a waist that would be just right for my hands to hold on to as I pounded into her. Waves of sun-kissed hair I could fist as she took me. Even the ridges of her spine somehow managed to be sexy.

Ridley's body twisted again, her other leg going up as she turned toward me. A smile pulled at her lips, twisting like her curves did. "Hey, Law Man."

Fuck me.

I thought it was bad seeing her from behind. That had nothing on those baby blues searing me to the spot. The way her tank dipped just enough for me to get a hint of the swells that would fit in my hands perfectly.

But Ridley was oblivious to my train of thought. "Just needed a little something to get my blood moving. I was sitting for too long." She effortlessly pushed to standing. "I think it's time for me to hit the interview circuit again."

All that fire blazing through me froze. "What?"

Ridley nodded, grabbing a notebook. "People are intimidated by a badge. But not usually by me. They'll open up more readily. I want to start with another visit with Coach Kerr and maybe Grady."

"No." The single word was out before I could stop it. But the moment it left my lips, I knew I'd made a colossal mistake.

Those blue eyes flashed as Ridley dropped the notebook to the table with a smack. "No?"

Hell.

"I just meant it's not smart. Not right now. We need to play this careful."

Her gaze narrowed on me. "It doesn't seem like *you're* playing it careful. You've talked to almost everyone on this list."

Ridley gestured to the wall of windows behind her that was now mostly covered in white butcher paper. It had become our de facto murder board. On one side was a timeline of all the cases. On the other was a list of every possible suspect.

"I have a gun and a badge," I argued.

"So what? That doesn't make it safe. Plenty of police officers are hurt in the line of duty."

"I'm prepared," I pushed back. "Ready for things to go sideways."

Ridley glared as she took three long strides into my personal space. "So am I. Public places, plenty of witnesses. I'm not an idiot, remember?"

"I know that, but—"

"But what?" she demanded.

She was close now. Too close. The heat from her body hit me in waves, right along with that damned burnt-orange scent. That smell was going to haunt me for the rest of my days.

"It's too risky." My voice had dropped, the rasp deepening. I knew it was a tell but there wasn't a damn thing I could do to stop it.

Ridley's gaze dropped to my mouth, holding there for a beat as if memorizing the shape. Then those blues lifted again, locking with my own eyes. "I know what I can handle."

There was only one thing I could do. Call that beautiful bluff.

I raised the stakes, closing the distance and pressing my body against hers. I could feel every rise and fall of her chest, the way those breaths came quicker now as her pupils dilated. Those perfectly pink lips parted.

"You don't know what you're playing at, Chaos."

Mischief flashed, but beneath it I could see her want, her need. "Don't I?"

She didn't wait then, just smashed through my wager with a royal flush. Her arms looped around my neck as her legs encircled my waist. Then her mouth was on mine.

Ridley took with wild abandon. There was no shy uncertainty with her. There was only need. A need I met with my own. And the moment her tongue stroked past my lips, I was gone.

She didn't just smell like oranges—she somehow tasted like them too. The kind fresh from the trees on the best orchard in the world. The bright, tangy flavor was one I could drown in for the rest of my days.

My tongue stroked hers, needing more, craving every last drop of her. My hips flexed against her, dick hardening to the point of pain. I could feel those perfect nipples pebble against my chest. But I wanted to taste them, to see if they were as golden as the rest of her.

Ridley moaned into my mouth and almost made me come in my pants like a goddamn horny teenager.

Fuck.

I tore my mouth away from hers, taking in those wild blue eyes.

"Don't," she whispered.

"It's a bad idea," I rasped. "We'd be playing with fire."

Those ocean eyes sparked. "Then let's watch it burn."

Chapter Thirty-Four
Ridley

EVERY LAST INCH OF MY BODY BUZZED AS I WAITED. Waited for Colt to tip one way or the other. Waited to see if he would burn the world down with me. If he would let some of that chaos reign.

But I wasn't a patient person. I never had been. Always the one to jump without looking how deep the water was below.

My legs tightened around Colt's waist, pulling him impossibly closer. And with that, I felt his length press against me, straining. My lips parted, crying out for breath, for him.

"I'm going to hell," he muttered.

And then his mouth was on me. Not my lips but my neck, trailing over the sensitive skin there, where the bruises had now mostly faded to nothing. His fingers tangled in the straps of my tank. "This goddamned shirt," he growled.

I pulled back slightly, breathless, but needing to see his face. "What'd my tank top ever do to you?"

"Been haunting my fucking dreams, that's what," Colt snapped. He slid one strap down and then another. "Been dying to know just how they all connected. Wondered if I snapped one, would they all come falling down?"

He tugged another and another before the fabric fell away, down to my waist, and my breasts were exposed to Colt. He stared down at them, tracing every detail with his gaze.

His hand lifted, thumb tracking over the underswell and then up. "Wondered if this was as golden as the rest of you." That thumb circled my nipple, and I sucked in a breath.

"Colt." His name was a plea. For what, I wasn't even sure. But I was desperate for it.

That callused thumb circled again, drawing the bud tighter, making me crave more. He twisted the peak, and I let out a sound that was more animal than human.

Colt's mouth lowered, pulling my nipple between his lips and sucking deep. A rush of wetness gathered between my thighs, and I rocked into him, craving a release from the building pressure. His teeth grazed my nipple, and I cried out.

His head lifted, eyes colliding with mine. "Fuck. Those sounds you make, Chaos. Need to hear what you sound like when I'm inside you."

My core tightened, but there was nothing to close around, only reminding me how much I craved Colt. How much I needed him. Maybe from the first moment I'd seen him. Those damn broad shoulders and that scowl that somehow managed to make him hotter.

But it was more than that. Some part of me knew it was, even if I didn't want to look at that piece too carefully, that sliver of connection that was so much deeper than anything else—how we understood each other's pain, loss.

My arms tightened around Colt's shoulders, and I pulled myself to him, not wanting to think about that tether. Right now the only thing I wanted to do was feel.

My mouth met his in a fever pitch. Our tongues dueled for supremacy, battling in a way I never wanted to end. But then Colt tipped the scales.

He moved forward, holding me to him with one hand while he shoved papers out of the way with the other. Then my back was hitting the cool wood of the table. The opposing temperatures only tugged at every nerve ending, coaxing them higher, making them cry out for more.

Colt stared down at me for a moment. His hand skimmed over my face, his thumb tracing my lips and then traveling down the delicate skin of my neck. He followed the line of my collarbone and dipped lower.

My back arched on instinct, nipples aching for Colt's touch. He gave me what I wanted with both hands now, thumbs circling. Then his fingers twisted, and I bucked against it all, more wetness rushing between my legs.

"The way you move. Like a goddamned work of art. Could spend a lifetime memorizing all the ways you bend and bow."

I shuddered at his words, the promise of them.

Colt's hands released my nipples and trailed lower. One traced the curve of my side while the other circled my navel. He took his time, teasing and exploring, but never going where I wanted.

"Colt," I ground out.

Those deep-brown eyes darkened. Some women would've misread the shift in color, been startled or maybe even scared. But that change only made my legs grip Colt's waist tighter.

"Don't. Rush. Me," he growled. His fingers traced the line of my shorts along my lower belly. "Need to know what you look like beneath all these damn workout clothes. If you taste as good as you smell."

Another shudder swept through me as my heart pounded against my ribs. "Please," I whispered.

His mouth curved the barest amount. "God, you're pretty when you beg. Think that deserves a reward."

Then both of Colt's fingers were in the band of my shorts. In one swift move, he jerked them down my legs. My bare ass hit the cold table, and I couldn't hold back my whimper.

But Colt was back, stepping between my knees and staring down at me. The only piece of clothing still left on my body was the tank top ringing my waist now. His gaze swept over the length of me, halting between my legs.

"Feet up on the table." His voice was low, coated in gravel, grit, and demand.

I shivered as I obeyed, lifting one leg and then the other. Everything about the position was vulnerable, the most intimate part of me on display for him.

Those dark eyes flashed, that hint of gold coming through. "So. Fucking. Gorgeous. Glistening. Just for me."

My lips parted as I sucked in a silent breath, tried to hold on to anything that would keep me grounded when it felt like I could just fly off the table.

Colt's thumb glided up my thigh, the rough callused feel only adding to the sensation. Then he parted me, sliding his finger along my slit and making a soft moan slip free. "Perfect." His finger traced my opening but never thrust inside.

"Colt." I knew I was begging, but I didn't give a damn at this point.

"Love the sound of my name on your lips."

Our eyes locked and I didn't look away. "Colt."

Two fingers stroked in. "So damn perfect she deserves another reward."

My back arched as he moved those fingers in and out, almost lazily, to a rhythm that was only his. But every drag across my walls was the most beautiful torture.

"Please," I whispered, my eyes fluttering closed as I tried to soak up every hint of sensation.

"Please, what?" he gritted out.

"Colt," I breathed.

"That's my girl." Then his fingers were gone.

I whimpered in protest, but the sound was stolen from my lips as Colt dropped to his knees. He gripped my thighs and tugged me down the table, placing my legs over his shoulders. "Don't come, Ridley. You tell me before you're going to come because the first time I make you shatter, I'm gonna be inside you."

His words vibrated over my core, the combination of sound and breath washing over me, but I didn't have a chance to protest, because his mouth was on me. His tongue circled my clit, teasing the flesh and coaxing it to attention.

His fingers were sliding in again, twisting with each flick of his wrist. The tip of his tongue delved in a precision attack, one that had me nearly breaking apart on the spot.

My breaths came faster, hands curling into fists as I tried to hold back my orgasm. Colt's lips closed around that bundle of nerves, sucking and flicking. My whole body convulsed.

"Colt," I begged. Everything in me cried out for release. Needing to break. Needing Colt to be the one to break me.

"Gonna come, Chaos?" The words whispered across my clit.

"Yes."

He was on his feet in a flash. I couldn't even pull myself together to watch him, to take in all the glory that was Colt. I heard a belt, then a zipper. The sound of a condom packet tearing, and then Colt was hovering over me. His tip bumped my entrance, and he stared down at me with those dark eyes.

Storm eyes.

Ones I could get lost at sea in, never to be found again. But I'd happily go down with that ship.

"Tell me I can have you."

There was only one answer, and it came out on an exhale. "Yes."

It was all Colt needed. He slid inside me on one long thrust.

It wasn't violent, but it wasn't gentle either. It was Colt. Powerful and just a little rough around the edges.

And it was everything I needed.

My back arched as he slammed into me again. My legs hooked around his waist as he took me, just trying to hold on. My walls fluttered.

"Not yet," Colt gritted out. "Need more of this heat."

That nearly did me in. I gripped the edge of the table above my head. Trying to hold on longer. To give Colt what he needed.

He let out a growl as his gaze swept over me, the way the move had exposed the swells of my breasts even more. All of me on display. For him.

The last strand of control snapped. Colt powered into me over and over. The arc of his hips striking that spot inside that had the world going fuzzy around me. My hands tightened on the edge of the table, the bite of pain helping keep that one thread of control.

"Ridley," Colt rasped.

And I knew.

I let go. I let everything I'd been holding back for weeks free. It wasn't a spiral or even a shattering. It was so much more.

It was chaos.

My whole body convulsed, curling around Colt in every way it could. Taking him deeper and planting him there. Demanding more.

And he gave it to me.

Colt's palm hit the table next to my head as he arched into me again and again. He came on a shout, and I took it all and more. Everything.

His chest heaved as I slowly released my grip on the table. My fingers had gone numb, and as blood returned to them, they began to tingle. A sensation that matched the rest of me.

Colt stared down at me for a long time, and the mask slowly slid back into place.

"Don't," I warned.

His face hardened. "Don't what?"

"Put that wall back up."

Colt slid out of me, and I couldn't help the small wince. His hands were gentle as they slid along my thighs. "Did I hurt you?"

I sat up, not giving a damn that I was completely naked, and Colt stood there in his tee and nothing else. "No. I feel fucking fantastic, but if you get all weird on me, it's really going to harsh my buzz."

His lips twitched. "*Harsh your buzz*?"

"You know what I mean. We are both grown adults who were having a little fun. Don't ruin that."

Colt stared at me for a long moment. "It's dangerous. We're working together. A lot of serious shit is going down, and—"

"And we need an outlet," I argued. Because damn it all to hell, I wanted more of Colt. Whatever he could give. "Friends with benefits."

Colt moved closer, his thumb tracing over my collarbone. "That what we are, Chaos? Friends?"

I bit my bottom lip. "Enemies with benefits?"

He chuckled but his fingers lifted, gently removing my lip from between my teeth. "Won't lie. I want more of you. All oranges set aflame."

My nipples pebbled again, and my breaths came quicker. "Then we set ground rules to keep it safe. I'm on the pill, and I've had a checkup."

Colt's eyes flashed as his thumb stroked my collarbone. "Been checked too."

"Good. That's the physical safety. No sleeping in the same bed."

Colt's expression went guarded. "No catching feelings that way."

"No starting to think this is something it's not."

He nodded in agreement.

"No hooking up with anyone else while this is going on," I said, trying to keep my voice even despite the fact that the idea of Colt with another woman made me nauseous. "Either of us have interest in someone else, we end this."

Those deep-brown eyes darkened to black. "That enough rules?"

I swallowed hard. "I think so."

"Good." Then he lunged, hauling me over his shoulder and striding down the hall.

"Colt," I squealed.

He slapped my ass, the sound reverberating against the walls. "I'm just damn glad you didn't make any rules about the shower."

Chapter Thirty-Five
Colt

I COULDN'T STOP STARING AT HER. OR TOUCHING HER. Or just breathing her in. That burnt-orange scent was everywhere now. The air in the dining-room-turned-office. The sheets as I went to sleep every night—alone. Singed into my goddamned skin.

"What are you scowling at?" Ridley asked, cutting into my spiraling thoughts.

I leaned back in my chair, trying to force nonchalance. "Nothing. We've just been over these case files a dozen times. I don't think it's going to bring anything new."

Ridley unwound her legs from a pretzel-like position. Today she wore jean shorts and a flowy sleeveless blouse with tiny flowers all over it. Her hair hung in loose waves around her, the color a little blonder than normal. Maybe because she'd worked most of the day outside yesterday. Torturing me in another of those damned tank tops as she lay on a towel reading the latest police report I'd gotten.

Her gaze roamed over me, a silent check-in. "You need to take a run?"

My scowl only deepened.

Ridley held up both hands in surrender. "Sorry. Geez."

I was the one who should've been sorry. But it annoyed me that she knew me so well. Knew that after hours at this table, I needed to move, to get the pain and death out of my system.

I twisted my head, making my neck crack. "It's not you." Only it was—it was everything about her.

"Will you come look at this tape for me?" Ridley asked.

Hell.

I didn't need to be closer. Didn't need to smell that tempting scent. Feel the heat that always came off her in waves. Be close enough to touch that skin.

But I went. Because not going would be admitting just how weak I was when it came to Ridley Sawyer Bennett.

I stood and moved behind her chair, locking my fingers around the back of it so I wouldn't be tempted to tangle them in those blond strands; then I turned my eyes to the laptop screen. A brand-new one, since I hadn't been able to recover her old one, hadn't been able to find the asshole who had hurt her.

That fact only stirred my annoyance further. It felt like everything surrounding me was a series of failures these days. I focused on the screen, the image there, trying to shove out every other thought. It was a video I'd seen before. Coach Kerr standing at a gas pump, filling up his SUV.

The footage was a little grainy, but you could see him clear as day. Those polo shirts he always wore. The ball cap pulled down low with *Wimbledon* stitched across the back. His license plate on display, confirming the vehicle's identity. The time stamp read 8:13. It was about as good as you could get in terms of an alibi.

Because during that time, Emerson was unconscious in the back of a truck. On her way to be hurt in some of the worst ways imaginable. My fingers tightened on the chair, and I closed my eyes for a moment.

Emerson was safe. She hadn't been hurt, not physically. But it didn't change the fact that her life had been forever altered.

"Something is off with this footage," Ridley said, voice low.

My eyes opened, narrowing on the screen. "What do you mean?"

I watched as Kerr turned, glancing at something over his shoulder. It was him. During the window of the crime. In addition to the tapes, the clerk on duty that night confirmed seeing him. We'd just been lucky they saved the old cassettes for a week before recording over them again.

Ridley didn't look up at me. She just kept her gaze locked on the screen. "Emerson was abducted May twenty-third, right?"

I nodded but then realized she couldn't see me. "Yeah. Right before Memorial Day weekend and school getting out for the summer."

"I've looked at everything about that day. Was it a full moon? What was the temperature like? The weather? What time did the sun set?"

"It was cold," I said automatically. "I remember I had a jacket on when I went to pick up Em."

Ridley nodded, turning to me. "There was a cold snap that lasted for three days. Looks like that's normal in the mountains. The wild swing of temperatures."

I frowned. "Sure. We can be in the eighties one day and the forties the next."

"It wasn't quite that drastic. But on the twenty-second, the high was seventy-two. On the twenty-third, the high was forty-eight, and that was in the height of sunshine. So why"—she turned to tap on the screen—"is Coach Kerr in shorts and a polo?"

My gut tightened, that prickle of awareness skating over my skin. "Could be that he was working out with the team. Maybe he forgot a coat."

Ridley tapped on her laptop screen. "There's a fleece right here on the back seat. Or if it was chilly, he could get back in the SUV while his gas tank fills. But he doesn't. He also doesn't shiver at all. Doesn't look the slightest bit cold. I looked up the temperature at eight o'clock on the night of the twenty-third. It was thirty-six degrees." She looked up at me. "Even if I'd just run a mile, I'd still want at least a sweatshirt if it was that cold."

Fucking hell.

I stared at the screen for a long moment. "That's video footage."

"With a timestamp only," Ridley argued.

I shook my head. "We have the original cassettes in evidence. They have the dates written on them. They were labeled each week when the gas station started over."

Ridley met my gaze dead-on. "And how difficult would it be to just write a new label with a different date?"

Everything in me tightened. I hadn't been a deputy at the time, but I'd talked to every officer who worked my sister's case. I'd talked to them multiple times. Lucian, the gas station clerk, in his early twenties, had been working nights that week. He told officers he'd seen Kerr at the pumps that night. And the owner of the gas station, Bill, had been the one to hand over the tapes. I couldn't see all of them being in on some sort of conspiracy. But still…

I released my hold on Ridley's chair. "I need to bring Kerr in for questioning."

She was on her feet in a flash. "I'm coming with you."

"The hell you are."

Ridley's expression went thunderous. "I thought we were past this. That we were teammates."

"This is an active investigation. You can't just come on a ride-along."

"I gave you the information that led to this."

"Yes, but—"

"Don't cut me out." Ridley's voice dropped low. It wasn't pleading exactly but something worse. The undercurrent said she believed I'd do the right thing.

I cursed. "Go to the station and meet me there. I'll tell Ryan to let you watch from observation."

Ridley's entire face lit up, like sunshine was pouring out of her goddamned skin. It nearly knocked me over, it was so bright. She stretched up onto her tiptoes, pressing her lips to my cheek before whispering in my ear, "Thanks, Law Man."

Chapter Thirty-Six
Ridley

I felt the undersheriff's gaze sweep over me as we stood in observation. It wasn't judgmental exactly; it was more curious, assessing. Sophie Ryan had met me in reception with a blank mask I knew she had to have learned from Colt.

When he had told me *Ryan* would meet me, I hadn't expected a woman. And certainly not one only a year or two older than me. She wore no makeup, and her hair was pulled back in a bun at the base of her neck. I understood the play. She was trying to be one of the guys as much as possible, so nothing that would accentuate her femaleness.

But there wasn't a damn thing she could do about those gorgeous green eyes. Or her beauty in general. But I also knew that if she was Colt's second-in-command, she had to be a damned good officer too.

That was why I let her look now. Didn't try to hide my fixation on the one-way mirror in front of me as I waited for Colt to bring Kerr in. There were a few officers behind us, their voices melding together in a low din. But I didn't join in.

I wasn't new to law enforcement stations. I knew the deal. The more silent I was, the more I'd learn. So I stayed still and listened.

Two of the guys were arguing about the coach. One saying he always knew the dude was a creep. The other eyeing me and saying it was ridiculous that they were bringing a guy in just because he wasn't wearing a coat.

"This goes much further, and Colt is going to have to step down."

The words were low, but the fact that they'd been said at all had me turning to the woman next to me.

Ryan met my gaze with more of that assessing stare, and I knew she'd gotten what she'd wanted: a true reaction out of me. "You care about him," she surmised.

It wasn't a question, but I still shifted under the weight of it. "He deserves to help find who's responsible. It'll help him finally heal."

Ryan was quiet for a long moment, mulling that over. "Is that why you do what you do? To help yourself heal?"

Annoyance flickered through me before I could fight it back. I wasn't thrilled that Colt had been spreading my business around, but I understood the need for it at the same time.

Ryan shook her head, reading that annoyance. "Colt didn't say a word. I looked into you on my own. And Trey might've pointed me in the right direction, didn't want me getting the wrong idea about you."

My jaw went the slightest bit slack.

She chuckled. "Come on. You've got my sheriff jumping through hoops, my town in a tizzy, and then you up and almost get yourself killed. I was curious."

I hated the way *my sheriff* ground at me. The way it had me wondering if there'd ever been anything more than professionalism between her and Colt. *Jealousy*, I realized. It wasn't an emotion I was all that familiar with.

I'd felt it occasionally growing up. How could I not when my sister was the star of everything she took on while I flitted from one thing to the next, never landing long enough to take hold? But never in a relationship. Not that I'd had any since Jared and I ended things that fiery night.

He'd tried to be there for me afterward. To mend the fissure between us. But I was too numb to even realize he was there.

After that there'd only been the occasional partner. A friend who'd become more for a time. A couple one-nighters. But mostly I was on my own. No chance for jealousy to rear its ugly head like it was doing now.

"So," Ryan prodded. "Is that why?"

I turned back to the woman next to me and decided to let her see. To give her the truth. "I won't know peace until my sister does, but at least I can help others find it in the meantime."

"Should've been a cop," Ryan muttered.

That had my interest piquing—Ryan had a story. I just wondered what it was.

Before I could ask a single question, the door to interrogation opened, and two men stepped inside. Colt's back was to the mirror, but I could see the lines of strain along his shoulders and up his neck. The way the muscles had so tightly corded, it looked like they could snap and fray with just a tap of a finger.

"Are we rolling?" Ryan snapped.

"Yeah, boss," one of the guys behind me said quickly.

"Good. Then shut the hell up."

Another of them snickered, but it quickly cut off with the sound of an elbow to the gut.

I ignored it all, my gaze locked on the image in front of me, trying to see Coach Kerr through fresh eyes—the gray in his dark hair and deeper lines around his eyes and mouth. I'd pinned them as smile lines, evidence of someone who made the action frequently. But just because someone smiled, that didn't mean they couldn't also be a monster.

His hazel gaze jumped around the room before landing on the mirror. He looked somewhere between Ryan and me. It was unsettling, having him stare at nothing but still so close to me. But I tried to look into those hazel eyes, tried to see if they were capable of ending so many lives, of causing untold pain.

Colt gestured to the chair on the opposite side of the table. "Have a seat. I need to ask you a few questions. Could always have a lawyer here with you. Do you *need* a lawyer, Bryan?"

The use of the coach's first name was a conscious choice. A way to make things seem normal, an everyday encounter, not an interrogation.

Kerr swallowed hard. "No…I don't need a lawyer. You know that, Colt."

Colt leaned back in his chair, letting silence sweep through the room. That quiet was like a boa constrictor, gliding along the floor, curling around Kerr, and then strangling him.

He swallowed again; this time the action was more pronounced. "What's this about?"

Colt was quiet for a moment longer before speaking. "Walk me through May twenty-third ten years ago."

Kerr's eyes shifted to the side and then back to Colt. "I've done it a million times. You have my interviews on video. All of them."

"Walk me through it *again*."

"All right. All right. I, um, we had practice like normal. Emerson stayed after like she always did. She had a spare set of keys to the equipment room, so I left her with the ball machine. She was practicing when I left."

Colt didn't move, and I knew he had to be pinning the coach to the spot with those storm eyes. "Was anyone else still there when you left?" Colt asked.

Kerr wiped his palms on his khakis. "No. No one else was there. I had to clean up the rest of the equipment before I left."

"But there's not all that much equipment, is there? Not when everyone has their own rackets and Emerson was still using the ball machine."

The coach shifted in his seat. "I watched her practice for a little while, gave her some pointers, and then left."

"Interesting. I don't remember you sharing that when you were questioned before."

"I—I probably forgot. It was a high-stress time."

"Yeah," Colt spat. "It must've been real high stress for you. Nothing like what it was for my sister who'd been fucking kidnapped, hit over the head, and thrown in the back of a truck."

"I didn't mean—"

"Of course you didn't. Now where did you go when you left the park?"

Kerr's breaths came faster now. "I drove around for a little bit. I was trying to brainstorm some new drills and training tactics. I always drive around to think."

Colt made a soft scoffing noise. It wasn't even a word, but it was like a physical blow to Kerr.

"God, he's good," Ryan muttered softly.

It was true. Colt was slowly but surely backing the coach into a corner.

"Then I went to the gas station because I was running low."

And now he had Kerr right where he wanted him. Like a spider weaving the perfect web.

Colt leaned back in his chair. I couldn't see his face, but I knew he was taking the coach in, using silence as a weapon. Kerr twisted in his seat, the metal squeaking with the action.

"You know, Bryan, it's interesting. Sometimes you look at something so many times that you stop truly seeing it. Has that ever happened to you?"

Kerr opened his mouth, then closed it, then opened it again. "I don't know. Maybe?"

Colt made a low humming noise. "Take the video of you at the gas station. I always fixated on the time. On seeing your face. Checking and rechecking that it was really you."

The coach began to tremble, his hands shaking so strongly he tucked them beneath the table.

Colt kept right on spinning his web, the strands weaving tighter, building the perfect trap. "I was so fixated on those tiny details that I missed the big picture. It took someone else looking at it all for me to truly see."

Kerr's throat worked as he struggled to swallow.

"Bryan, do you know what the temperature was on May twenty-third, ten years ago?" Colt asked. His tone sounded like he was truly curious.

Kerr's brow furrowed. His nerves didn't lessen any, but there was genuine confusion in the mix now too. Careless little fly, not seeing where he was headed. "No…I—"

"It was thirty-six degrees," Colt said, cutting him off.

"Okay…"

Colt's head turned slightly, just enough so that I could see the tiny slip of a smile that broke through. "I've lived in Shady Cove my whole life. Gotten pretty used to those cold snaps." Any hint of a grin vanished in a flash. "But I still don't stand around outside waiting for my tank to fill when it's thirty-six degrees out. Especially when I'm wearing a fucking polo shirt and shorts. And I sure as hell would at least get the fleece out of my back seat."

Kerr froze. No part of him moved other than the tiny flutter in his chest. The beat of those trapped wings against his ribs.

Colt leaned forward, forearms resting on the aged metal table with peeling corners. "So it would make a hell of a lot more sense if that video was actually from the night before. An evening when the temperature was sixty-two degrees at eight o'clock. That's practically balmy, don't you think, Bry?"

It was the *Bry* that did it to me. I couldn't help the grin that spread across my face. God, Colt *was* good. I'd trapped an interviewee in a lie or two before. I'd even broken someone on record. But watching Colt work was a thing of beauty.

His voice dropped to what was almost a stage whisper. "So tell me. If I show that picture to everyone on the tennis team, what will they say? Was that the outfit you wore the night Emerson was abducted? Or were you wearing something else altogether?"

There were a few whispered *damns* behind me, but to my left, Ryan didn't make a sound. She was too riveted by the scene in front of us.

Sweat broke out across Kerr's brow as his trembling intensified. For a moment I thought he might fall right out of the chair. And then he broke.

Big racking sobs. The kind that looked like waves overtaking the body. So brutal it almost seemed like they could break the man's bones.

"I-I—I didn't—it wasn't me. I swear!" Kerr cried.

"You weren't at the gas station the night Emerson was taken, were you?" Colt pressed.

The coach shook his head. "N-no. I wasn't. I-I paid Lucian to lie. To switch the date on the tapes. Because he knew I didn't do it. That I would never—couldn't hurt Em—"

"Don't say her name," Colt growled.

Kerr's mouth snapped closed.

"Where were you that night?"

The sheer demand in Colt's voice had me wrapping my arms around myself, squeezing hard as I waited. I stared at the man as a million questions flew through my head, but there was only one that stayed.

Was this the man who killed my sister?

As I stared at him, all I saw was weakness. The fear quaking through him. I couldn't imagine someone like this doing the terrible things I'd linked together. But wasn't that monster weak too? It was the ultimate weakness to dominate those less powerful than you. To sneak and drug and wound, to do so much worse. So maybe this was the exact face of the monster who'd been masked for so long.

"I was having an affair." The words tumbled out of Kerr's mouth so quickly it took a second for me to understand them.

Colt straightened, head turning just enough so that I could see the flutter of muscle along his jaw. "Bullshit. You would've said. No one would take a murder charge over their wife finding out they were fucking around."

Kerr's hands tightened in his lap, knuckles bleaching white as the blood drained from his face. "It was with a student."

The room around me went deathly silent. No one even breathed. One beat. Then two. Three.

"Who?" Colt growled low.

"Tara Gibson," Kerr whispered. "She was seventeen. It was legal in most states, but—"

"Not in California, you sack of shit," Colt snarled. "You knew your ass would be fired, and you'd be blacklisted from any future teaching or coaching jobs. Not to mention your ass would've ended up in jail, and they don't take too kindly to men like you there."

The coach's head lifted. "You won't tell, right? Promise me you won't tell. My wife—"

Colt scoffed. "You're disgusting. She was your student, your athlete. Not only were you twenty-five years her senior, but you were in a position of power over her. Your wife is the least of your worries."

"Colt—"

He shoved back his chair and stood. "Stay there."

"Where are you going?" Kerr's eyes were wild now as his gaze jumped around the room.

"To verify your fucked-up story," Colt snapped, stalking out of the room.

I was already moving for the door, Ryan on my heels. I felt Colt before I saw him, the furious energy charging through the hallway.

The moment our eyes locked, I felt his pain. Those dark orbs were now swirling pools of black, nothing but agony in their depths.

I could feel Ryan at my back, the other officers spilling into the hall behind us. But all I could see was Colt. His pain and fury. Emotions I knew all too well.

I was moving before I could think, getting right up into his space before I could stop myself. I wanted to throw my arms around him and tell him it would be okay. But I wasn't sure if that was true.

Colt's head dipped, those pools of shadow searching, desperate for something to hold on to.

So I gave it to him.

Being a rule breaker wasn't anything new for me. So I ignored that we were in Colt's place of work. That his subordinates were behind me.

I slid my fingers through his, linking us together. I squeezed with everything I had. Because I wanted to tell him one thing. The only thing I'd never truly had but wanted so damn badly.

That he wasn't alone.

Chapter Thirty-Seven
Colt

FIRE BLAZED THROUGH ME, AN INFERNO OF PAIN, FURY, and failure. So much of it I could barely draw a full breath. My vision blurred, the hallway going in and out of focus.

But there she was.

Storming toward me like true chaos in human form. And the moment her hand slid into mine, I could breathe again. It shouldn't have been possible for chaos to be so calming, but it was. She was.

Ridley.

The last woman in the world that should've been my comfort in all this. The one who was ripping all the wounds open again. But I was starting to see it was so she could heal the infection that had taken root there—one that had spread. One it felt like she'd gotten to just in time.

A throat cleared behind Ridley, and I forced my gaze away from her face, from her comfort. But she didn't let go of my hand.

Ryan stood there; the mask she had become so good at wearing had cracks in places, and anger seeped through. If there was one thing she hated, it was men abusing their power. "Let me talk to Tara. I think that's a conversation that might be easier with me."

Ryan rarely made a case for using her status as a woman. It wasn't something she liked to point out, probably because being a woman in law enforcement came with its own sets of challenges. But she was right to use it here.

I nodded quickly. "Okay. You call me the minute you're done. And I want this prick held until then."

"On it, Sheriff," Marshall called, moving to interrogation.

He'd sit with the asshole, give Kerr a call to his lawyer if he asked for it. And he should've asked. My stomach roiled as a fresh wave of fury pulsed through me.

Ridley's grip on my hand tightened as she pitched her voice low. "Let's go outside and get some air."

She knew I was a second away from losing it. From tearing every photo and award off the walls and smashing them to pieces. From going into that room and pummeling Kerr because he *was* a monster. Just not the one I was looking for.

Ridley tugged me toward reception before I could say a word, but I didn't miss the way Ryan's gaze dropped to our joined hands, the other officers' too. I'd have the gossip mill working overtime. Not what I needed, but I didn't give a damn.

Part of me was aware of the people we passed, the sounds of the station. But it wasn't until we were outside, the sun streaming down, the fresh scent of the redwoods wrapping around us, that my vision cleared.

Ridley dropped my hand, but it was only so she could press her palms to my cheeks. "Look at me."

My back teeth gnashed together, but I forced my gaze to hers, to those beautiful, hypnotic blues.

"We're going to get him," she vowed.

"I know." Because I knew both of us were too damned determined for it to be any other way. "But what else are we going to find along the way? How many monsters? I'm not sure I can handle knowing the reality behind the people I've been living alongside my entire life."

Empathy washed across Ridley's expression. "It's like rebreaking a bone. Hurts more than the first time, but it's necessary to get it to heal right. We're digging them all out. Bringing the monsters out so they can't hide anymore, can't *hurt* anyone anymore."

And, God, I did want that. Didn't want there to be a soul in Shady Cove that was trying to do others harm. But I knew that was an impossible task. We'd just have to take what we could and keep doing the work.

My phone let out a series of dings in my back pocket, and Ridley's hands dropped from my face. I missed their heat, their demanding strength when it felt like my own was faltering. But I wasn't ready to ask for them back either.

Instead, I pulled out my phone.

Shortcake: Is my brother open to bribery?

An ache took root in my chest. Emerson had no idea what had happened today. How close I'd thought I was. My fingers flew over the screen.

Me: I'm an officer of the law.

Shortcake: I'm taking that as a yes then.

Me: I'm not above arresting you.

Shortcake: Arrest me after you come over here and eat fried chicken, coleslaw, and biscuits. Bring Ridley. Trey's coming too.

I stared at my phone for a long moment, trying to figure out how the hell I felt about this. And what it meant.

"What is it?" Ridley asked, but she was already tipping my phone down so she could read the screen upside down.

I jerked it out of her grasp, a grin tugging at my mouth. "Nosy much?"

She smiled up at me, and it hit me somewhere in the solar plexus. The kind of pain you got from holding your breath for too long. Her blue eyes twinkled. "I get the best info from being nosy."

I rubbed at that spot on my chest, trying to clear the sensation. "Em wants us to come over for lunch."

Ridley's brows flew up, but the reaction was quickly followed by a wariness that settled over her features. "And you don't want me to go."

"No," I said quickly. "I'm not sure," I finally admitted.

I didn't miss the flicker of hurt in Ridley's expression. It ground the guilt in deeper.

"I'd like to get to know her. Not because of who she is to this case but because of who she is to you," Ridley said softly.

Fuck. I was the world's biggest asshole.

I cleared my throat as I shoved my phone into my pocket. "All right."

"Easy as that?" Ridley challenged.

Nothing about this was easy. But it was the least I could do to try to make things right when I kept fucking up. "Let's go."

I inclined my head toward my SUV. I shouldn't be leaving the station. Not with everything going on. But it wasn't like there was something I could do other than wait—for Ryan to take Tara's statement, for Kerr to slip and tell us more messed-up shit he'd done.

All of that would be here in another couple of hours. And seeing Em would help. Would remind me that she was safe, as okay as she could be.

"I've got my van here," Ridley reminded me.

One corner of my mouth kicked up the barest amount. "Hope you parked in an oversized spot so you don't get a ticket."

She glared at me. "I will sic Tater on you in the middle of the night."

I held up both hands in mock surrender. "I solemnly swear not to write you a ticket."

"Glad to see Tater and I are intimidating enough to keep you in line."

My lips twitched. "It's not you. It's the damn cat. I see murder in her eyes."

"You love Tater. Don't deny it."

I climbed behind the wheel, waiting for Ridley. "Look what she did to me when I tried to give her a treat yesterday." I held up my finger with a series of puncture wounds for Ridley to examine.

"It's barely a scratch," she argued as I pulled out of the station's parking lot.

"I probably have some disease," I shot back.

"We could make a pit stop at the doctor," Ridley offered. "Get you some rabies shots."

I instantly fisted my hand, hiding the injuries. "Keep your needles away from me."

She laughed, the sound lightening a little more of the weight that was bearing down on me. Scattering some of the shadows that had made their home in my chest. There was something about Ridley that always did that. Sometimes it was something ridiculous or understanding or fierce. The methods were as all over the place as she was, but they always reached me.

Ridley chattered on about the risks of rabies, telling a story about a friend who had to get the shots after trying to feed a squirrel a peanut on their campus quad. And I let her wash away the worst of the day with her presence alone.

It didn't take long for us to get to Emerson's house. Trey's truck was already parked outside, and I pulled in next to it but didn't shut off the engine right away. Instead I stared at the yellow house. Em had painted it with my and Trey's help.

"She doesn't usually let people inside," I finally said. "Just Trey and me."

Ridley didn't say anything at first, just took in my statement. "I'm good with moving at Emerson's pace. If it's too much, I'll take that cute dog of hers outside to play fetch and admire her incredible flowers."

I turned to Ridley, feeling things I sure as hell shouldn't have been, given our agreement. "Thanks, Chaos."

"Come on," she urged. "I'm hungry."

Ridley was out of my SUV before I could say another word. She'd let the events of the day slide off her somehow. Maybe she'd learned that skill by covering so many cases. Living in the pain of the victims and their loved ones, but somehow figuring out how to let it go when she needed to and focus on the good.

I climbed out of my vehicle and met Ridley at the bottom of the steps. But before I could say anything, the door opened, and Emerson was there. I knew her well enough to see the nerves. The way her fingers twisted in a kitchen towel as Bear leaned into her.

Something told me that Ridley saw it too because her smile widened. "Please tell me that massive floof of a dog likes to be cuddled."

Em chuckled, her grip on the towel loosening a fraction. "He thinks he's a lapdog."

Ridley clapped, then hurried up the steps and crouched. "What's his name?"

"Bear," Emerson said, giving the dog a pat to tell him he could go to the newcomer.

"Bear," Ridley said wistfully. "The most perfect name for the bestest boy."

Bear charged over to her, knocking Ridley to her butt. But she just laughed as she threw her arms around the beast and pressed her face into his neck. "He really does go right for the lap," Ridley said, her voice muffled by all the fur. She scratched and rubbed, making Bear's day. "Now don't think I'm going to sneak you table scraps just because you're giving me cuddles."

Emerson grinned. "He's not going to leave your side now. You've got a friend for life."

Ridley looked up at my sister from her spot, still covered with over one hundred pounds of Bernese mountain dog. "My evil plan works."

And it had. But none of it was evil. I saw it now, her approach. Making it about Bear so Emerson wouldn't be overwhelmed by a new person's focus on her.

"You might not be saying that when he launches into your lap at lunch," Emerson warned. "I hope you guys are hungry because I made enough to feed an army. Trey's just setting it all on the back deck. Come on through."

More of the nerves had slid out of Emerson. Her muscles were looser, her grip on the towel light.

I reached down and pulled Ridley to her feet. It took some doing, since Bear didn't want to let her go. And I didn't blame the dog. When Ridley finally stood, she knocked into my chest with an *oomph*. Her eyes shot to mine, and I couldn't move, I was frozen to the spot by that hypnotic stare.

Hell, yes, I was feeling things I shouldn't be. Feeling more. Feeling everything. For a woman who was only temporary, passing through on a mission that could bring my family and me healing. Or leave us in wreckage in her wake.

Chapter Thirty-Eight
Ridley

I WATCHED AS A MILLION UNNAMED EMOTIONS SWEPT through Colt's stormy gaze, each one flickering to life and then disappearing so fast that I couldn't grab hold of a single one. But it didn't stop me from trying. Because I wanted every piece of him.

And that knowledge was dangerous. He was dangerous.

Bear barked and I jumped, forcing a laugh. "No need to be jealous, buddy. I've got all the pets for you."

I followed the dog and Emerson into the house, trying to shake off the lingering feelings clinging to me. As I walked down the long hallway toward the kitchen, I couldn't help but slow my steps. There was art everywhere. Lots of different media but all of it amazing.

As I reached the kitchen, I found Emerson grabbing a pitcher of what looked like iced tea. "You've got great taste in art," I told her.

Emerson's cheeks tinged pink. "Thank you."

The screen door slapped shut as Trey strode inside from the back porch. "What she's not telling you is that she did them all."

I turned back to Emerson, gaping. "*All* of them?"

She shrugged, heading for the back door. "It's a nice outlet, and it gets my creative juices going for work projects."

I took the basket of rolls Trey handed me and followed Emerson outside, Bear on my heels. "Work projects?"

She nodded, setting the pitcher down. "I'm a graphic designer. Mostly web design but a few general branding clients as well."

The perfect job to do from the safety of your home.

Trey crossed behind Emerson, giving her shoulder a squeeze before setting a bowl of coleslaw on the table. "I keep telling her she should set up a site to sell her art."

"You really should," I agreed. "If I had walls, I'd buy some." I frowned as I tried to picture my interior space despite its recent destruction. "I might be able to fit one of the smaller ones. One of those wildflower watercolors by the bathroom?"

"Make her a strong offer," Trey chided.

I grinned. "I'd never lowball her. They're too good. Seven fifty?"

Emerson's eyes went wide. "Dollars?" she squeaked.

"Definitely not cents," I said with a laugh.

Trey smacked a hand on the table. "Sold!" He glanced at Emerson. "Right?"

She shook her head. "That's too much."

"I've traveled all over and always poke my head in galleries along the way. It's not," I told her. "You could be making bank if you sold them online."

Colt moved into our huddle, a frown on his face. "I don't know if that's a good idea."

"Why the hell not?" Trey challenged.

"It puts Em out there. Public. If her history got out there along with it, it could make her a target."

I watched as Emerson's shoulders slumped, a little of that shocked-but-happy surprise bleeding out of her.

I shifted closer to Colt and slowly stepped down on his foot, *hard*. His gaze flew to me, confusion there. "What?"

I glared back, trying to make a silent point.

"What your houseguest is trying to say more delicately than I will is that you're being a dick," Trey said.

A muscle ticked along Colt's jaw. "I'm being cautious."

I kept right on glaring at him but spoke to Trey. "I have no problem telling Law Man that he's being a giant dick. He likes to do that often. Sometimes in good ways, other times not so much."

Emerson choked on a laugh. "I have been wondering what this roommate situation entailed."

"Friends with benefits. My kinda houseguest," Trey said with a grin.

"Jesus," Colt muttered. "Is nothing private anymore?"

I turned to Trey with a smirk. "*Enemies with benefits* would be more accurate."

He barked out a laugh. "I knew I liked you."

"Would you three quit it?" Colt gritted out.

Emerson's hazel eyes danced. "Come on, don't pout. We're just having a little fun."

"I don't pout," he shot back.

I reached up and grabbed his bottom lip. "I don't know, this was sticking out pretty far."

Colt grabbed my wrist, tugging me to him fast and hard. "Chaos," he growled, but there was an amber heat in his eyes. "Careful. You're playing with fire."

My breath hitched. "You should know by now, Law Man, I'm not afraid of getting burned."

I glanced over at Colt as he drove. The sun hung lower in the sky now, its heat having baked the earth all afternoon. We'd spent hours at Emerson's. Hours I'd loved because I adored Colt's sister. More than that, I admired the hell out of her. She had an incredible strength and, more than that, an intelligence that she'd used to make herself feel safe despite what she'd been through.

Colt had gone quieter after getting a call from Ryan. He'd stepped inside, away from prying ears, to take it. And he'd done his best to hide the anger when he'd come back out. But I knew the change had put Trey and Emerson on edge, wondering what was going on.

"What did she say?" I finally asked, breaking into Colt's spiraling thoughts.

His fingers tightened on the wheel. "Who?"

"Let's not play that game. We're both smarter than that."

Colt sighed, making the turn up the mountain road that led to his house. "Tara confirmed their relationship. Broke down while talking to Ryan. All sorts of guilt and confusion. It's been haunting her for years, getting mixed up with Kerr."

"Bastard," I muttered.

"He made her feel like the whole thing was her fault. That she tempted him into cheating on his wife, into starting a relationship that could've gotten him fired."

I stared out at the forest around us as we drove, trying to take on its calm. "Now she can let it out, finally process what she needs to."

Colt's gaze flicked my way. "Excising the wound."

I shifted in my seat so I could really take him in. "What do you mean?"

"Took me a while, but I realized that's what you do. You find where the hurt and sick is and cut it out. It means reopening the wound, but it also means healing."

I stared at him for a long moment. "That's incredibly morbid and kind of gross but also…beautiful."

Colt chuckled as he made the final turn toward his cabin. "It's also accurate."

That thing inside me shifted. The one that cared a little too much that Colt saw what I was doing as *good.* That he got me. I forced my gaze away, toward the cabin. "Did she corroborate his alibi?"

"Unfortunately, yes," Colt said, pulling to a stop in front of his house.

We both sat in silence for a long time, letting the weight of the day settle in. "I wanted it to be him," I finally admitted. What a horrible thing to wish on a person, even someone like Bryan Kerr.

Colt stared straight ahead. "Me too."

I could feel his pain calling out to me for comfort. I wanted to take his hand, to weave my fingers through his. But there'd been too much of that today already. Physical acts but emotionally intimate. Not the sort of thing enemies with benefits did.

"Come on," I ordered, shoving my door open. I hopped out of the SUV but didn't head for the front door. Instead, I took the path around the side of the house, hoping Colt would follow.

A door slammed behind me. "Where are you going?"

I turned, walking backward, and grabbed the hem of my flowy tank top. It was almost four, but the sun had been warming everything for hours. I tugged the shirt over my head and dropped it on the steps to the back deck.

Those deep-brown eyes heated to warm amber. "What the hell are you doing?"

My lips twitched. "What I'm good at. Creating a little chaos."

Colt barked out a laugh. "You are damn good at that."

I jogged up the steps and my fingers locked in my shorts, my gaze cutting to the man following me. So damn gorgeous with that dark hair and those dark eyes. The angular jaw and scruff my fingers ached to run over. I didn't look away as I stood on the deck and pulled my shorts down. I waited there in nothing but my bralette and thong and watched those eyes turn from amber to gold fire.

"Ridley," Colt growled.

I grinned, climbing up onto the deck's railing. "Come on, Law Man. Live a little."

And then I jumped in.

Chapter Thirty-Nine
Ridley

THE WATER HIT ME WITH A SHOCK OF COLD, THE KIND of freezing that stole all the air from your lungs. I burst to the surface with a stream of curses, only to be greeted by Colt's smirking face.

"That water is pure snowmelt this time of year."

I treaded water, my body getting used to the arctic temperatures. "Just a second of pain for a world of bliss." I flipped to my back, taking in the sky, the way the clouds floated across the blue in cotton puffballs. It was almost hypnotic. "Come on, Law Man. A little cold never hurt anyone."

I twisted my body so I could watch him out of the corner of my eye. That muscle in his jaw began to tick, but then he disappeared. A second later he was back, the gun at his hip gone and his fingers going to that uniform shirt that should've been ugly but somehow managed to be hot as hell on him.

Tugging myself upright, I treaded water again so I could take in the show. I didn't often let myself watch Colt like this. When we came together, it was usually a fever pitch of need. There were no slow stares and lingering touches. But now, I let myself watch.

Colt's shirt slid from his body. Then he grabbed his white tee from behind his head and tugged it up and over. As it fell to the deck, I couldn't have forced my gaze away if I'd tried. That chest and those shoulders could do me in. All warm, tan muscles with a dusting of hair across his pecs. Hair I'd felt as he took me but hadn't let my fingers trail through.

Colt's fingers deftly unbuckled his belt as he kicked off his shoes. The pants dropped, revealing black boxer briefs. Then the pants and socks were gone altogether, and he was climbing the railing. "If I break my neck pulling this ridiculous stunt, I'm going to haunt your ass."

I grinned up at him. "I could be into a little ass play."

Those eyes darkened again to that shadowy brown that was full of promise. Then Colt launched himself from the railing. But he didn't go for an easy jump. He did some sort of flip that landed in a cannonball, sending a fresh wave of water over me.

But Colt didn't surface. I turned in circles trying to see where he might've popped up, but he was nowhere to be found. My heart picked up speed, and just as I was about to dive down, a hand locked around my ankle and tugged.

I shrieked as Colt popped up right in front of me, laughing. I splashed water in his face. "I'm going to kill you for that."

He grinned, and it had a boyish quality to it. The kind that reminded you of innocent mischief and the teasing tug of pigtails. He shook the water out of his hair, and it coursed down his face in rivulets. "You wanted me to live a little."

"Yeah, live. Not scare twenty years off my life."

Colt pulled me to him, then swam us close enough to shore that he could stand, the grin still on his face. "Sorry, Chaos."

My legs wrapped around his waist. "You're not sorry at all."

That grin widened. "Maybe not."

His fingers dug into my ass, massaging there. My body responded instantly, heating at his touch, leaning into him in a quest for more. My fingers threaded through his hair, almost midnight now that it was wet, and tugged on the ends of the strands.

"Need something, Chaos?" That rasp to his voice was back, the one that had skated over my skin in a pleasant shiver since the first time I heard it.

The only problem was that I was becoming addicted to the sensation. It was a dependency I didn't want to study too closely, so I did the only thing I could. I kissed Colt.

He tasted like a mix of iced tea and mint, and his scent of bergamot and cloves swirled around me. Colt met my kiss in that duel for supremacy I could always count on him for. It was as if we were always starving for each other. Maybe because we knew this thing between us had an expiration date. Only, we had no idea what that date was.

Today had been a reminder of that. I could've just as easily been wrapping up the case, mapping out the lineup of final podcast episodes. But instead I was in this lake, with Colt.

And he was making me *feel.*

I was good at doing things that reminded me I was still alive, still breathing. But no one and nothing made me feel more alive than Colt.

Remembering that spurred me on, my legs tightening around his waist. I felt his length press against my core and moaned into his mouth as I rocked against him. I searched for friction, for pressure, but what I really needed was him.

Colt tore his mouth away from mine. "Chaos," he growled, the warning clear in his voice.

I searched those dark eyes. "Remind me I'm alive."

He must've read the desperation in my voice, the need, because something shifted in him. His hands tightened on my ass, pulling me harder against him, showing me how much he needed me too.

"You feel how much I want you? How I'm dying to be inside that tight heat, stretching you, taking you?"

My walls fluttered, crying out for exactly that. "Yes."

One of Colt's hands left my ass, skimming up my waist to cup my breast. "Your gorgeous fuckin' nipples are already hard enough to cut stone. Cheeks flushed, lips parted. Most beautiful sight I've ever seen."

"Colt," I breathed.

"You know what hearing my name on your lips does to me."

I did. But what he didn't know was that it did something to me too. The promise of it.

"Take me," I whispered.

It was all he needed. That hand dropped from my breast, curving around my waist to hold me as he tugged my underwear free with the other. Then he reached for his boxer briefs, pulling them down. His tip bumped against my entrance as my legs encircled him again.

Those dark eyes flashed, all heat and promise. "Tell me again."

"Take me."

He did.

Colt's arm tightened around me, pulling me down onto him as his hips rose up to meet me. My lips parted, my head tipping back as he filled me. The stretch was heaven, taking me right to my limits and reminding me exactly what I needed, that I was here, breathing.

Colt slammed into me again and my legs tightened, spurring him on, desperate for even more. His fingers slid into my hair, tightening on the strands. My head tipped back even farther, taking in that glorious late-afternoon sky.

The beauty of it all was almost more than I could handle. But I focused on every sensation, not wanting to lose a single one. The cold water sliding over my heated skin. Colt's fingers gripping my hair. His cock moving inside me.

Then Colt's head dipped. His lips closed around my nipple through the thin fabric of my bra. That nearly took me over the edge as he hummed around the bud.

His hips angled, hitting that spot where I needed him most. And then his teeth grazed my nipple. That hint of pain, the sensation that made all others sweeter, took me over.

My core clamped down around him as I let out a sound that didn't resemble anything human. But I didn't care. I wasn't hiding from him. I could be who I needed to be.

Wave after wave rolled through me as Colt kept moving, thrusting deeper until his fingers fisted my hair, his lips moving to my throat, and he released inside me. We rode every ounce of pleasure the other gave until there was nothing left but shallow breaths and gentle hands.

Colt pressed a kiss to the column of my throat as he finally pulled out of me. "Thank you. I think I needed that reminder too."

We were both processing the day, in our own ways and together. And there was something about that truth that had an ache taking root in my chest. But I smiled at the man opposite me. "Nothing like a little lake action to remind you you're alive."

Colt chuckled. "Pretty sure your underwear's floating behind you."

I laughed as I twisted in his arms, grabbing for them. "I'm not putting these back on. Nothing sounds worse than cold undies."

He grinned back at me, looking lighter than before. "I'm kind of partial to you underwearless."

"You would be." I brushed the hair back from his face with one hand, my fingers tracking down to his scruff and feeling the prickle of it the way I'd wanted to earlier. "You're something to look at."

Colt quirked a brow. "Am I, now?"

"Quite the specimen."

"Careful, this could go to my head."

My thumb traced below his bottom lip, following the line of scruff. "I like seeing you like this. Relaxed, happy."

That look faltered for a minute, but Colt held it. The quality changed but not the root. "We used to come here all the time. Mom, Em, and me. It was our spot. There was an old run-down cabin where my place sits, but no one lived up here."

I stilled, a mixture of warmth and pain sweeping through me. My family had our own special lake spot and the memories that went along with it. That joy mixed with sorrow came on every time I ventured to a similar spot. But this was more.

Colt looked at me, but I knew it wasn't me he was seeing anymore. "After everything that happened to Em and she didn't want to leave the house much, I would still come out here. Just to think or try to silence the guilt."

That pain beat out the warmth as I looked at the man who carried so much on his shoulders. So I did the only thing I could: I showed him that he wasn't alone. "I made Avery go to the party that night."

Colt blinked a few times, trying to bring me back into focus.

"She hated the parties the frats put on, but I wanted her to get out and experience college before we graduated. If I hadn't..."

Colt's hand slipped beneath my tangle of wet hair, and he squeezed my neck. "If you hadn't, he would've taken her another time."

"I know," I croaked. "And I could say the same to you."

Colt's face softened. "You're a smooth one."

"I try." I stared at him for a long moment, soaking in his heat, in such contrast to the chilly water of the lake. "I've never told anyone that."

His brow creased as his thumb stroked the column of my neck. "What?"

"That I forced Avery to go. Not the cops. Not my parents. No one."

Colt's thumb stilled.

"They still blame me. My parents. Dad never said anything, but one of the times Mom lost it and ended up in the hospital, she screamed at me, *Why didn't you stay with her? You lost my baby!*" I could still hear the words. They were permanently etched into my brain, even if she didn't remember saying them.

Colt's fingers tightened on my neck, not painfully but in a way where I could feel the anger rising in him. "She was hurting," he rasped. "And sometimes when people can't deal with their own pain, they have to spew it onto other people. Doesn't excuse it, but sometimes just understanding that helps."

I searched his dark depths. "Did your mom do that?"

He shook his head. "She went inward. Stopped connecting. Don't get me wrong—she did everything a mom was supposed to do, but it was like she wasn't all there. I think she had to put up a wall, hoping she'd never feel that sort of pain again."

"I think that's how my dad is." I let my arms curl around Colt's shoulders, soaking up their strength. "He'll check in occasionally, but he isn't really *there*."

Colt's thumb picked up its ministrations again, that rough pad sweeping over the delicate skin of my throat. "Things like this, they change you."

"I miss them," I admitted. "It's bad enough how much it hurts missing Avery. But it's somehow worse missing them because they're still here. Right in front of my face. But still...gone."

Colt's arm tightened around my waist. "But you're still here. Still fighting. For them and for Avery."

My eyes burned, but I didn't let any tears come. "I am."

"And you're not alone."

I stiffened. "Colt—"

He squeezed my waist to cut off my words. "You've built a community around you. One you carry with you wherever you go. And then you make more as you go. Dean's half in love with you. My damn dog is all the way there. You've got Sam reaming me out for giving you a hard time, and even his chess buddy Norm has started taking your side. Mira and Celia are not far behind. Hell, even that biker, Ace, asked me what I was doing to find the guy who hurt you. My sister adores you, and my best friend since birth took your side before he even met you."

That had me choking on a laugh. "Sorry about that."

Colt sent me a mock glare. "You should be." His fingers skated along my ribs. "Ridley. You're never alone because you carry your sister with you."

I sucked in a breath so sharp it sliced at my throat and lungs.

"She's always been a piece of you, and she always will be. And you honor her every day of your life."

I struggled to speak, wanting to so badly but also not wanting to lose it. "That's all I want. To do her proud. To live for us both."

"You do." Colt dropped his forehead to mine. "I promise you do."

We stayed there for a long moment, neither of us moving, until finally the cold won out and I shivered.

Colt pulled me tighter against him and started toward shore. "Come on. Let's get you warm." He kept hold of me as he walked out of the water, my legs hooked around his waist. "If there are any hikers out on the lake trail, they're getting a real nice ass shot."

I choked on a laugh. "We all deserve rewards for getting out on the trail."

Colt just shook his head, but I could feel his grin against my cheek. "Making the most of every day, right?" he asked.

"Even if that means showing the world my ass."

He chuckled as he set me down on the deck. "Let me grab us some towels."

I shivered as the mountain air hit me but moved to pick up my discarded clothes as Bowser charged out the back door. I pulled on my shirt and paused to greet him, giving him a good rubdown. "There's my boy. Were you good today? You want to play fetch in a bit?"

Bowser wagged and barked, then ran down the steps to go do his business. I fished my phone out of my pocket, seeing a series of texts. But one name caught my eye.

I hadn't heard from Baker since the scene at the hospital. I'd simply continued recording my episodes and took the chicken's way out by letting Sully deal with him. Thankfully, my editor had been willing to take one for the team these past couple of weeks, but it looked like that reprieve was over.

Baker: What the hell is going on with your Instagram? Is this some sort of stunt?

I frowned, pulling up the social media app. My feed looked normal, but then I clicked on a photo. The comments were flooded with unfamiliar handles that had a sick feeling spreading through me.

AveryAnnihilator123,
SerialSlasher69,
EmersonsEverything88.

The list went on and on, each comment worse than the one before it.

Careful where you put your nose Ridley or it won't be
a w@rning next time.
Go spread your lgs somewhere else podcast slût.
Two Gs to whoever teaches Ridley a lesson.

But my heart stopped when I saw the most recent comment.

I wonder, will Ridley's screams sound the same as her sister's? I can't wait to find out.

Chapter Forty
Colt

Grabbing the towels from the closet, I headed back to the deck, ignoring the fact that I was getting water all over my house. But after an afternoon with Ridley, I shouldn't have been surprised. Chaos reigned in her wake, but it was the beautiful kind, the type of disarray that meant you were truly living.

I stepped outside, letting the screen door snap closed behind me as Bowser nosed at Ridley's leg. But her hand didn't drop to pet him the way it normally did. She didn't move at all, nothing except the small shiver that racked through her as her now-wet shirt clung to her body.

My pace quickened, and I wrapped one of the towels around her. Ridley still didn't move or make a sound. I followed her line of sight to the phone in her hands. She gripped it so tightly her knuckles looked like they'd lost all blood flow.

That's when I saw it. The vile comment at the bottom of the screen.

I wonder, will Ridley's screams sound the same as her sister's? I can't wait to find out.

Bile surged, rage hot on its heels. "What the fuck?" The words were more growl than anything else.

Ridley whirled as if just realizing I was there. She didn't make a move to attack, but her eyes were wide and her typically tan face was a sickly shade of pale. "I—there's—a lot—" She wasn't making sense, but it didn't matter.

"Inside," I ordered. Even Bowser seemed to understand my tone.

I grabbed my discarded clothes and guided Ridley quickly toward the back door. But my head was on a swivel, looking for anything out of the ordinary, anyone who might be watching.

Hell.

Stripping down and jumping off my deck had been the height of recklessness when just a couple of weeks ago, Ridley had been attacked. I knew there was someone out there who wanted to do her harm. I should've been a hell of a lot more cautious than risking the kind of moments we'd just shared in that lake.

Slamming the door, I quickly locked it and set the alarm. I took Ridley's hand and led her down the hallway to my bedroom. She didn't say a word as I headed for my closet. I reemerged with a thick gray bathrobe. Gently, I slid one of her arms into it and then the other.

Ridley shivered, then stared down at the garment. "You have a bathrobe."

"Yes," I said, a hint of defensiveness making its way into my tone.

"It's fluffy," she mumbled, skating her hand over the fabric.

"Comfortable," I amended.

"Cozy."

I grunted and took her face in my hands. "Will you be okay for a minute?"

Ridley nodded. "Not gonna break."

"That's my girl." I released her and slipped back into the closet, quickly changing into jeans and a tee. But I left the door open. I couldn't stand not having eyes on Ridley for even a second. My alarm was set and the doors were locked, but I still wasn't about to risk it.

The second I was changed, I headed back out to my bedroom and took Ridley's hand, leading her back to the living room. The moment we sat on the couch, Bowser dropped his head into Ridley's lap. Her free hand immediately began to scratch and pet, but her other still held the phone in a death grip.

I tried to keep my voice steady, calm, even as anger surged in fiery waves. "Can I have it?"

Ridley didn't make a move to hand the device to me for a moment, just kept petting Bowser. Finally, she flipped the device over and punched in a passcode. She didn't make any attempt to keep the code from me, but whether that was from shock or her simply telling me she had nothing to hide, I wasn't sure.

I gently took the phone from her. The Instagram app was still open. I fought to keep my expression as neutral as possible as I took in the endless stream of comments. There were countless screen names with threats and other disgusting messages.

The use of Emerson's name in more than a handful had me pulling out my own phone and assigning an officer to sit outside her house for the night. But it wasn't long before I saw a pattern. There were only about twelve unique phrases and even fewer names. It looked as if someone had put them all in a jar and kept mixing them up to use over and over again. A computer program of some sort maybe?

Ridley's phone dinged in my hand, and I scowled at the screen.

Baker: For fuck's sake, call me. We need to get a handle on this.

This prick needed to take a flying leap.

"I need to call him," Ridley said. Her voice wasn't quiet. It was robotic. So unlike her.

"The hell you do."

That had her pulling up, a little life flooding back into her cheeks. "He'll never leave me alone otherwise."

"Maybe he's the one who's leaving the comments in the first place."

Ridley's jaw went slack as shock set in, but it quickly fled as she mulled over the idea. "It's possible. He likes any sort of press attention."

"There's a pattern in these. A few root phrases. I'm guessing it was done with a software program. I want to get your phone to our tech team—"

Ridley snatched it out of my hold. "No."

I pinned her with a stare. "This isn't something you can just brush off."

"I know that. And I'll give you my Instagram login and password, but you don't get my actual phone. I need it. It has access to the tip line app, and it's how I'm in contact with sources."

My molars ground together as I struggled not to lash out in search of control. "Maybe you should be taking a break from all that."

Ridley sent me a look that asked if I was a moron.

I should've guessed as much. These past couple of weeks, while we'd put as many pieces together as we could, Ridley was doing the same on her show. She even interviewed a psychologist who specialized in the developing criminal mind. If she didn't pause after an attack and concussion, she wasn't going to pause for anything.

"Fuck," I muttered.

"I have a friend who can help. He's good with computers and all things tech," Ridley assured me.

My eyes narrowed. "What kind of friend?"

She sent me a wincing smile. "One that bends the rules of legalities but gets excellent results. The white hat I told you about before."

"Jesus." I dropped my head to my hand, pinching the bridge of my nose.

"My contact can find out what's going on. Probably even track this creep's IP address."

My spine snapped straight. "None of which I'd be able to use because it was gotten illegally."

Those blue eyes twinkled, and while I was happy as hell to see Ridley find a little more of her fire, I didn't want to even guess what she was about to suggest.

"I happen to know that anonymous tips are made to law enforcement at every level, even the FBI. And those tips are admissible in court as long as law enforcement doesn't know for a fact they were obtained illegally."

I stared at the woman next to me. "I'm a little scared of you. You know that?"

She just grinned wider, as if I'd told her she was the most beautiful woman in the world. "Thank you."

"It wasn't a compliment," I muttered.

"Actually, it was," Ridley shot back, taking the phone back and typing out a text. Moments later she received a *ding* back. She bit her bottom lip as she chatted back and forth with whoever it was. "He's on it."

"And how the hell do you know this *contact*?"

Ridley shrugged. "He came forward with some files that helped me break another case two years ago. He helps how he can now."

"Have you ever met him?"

She shook her head. "I don't even know where he lives."

"Goddamn it. He could be the unsub." I pushed to my feet, wondering how the hell I was going to get the location on a hacker.

"Law Man, breathe." Ridley stood, crossing to me and placing a hand on my chest.

"I don't want to breathe," I gritted out. "You could've been talking with the monster like he's your BFF."

Her lips twitched.

"It's not fucking funny."

"He's a consultant with the FBI."

I stilled. "He what?"

"Consults with the FBI. I verified it with them. But I don't like making that public knowledge. For his protection."

"I'm. Not. The. Public," I growled.

Ridley winced. "Sorry. I know. I'm just used to not telling people, so I didn't think."

I let out a long breath. "Okay. But I'm running him by my own contact who used to be with the Bureau. Anson will know if he's legit."

Ridley's phone rang with the theme song of *Jaws*. She scowled as she hit *accept*. "I'm dealing with it, Baker. Just give me a second."

I could hear him go off on a tear on the other end of the line, but Ridley didn't cower.

"No, I'm not going to LA. And no, I don't need your security detail. I've got my guy on it, and I'm staying somewhere safe."

I couldn't hear the muffled words on the other end of the line, but Ridley's scowl deepened.

"If you say another word about Colt, I will use that emergency clause in my contract and drop your ass midseason; don't think I won't." She paused as Baker kept talking, her shoulders relaxing. Then they stiffened right back up again. "You're still here?"

Another pause. "Fine. I can meet you in an hour. The Whiskey Barrel."

My whole body tensed as Ridley hit *end* on the call. "Tell me you didn't just say you'd meet that asshole."

Ridley lifted her blue gaze to meet mine. "If we want to figure out if he left those comments, I need to ask him to his face. Baker is a lot of things, but a good liar isn't one of them. If he's bullshitting, I'll know."

But doing so would mean leaving Ridley exposed. And we already knew there was at least one person who wasn't afraid to hurt her to get what he wanted. What if there were more?

Chapter Forty-One
Ridley

My gaze kept wandering to the man next to me as if it had a mind of its own. But Colt's never strayed from the pavement ahead of us. His hands held the wheel in a death grip. His jaw wound tight, the muscle along it twitching every so often. And those eyes—they somehow managed to be even darker than before.

I pulled a leg up, my arms curling around it and my chin resting on my knee as my sundress billowed around me. "Stop glaring at the road. It didn't do anything to you."

That twitching was back, quicker than before. "Bad ideas piss me off."

I sighed. "Colt. We're going to a bar. A public place with plenty of people. I get that I need to be careful, but I also need to see this through."

For so many reasons.

His grip on the wheel softened ever so slightly, and he cast a look in my direction. "I don't want anything to happen to you."

I froze. Everything in me tightened, warring between fighting and fleeing, while another part of me wanted to do something else altogether. That part of me wanted to roll around in Colt's words, to read promises in them that weren't even there. We hadn't once discussed the possibility of this being more. And even if we had, I might be too terrified to reach for it because I knew what it meant to lose someone you loved, and I wasn't sure I could survive that again.

I released my hold on my leg, dropping my foot back to the floorboard. "I'll be careful. Promise."

"Good," Colt said, though it was more of a grunt, that gruffness coming right back around.

"You can keep an eye on me from the bar—"

"The hell I am. I'll be right next to you."

"Colt—"

His gaze jerked to me as he stopped at a light. "By your side."

"Baker's never going to trip himself up if you're right there. I need to get a good read on him. And we have some things to settle."

Colt's dark gaze held me for one beat and then another. "You don't go anywhere else with him."

"Not without you, Law Man."

He let out a long breath as he eased off the brake. "This is a horrible idea."

But he was going along with it anyway. Because Colt knew how important it was for me to have control over this area of my life. Not to give it up, no matter how many threats loomed.

As if my thoughts conjured the subject, my phone dinged.

Dex: Did a deep dive on your IG. The accounts are part of a bot software. It's expensive, but anyone can purchase it. It hides the user's IP address and creates a variety of accounts and comments that then spam the victim. There are a few options for the actual software so I'll keep digging, see if I can break in and find out who used it.

Damn. I'd hoped he'd be able to come back with a name. And if I was honest, I didn't think this sounded like Baker. He might like the outcome of more attention on the podcast that threats like these could bring, but tech was not his thing. He had his own Instagram profile, but it was a mixture of mirror selfies and photos with people he thought would improve his clout.

"Who was it?" Colt asked.

"Dex. My contact. He figured out the profiles were created with software that hides the actual user and spams people. Just like you thought."

Colt's jaw simply worked back and forth as I quickly typed out a text to Dex in return.

Me: Thank you. I really appreciate it.

Dex: Be careful until we find out where this asshole is.

My hand moved to the pocket of my dress. God bless pockets in dresses. Mine housed two very important things—Chapstick and my tiny Taser.

Colt pulled into a parking spot next to a row of motorcycles outside The Whiskey Barrel and shut off the engine, but he made no move to get out of the SUV. Instead, he turned to me. "Walk me through the plan."

"We head in. I talk to Baker, try to get a feel if he was the one who sent those spam bots after me, while at the same time making nice so we can finish this season."

That had Colt scowling. "If he's the one who programmed the software to say all that awful stuff, why the hell would you want to finish the season with him?"

"Because you never know if the public might come through with tips. If I pull out now, we lose the six episodes that are already up. All my subscribers and reviews. I'd have to start from scratch in the middle of a story. It's better to play along so Baker won't suspect a damn thing when I pull out of our contract the moment this season is done."

Colt's brows lifted. "You're leaving him."

I nodded. "He went too far at the hospital. He's always been pushy, but it's delving into manipulative waters, and I'm not down with that."

"Good," he clipped. "That guy is a prick."

My lips twitched. "A soul or two might've called you the same."

Those dark eyes heated to warm amber as Colt slid his hand into my hair. He tugged on the strands, tipping my head back to give himself access to my mouth as he leaned in. "Prick, huh?"

His lips hovered over mine, just shy of where I wanted them. "Maybe," I whispered.

Colt's mouth took mine. It wasn't gentle—it was all need and dominance. But I didn't let him take over. I gave as good as I got, my tongue twisting with Colt's, stroking, teasing, demanding more.

When he broke away, I gasped for breath and then glared at him. "Seriously?"

Colt sent me a cocky grin. "Just a little reminder of what's waiting at home, so you don't take too long."

"Overbearing alpha males who are too good with their tongues," I grumbled as I slid from the SUV. Colt's chuckle sounded behind me as I headed for the bar's door, but I ignored it.

I couldn't ignore when his hand caught mine and he slowed me to a stop. His lips brushed mine again. "Should've told you before now. You look beautiful. A kind of beauty that would make any man stop in his tracks. But it's only matched by your fierceness." Those brown eyes sparked gold. "Show no mercy, Chaos."

My lips parted on a silent inhale as I stared up at Colt. This man would be my ruin. The way he made my body come alive with the barest touch. How deeply he believed in me, believed in what I was capable of.

"No mercy," I whispered.

Colt squeezed my hand twice and then released it, moving to the door. He held it open for me like a true gentleman. But that was part of his pull—the mix of polite care and ruthless demand. It was a heady combination.

I tried to ignore my swirling thoughts of Colt and stepped into the now-familiar bar. It was more crowded than I'd ever seen it. But that made sense; we were heading into a weekend, and the closer we got to true summer, the more tourists would descend on the small town.

I saw some familiar faces. Norm and Sam, the chess-playing duo, were at a table with beers as Mira and Celia sipped beers next to them. Ezra sat with a woman at the bar, nursing cocktails of some sort. The bikers, including the Jack-loving Ace, were in a corner. And Trey slung drinks behind the bar.

A hand pressed into my back as Colt bent, his lips brushing my ear. "I'll be at the bar."

I nodded, quickly searching out Baker. It didn't take me long to find him. His blond hair, which looked fake in the lights of the bar, stood out. I wove my way through the crowd until I got to the table in the corner.

The way the four-top was angled, the only seat that gave me a good vantage point meant sitting next to him. Not next to him like we were a couple on a date, but on two edges of a corner. Still too close for comfort. But I lowered myself to the chair anyway.

"You're late," Baker snapped.

I rolled my eyes. "Your watch is always set five minutes early."

He grumbled something under his breath. "I ordered you french fries and that god-awful whiskey you love so much."

Baker's knowledge of my favorite things had me softening

toward him slightly. When he'd first picked me up under his production company, he'd come on the road with me for a week. He'd been appalled by what I consumed. At that point in time, I was living out of vending machines and drive-throughs, but I'd also been twenty-three, and nothing could hold me back. Not even living on eighty-two million chemical concoctions.

"Thank you." I leaned back in my chair. "What are you still doing here?"

Annoyance flicked through his gray eyes. "Trying to make sure my star podcaster doesn't bite it because she's being absolutely reckless."

That bit of warmth I'd started to feel toward my boss quickly died. "Gee, thanks. It's great to know you care."

Baker stared back at me and then sighed. "You know I care, Ridley. I wouldn't be in this godforsaken dot on a map if I didn't. But I don't want to see you tank your career or worse. You're not being careful."

"I am being careful," I argued. "I'm staying with the freaking sheriff. I'm not going out after dark. I'm watching my back."

And I'd continue taking those precautions, because ending up dead wasn't something I especially wanted to happen. But I also wasn't going to back down. Not when I had the chance to bring Avery peace and possibly bring my family healing, not to mention all the other victims and their families.

Baker opened his mouth to say something else, but we were interrupted by a waitress in her forties. She held her tray with an expertise that spoke of years on the job. "Here you go, honeys. One Grey Goose and soda, one Ransom, and a basket of fries. Here's some ketchup too. You need anything else?"

"We're fine," Baker gritted.

I smiled up at the woman. "Thank you so much."

She sent me a wink. "Just flag me down if you need refills or anything else."

"Small towns," Baker groused.

"Aren't they the best?" I asked, popping a fry into my mouth.

He wrinkled his nose. "No thank you."

I just shrugged and ate another fry.

"We need to discuss your Instagram. I've talked to my security team. They'd like you to move into a more secure location than whatever measly excuse for a house that sheriff lives in. Two-man security detail and—"

"No," I cut him off. "I already told you, I'm not doing that."

"Ridley, don't be an idiot."

"I'm not. But I'm also not going to follow your orders just because you barked them at me. Anyone could be responsible for those comments. Hell, you could've posted them just because you wanted more eyes on the show."

Redness crept up Baker's neck. "Did you just accuse me of harassment?"

I watched every flicker of reaction, trying to figure out if it was him. "I didn't accuse you. I simply pointed out that just about anyone on this planet could be responsible. Even you."

That redness grew and expanded, deepening in tone. "I am not a child throwing a tantrum. And I don't need to use the tactics of one to get what I want. I have the most-listened-to lineup of programs. The top rated. The most awarded."

And none of those were things he gave his creators credit for; it was always Baker's doing. How I'd stayed with him for as long as I had, I'd never know.

"I won't stand for you throwing these ridiculous accusations my way," Baker snapped.

I took a sip of my whiskey, letting that familiar smoky heat sweep through me and waited for Baker's temper to ease, not taking my eyes off him for a second. The reaction thus far was typical Baker—rage at me thinking him anything less than perfect.

Any other time I'd caught him up to no good, he got squirrelly, almost petulant. And that wasn't his demeanor now.

"You aren't going to say anything to that?" he demanded.

I gentled my tone, trying for another approach. "I told you, I was simply making a point that the culprit could be anyone. So we all need to be careful. It could be someone out for you and your shows just as easily as it could be someone out to get me."

Baker stiffened as he processed the thought. He instantly pulled out his phone, fingers flying across the screen. As the device dipped down, I could see he had Instagram open. He was checking each of the podcasts under his umbrella. Unless he'd become an amazing actor over the past few weeks, it wasn't him.

When he was done, he took a sip of his drink and looked up. "Every other podcast is fine. Which just goes to show that *you* need a security detail and help."

I tensed at the word *help*, knowing what it could mean.

"I have the guys from *Reality Rampage* arriving on Monday. We'll be doing a crossover event. People will love it, and you won't have to do a single interview alone."

Anger built, sparks catching fire somewhere low. I'd listened to exactly one episode of Baker's new show. The guys who hosted it had zero respect for what victims or their families had endured. They made crass jokes and took nothing seriously. But worst of all, they didn't give a damn about lives being lost or forever changed.

"No." My voice was low, barely audible above the noise of the bar, but it carried a finality no one could ignore.

Baker's spine stiffened. "Excuse me?"

"I said no." My fingers tightened around my glass as I tried to keep my voice even. "I am not working with them. You know why this job is important to me. You know why what I do is sacred. To them it's nothing but a joke."

"Stop being so dramatic, Ridley. The guys know how to entertain, that's all. And it wouldn't hurt you to learn a little of that."

I stared back at the man I'd worked with for almost four years now. I remembered the night I'd broken down to him about Avery, telling him why bringing these stories to light meant so much to me. Maybe he'd never actually cared at all.

"I quit." The words were out of my mouth before I could stop them. But the moment I gave them voice, I felt free.

Baker scoffed. "Don't be ridiculous."

"I. Quit." I spoke each word like it was a complete sentence. "We each have an out clause in our contract. I'm using mine effective immediately."

"Come on, Ridley. There's no need to throw a tantrum. Just—"

"I'm not. This hasn't been working for a long time. Maybe it never did. But either way, I'm done. *We're* done."

At least I'd get to keep the name. It was in my contract. But I'd have to start fresh when it came to subscribers and reviews. It didn't matter that I'd have to start from scratch or find a whole new staff of people to work with. I didn't care if I had to crawl up a mountain on bloodied knees, I'd do it. Just to be free of Baker. To know that the work I did was to help.

Baker lashed out, his hand gripping my wrist so hard it startled a gasp out of me. The sound only made him tighten his hold as he pulled me in. "Don't think you can just walk away from me, you little cunt. I have poured hundreds of thousands of dollars into building you. And I can pour just as much into tearing you down."

A shadow swept over the table and a furious voice cut through the din of the bar. "Let. Her. Go. Or I'll happily remove your balls from your body."

Chapter Forty-Two
Colt

I HADN'T TAKEN MY EYES OFF RIDLEY FOR MORE THAN A handful of seconds since we'd gotten to the bar. Nothing longer than a hello and chin lift to Trey when I'd sat my ass on a stool at the end of the mahogany closest to her and Baker's table. And now I was damn glad I'd picked that seat.

Because I'd seen those first flickers of annoyance pass over the bastard's face. I'd seen it ebb and flow, retreat and come storming back in. I'd seen it morph into fury at something Ridley said to him. And I'd been out of my seat before he'd grabbed her.

The moment his hand latched onto Ridley's wrist, a red haze slipped over my vision. It took everything in me not to reach over the table and grab him by the throat. I would've arrested someone else for doing the same, but all I could think about was how he was touching Ridley without her permission, hurting her.

Baker's gaze jerked to me. "This is none of your goddamned business, hick."

I didn't give a damn what he thought of me, what insults he might hurl my way. All I cared about was Ridley. "I'll give you three seconds."

He scoffed, gripping Ridley's wrist tighter. "You can't do

a damn thing. My lawyers would have your ass in a sling. I'm untouchable."

"Are you sure about that?" Ridley snarled.

One second Baker had her wrist in a tight hold, and a moment later, he was twitching and crying out in pain. He curled in on himself and fell to the floor, yelling and sobbing.

The whole bar went quiet around us, the only sounds the strains of some retro rock 'n' roll and Baker's cries. But I was already moving to Ridley, helping her out of the chair, hands going to her wrist. "Are you okay? Do you think it's broken?"

She shook her head. "I'm fine." She flexed her hand, twisting her wrist as if to prove it. Then she held up her other hand and grinned. "Pretty sure I tased his balls."

My eyes went wide as I took in the small pink device that looked more like a flashlight than a Taser. "Seriously?"

Ridley shrugged, still grinning. "You gave me the idea with that whole remove-your-balls-from-your-body threat."

"Should've known you'd take that literally," I mumbled.

Trey moved toward our huddle. "Deputies are on the way. You okay, Ridley?"

She sent Baker a withering stare as he still writhed on the floor, and tucked the Taser back into her pocket. "I'm fine. Sorry about the drama."

Trey glanced at the man on the floor and then pressed his lips together to keep from laughing. "Never seen a fall quite like that one."

"A-plus on form," Patty called as she tucked her tray under her arm and offered Ridley a high five.

Ridley choked on a laugh and hit Patty's palm with her good hand. "Thanks."

Patty glared at Baker, whose cries had softened but he made no move to get up. "Rude as anything. Should've known he was up to no good."

"Sorry you had to deal with him," Ridley said.

"Not your fault, hon. Just glad to see the dirt where it belongs."

A few of the bikers hooted at that.

"Need any backup, Ridley?" Ace called. "I got a man who can take the trash out."

"I can help," Norm offered.

"Jesus," I muttered. "You've got bikers and senior citizens teaming up to off your enemies?"

Ridley just smiled up at me innocently. "I like making friends."

"Fucking hell," I mumbled as Ryan and Deputy Marshall charged into the bar.

Ryan scanned the room and started moving the second she saw us. "What happened now?"

"He assaulted Ridley. She tased him," I answered, trying to fill her in as succinctly as possible.

"Tased him in the balls," Ridley added helpfully. "You're leaving out the best part."

Ryan's eyes widened as Sam yelled, "You show 'em, sweetheart."

Ridley just waved at the chess-playing troublemaker.

I groaned and glanced at Trey. "Could you get Ridley some ice for her wrist?"

"Coming right up," he said, heading for the bar.

"I'm okay," Ridley assured me.

I pinned her with a look. "We don't want it swelling."

"She broke my balls," Baker wailed. "Arrest her."

Ryan tried to cover her laugh with a cough. "What do ruptured balls fall under in the penal code anyway?"

Ridley pressed her lips together to try to hold her laugh in but failed miserably. "*Penal code.*"

"I give up," I muttered. "Marshall, will you arrest this asshole and get him medical attention if he needs it?"

"You got it, Sheriff. Just as long as I don't gotta look at his balls."

"Fuck me," I muttered.

But Marshall hauled Baker to his feet, reading him his rights as he yelled. Baker glared at Ridley. "You're going to regret this. My reach goes farther than you know. I can get to you anywhere—"

"Get him out of here," I yelled. "And add *threatening a witness* to his charges."

All amusement fled from Ryan's face. "Walk me through what happened."

Ridley did as she asked, not getting rattled until she shared why she was so mad about what Baker was attempting to force her to do.

"It matters to me, this work," Ridley said quietly, her throat working as she tried to keep her composure. "I take it seriously. People open up to me. They share their pain. And it means everything to me to be the holder of it, to try to find them peace. I wasn't about to let him bastardize that."

I couldn't stop myself from touching her now. I knew it went against our rules, but I did it anyway. My arm curled around her shoulders as if that could give her strength, protection. But the truth was, Ridley was stronger than anyone I'd ever known.

Ryan's eyes flashed. "What you do, it's something worth fighting for."

"Thank you," Ridley croaked.

"I've got everything we need for now," Ryan said. "I'll give you a ring tomorrow if I have any other questions."

"Thanks, Ryan," I said. "I'll be in tomorrow morning."

She nodded and headed for the door.

"Here you go," Trey said, handing Ridley some ice wrapped in a towel. "You can take this home."

Ridley sent him a grateful smile. "At least I didn't break any furniture."

He chuckled. "Would've been worth it if you did."

"Come on. Let's get home," I said.

Trey's brows lifted at that, and he sent me a pointed look. I tried to ignore my best friend. It was just a word, a slip of the tongue.

Home.

But as I guided Ridley toward the door, I couldn't ignore the fact that my cabin had never felt like home until Ridley filled the space with light. Her papers spread out over the dining table. Her scent clinging to the walls. Her damn cat attacking me every time I gave it a new toy.

She made everything better. But when this case was done, she'd leave. And I'd be left with nothing but a bittersweet memory.

Chapter Forty-Three
Ridley

Colt was being weird. It wasn't like he was normally a chatterbox, but he was quieter than normal, lost in his head as the late morning sun streamed in through the vehicle's window.

I reached over his SUV's console and pinched his side.

"Ow, shit." He twisted out of my grasp and sent me a scowl. "What? It's not enough that your cat almost took my hand off this morning?"

"It was just a—"

"If you say *tooth hug*, I'm going to put that cat up for adoption."

"Colter Brooks, you did not just say that."

His lips twitched. "Full-naming me? Must mean business."

"Damn straight, I do. Do not threaten Princess Tater."

He chuckled, and the action sent warmth spreading through me, the kind of heat that was only his.

"Love that sound," I said softly.

Colt glanced over at me in question. "My laugh?"

I nodded. "Something about it. It's gritty and imperfect but more real somehow."

He turned onto Emerson's road, his fingers tightening on the wheel. "Feel the same way about your smile. It twists more to one side than the other, but it just makes me want to memorize the shape."

Pain speared through me. Somewhere along the line, I'd messed up. Because this thing between Colt and me wasn't just fun and games. It was that, but it was so much more. He saw things in me that no one had ever taken the time to recognize. He understood the colors I painted my world with because he spoke the language of my pain.

And now I couldn't imagine walking away from him.

But I'd have to. Whether that was in three days or three months, it wouldn't matter. It would kill a piece of me—the piece I was beginning to love most.

Colt pulled to a stop in front of the sunny-yellow house. His hands didn't leave the wheel for a moment. His strong fingers flexed around it, then readjusted and flexed again. Finally, he put his SUV in park and turned to me. "Why don't you come to the station with me instead? You can hole up in one of the conference rooms to work."

One corner of my mouth kicked up. "First you don't want me at your house alone. Now staying at Emerson's isn't enough, even though Trey's going to be here too."

Colt grimaced at the space between us. "Don't like that Baker's out on bail and we still don't know who attacked you." He reached out, tracing the faint marks on my wrist that I knew would deepen to a darker bruise by tomorrow. "Hate that this happened to you."

"I don't."

Colt's gaze flew to my face. "Why the hell not?"

"Because it showed me what I needed to see. I severed a business relationship that I never should've started. But if Baker hadn't grabbed me, said what he did, I would've always wondered if I'd done the right thing. Now, I know I did."

Colt stared at me for a long moment, his gaze roaming over my face in a gentle caress. "You always see the silver lining."

My lips pulled into a full smile. "I try. Now kiss me and go catch up on all the work you've been missing because of me."

That familiar scowl was back. "Bossy."

I leaned across the console, my mouth just a breath away from his. "You like me that way."

"Damn straight I do." Colt closed the distance, his hand delving into my hair as I opened for him. His tongue stroked mine, reminding me just how quickly he could spark my body to life.

I pulled away, trying to cut the kiss short so I didn't climb on top of him in the middle of Emerson's driveway. "Have a good day, Law Man."

I was out of the vehicle before he could say another word. I slung my bag over my shoulder and jogged up the steps. Before I reached the porch, the front door opened. Emerson was there, a hint of anxiety bleeding into her features.

A weight settled into my stomach. I'd thought she'd gotten used to me from all the time I'd spent here the other day. I'd had the sense that she trusted me, but maybe I'd been wrong. The last thing I wanted was to cause her any more pain.

I opened my mouth to tell Emerson I could go to the station with Colt, but my words were cut off as she rushed out and pulled me into a hard hug.

"You're okay? He didn't hurt you? Trey said you were all right, but he can hedge to protect me sometimes." Emerson released her hold on me but quickly gripped my shoulders as she did a head-to-toe sweep.

I couldn't help it; I beamed back at her.

Her brows quirked. "You smile at the reminder of some douchebag grabbing you?"

I shook my head. "I'm smiling because it's nice to have

someone care, and at the reminder that I tased that douchebag's balls."

Emerson burst out laughing. "Trey *did* tell me that part. Come on inside. I've got tea brewing." She gave Colt a wave as Bear weaved around us, and then we headed in.

Emerson led me toward a warm and inviting living room. The space was a patchwork of colors that all somehow managed to work. And the huge picture window that looked out on the backyard only added to the effect.

Through the window, I caught sight of Trey working in the garden. A wheelbarrow sat to the side, already half-full of what looked like weeds. And I didn't miss that Trey himself had lost his T-shirt somewhere along the line.

As I lowered myself into one of the two overstuffed chairs by the window, I noticed Emerson's gaze lingering on Trey. I didn't blame her. If I hadn't been so caught up in her brother, I would've taken advantage of that view a little longer.

A yapping bark made Emerson jump, her gaze pulling from the window, her cheeks flaming. I bent down to greet the little barker. He looked to be more fluff than dog.

"Who's this?" I asked as I lifted the little Yorkie up into my lap.

Emerson reached for the tea to pour us each a cup. "I forgot you didn't get to meet Saber the other day. He's named for his vicious snaggletooth."

I grinned down at the little guy, who did indeed have a single tooth that seemed to hang over his lip. "Nice to meet you, Saber." I gave him a scratch behind the ears, and he immediately curled up in my lap.

"He'll never let you stop now," Emerson warned.

"Just fine with me. I've got a cat who's the same way."

She slid a beautiful cup and saucer in my direction. "Sugar? Milk? Honey?"

"Just the tea is perfect."

Emerson studied me again, a little of the levity leaving her. "You're really all right?"

"I am. Promise. Well, other than the fact that I'll have to start this season of my podcast from scratch since I left his company." I slumped back into the chair. I hadn't really given myself a chance to think about how I was going to continue telling Emerson's story without the episodes Baker had under his control.

Emerson lifted her cup to her lips, blowing gently on the liquid inside. "Is that so bad?"

I worried the corner of my lip for a moment, mulling that over. "Rehashing what I've already covered is bound to lose me listeners who've already heard the information. But if I jump in where I left off, I could confuse people who are new."

She took a sip of tea, mulling that over. "What if you began where you started with me?"

I shifted in my seat, Saber sending me a dirty look. "What do you mean?"

"What if you start by linking the cases instead of with my case alone? That's bound to get people invested. Then you can weave in the information you've already covered little by little. People who have listened already probably won't even notice because it'll be mixed in with the new stuff."

I was quiet for a long moment. "You want a job as a podcast producer?"

Emerson chuckled as she set her tea down. "I think I've got enough on my plate."

I stared at the tea in my cup, watching the deep orange liquid swirl. "I've never talked about my sister on the show. Feels like ripping out a piece of myself and putting it on display."

"It's going to connect you with your listeners," Emerson said softly. "Bond you to them. Because you're brave enough to share that pain."

My gaze lifted to hers. "I hope it's the right thing to do. And that I can get through it."

Emerson reached across the table and took my hand, squeezing it hard. "You're Ridley Sawyer, taser of douchebags and tamer of ornery brothers. You can do anything."

I choked on a laugh as I squeezed Emerson's hand back. I just hoped she was right.

I sat in the back of my van and pulled the absorption panels into place. The hexagonal foam pieces doubled as décor during my travels but were necessary to cut down on echoing and excess noise. Even though I'd recorded a few podcast episodes from Colt's driveway, this one felt different. Rawer, more real.

An alert for a video call sounded from my brand-new desktop. I braced, hoping like hell Baker wasn't trying to call, but I relaxed when I saw Sully's name on the screen. I hit *accept* and his lined face filled my monitor.

"How ya feelin'?" he asked, leaning toward his computer's camera.

I could see the concern in Sully's face, feel it in his words. That knowledge felt like a warm blanket wrapping around me. I might've blown up one part of my professional life, but I still had good people around me.

"I'm as ready as I'll ever be." But just saying the words out loud had butterflies taking flight in my stomach.

Sully grinned, that small gap between his two front teeth showing. "Hell yes, you are."

I studied my editor of four years. "Are you sure you want to come with me on this? It'll mean losing a couple of other gigs." I was sure Baker would fire Sully the second he realized Sully was still editing for me.

Sully's face screwed up as if he'd tasted something bad. "That prick can shove it. If I never have to edit another of his shows, I will die a happy man."

I chuckled. "Tell me how you really feel."

But Sully didn't laugh with me; instead his expression went serious. "I'm glad you got out from under his thumb, Rids. You deserve a hell of a lot better than he's been giving you. I'm just sorry it got to this point."

My throat burned. "Thanks for having my back, Sull."

"Always, kiddo. Always. You want me to stay on while you record?"

I shook my head. "I'm good." I couldn't stand the thought of someone watching me while I gave voice to everything I'd been working on for so long, while I laid my pain bare for the whole world to hear.

"All right, then. Just shoot me a text when you're done, and I'll get to work."

"Sully, it's after midnight in New York. Just do it in the morning."

It was his turn to shake his head. "This is important. I want to get it up first thing tomorrow morning, and you know I'm a night owl."

I sighed. "Okay. But call it if you get too tired."

"Will do, boss."

My lips twitched. "G'night."

"Good luck," Sully said as he hit *end* on the call.

The moment he was gone, I began checking my equipment. The mic was secured in the stand. The cable from that to my audio interface was good. And the USB from that to my computer was ready to go.

I opened Pro Tools and switched on the mic. "Testing one, two, three."

Sound was good. Right in range. But then again, my body had memorized just how far from the mic I needed to be.

I stared at the screen, licking my suddenly dry lips. My gaze dropped to my notes, the intro I'd written and rewritten countless times as I'd worked at Emerson's. But now it didn't seem right.

I turned my head slightly, just enough so I could see a sliver of night sky, the string of lights that centered me. And then I spoke.

"Hi there, podcastlandia. This is Ridley Sawyer, host of *Sounds Like Serial*. You're probably wondering why the show looks a little different and why we're not on the True Crime Channel anymore."

I traced a strand of stars with my gaze, focusing on them. "The truth is, it was time for me to go out on my own. To follow the path that called to me without the pressure of other voices. But most of all, it's time for me to tell you why I do what I do."

The stars went fuzzy as I sucked in a long breath, trying to fill my lungs with all the strength they would need for what was to come. "The night before our college graduation, my twin sister, Avery, disappeared. The only thing left behind was a blood-smeared key chain and signs of a struggle on a wooded path."

The blur of stars slipped away until all I could see was Avery. Her blue eyes, which were just a bit grayer than mine. The way her nose crinkled when she smiled. How that one lock of hair never quite curled into submission the way she wanted.

"She was an amazing human being. Kind, smart, talented. But more than that, she was loved. By her friends, by our parents, by me. She left a hole in our lives that will never be filled. We will never stop missing her. But maybe we can help her find peace by bringing her killer to justice. And I'd like you to help me do that."

So I laid it out. Peeled back every agonizing layer until there was nothing left. I gave them everything. And I just prayed that it would be enough.

Chapter Forty-Four
Colt

I PACED BACK AND FORTH ACROSS THE LIVING ROOM, checking through the front windows every third or so pass. It was almost eleven now, and Ridley had been in that damn van recording for hours. I could still see the light on in the vehicle, knew she was still at work, but I couldn't help worrying.

That worry grated. Ridley had been doing this for years. She was perfectly capable of covering a story without it wrecking her.

But I knew this one was different. That it was taking more than a piece of her. It was taking countless pieces.

And I hated that. Wanted there to be something I could do to help, to soothe her. But I wasn't sure there was. The most I could do was help her to weave together the strands we'd uncovered.

I knew when this episode went up, her tip line would be flooded with new strands to investigate. I just hoped there'd be ones of value amidst all the attention seekers out there. Ones that might help us find the answers we both so desperately needed.

But as I stood at my front window, staring out into the dark, I suddenly wasn't so sure it was worth the price. A month ago, I would've given anything to give Emerson the peace she needed, the knowledge she was safe, that her monster was behind bars. Now I hesitated. Paused at the idea of causing Ridley pain to ease Emerson's.

Because Ridley had become so much more than simply a wild flash of color and energy, throwing my life into chaos. She thought we needed to find the monster to get any real healing, but just her presence was healing me. I was starting to see things through new eyes because of her outlook on life.

I also knew that if I tried to clip Ridley's wings, she'd never forgive me. I had to let her fight the battle in her way. I could just be there to stand beside her and tend her wounds in the aftermath.

The light in the van went out, and I braced myself, my muscles winding so tight they felt as if they might snap. I didn't move from the window, couldn't have even if I'd tried. I watched as Ridley climbed out of her van, locking the door behind her. She started down the path toward the house but then stopped midway.

Ridley tipped her head back and stared at the sky. The moonlight cast her in a silvery glow that exposed all the scars of the wounds I knew she'd just reopened. All for the sake of helping to end a monster's reign.

I wanted to run out there and beg her to stop. To wrap her in my arms and shield her from all this agony and suffering. But I knew I couldn't.

So I watched.

I watched as Ridley closed her eyes and sucked in a breath. As she pulled in strength and fortified her shields.

God, there was so much beauty in that strength, but also in that pain, because that was what made her so damned strong.

Ridley tipped her head back down and stared at my front door for a long moment before starting toward the cabin. I hated that moment of hesitation, but I understood it just the same. Because we were both trying to hold ourselves back from whatever this had become. It was so much more than enemies with benefits or whatever other ridiculous term she'd coined. And I was done pretending otherwise.

I moved from the window, crossing to the front door and opening it. The light overhead cast Ridley in a warm glow as she approached. "Did I make it in time for curfew, Law Man?"

I ignored her quip and pulled her into my arms. I didn't say a word, simply held her and let her know I was there.

Ridley's body shuddered against me, and for a moment I thought she might let that shell break. Crack enough to truly let me in. But just as quickly as she wavered, those walls were reinforced. She kissed the underside of my jaw and slid out of my hold. "I'm exhausted. Can I fill you in on everything in the morning? The episode should be up then too."

Annoyance flickered through me as I locked the door and set the alarm, some part of me wanting to smash through every wall Ridley erected between us. "Chaos," I started.

She turned halfway down the hall. "Please, Colt. Just give me tonight to get my head on straight."

Pain burned through me, but it was the pleading that did me in. "Okay."

Then I watched as she disappeared into the guest room and shut the door. The snick of the latch echoed in the silence, sounding more like a gunshot than the closing of the door. The noise rang in my ears as I forced myself to walk past her door and into my own room.

But sleep didn't find me. I stared at my ceiling for hours, listening to Bowser's snores from his bed in the corner. It was because of those ridiculously loud snores that I wasn't sure what I was hearing at first.

The sound teased my ears, resembling some sort of animal in distress. Then it got louder. Whimpering. Not animal but human.

I was on my feet before I could consider the wisdom of it, moving from my room to Ridley's, the sound only getting louder until a cry pierced the air. I didn't stop to knock, simply threw the door to her room open.

Ridley tossed and turned under the covers as if she were battling some sort of invisible demon. And maybe she was. I dropped to the bed, my hands landing gently on her shoulders. "Ridley."

She batted at me, striking out as if I were an attacker.

"It's okay. It's just me. You're having a bad dream."

Ridley didn't wake, too caught up in the throes of unconsciousness.

I squeezed her shoulders a little harder. "You're safe. Come back to me, Chaos."

Her eyes flew open, and she blinked a few times. The moment Ridley registered it was me, she threw herself at me. I caught her with an *oomph* as she shook against me.

The sobs came then, racking her body. Nothing about them was gentle, each one more violent than the one before.

I cursed as I slid onto the bed, keeping hold of Ridley as I did so. I cradled her to my chest, rocking her. My hand trailed up and down her spine. "Let it out. You're safe now. It's okay."

"It's not." The words were barely discernible through her cries.

"Tell me." It was a command but also a plea, to give me a piece of her pain to hold awhile.

It took her a couple of tries before she could get the words out, but finally the sobs eased enough. "It's always the same," she whispered. "Avery's in the middle of the lake. I can't see her, but I know she's there. She's screaming for me. But I'm stuck in the shallows. It's like there's quicksand holding me there. I'm fighting and fighting, but it just makes it worse."

"Fuck," I rasped, holding her tighter to me.

"I can never get to her." Ridley's tears fell against my bare chest, soaking the skin there as I stroked her back.

"How hard you fight is a mark of how much you love her."

Ridley's head tipped back a fraction, her gaze colliding with mine. "But it's never enough."

I brushed the blond strands away from her face. "Maybe you just need a little help."

Her brow furrowed in confusion.

"A little help to get out of that quicksand, to get beyond the shallows. But you have to take the hand that's reaching out."

A fresh wave of tears filled Ridley's eyes. "I'm scared."

"I know," I whispered. "But I'm right here waiting."

She didn't look away, just lay there, her chest rising and falling in ragged breaths. Then her hand moved, sliding down my arm until her fingers linked with mine. I closed my hand around hers, soaking in the feel, the gift that was her taking hold.

My lips ghosted across Ridley's temple. "Sleep. I'm right here. Not going anywhere."

Her gaze jerked to mine again. "What about the no-sleeping-in-the-same-bed rule?"

I chuckled, the sound moving from my chest to hers. "Haven't you figured it out yet, Chaos? You've had me breaking all the rules since the day I met you."

Chapter Forty-Five
Ridley

I BLINKED AGAINST THE BRIGHT SUNLIGHT, THE BEAMS making me squint. How late had I slept? Maybe the brightness of the sun was why I was so damned hot.

And then I felt it.

Colt. He was everywhere. Under me. Over me. Against me.

That scent of bergamot and cloves invaded my senses like a full-on attack. And as his hips flexed against my backside, I couldn't help the moan that slipped out of my lips. The feel of him, that hardness against me, was too much.

Colt's fingers pulled the hair away from my neck, and then his lips were there, skating over my tender skin. "You sleep okay?"

I nodded, not trusting my voice. The truth was that I'd slept better than I had in years. Since that night. Colt had kept his promise, like always—he'd stayed.

His arm slid beneath the covers, fingers trailing up my bare thigh. "How do you feel?"

"Fine," I croaked. "Good, I mean."

"Hmmm." The sound Colt made buzzed against my neck. "Think I could make you feel a little better?"

Hell.

I needed to say no, to put some distance between us after last night. He was too close, in every definition of the word. And I knew what could happen when people were too close. It could destroy me when I lost him.

And I would lose Colt. One way or another, it would happen eventually.

"Colt—"

"I'm busy," he said, nipping at my pulse point as his fingers explored higher up my thigh.

My breaths came in short, quick pants. My nipples pebbled against the cotton of my tee. Those damn traitorous peaks. I arched back into him, unable to resist.

Colt cursed, and his other hand came from underneath me, palming my breast and tweaking my nipple. "You live to torture me, don't you?"

I couldn't help the small smile that came to my lips. "Maybe."

He nipped and licked his way up the column of my neck. "Dangerous. Lethal."

My heart pounded against my ribs. Because that was what Colt was to me.

His fingers trailed higher up my thigh, freezing as he came to the apex. "Tell me you aren't sleeping in just a T-shirt."

I bit my bottom lip. "I'm not sleeping in just a T-shirt."

He flipped me to my back, hovering over me. "You little liar."

I grinned up at him, a giggle slipping free.

Colt's eyes darkened. "*My* T-shirt."

I froze. I'd forgotten I'd put the old, worn cotton tee on last night in the search for comfort. "It's soft," I said defensively, trying to deny my real reason for slipping it on.

Those shadowy depths skated over me. "Love the look of you in my clothes."

"Colt—"

He stole the sentence off my lips as he jerked the tee up and over my head. He flipped it behind me, making me arch on instinct, my breasts raising up higher. "Grab the headboard, Chaos."

I sucked in a sharp breath as my blood heated. Shadows danced in Colt's eyes, ones that held a delicious promise. He was like a drug. I kept telling myself just one more taste would be enough. One more night where I lost myself to the feel of him. One more endless moment of *feeling*.

I'd made countless promises to Avery that I would live. And no one made me feel more alive than Colter Brooks.

My hands lifted to the rustic metal bars above my head, the ones that fit so well with the rest of the décor in the room. But décor was the last thing on my mind as the rough texture bit into my palms. There was something about that, the friction of the metal against my skin as I waited for what Colt would do next.

I didn't have to wait long.

Colt's head came down, his mouth closing around my nipple as his hand dipped between my thighs. My back arched further, seeking everything that was him. His hands, his tongue, the slight graze of his teeth.

Another moan slipped free, and I didn't try to hold it back. I let it fly and pushed my hips into Colt's hand.

"My greedy girl," he growled against my breast.

And I was. For him.

Two fingers slid inside on an easy glide as his tongue circled my nipple.

"Colt," I breathed.

Those fingers swirled, stretching me. The slight burn melted into smoky heat—a heat I only wanted to sink deeper into.

A third finger joined the first two, and my mouth fell open, no words slipping free. I could only grip the bars above me harder as I tried to hold on, to soak up every ounce of sensation.

Then Colt's mouth was gone, but his fingers kept working. That circle, then slide. The curving drag of fingertips down my walls until I was ready to beg.

As if he could read my mind, Colt's other hand slid along my jaw. "Need more?"

I sucked in air, desperate for something to cling to. "Yes."

"But not just *any* more. Tell me who you want."

My head jerked, searching for those shadowy eyes. And when I found them, they burned. Branded me in a way that I knew I'd never be the same. I knew what Colt wanted. And the damn bastard played dirty.

But I couldn't lie to him. Not while staring into those depths I knew housed a soul that understood mine. Depths that truly *saw* me.

"I want…*you*." The words tumbled out between pants.

Colt's fingers were gone in a flash and his boxer briefs shucked in a split second. His tip bumped against my entrance as he stared down at me. "Tell me again."

"You, Colt. I need *you*." Those words nearly broke me as the bars bit into my palms. Because they were true. And it was more than his body that I craved. It was everything about the man. The surly demeanor that hid the most tender caring. That gruff protective streak that shielded everyone he cared about.

He planted one hand on the bed as his other covered one of mine, encircling a bar on the metal headboard. And those shadowy eyes didn't look away as he thrust inside me.

My lips parted at the feel of him. All of Colt. My eyes watered as I struggled to adjust to his size.

"Fucking perfect," he breathed, those eyes I loved falling closed for the briefest second as he soaked in the feel of me.

There was power in that. A surge of heady strength that had my walls tightening around him.

Colt cursed, his eyes flying open again. "My girl wants to play."

My hips rose up to meet him in answer, and he didn't wait. Colt slid out on a delicious glide and thrust back in with more force this time.

"Hold tight," he warned, those fingers gripping mine around the bar harder. And then he took me again.

The force of it was just shy of too much. But I wanted him to tip over that scale. I wanted to always carry a piece of him with me, to always remember what it was like to be his.

My legs tightened around him, heels digging in and silently asking for more. And Colt gave it to me. He took me like a man possessed. Each thrust deeper, tipping the scale into those slight flickers of pain. A pain that was ours—a pain that only drove the pleasure higher.

Because there couldn't be one without the other. And if there was one thing Colt and I had both learned, it was that. Loss and hurt could turn you bitter, or it could make you appreciate love and life that much more.

"Eyes on me," he ground out, his hand gripping mine tighter. "Let me in, Chaos."

My heart hammered against my ribs. Of course it wasn't good enough for Colt to simply have my body. He wanted all of me. My heart. My mind. My goddamned soul. All those pieces I kept hidden from the rest of world.

But he should've known he already had them. And finally, I let him see it.

"Colt," I rasped as I let the walls down. Every shield I'd reinforced with steel to keep from being hurt again, all of it was useless in the face of all this man was.

"There she is," he breathed, his forehead dropping to mine as he arced into me again.

My walls clamped down, demanding more, demanding *everything*. And wanting to take that everything and hold it close.

A nonsensical sound slipped from Colt's lips as he came. Guttural. Animalistic.

I took it all. Each wave of my orgasm pulling him deeper, closer, burning him into me. A forever brand. One I'd wear with pride.

We collapsed together, Colt rolling us so I was on top of him, taking care of me even in this. His fingers trailed up my back, tracing the bumps of my spine. "Never felt anything like this."

My grip on him tightened instinctively as my fear raged. "Me either," I croaked.

"Scares the hell out of you."

I nodded against his chest.

"Don't worry. I'll be right here for as long as you'll have me."

That fear only dug in deeper at the thought of losing the beauty that was this man. "And he always keeps his promises."

"Damn straight," Colt said, his lips brushing my temple.

A barked meow sounded, and out of the corner of my eye, I saw a flash of fur. "Tater! No—"

But it was too late. She hurled herself onto the bed and sank her teeth right into Colt's ear.

Chapter Forty-Six
Colt

"It's not fucking funny," I said, scowling as I shoved a spoonful of cereal into my mouth.

Ridley's lips twitched as she sat cross-legged in the chair opposite me at the kitchen table. "Depends on where you're sitting, I guess."

I lowered the spoon from my mouth and used it to point to my ear. An ear that was bandaged, thanks to that serial-killer cat. "Look at my ear."

She choked on a laugh. "Maybe she thought you secretly wanted an ear piercing."

I glared at the ridiculous woman opposite me. "Has anything about me ever led you to believe that I secretly wanted an ear piercing?"

Ridley's blue eyes danced as she grinned. "Okay, maybe she was marking her territory. She obviously loves you."

I dropped the spoon into my bowl with a clatter. "Her love is toxic. No, deadly. She's going to end up on one of your true-crime podcasts but for cats."

"He doesn't mean it, Tater," Ridley yelled in the direction of her room.

I swore I heard a hiss in response.

Ridley turned back to me, amusement still in her eyes but some anxiety there too. While I'd caught up on a little paperwork, she'd proofed the podcast episode she'd recorded last night and hit *publish*. She pulled a knee to her chest, hugging it tight. "I'm scared to look."

I moved then, always unable to stay away from Ridley in any sort of discomfort, even if it was simply nerves. I crossed to her, lifting her from the chair and then settling us both into it again.

"I don't know what it says about my dedication to the feminist cause that I like when you manhandle me," she grumbled.

I chuckled. "It says you need others to respect that you can do it yourself, but sometimes it's nice to have someone do it for you."

Ridley burrowed into me, seeming suddenly small. "A good way to think about it."

I held her to me, running a hand up and down her back. "You want to look together?"

"Yes," she said on an exhale. I reached for her phone, and she slapped it out of my hand. "Not yet!"

"Ridley," I soothed her, trying not to laugh at her ridiculousness, no matter how damn adorable it was. "Whatever's on the internet is on there. Whether we look or not doesn't change that there are going to be some kind souls and some assholes."

She pulled back a fraction, looking up at me. "That's a hell of a poem, Law Man."

"Simple truths." I slid my hand along her jaw and took her mouth with mine. My tongue stroked in, and I didn't miss a moment of drowning in her taste. When I pulled back, her eyes were just slightly hazy. "Let's do this. You and me."

Ridley's hand tightened on my uniform shirt. "You and me."

I lifted the phone, and she tapped in the code. Nibbling on her bottom lip, she toggled to Instagram and then to her profile.

She clicked on a video that she'd obviously recorded that morning, talking about the new episodes.

"Hello, internet friends," it began but was quickly cut off as she opened the comments section, and it filled the screen. I could feel the tension in her body as her muscles wound tight.

Mine soon followed at the sight of the first comment.

Crybaby bitch.

Fucking hell. Why were some human beings so awful? But then I caught sight of another.

Thank you for your bravery. My best friend has been missing for eight years, and no one gets how your life just stops. How part of you will always be stuck in that moment. You get it. You care. Keep fighting. #BringAveryHome

Ridley scrolled from one comment to the next. I lost count in the sixties because there was no end in sight. And there were certainly assholes. And creeps. But more, there was so much support and love.

You've fought for countless others. Now it's our turn to fight for you. #BringAveryHome

If anyone can find your sister, it's you. You've got this Ridley! #BringAveryHome

When Ridley tapped the hashtag, it already had over thirteen thousand entries. People who were spreading the word and sharing Avery's story—and Ridley's too. Because they cared.

I didn't realize Ridley was crying until I felt the drops hit my arm. Curving around her, I saw the tracks of silent of tears left on her cheeks. But it wasn't grief in her eyes—it was something else entirely.

"They're with me. They're helping," she whispered.

I pulled Ridley tighter against my chest. "Of course they are. And it's because of everything you've done for others. They see everything you've given, and now they're giving a little of it back."

Ridley looked up at me, so much hope in those blue eyes. "Do you think it'll help?"

Just a couple of months ago, I would've shot the idea down. I wouldn't have thought there was any way countless internet sleuths would ever break a case. But that was before Ridley. Before I was reminded of the good in people. That pain didn't always change us for the worse; it could change us for the better too.

"With all the people you're reaching, all the people they're reaching in return? We're going to have our best shot yet."

Ridley beamed, the echoes of her tears still glimmering on her cheeks. "We're going to find her."

I dropped my forehead to hers. God, I hoped so. For all of us.

My phone dinged, pulling me out of the moment, and I snatched it up from the table, reading the incoming text. My whole body tensed, going solid beneath Ridley.

She twisted in my lap, concern lining her features. "What is it?"

I swallowed, trying to clear my throat. But it didn't do any good. "It's Emerson. She wants you to interview her. She wants to tell her story."

Chapter Forty-Seven
Ridley

THE TENSION IN THE AIR WAS A LIVING, BREATHING thing. An invisible smoke that polluted everything around it, making it hard to take in a full breath. Or maybe it was simply that we'd turned off the AC in Emerson's adorable home, making the living room stuffy in the eighty-degree heat.

I wanted it to be the latter. Needed it to be that. But as I stole a sidelong look at the woman I now considered a friend, I knew that was a hopeful lie.

Emerson wore an oversized pink T-shirt that had tiny hearts all over it and sweats with a rainbow down the side. But nothing about her outfit matched her demeanor. Her typically fair complexion was even paler than normal, an almost gray hue beneath it.

Her lack of color had her brother asking her at least half a dozen times if she needed to sit or something to eat or drink. Right up until she bit his head off. He shut his mouth altogether, and Emerson picked up her pacing. Back and forth across the living room as she wrung her hands.

Trey simply stood in the corner, watching Emerson mostly, but occasionally his gaze would move to me. It was as if he was making sure I wasn't hiding weapons or anything else that might hurt Em in the gear I was setting up.

While my microphones weren't going to start spitting bullets anytime soon, I couldn't make any promises about the emotional toll my presence and gear might inflict. And that had guilt stewing somewhere deep. I might've been willing to cut myself open in search of peace and the protection of innocent lives, but Emerson might not be there yet.

Her gaze locked on mine, and she didn't look away. "I can do this. I *need* to do it."

I understood that. There'd been a freedom that had come from sharing Avery's story, my story—unmistakably *our* story now. Even before I'd seen the outpouring of love from my listeners, I'd felt more empowered by simply sharing my truth. And I could only hope Emerson would feel the same way.

"All right," I said, doing my best to give her an encouraging smile. "I'm almost set up. You can take that seat there." I pointed to the overstuffed chair she'd sat in yesterday when we had tea. So much had happened in the past twenty-four hours, that felt like a lifetime ago.

"Here," Emerson said quickly. "Let me move the yearbooks." She hurried over and grabbed the stack of books. "I was trying to jog my memory last night, get back to that time."

"That's good," I encouraged. "I'd actually love to take a look at those after we talk. The ones Dean checked out for me at the library went MIA along with my laptop and some other stuff."

Emerson winced at the reminder of what had happened to me. "Of course." She moved the yearbooks to the coffee table and sat as I hooked up the final cable.

As I opened Pro Tools on my new laptop, I felt eyes on me. I knew the owner of the gaze without even looking, but when I finally sought out the source, a different sort of shadow greeted me. Pain swirled in Colt's dark-brown irises, and there wasn't a damn thing I could do to stop it. But I still tried.

"Do you want to take a walk while we record?" I asked.

His stare hardened. "No."

"Dial it back a notch," Trey clipped.

Colt's glare moved to his best friend, but he didn't say a word.

I decided to leave them in their stare-off and focused on Emerson as I sat. "How are you feeling?"

She swallowed, then picked up the glass of water and took a sip. "I'm okay."

"If at any time you want to stop, just say the word. You also get final say on what makes it into the episode. I'll give you a cut before we release it, and if there's anything you want out, we take it out. No questions asked."

Trey took a step forward, reaching out to squeeze Emerson's shoulder. "You've got this, Emmie. We're right here with you."

Colt didn't say a word.

I didn't search out his eyes this time. I had to let him deal with the onslaught of memories however he needed to. Instead, I kept my focus on Emerson as I hit record. "Go ahead and talk normally so I can test the levels."

She glanced down at the microphone like it was some sort of two-headed snake, and I didn't blame her. "I don't have to lean closer or anything?" Emerson asked.

I shook my head as I watched the levels on the screen. "These are good at picking up voices as long as there isn't a lot of ambient noise." I slid her mic back a fraction. "Try one more time."

"Testing one, two, three." Emerson sent me a wobbly smile. "Isn't that what all the professionals say?"

I chuckled, even though it was forced. "You're hired."

Her smile got wider, a little steadier. "Let's do this."

I reached across the table and squeezed Emerson's hand. I

wanted to give her that same touch point Trey had, to let her know that I'd be with her every step of the way. She wasn't alone. "Would you mind telling the listeners your name?"

"H-hi. I'm Emerson Sinclair."

I let out a breath as I released her hand and sat back. "Thanks for talking to me today." My gaze shifted so she hopefully didn't feel as much pressure. "I've had the privilege of getting to know Emerson over the last several weeks, and I can tell you a few things about her. She's one of the strongest people I've ever met and an incredibly talented artist; she makes one hell of an amazing fried chicken lunch, and she has some of the cutest dogs on the planet."

A laugh startled out of Emerson. "This one here is definitely the most ferocious."

I grinned back at her. "How could I forget Saber's vicious snaggletooth?"

"He's wondering that right about now."

"Apologies to Saber the ferocious Yorkie." But there was only so long I could talk about adorable dogs and amazing paintings. At some point we'd have to go to the hard places, and it was better to get it done. "Emerson, can you tell me what life was like when you were sixteen?"

Her fingers dug into the arms of the chair in a way that would leave permanent marks behind. "I think it was a pretty stereotypical teenage existence in a small town. I went to school, played sports, had an after-school job. I really wanted to save up for a car, so I didn't have to bum rides from my big brother all the time."

Emerson's gaze moved to Colt, and I couldn't help but follow. His smile was strained, so much pain and pride in his eyes.

"I don't know if you were exactly stereotypical. You were in the National Honor Society and a state champion tennis player," I continued.

Her cheeks pinked. "It feels like a million years ago, but I tried my best at school, even those pesky science classes I hated. But I—I loved tennis."

Emerson's voice hitched as she spoke about the sport. She went on to share how she'd joined the team on a whim in middle school and caught the bug. How she'd worked year-round to improve, making varsity her freshman year of high school.

My fingers tightened on my knees as I prepared to dive in, knowing it would hurt Em and that I'd feel it all with her. "Was it that dedication to improvement that had you practicing late on the night of May twenty-third?"

Emerson's hand trembled as she grabbed for her water and took another sip, but I gave no signs of rushing her. This was at her pace or not at all. "I practiced late every night," she said. "I did every camp and special clinic, anything to improve."

"Can you walk me through that night in particular?" I asked gently.

Emerson nodded, but it took her a moment to speak. "I hit balls for about an hour after practice ended. The lights on the courts were always pretty decent, so it didn't matter that it had gotten dark."

The tremor was back, but it had spread through Emerson now, taking root in her muscles. "Coach gave me an extra key to the equipment room, so I could put the ball machine away when I was done. I didn't see anyone when I did, didn't hear anything out of place. There was no part of me that was on alert. Maybe because Shady Cove had always been such a safe place, somewhere we could walk to school without a parent and ride our bikes like little terrors."

Emerson licked her lips as tears filled her eyes. "But it wasn't safe that day."

I still didn't rush her. I waited until she was ready to keep going, trying to assure her that I was right there with her.

She took a deep breath and closed her eyes, a single tear sliding down her cheek. "I bent to put my racket in my bag, and that's when I heard it. It wasn't the snap of a twig like in the movies. It was a rush of feet, but not heavy. Almost like a track star or one of those football players who almost look like they're dancing."

Her eyes opened, more tears spilling out now. "I didn't see a thing. Was just about to look up when the first blow hit so hard I saw stars. I tried to scream." The tears came faster now. "I swear I tried to fight him. But he was so strong." Her body shook from the memory, the tears, or maybe some combination of the two.

Colt pushed to his feet. "That's enough. That's fucking enough."

"Colt," Trey warned, his voice low.

"What?" Colt snapped. "I'm not going to sit here and not say a word while my sister's fucking crying. She already won't leave the house. This is just going to make it worse."

Emerson froze, her arms curling around herself as the tears tracked down her cheeks. "It's my choice," she choked out.

"She's right," Trey said, stepping into Colt's space.

His gaze jumped between the three of us. "Fine," he spat. "But I sure as hell don't have to watch it."

I hit stop on the recording, pushing to stand and heading toward the back door after Colt.

Trey caught my arm. "I wouldn't. He's gonna say something he doesn't mean, and he'll hate himself for it later."

"Maybe," I agreed. "But I'm not going to leave him alone in his pain. Even when he hated me, he *never* did that."

My words had Trey releasing his hold on me, and I hurried through the kitchen to the back deck. I didn't see Colt at first. He'd already made it through the garden to the edge of the tree line.

He looked so much like a little boy in that moment. One who'd been knocked down by the schoolyard bully. Defeated and dejected. Hopeless.

My heart ached for that boy. For the Colt who'd been barely a man when his sister was taken. When his world had fractured and he'd blamed himself for it.

I hurried across the grass and through the maze of flowers until I got to him. I knew my words wouldn't do a damn thing, so I wrapped my arms around him from behind, pressing my cheek to his back. I braced for rejection, for cruel words hurled out of anger, but they didn't come.

Instead, his body shook. Silent sobs racking through him.

My heart, which ached, shattered then—for this beautiful man still holding on to so much guilt.

"He fucking hit her. Over and over until she passed out. And I wasn't there. Too caught up in pool with my buddies after work and not watching the goddamned time. I wasn't there."

I moved again, curving around him until we were front to front and I could put my palms on his face. "It wasn't your fault."

"I know. But I still wasn't there." Tears tracked down his cheeks, and I felt it then. The weight of Colt coming to terms with his grief, finally. Once he realized the responsibility wasn't on his shoulders, he could deal with the pain of it happening at all. To his little sister. The person he loved most in this world.

I took that pain on with him. Held his scruffy face in my hands and helped him shoulder it. And as those shadowed eyes met mine, I gave him the last piece of me. "I love you, Colt."

His body jerked. "Chaos."

"I love you." My own cheeks were wet now, the overload of emotions only having one way out.

Colt's throat worked as he swallowed. "Think I loved you from the moment you told me the cat had fucking AC in that van."

A laugh burst out of me, the last sound I was expecting. "Is it fitting that I'm laughing and crying when I've told you I love you?"

He pulled me into him. "Baby, you're chaos. Of course it is."

And then he kissed me, our tears mixing on our tongues but sealing us together with something stronger than we'd ever experienced before. And when he pulled back, he brushed the hair away from my face. "Best gift I've ever received, meeting you."

"Me too," I whispered.

We stood there for a long moment, and then Colt finally broke the silence. "I gotta go make things right with Em."

"Go." I held on for one moment longer and released him. "I'll just be a second."

Colt hesitated, so I shoved him in the direction of the house. "*Go*, or I'll tell Trey you're a lovesick fool."

Colt shook his head but grinned and took off at a jog for the house.

I watched him go even after he disappeared inside. The fear was still there—the fact that part of my heart was beating outside my body. I felt a little sick at the thought. But I didn't let it win. Because that thing between Colt and me, that love, would always be worth fighting for.

I slid my phone out of my pocket. My fingers itched to type out a text to my sister to tell her I loved her. It knocked me sideways. Because that was the urge every time something big happened. Sometimes I would type out a text just to pretend it would somehow get to her.

The wind picked up, and the leaves around me rustled, but something in the air shifted. It wasn't even a sound, but a feeling. I turned, searching for the source. But I wasn't fast enough.

Something punched into my side, and pain speared through me, a burning agony. I started to crumple to the ground, my vision going blurry, but something caught me. No, some*one*.

Strong arms jerked me up as they started dragging me back. "I should've known you weren't special like your sister. Just a whore like all the rest of them."

Chapter Forty-Eight
Colt

I STEPPED INSIDE THE HOUSE I'D GROWN UP IN. THE scent of it had changed slightly over the years; there was lilac lacing it now, a scent Emerson favored. But the roots of it were the same. It wasn't anything I could put a name to; all I knew was that it meant *home.*

Walking through the kitchen, I steeled myself. The riot of emotions pulsing through me was almost more than I could bear. The pain of all Emerson had endured and the joy of all Ridley had given me melded together into something that only heightened both.

But that was life. There couldn't be true happiness without grief, no pleasure without pain. Each one made us recognize the other in equal measure.

Rounding the corner, I found Emerson standing in the living room alone. Her arms were wrapped around her waist as if she were trying to hold herself together as she stared at a painting. I knew it was one of her own. A favorite.

It was a landscape of the lake my house was now on. One she'd painted from a combination of memory and photos. The canvas was cast mostly in dark purples, blues, and greens, with stars dotting the two upper corners. But the sun was just beginning to come up over the horizon, giving a glow to the center of the piece.

Hope.

I saw it more clearly now, how all Emerson's artwork had that quality—how she was painting it for herself, creating it when the world had stolen so much.

"Em," I said, voice raw.

She turned, not fast but not stalling—in a measured way, almost as if the weight of the world was on her shoulders. She wasn't crying anymore, but her eyes were red and puffy.

"Where's Trey?" I asked.

Emerson swallowed, her fingers digging into her sides. "I told him I needed a minute. He went out front to return a call."

I nodded absently, feeling the emptiness of the room, the lack of distraction. "I'm sorry I lost it."

Emerson shook her head, those blond strands shifting over her features. "I need you to believe in me."

I felt the blood drain from my face as a pit took root in my stomach. "I do—"

"You don't." Her words weren't any louder than a moment before, but they had a bite to them. "I know not leaving this house might make me seem weak—"

"It doesn't," I argued.

She held up a hand. "It makes you think I'm delicate, that I could break. So you step in and try to fix everything for me. But the more you do, the less I have to *try*. And I need to stretch myself, Colt. I need the challenge of trying to accomplish new things. That's what this was." Emerson gestured to all the recording gear.

"The urge to shield you is never going to stop," I admitted. She opened her mouth to argue, but I kept going. "That's partially because I have a lot of guilt around what happened. Guilt for being late. For not being there when you needed me most."

"Colt—"

"But mostly because I love you and you're never going to stop being one of the most important people in my life. You're my *sister*. The only family I have left. The idea of anything else happening to you *kills* me."

Emerson's eyes glittered with unshed tears again. "I love you too. You're the best big brother around."

"I don't know about that. But I'm going to try to do better. And the first part of that is standing with you while you tell your story. Because doing that is going to touch people. It's going to help some of them feel not so alone because of what's happened to them. It's going to inspire others to help solve this case. It's going to be fucking hard, but it's also going to be worth it. And I *know* you can do it."

She flew at me then, her slight body colliding with mine as she held on with all her might. "I love you too, Colt. This is all I've ever needed. Just knowing you're with me."

"Always, Shortcake."

"I hope this means you pulled your head out of your ass," Trey called from the entryway to the living room.

Emerson released me and sent him a smile as she wiped the remnants of her tears away. "We're good."

Trey arched a brow at me. "What about your girl? You fuck that up?"

I flipped him off. "We're good too. Better than. She was just giving Em and me a moment."

I glanced out the big picture window toward the garden. I had to move closer to it to see where she was, but when I did, there was no one. Not a single soul in that garden or the forest around it that I could see.

Panic hit hard and fast, but I tried to breathe through it. There were a million explanations. She'd walked into the woods or around the front of the house.

But I was already moving, storming through the kitchen and out the back door as Trey yelled my name. My pace picked up to a jog as I hit the deck, my head on a swivel. But there was no sign of her anywhere.

That panic dug in, holding my lungs hostage and making them burn, and then I was running. I headed straight for the spot in the back garden. The one where Ridley had told me she loved me.

My Chaos.

The only one who would tell me she loved me in the worst and best moment of my life. But she wasn't there either. I scanned the area with new eyes. Assessing ones, slipping into law-enforcement mode.

My gaze caught on it then. The disruption of earth in two lines. Drag marks.

Everything in me seized, but I didn't move. I crouched, taking them in and froze.

"What the hell is going on?" Trey demanded, slightly out of breath from running after me.

"Her phone," I croaked, not able to look away.

I felt Trey lean over me then, trying to see what I did. His hand landed on my shoulder, then convulsed in a death grip. "Is that blood?"

Chapter Forty-Nine
Ridley

Waves of hot and cold battled through me, one taking hold and then getting washed away by the other. I groaned, trying to roll to my side. *Do I have the flu?* I hated being sick. Especially when said sickness included a fever.

As I moved, white-hot pain speared through me. I wanted to scream, to cry out, but the only sound that came was a sluggish moan. I shifted to my back, and the pain eased a fraction, but an intense burning still radiated from my side.

What the hell happened?

My eyelids fluttered, their movement scraping against eyes that felt far too dry. It was only light and shape and color at first. Nothing made sense.

Then my surroundings began to compute. The room was dark. Not completely, but shades were drawn, and only a small desk lamp illuminated the space.

My brows pulled together in an almost painful contraction. I was on a hard floor, and nothing around me was familiar. There was a desk and bench seating behind it on the opposite side. But everything was incredibly narrow. And up ahead were two captain's chairs, a steering wheel, and a covered windshield.

An RV?

My gaze flipped to the other side, and I was greeted with a kitchen and small dinette. Past it was a small hallway with three closed doors. My mouth went dry as my heart pounded against my ribs.

None of this was familiar.

I frantically searched my memory for the last thing I could grab hold of. Emerson's house. The podcast interview. Telling Colt I loved him in the garden, and then—

I jerked upright, and a blinding pain stole my breath. I couldn't hold back the whimper that left my lips at the agony. I fumbled, trying to search out the injury, but found I couldn't because my hands were bound with coarse rope.

Fuck. Fuck. Fuck.

The curse was chanted over and over in my head. Someone had attacked me. Had—I looked down at my shirt and the dark brownish-red stain—*stabbed* me.

A wave of wooziness swept over me, and I squeezed my eyes closed. *Just breathe. In and out. Nice and easy.*

I didn't want to think about what could happen if I passed out again. Slowly, I opened my eyes and tried to take stock of my injury. There wasn't a huge amount of blood on my shirt, but holy hell did it hurt.

Slowly, I used my bound hands as best as I could to lift the cotton. I tried not to let the nausea take me under as I caught sight of the wound. It was so thin and precise, but blood still oozed from the puncture.

I let my shirt quickly drop and pressed my hands to my side. A fresh wave of pain rocked through me, and I opened my mouth in a silent scream as black dots danced in front of my vision. I tried to focus on my breath, but the agony was too much.

I wasn't sure how long it took for the pain to ease a fraction, enough so that I was breathing normally again, but when it did, my surroundings came into better focus. It was an RV. A nice one from the looks of it, and I knew how expensive vehicles you lived in could be.

But I needed out of it. Now.

The man's voice echoed in my head. *I should've known you weren't special like your sister. Just a whore like all the rest of them.*

The panic was back in full force as blood roared in my ears. I couldn't think about those words. Because if I let myself come to terms with the knowledge that the man who'd taken Avery—killed her—had me, I'd be paralyzed.

Just breathe.

That was what I had to do first and foremost. I focused on the inhales and exhales. Not too fast or too slow.

Once they were steady again, I looked down at my wrists and ankles. The rope was so tight, my fingers and toes tingled, but that didn't mean there wasn't a way out. I tried to move my legs closer and that's when I saw it.

The chain.

The rope around my ankles was connected to a short chain that was fastened to a bracket in the wall. Something that spoke of preparation, of doing this exact thing countless times before.

Just breathe.

I spoke the words in my mind over and over. And as my breathing evened out, I started searching again. This time for a tool. Anything that might be strong enough to slice or fray these ropes. They were the kind with rough strands that were always weakening and falling away; there was just an endless supply of them.

I glanced toward the kitchen and blanched. Even if the chain reached that far, there were locks on the cabinets. This man had kept people here. Young women. Girls.

Just breathe.

I turned toward the desk, trying to take stock of its contents. The surface was mostly clear except for a computer monitor. It had one of those screensavers that morphed from landscape to cityscape but told me nothing.

Then I frowned, nose scrunching. There was hair on the desk. The worst possible reason for such a thing filled my mind, but then I realized it was a wig. A mix of blond and gray. And then what looked like skin but I finally realized were prosthetics.

My breath caught in my throat as my body seized at the package of grape gum. Memories from the night I was attacked filled my mind, that sweet smell. Only it wasn't just sweet—now I could identify it as grape. Like the gum I remembered chewing as a kid. And then I looked at the opposite wall.

A ringing started in my ears as my whole body buzzed. Buzzed because I wasn't breathing, and I knew I needed to. But I couldn't.

Because I recognized that view. I'd seen it countless times on the other end of video calls, set at different times of day and weather. And I'd never known it was completely fake.

"Ah, she's finally awake."

I whirled at the voice. I should've recognized it earlier. Should've known. But it was different somehow. Younger? The face that greeted me certainly was. No paunch or jowls. No wrinkles at all. He didn't look decades older than me. Not now. But I knew those eyes, even if they had morphed with disgust.

"Sully?" I croaked.

Chapter Fifty
Colt

CHAOS REIGNED AROUND ME. BUT IT WASN'T THE WARM, ridiculous, light-filled chaos that Ridley embodied. Countless officers circled Emerson's backyard, ones I recognized and ones from the state who were unfamiliar. Evidence techs swarmed through the garden as they tried to find anything that might give us a lead.

"What did the closest traffic cameras give us?" Ryan asked Deputy Marshall, a clipped tone to her words.

Marshall lifted his phone. "A white Acura and silver pickup heading south. A gray Jeep heading north."

"Which tells us nothing," I growled.

Ryan turned to me, her face impassive, but I saw the sympathy in her eyes. "It's a part of the puzzle," she reminded me. "The more information we gather, the quicker we'll find her."

I knew she was trying to help, was doing everything she could. The state police were already here, marked by the lead detective side-eyeing me for getting any information on the case. She'd placed a call to the FBI, who was looking over Ridley's findings with fresh eyes. And I'd texted my friend Anson, who used to be with the Behavioral Analysis Unit, to see if he could put in a word.

But none of that was enough. Not even close.

As if Ryan read that, she gave my arm a quick squeeze. "Why don't you try talking to Emerson again? She could've remembered something. I'll come find you if we get anything new."

It was a brush-off, and I fucking knew it. But if I stayed out here, I'd end up decking someone. Probably Detective Holden from the state police. So I didn't say a word, simply stalked off toward the back door.

It slammed behind me as I strode inside and toward the living room. Emerson and Trey were huddled on the couch, a yearbook in each of their laps.

"Anything?" Emerson asked, her face pale.

I shook my head.

Trey muttered a curse under his breath. "Word's spreading. Got a call from Sam. Celia's setting up search parties, and he and Norm are helping."

It was my turn to curse. "Just what we need. I hope like hell you told them that if they see *anything* they need to call 911."

"Of course I did," Trey shot back. "Though they got backup. Got a text from Ace, and he and the Devils are riding with them."

A burn lit somewhere deep. Of course Ridley had made friends with a motorcycle club that lived a less-than-legal lifestyle. And of course they were riding out for her. Because that was the sort of person she was. Made every single soul that crossed her path fall in love with her.

My chest seized in a vicious squeeze, and I gripped the back of the overstuffed chair, just trying to hold on.

"Colt," Emerson whispered.

I swallowed down all that pain, that fear, that fury, and forced my gaze to my sister. "Anything coming up?"

She shook her head. "I'm trying but…"

"It's okay," I told her, but we both knew it was a lie. We needed something, anything. Because this all had to be linked. Ridley had gotten too close, and now she was gone.

"We keep going," Trey said, beginning to flip through the yearbook he had again.

Emerson nodded, staring down at her own pages. "Everyone looks suspicious now."

Trey stopped on a spread about the tennis team. "Someone got eyes on Coach Kerr?" he growled.

Emerson straightened. "Coach? Why?"

I winced. Word had made it around town about the coach and his relationship with Tara Gibson when she was underage, but I'd avoided the topic with Emerson so far. "A deputy found him coming out of his lawyer's office two towns over. He couldn't have done this."

Trey's jaw worked back and forth but he didn't say a word.

"Will someone tell me what's going on?" Em demanded.

I sighed. "Kerr faked his alibi for the night you were taken."

"What?" she whispered.

"But it wasn't for the reason we thought. He was at a motel with Tara Gibson."

Emerson's jaw went slack. "But—but she was only seventeen."

"I know," I said, a sick feeling swirling in my stomach.

"What about him?" Trey asked, tapping a photo in the yearbook.

It was a shot of Emerson with a guy I didn't recognize. He was young. Maybe five or six years older than her, and it looked like he was instructing her on a swing.

Emerson frowned down at the book. "That was one of those clinics Coach signed us up for. Shawn Sullivan. He was All-American, just out of college. He—"

Emerson's words cut off as she started to shake. Trey dropped the book, his arm going around her. "Emmie, what's wrong?"

She stared straight ahead, but I knew she wasn't seeing the room in front of her. "Grape Bubblicious."

Everything in me stilled and then instantly went wired. It was the one thing law enforcement had kept from the press. The scent of grape Emerson had identified.

"He always chewed grape Bubblicious gum. Always." Emerson's gaze shot to me. "Was it him? Was it Shawn?"

I was already moving, crossing to the back door and shouting for Ryan. She and Marshall were inside in a flash.

"Em remembered something," I clipped. "Shawn Sullivan ran a tennis clinic for her team. Always chewed grape gum." A memory flashed, Ridley recounting her attack at the campground. "And Ridley—" My voice cracked on her name. "She said that she smelled something sweet on the guy's breath who attacked her."

Ryan's eyes flashed as she turned to Marshall. "Run him."

He pulled out his phone, opening one of the apps we used. "Do you know where he's from or his birthday?"

Emerson shook her head. Her whole body was trembling, and her breathing was shallow as Trey held on to her. Whether it was the memories or having new people in her space, I didn't know.

"I think I got him," Marshall said. "Tennis All-American?"

"That's him," I clipped.

Marshall scanned the screen as he scrolled. "Nothing on his official record, but he was questioned in a rape case in college. Looks like they circled him for a while but nothing stuck. No charges were ever filed."

He switched to another internet browser page. "He's got a website. Offers tennis clinics to high schools, colleges, and universities."

My muscles started to buzz as rage burned. "The perfect cover for traveling the country and abducting women to rape and kill them."

Just saying the words killed something in me. What was happening to Ridley in this very moment?

"Get Sanchez and Geary, and track it. Every woman on Ridley's list. We need to see if it lines up," Ryan ordered.

But we needed something else. "Where the hell is Shawn Sullivan right now?" I growled. "If he's holed up somewhere, there has to be a trace. We have to find him."

I just hoped like hell it wouldn't be too late.

Chapter Fifty-One
Ridley

Waves of emotion and sensation warred against each other as a man I both recognized and didn't prowled toward me from the back of the RV—burning heat and shattering cold, disorienting confusion and terrifying panic.

My mind struggled to put the pieces together, to recognize the man in front of me. But none of it made sense.

Sully's face twisted into a grin that was as far from warm and comforting as you could get. "What's the matter, Rids? Don't recognize me without the old-man getup?"

I wanted to look at what I'd seen on the table, the wig and the prosthetics, but I was too terrified to take my gaze off the man getting closer and closer. It wasn't just the absence of wrinkles, graying hair, and a paunch. Sully even moved differently now, more agilely. Like he could strike at any moment.

"Who. Are. You?" I croaked, the pain in my side intensifying as I struggled to catch my breath.

The man I knew as Sully made a tsking sound. "Come on now, Rids. You know me. But you should've been paying closer attention. Because you saw me before I ever started editing your goddamned show."

I stiffened, the pain spreading out in waves. "When?"

That grin spread so wide his mouth twitched at the sides like it was hard for him to hold it. "You know, you've always had shit taste in men."

My hands convulsed as I tried to pull at my bindings, as if somehow I could break them with the power of my fear.

"Jared was almost as shitty a tennis player as he was a boyfriend."

I squinted at Sully, trying to place this younger version of him. "You weren't on the tennis team with him."

Sully scoffed. "Thank God, no. But I did try to teach that little shit a thing or two."

A coach? I flipped through images of the coaching staff in my mind, but I couldn't place him there either.

"I'm disappointed in you," Sully singsonged as he leaned against the kitchen counter. "I taught a clinic to your boyfriend's pathetic team. You and Avery came to watch at the end. Both so beautiful. But I knew right away that *she* was the special one. Shy. Reserved. *Perfect.*"

My body shook at the way he spoke about my sister. There was an intimacy there that turned my stomach. And it was a lie. "You didn't know her," I wheezed.

Sully's spine snapped straight. "I knew her better than anyone. Followed her for weeks before I took her. Learned every last detail. And I'm the only one who knows what she sounds like when she *really* screams."

Bile surged up my throat. It was him. The man who'd stolen my sister from me.

"I let you in," I croaked as tears pooled in my eyes. That made it all worse. I'd sent Christmas gifts and birthday cards to the man who'd ended Avery in the worst ways imaginable.

Sully tipped his head back and cackled like he'd heard the funniest joke of all time. "That's the best part about it, Rids. You're a living, breathing reminder of possibly my favorite kill. Hell, I know it is, and that's thanks to you."

I shuddered, pulling the rope tauter as I struggled to get free.

"It's you reminding me of her that makes it the best one. I get to relive it all every time I hear your voice. It was worth those countless months of classes on audio editing. Worth playing the idiot fan of your show to get in on the ground floor. Because every time you speak, it's like she's still here. It's really too bad I have to kill you and lose that. But maybe killing you is going to be the best of all. Because it'll be like killing her all over again."

Fear clogged my throat as the threat of more tears burned the backs of my eyes. "Don't," I whispered.

The grin was back. "Oh, Rids. I'm going to love hearing you beg. Feeling the slice of my knife through your throat when I finally end it all."

My whole body shook. I couldn't stop it. But I wouldn't give him my begging or my pleas. I'd swallow them down and take whatever pain was to come. "How many?"

Sully's head quirked to the side. "How many what?"

"How many people have you killed?" My voice sounded calmer than it had any right to, even as my body trembled.

He tapped his fingers against the countertop in a staccato rhythm. "Now you ask the right questions. This is good. It'll prepare us."

"Prepare us?" I croaked.

Sully inclined his head toward the desk where his computer sat, and that's when I noticed the microphones off to the side. "We're going to record the best podcast episode of your life. Pull all the pieces together right before I bury you in the woods and head for Mexico."

My heart pounded against my ribs. Time. I had time. I'd draw out the episode for as long as I could and break free. "I need the backstory so I know what questions to ask."

"Always impatient. I can't spoil the show, but I'll give you some clues. Thirty-four that you should've found. Thirty-four perfect specimens that will live forever in my memory."

He rubbed his fingertips together as if sifting through memories. "Traveling the country for my tennis clinics really did give me the perfect cover. The perfect way to get on campuses and school grounds so I could find them."

My stomach soured, bile churning as I struggled to keep whatever I'd last eaten down.

"I don't really keep track of the others." Sully spoke the words so casually, as if he were talking about pieces of trash rather than human beings.

"The others?" A fresh wave of nausea slid through me.

"The ones I ended just to take the edge off. They didn't matter." Sully ran a hand through his blond hair free of any gray. "I have to give it to you. Finding those early women, the ones before I discovered who I *really* was meant to be, was something." His blue-gray eyes hardened to stone. "Maybe I'll revisit Emerson before I leave. Show her who I *really* am."

I jerked, my legs snapping the ropes and chains tight. A fresh wave of pain washed over me, but on its heels was resolve. That wasn't going to happen. I'd get free. Get help.

Sully laughed, his eyes lighting with a perverse joy. "Like that fight. Not all my girls had fight. That's what happens with the shy ones. Some are surprising, give you a nice battle. But others just lie there like a dead fish."

I twisted, my teeth grinding together, and when I did, I felt something dig into my hip. The Taser I usually carried was gone, but something else was still in my pocket. I shifted again, trying to feel what it was.

Avery's key chain—the lacrosse sticks I'd given her for her sixteenth birthday.

It wasn't a lot, but it was something. If I clutched it between my hands, it might be enough to hurt Sully if I got him in the face.

"What? Cat got your tongue, Rids?" Sully taunted.

My gaze shot to him. "Just wondering how pathetic someone has to be that this is what they have to resort to."

Fury contorted Sully's expression, and he shot forward, slapping me so hard I flew to the floor.

"You little cunt. I'm going to—" His words cut off as a loud ringing sounded. Sully pulled out his phone and glared at the screen. "I need to take this. Scream all you want. The RV's soundproofed. And we're on the bluffs miles away from town, and there's no one around."

I shuddered at that knowledge as Sully opened the door and stepped outside. I tried to pull up a map in my mind of where the bluffs were. I knew they were north of town and that Em's house was on the outskirts in that direction. If I got free, I just hoped like hell I could use landmarks to point me in the right direction.

My face throbbed as I pushed myself to sitting. Everything hurt now, and the world was going a little fuzzy, but I slid my fingers into my pocket, fumbling around for the key chain as the ropes cut into my wrists. My fingertips grazed the metal edge and I finally grabbed hold.

Tugging it free, I studied the metal piece. One of the stick's edges was sharpest. It would do real damage if I caught Sully in the eye, but I wondered if it might be strong enough to get through the rope at my ankles.

I studied how the chain was connected to that rope and hope surged. Only one loop was threaded through the chain. If I could start to fray that one, maybe I could get free.

I got to work, sawing at the strands and straining to hear

any signs of Sully. But I believed him about the soundproofing; I couldn't hear a damn thing.

My fingers cramped as a few of the braided threads broke. I quickly switched hands, taking stock of the blood on my fingers. But I didn't register the pain of my cuts. I was too focused.

I gripped the rope with my now-injured hand, sawing with the other. The tension helped, and two more pieces of the braided cord snapped.

Hope surged and I sawed harder. The pain started to break through, but I didn't stop. Two more to go. I could do this.

The door rattled and tears sprang free. *No, no, no. Not yet.*

The rope snapped and the chain fell to the ground. I dropped the key chain, grabbing at the rope and pulling my ankles free even though my hands were still bound.

I leapt to my feet, and the world swam, but I didn't stop. I braced myself in the doorway and waited until the door just began to open—and then I kicked with all my might.

The door slammed into Sully's face, sending him stumbling back with a shouted curse. But I didn't hesitate. I ran.

My side screamed in agony as Sully cursed again, scrambling to his feet.

I knew I didn't have much time. I had to get to a place I could hide. I ran toward the thickest trees, but Sully was on my trail.

A shot sounded, cracking the air, and I ducked on instinct.

"I'll kill you and make it hurt," Sully bellowed.

He was already going to do that, and I'd rather die fighting. For me. For Emerson. For Avery.

I pushed my muscles harder, my vision blurring as I searched for anywhere to hide. But before long, the trees grew thinner. Then I broke into an opening—an opening that led to cliffs.

I skidded to a stop as another bullet pierced the air. I didn't want to turn and look. All I could do was stare at the water below.

A crystal-blue lake that was too far down to offer rescue. I was trapped.

My eyes stung as pain grabbed hold, but I forced myself to turn around.

Sully stood there, blood streaming down his face from what looked like a broken nose. He leveled the gun at my head. "What's it going to be, Ridley?"

Chapter Fifty-Two
Colt

THE LEAD DETECTIVE FROM THE STATE POLICE STOOD ON the back deck, hands on his hips, staring down his nose at me. "You want me to start a statewide manhunt for someone because your sister remembered someone chewed grape gum?"

I bit the inside of my cheek so hard I tasted blood. "He fits the profile."

"A made-up profile from cases we aren't even sure are related," Detective Holden spat. "And between you and me, your sister doesn't seem all that stable. Her testimony probably wouldn't even hold up in court."

A whole different sort of fury surged. My fingers clenched, knuckles itching to collide with Holden's nose. As if reading my mind, Ryan stepped in front of me. "We've already put Shawn Sullivan in the vicinity of four other missing women just weeks before they disappeared."

Holden scrubbed a hand over his face before shaking his head. "Come talk to me again when you've put him at the scene of the disappearance. We're wrapping up and heading back to headquarters. We'll keep *you* in the loop of the investigation."

He shot that last sentence at Ryan specifically. Because he'd wanted me off the premises of the crime scene from the moment he'd arrived. It was just too bad for him that it was my sister's house.

"I found something," Marshall called, running up the steps to the back deck.

My hands fisted tighter as I tried to hold on to control. But I could feel it slipping. Too many awful images flew through my head. Ones I knew because of all the crime scene photos I'd studied over the past month.

Knowledge was supposed to mean power, but I'd never felt more powerless. Those images flashed in my mind, but instead it was Ridley's face on their lifeless bodies.

"Tell me," I snarled.

Marshall didn't deserve my rage, but he didn't take it personally. He knew I was holding on by a fraying thread. Instead, he started talking. "We got a hit on the gray Jeep. It's registered to an LLC. The same LLC that reserved the single campsite at the bluffs for the next two weeks. It took a little digging, but that LLC has a single member."

"Shawn Sullivan," Ryan finished for him.

Marshall nodded.

But I was already moving. Running for my SUV. I didn't give a damn about protocol or procedure. All I could see was Ridley.

I was halfway to my vehicle when a hand caught my arm. Ryan jerked me to a stop as deputies donned their Kevlar and moved to their squad cars and SUVs. "You know you can't go."

"The hell I can't," I growled.

"And what happens when we take him down and the whole arrest is called into question because you were the one to do it?" Ryan challenged. "What happens if we lose him because of *you*? How are you going to explain that to the families of those missing women? To the family of the one who disappears next?"

Rage blasted through me, but I knew she was right. I also knew I couldn't *not* go. I had to be there for Ridley when she needed me. "Don't cut me out. Let me be there in the end. She needs me."

Indecision swept over Ryan's face until she finally relented. "You ride with me. I don't even want any record of your official vehicle on the premises."

I jerked my head in a nod and ran to my SUV to grab my vest. Pulling it over my head, I secured the sides and slid into Ryan's sedan. She was already behind the wheel and barking orders over the radio.

The instructions were to go in quiet, no lights or sirens, nothing that would spook Sullivan. Ryan led the parade of law enforcement vehicles, all of us making the trip in record time. As she pulled to a stop at the campsite, my stomach hollowed out.

A gray Jeep and a large RV stood sentry. The RV's door was wide-open and flapping in the wind. But it was more than the ghostly reception that had me frozen to the spot. It was that they were familiar.

"I've seen that RV before," I choked out.

"Where?" Ryan clipped.

"At Ridley's campsite. I'm not sure when that was exactly. Before her attack." My gut soured. I'd missed it. Hadn't thought back to that fancy RV I'd seen previously, thought to check the camp's registry. "He's been watching her all this time."

"Hold it together, Colt. If you don't, I'm going to have to cuff you to this squad car, and I really don't want to have to do that."

"I missed it. Should've seen…"

"But you're seeing now," Ryan reminded me. "So let's go get your girl."

We were out of the car in a flash, Ryan whispering orders into her radio as officers fanned out.

"I've got blood," an officer with only a few months on the job said as he and Marshall approached the RV.

Marshall slipped inside, Sanchez on his heels. Seconds later we heard a *clear* over the radio.

"Blood trail, broken vegetation," another deputy called from the tree line.

All I could hear was the word *blood* over and over. It haunted me with each pound of my heart until finally my body went numb altogether.

I fell in line behind a handful of officers, Ryan leading the charge through the woods. She had search and rescue training that I knew helped her to see the lay of the land now. Broken branches and trampled underbrush that I prayed would lead us to Ridley. A Ridley who was safe and unharmed.

A shot shattered the silence, and the numbness disappeared in a split second, replaced by a terror I'd never known. Different than when I'd realized Emerson was missing. This terror was deeper, more vicious, because I knew the monster who'd taken Ridley. And that monster had a gun.

Every single officer broke into a run. Ryan's voice crackled across the radio, shouting orders. But all I could think about was Ridley.

Ryan hit the clearing before the bluff, gun raised. "Shawn Sullivan, this is the Mason County Sheriff's Department. Lower your weapon."

A laugh split the air, a sickening cackle that only spurred my muscles on until I broke through the trees. I saw it then.

The image my nightmares were made of.

Shawn had Ridley by the hair on the edge of the bluff, a gun pressed to the underside of her chin. This spot was one favored by especially adventurous tourists. Occasionally rock climbers rappelled down the cliff's edge, but that was with ropes and spotters.

The drop was over one hundred and fifty feet into the lake

below—you hit that water wrong, and you'd be dead before you realized how cold it was.

Shawn jerked Ridley's head back in a vicious snap, and she cried out in pain. That's when I saw the blood. It had seeped through her tank top and shorts, and trailed down her leg.

He'd hurt her. Cut her.

"Lower your weapon, Shawn. And we can all walk away."

He laughed again, that same sick twistedness to his tone. "Sophie Ryan. Second-in-command. I wonder if you'll get to take the sheriff's job when they realize how badly he bungled this."

My fingers itched to pull my weapon, to be the one to end this bastard, but I couldn't. I had to trust that my people had every available shot. I had to believe in everything I'd bled into them.

Ridley's gaze connected with mine as tears welled in her eyes. "Love you, Law Man."

Shawn gripped her hair harder, shaking Ridley like a rag doll. "You don't get to love him, you whore. You don't deserve any of this. My plan was perfect until you. You're going to pay for this."

"Shawn," Ryan warned, raising her weapon higher.

Ridley's eyes didn't move from mine. "Beyond the shallows, remember?"

Everything slowed. Heartbeats thundered in my ears as my mind connected the dots a split second before Ridley acted. A *no* was on my lips, but it was too late.

She reared her head back and slammed her forehead into Shawn's already bloodied nose. He howled in pain, his hold on her loosening for the barest second. It was only a moment, but Ridley didn't waste it. She shoved back, away from Shawn—and over the bluff.

Bullets pierced the air, but I was already running. Because she believed I'd be there to catch her when she fell.

So there was only one thing to do.

Jump.

Chapter Fifty-Three
Ridley

My head felt like it was full of cotton. No, not just my head, my mouth too. And maybe my ears. I groaned, trying to roll over, but couldn't.

"Easy, Chaos. I'm right here. Always, remember?"

That voice.

God, I wanted to see the owner of that voice. Some part of my brain recognized it as belonging to the man I loved before I could put a name to it. Because he was so much more than a name. He was the one who made me feel safe, seen, understood.

My eyes flew open, the bright sun making me wince and blink.

"Take it nice and easy," he murmured, his hands brushing my hair away from my face.

"Colt," I croaked.

He might be more than a name, but I loved that name too.

"Take it slow. No big movements. You've got some stitches."

I took in more of my surroundings now. Windows with industrial-looking blinds. A faint beeping emanating from a heart monitor. An IV. *Hospital.* I was in the hospital.

"You've been in and out for the past two days," Colt explained.

And it was then that I saw the weight of that. The dark circles under his eyes. The scruff that had gotten thicker again.

His Adam's apple bobbed as he swallowed. "They had to remove your spleen. There was a rupture. But you're going to be fine. Just need a few days to recover."

My brows pulled together, and the action made something on my forehead hurt, like I'd hit my head somehow. That tiny flicker of discomfort sent me hurtling back. The RV. The man I thought I knew. Running through the woods. My sister.

"Sully," I rasped, a whole different kind of pain sweeping through me.

A mixture of emotions played across Colt's face. "He's gone. He's never going to hurt another soul."

My chest seized. "Did you—have they—" I wasn't sure how to phrase what I needed to, but Colt could read me without words.

"The FBI has been going over his RV and a storage unit in Alabama for the past thirty or so hours. He kept journals. Maps. Trophies. It turns out his mother was a high-achieving athlete, blond, beautiful. She walked out on him and his father when he was quite young. And it sounds like his dad filled his head with a lot of opinions on women like that—they were both special and the devil incarnate. But there's a history of behavioral issues reaching back to when Shawn was in middle school, ones that should've been a red flag."

Nausea swept through me. "Keep going," I whispered. I needed it all. The Band-Aid ripped off.

"Local law enforcement is searching for twenty-six bodies, the twenty-six he killed out of the thirty-four he victimized." Colt's voice was even, calm, but I knew that wasn't close to how he was feeling.

"He said there were others, but he didn't keep track." The memories kept coming back in flashes, grotesque and terrifying snapshots.

Colt's hands slipped from my face as he straightened. "That's not entirely true. He took driver's licenses from all his kills. They're putting the pieces together. Those families will get their closure."

My eyes burned but I fought back the tears. "Avery?"

Colt moved back to my side, dropping into the chair at my bedside and taking my hand. "Arizona State Police found remains with a necklace that matched the description you gave."

A single tear slid down my cheek. "The silver disc with the lacrosse sticks. The one I gave her for high school graduation."

Colt nodded, lifting my fingers to his lips so that they ghosted along my skin as he spoke. "They're running tests as quickly as possible, but—"

"It's her." I knew it in my bones, my soul, some part of me shifting. "We'll get to put her to rest."

"You'll get to put her to rest," Colt echoed.

"Emerson," I rasped. "Is she okay?"

Those shadows were back in Colt's eyes. "She's worried about you. I think she'll be better now that I can tell her you're awake. She wanted to come, but—"

"No. That's too much, too quick."

The tension in Colt's shoulders eased a fraction. "It'll help. Knowing you said that."

Another memory flickered in my mind. The water. Strong arms pulling me toward the surface. The command to *breathe*.

My eyes flared. "You pulled me out…"

Those shadows danced in his dark depths, but there was heat in them too. "What choice did I have? You jumped off a fucking cliff."

My eyes narrowed. "You didn't have to jump after me."

Colt's hand tightened around mine. "Always going to jump after you."

The tears came a little faster now. "Love you, Law Man."

"Why do you always have to be the one to say it first?" he asked, exasperation lacing his tone.

My eyes danced. "Because you're too slow on the draw."

"I am *not* slow on the draw—"

"They're bickering," an older feminine voice called from the hallway. "Bickering is always a good sign. That was always a precursor to a good time."

"No one needs to hear about our sex life," Norm muttered.

Celia stepped through the doorway, a picnic basket in hand but scowling at Norm. "Oh, shove it, you stodgy old bear."

"Both of you shove it. I gotta see my girl," Sam called, pushing past them and toward my bedside.

"*Your* girl?" Colt asked, glaring at the man old enough to be my grandfather.

"Damn straight, son. Now how are you feeling, Ridley? Do you need me to get the doctor?"

"I brought lunch and dinner," Celia said, pushing in behind him. "You'll never get healed up eating this hospital food."

"Careful," Norm warned. "Her cooking could kill you."

"Oh, shut up. You certainly ate it all last night," Celia shot back. "And it's from Ezra. He wanted to make sure you were taken care of."

"Celia might've brought the food, but I brought your favorite booze," a deep voice called from the doorway. Ace stood there, motorcycle vest on, holding up a bottle of Ransom whiskey and Dean following behind him, a grin on his boyish face.

"You're going to get us all kicked out," Celia bit out.

They started to argue about whether or not whiskey was a banishable offense, and I couldn't help turning to Colt, so much warmth spreading through me.

He dipped his head, pressing his lips to our joined fingers. And I knew, after years of searching, I'd found my home.

Chapter Fifty-Four
Ridley

Four months later

I STOOD BAREFOOT AT THE EDGE OF CONSTELLATION Lake, Colt's lake, the water lapping at my feet, staring out at the horizon as the sun sank lower behind the mountains. It was breathtaking, the beauty of this spot, one that had been so special to Colt all his life and one where I'd found peace too.

A place that had become *ours*.

A place that I'd decided to stay because it was home—thanks to Colt and the people I'd found here. It wasn't the perfect place. There had been more than a little pain in Shady Cove. But there were also people devoted to making it right.

Sophie and Colt had set out making sure that Tara was able to file a civil case against Coach Kerr for statutory rape. But it was Dean who'd found the other piece of the puzzle as he'd set to work on his own podcast. The coach had been dealing opiates and steroids and using students to peddle it.

You might suspect a teenager of dealing some pot in a small town, but the harder stuff? No one had considered they'd been part of the drug problem in the county. And more than that, Kerr had confessed to injecting Jason Kipp with the dose that had sent him stumbling off the side of that lookout. All because Jason had wanted out of Kerr's drug-peddling circle.

Kerr wouldn't be getting out of prison anytime soon, and that was just fine with the people of Shady Cove. They were healing. And Emerson was included in that. She wasn't quite ready for expeditions away from home, but she was spending more time outside, with Trey, and that was the first step.

I was finding that healing too, those first embers of peace. When I placed a hand over my heart, I could feel Avery there. She'd always be with me, no matter where I went. And that would always be far and wide because, despite everything that had happened, I was still determined to give victims a voice.

Now it would just be with Colt at my side. We'd work the cases from here, and then I'd head out on location for a week or two, always eager to return home when I was done—to come back to him.

A throat cleared, pulling me from my thoughts, and I turned to find my dad. He looked different. Not the father he was before Avery vanished or the one in the first years after she was gone; he was someone else entirely. And while I loved all three versions, I liked this one the most.

"You ready?" he asked, a tender smile pulling at his lips. "Your mom is just getting the candles."

I nodded, countless emotions shifting through my chest. "Thanks for doing this."

We'd had a memorial back in Ohio after the officials released Avery to us. I got to hear countless stories about all the lives my sister had touched, all the ways she would live on through that. But there was something I needed to do for me, for us, and the bond that would always be only ours.

My dad moved into my space, something he did easily now.

He pulled me into his arms, resting his chin on my head. "She'd be so proud of you. And she'd love us remembering her this way."

My throat constricted, but it wasn't with pain now. It was with an abundance of gratitude. I'd gotten the privilege of loving Avery for twenty-two years in this life and forever in the next. "I miss her," I whispered.

"That's never going to stop," Dad croaked.

"It's the mark of loving her so deeply."

"It is," he echoed, releasing me at the sound of voices.

We turned to find Colt and my mom walking toward us, Bowser and Tater bounding around them. Colt's and my creatures had found their rhythm too. They got along best when causing us massive amounts of trouble, but we'd take it however we could get it.

I took their arrival as my sign. I bent to pick up the wreath of wildflowers, one with pale pinks I knew Avery would love. It housed a packet of ashes—one made of a special material that would dissolve slowly in the water once she made it beyond the shallows, to where she'd finally find her peace.

As I straightened, strong arms engulfed me, pulling me into a body that was always my refuge. Colt's lips brushed my temple. "You okay?"

I nodded against his chest. "It's time."

My mom sent me a wobbly smile as the sun sank beneath the mountains and the first stars began to glimmer. "Those starry skies were always her favorite."

My eyes filled as I returned her smile. "From the first perfect constellation on our ceiling."

Mom laughed, some tears leaking out with it. "I cursed getting you girls those glow-in-the-dark stickers. You put them everywhere."

I swallowed down the memories, holding them close. "But now they'll light her way home."

My mom nodded, sniffling as she lit the candles Colt held. He in turn gave one to her and my dad, while he held on to the other. We all stood there quietly for a moment, the animals stilling as if reading our mood. I held the wreath with one hand and placed the other over my heart.

"I carry you always," I whispered.

Stepping out of Colt's hold, I moved into the water, its cooling temperatures swirling up to my knees. I set the wreath down and, with a gentle push, finally set Avery free.

Colt met me in the shallows, as he always did, my feet sinking into the sandy floor, the earth closing over the tops of my toes. But I felt no panic. Only peace. Because I knew Colt would always lead me out of the shallows and into that bit of starlight we'd stolen for ourselves.

Epilogue
Ridley

One year later

I didn't want to brag, but I had the best view in the house. This massive three-paned window in Emerson's art studio looked out on her backyard, one that Trey had tended for her all the years she couldn't do it herself, which they were now tending together. Because Emerson was getting braver and braver when it came to living a life outside of these four walls.

But today would be a stretch of that bravery. Because all my and Colt's loved ones were filling the back garden. When Colt had asked me to marry him, there were only two places I considered: by our cabin on the lake or here, the first place I'd told Colt I loved him.

He'd wanted me to be sure. Certain that nothing from my attack would taint this day for me. But how could it when we were surrounded by so much love?

I grinned as I saw Dean in a black-on-black suit, complete with black nail polish. He was giving Ace the hard press. Ace was Dean's mentor, and I knew Dean had his heart set on covering the Devils motorcycle club in his next podcast season. Thankfully, Ace found him amusing instead of thinking him a threat. And I had to say he looked quite dapper in a black dress shirt with tiny skull buttons.

But he didn't have anything on my Sam. My surrogate grandfather, who'd taken it upon himself to teach me chess, was wearing his usual snazzy suspenders adorned with chess pieces and a red bow tie. He chatted with Mira, who was a vision in a sundress covered in delicate flowers. Maybe they would be the next two to pair up.

Norm and Celia had shocked the hell out of us when they'd eloped to Vegas and come back hitched. They still fought like cats and dogs, leaving Norm on the couch half the time. But Celia said it kept them young.

Movement caught my attention. Trey and Emerson on the edge of the grass. His head was bent, and even from this distance, I could tell he spoke gentle words to her. It wasn't a gentleness borne of thinking she was weak. It was one that came because of her importance to him.

Trey's hand lifted, brushing a stray strand of hair back from Emerson's face. I grinned so widely I thought my face might crack in two.

"What's got you grinning like a fool?" my mom asked as she slipped inside the studio.

I motioned her over to me, wrapping an arm around her waist. She'd put on healthy weight in the past sixteen months and gained back the muscle she'd lost by staying locked up inside for so long. But her body wasn't the only thing that was healing—her heart was too. And our relationship had mended with it.

I tipped my head against hers as I pointed to Trey and Emerson. She let out a soft squeal, the sound more befitting a young teen than a woman in her late sixties. "Are they…?"

"I'm not sure," I told her honestly. "But they watch each other.

Sometimes I swear they orbit one another as if the other is the sun."

My mom sighed. "That kind of love."

"It's a beautiful thing."

She turned to me then, brushing my hair away from my face. I'd left it wild because Colt liked it that way. There'd be no fancy updos or makeup artists on hand. It simply wasn't me. But I was wearing lace.

I'd found the dress in a secondhand shop while on location for a case. Something about the little store in Biloxi had called to me, and I'd wandered inside. I'd found the rack of wedding dresses in the back corner, and this one had nearly jumped into my hands.

The cream lace was almost a soft peach, and it had a bohemian vibe that matched me perfectly. It was fitting—giving something a second life spoke to me on so many levels.

"You're beautiful. The home you've built is beautiful. And so is the family," my mom whispered.

My eyes welled. "I wish she were here."

God, did I ever want that. More than anything. To have Avery join me at the end of the aisle, holding my bouquet of wildflowers for me. To have her as a part of this family.

"Oh, baby." My mom pulled me into her arms. "She is here. *You* taught me that."

She was. I knew that. She'd been the one who'd gotten me through my darkest moments, and I felt her in all the best ones. She was here today too. Just like she'd be with me every moment after.

A soft knock sounded on the door, and Mom released me, crossing to it. She opened it a fraction. "Colter Brooks, you can't be here. It's bad luck to see the bride before the wedding."

I couldn't help but laugh. "Watch out, Law Man; she's full-naming you."

I heard his answering chuckle from the other side of the door. "I'm going to go ahead and say we've already gotten through our dose of bad luck. And I need to give Chaos her wedding present."

My mom frowned but nodded. "Oh, all right. But not too long; we're about to start."

She hurried out of the room, leaving Colt to come inside. The moment I saw him in his dark-blue suit, I nearly died on the spot. He'd never looked more gorgeous. His dark hair was tamed but had dried with that slight wave I loved. And he'd left just a little scruff at my begging.

"Have I ever told you that you have *great* shoulders, Law Man?"

"Ridley," he growled. "I do not have time to fuck you before this ceremony."

A laugh bubbled out of me. "Fair enough."

He came to a stop a few steps from me, those storm eyes roaming over me. "Never seen a more beautiful sight. Not once. I'm the luckiest bastard alive."

My mouth curved. "Come here."

Colt listened to me for once in his life and closed the distance. His fingers tangled in my locks, and his mouth took mine with comfortable ease. A mix of heart and heat, and everything I needed to remember exactly what we were building.

When he eased back, those dark eyes searched mine. "Got you something I thought you might want to carry with your bouquet."

My brows pulled together in puzzlement. I already had my *borrowed* and *blue* thanks to Mom, and my *new* were the cowboy boots on my feet. So I had no idea what he might be adding to the array.

Colt slipped a hand into his pocket and pulled out something I'd palmed in my hand too many times to count. Something I'd traced as often as I breathed. Something I'd thought I would never get back.

"The FBI said I couldn't have it," I croaked, taking in the key chain that had once been Avery's, the same key chain that had set me free.

"They made an exception," he rasped.

"Colter Brooks, did you threaten to kill someone to get this?"

"Full-naming me, baby?" he asked, amusement clear in his voice.

"Yes, because I don't want the FBI busting into my wedding to take you down."

Colt grinned and lifted my hand, sliding the key ring onto the same finger as the diamond he'd put there. "I wanted you to have her, today of all days."

The tears crested, a couple spilling down my cheeks. "Colt."

"She's with us. Had a talk with her this morning. Thanked her for bringing you to me. For giving me back a life with light and joy and belief in the good."

More tears fell. "Colt, you helped me find all the missing pieces. Even the ones I didn't realize I needed."

He brushed his lips against mine, taking my tears with him. "Love you, Chaos."

"Love you, Law Man."

He searched my eyes. "Want to go make that permanent?"

"Never been more ready for anything."

Reading Group Guide

1. Ridley's sister disappears at the beginning of the book. How has this influenced Ridley's life and changed her career trajectory? Do you think the main goal of Ridley's career is to find her sister?

2. Why do you think Ridley and Colt are drawn to each other? Do you think it is purely a physical attraction at first, or are they linked in a greater way?

3. Why do you think Colt finally lays off Ridley when he realizes her sister was kidnapped too? Do you think he finally starts to understand what she's trying to do?

4. Why do you think Emerson trusts Ridley more than others? What has Ridley given or said to Em to make her want to trust and believe her?

5. Colt accuses Ridley of a crime after apologizing for his initial bad behavior toward her. Why do you think Ridley doesn't want to forgive him this time around? How has he hurt her?

6. Why do you think Colt offers Ridley a place to stay at his house after her attack? Do you think Ridley starts to realize how she truly feels about him while she stays with him? What are they providing for each other during this time?

7. Colt finally starts to let Ridley have more say in the investigation once he gets to know her better while she's living in his house. What do you think it means to Ridley to have someone believe her? Why do you think Colt has more empathy for Ridley than others previously have?

8. What does Ridley do for Emerson that creates a bond between them? Why do you think Emerson decides to tell Ridley her story?

9. Ridley is kidnapped at the end of the story, and she discovers that she has known the murderer for years. How do you think Sully pulled off all his lies? Why did he target Ridley and Avery?

10. Colt saves Ridley and she finally has peace over her sister's disappearance. Do you think Avery helped to bring Colt and Ridley together?

Author Q&A

Hi, Catherine! This is such a beautiful, suspenseful story. When you started your career as an author, were you always interested in writing romantic suspense?

I have loved books with mysteries since I discovered Nancy Drew and the Baby-Sitters Club: Mysteries. There is just something about suspense that heightens all the other story elements, and I knew when I started writing that mystery and suspense would have to be a part of what I created.

Where do you get your story ideas? Do they come to you in the middle of the night, or are they fleshed out through many months of work?

I always describe my process like a jigsaw puzzle. An element can come from anywhere: true-crime podcast, small-town news article, someone I see walking down the street. I'll start keeping a list of pieces in my phone for a book and add to it over time until it's completely fleshed out and I'm ready to plot the entire thing.

I love Ridley's fierceness and loyalty and Colt's strong desire to protect. Do you have a favorite character in *All the Missing Pieces*?

For me, it's Emerson. Her quiet strength and growth over the story were so fun to write. And I admire her so damn much. Plus, I think she is the missing piece that brought Ridley and Colt together.

Many characters in *All the Missing Pieces* accuse Ridley of bringing up trauma and sticking her nose where it doesn't belong. How did you walk the line between Ridley helping others, but also potentially hurting them by bringing up past trauma?

It's all about consent. Ridley is a champion of the truth, but she never pushes anyone to talk about something they aren't ready to discuss, even when it hurts her case.

Was it difficult to write Emerson, a character who has had a great trauma happen in her life? How did you approach writing her character?

I am a self-professed theater nerd and studied acting for many years, which meant a lot of learning how to break down scripts and find inroads with characters. It always began with me finding one way in which the character and I were similar. The same is true when writing. I always have to find that hook into the character and build out from there. In Emerson's case, the building-out process included research and a sensitivity reader to make sure I could get those trauma pieces as accurate as possible.

Most of your books take place on the west coast of America. What do you love about the west coast?

I am a Pacific Northwest girlie at heart. Anywhere from upper

NorCal through Washington. For me, the landscape is so specific and a little wild. I think it becomes a character in the books, and I absolutely love that.

Acknowledgments

If you've read one of my books before, you know I'm partial to the acknowledgments portion of the story. I love the practice of sitting down at the end of that first round of edits and thinking about all the people who helped turn a spark of an idea into a bound and published book headed for shelves.

First, I'd be remiss if I didn't thank the inspiration for this story...PODCASTS. I am huge true-crime podcast fangirl, and podcast fangirl in general. So I have to give a shout-out to some of my favorites. *Armchair Expert*, my first listen each and every week, and a show that makes me move through the human experience with more thoughtfulness and empathy. And of course, my true-crime favorites: *Up and Vanished*, *Serial*, *To Live and Die in LA*, *Your Own Backyard*, *The Teacher's Pet*, *Dirty John*, *Sweet Bobby*, and probably eighty-two million more.

A massive thank-you to my very own audio experts, Willow and Nate, for answering endless questions about podcasting and recording in general, and for reading all the passages where Ridley was recording to make sure I didn't bungle anything too badly.

This book has had so many loving hands on it, helping me to make it the best it could possibly be, and they all deserve epic rounds of applause. Kimberly, thank you for loving this idea and championing the story. I'm so lucky to have you in my corner. Gretchen, thank you from the bottom of my heart for your excitement about this book, along with your insights, ideas, and answering of endless questions. Tooth hugs and candy addictions forever! Aimee, thank you for loving this book, your perspective, and helping to make it sing. To my fearless betas who read this story in its roughest form: Jess, Jill, Kelly, Kristie, Tori, Sam, and Trisha. To Chelle and Julie for being a final set of eyes and always making my words sing. And to everyone at Sourcebooks Casablanca who has been so warm, welcoming, and endlessly supportive, but especially Christa, Gretchen, Alyssa, and Katie.

Romance books have given me a lot of things, but at the top of that list are incredible friends that I am so lucky to have in my life. An extra-special thank-you to Samantha Young for handholding through my first traditionally published book; I truly wouldn't have made it through without you from start to finish.

To Elsie Silver, who screamed even louder for me than I did for myself when this deal came through, and made sure the book actually got finished. To Rebecca Jenshak, who talked me through countless edits (and one spiral) and assured me I could do it when I wanted to throw in the towel. To Laura Pavlov, who made me laugh during a time when stress had me wanting to hide under the covers, and played the *Rocky* theme song as many times as I needed. To Willow Aster, who lent me her podcast expertise, her kindness, and her encouragement. To Kandi Steiner, for countless voice-memo pep talks as only she can. To the Lance Bass Fan Club: Lauren Asher, Ana Huang, and Elsie Silver, for helping me navigate the trad world for the first time and always sending the best NSYNC memes. To Jess, who always supports and listens through endless plotting voice memos. To Paige, who makes me cackle with story times and possible plot twists. Thank you all for walking this path with me. I love you to the moon and back.

To the most amazing hype squad ever, my STS soul sisters Hollis, Jael, and Paige, thank you for the gift of true friendship and sisterhood. I always feel the most supported and celebrated thanks to you.

To all my incredible family and friends who have cheered and supported me through all the ups and downs of the past few months, I am incredibly grateful for each and every one of you, but especially my mom. Thank you for all you do.

The crew that helps bring my words to life and gets them out into the world is pretty darn epic. Thank you to Devyn, Jess, Tori, Kimberly, Joy, and my team at Brower Literary. Your hard work is so appreciated!

To all the reviewers and content creators who have taken a chance on my words...THANK YOU! Your championing of my stories means more than I can say. And to my launch and influencer teams, thank you for your kindness, support, and sharing my books with the world.

Ladies of Catherine Cowles Reader Group, you're my favorite place to hang out on the internet! Thank you for your support, encouragement, and willingness to always dish about your latest book boyfriends. You're the freaking best!

Lastly, thank YOU! Yes, YOU. I'm so grateful you're reading this book and making my author dreams come true. I love you for that. A whole lot!

About the Author

Writer of words. Drinker of Diet Cokes. Lover of all things cute and furry, especially her dog. *USA Today* bestselling author Catherine Cowles has had her nose in a book since the time she could read and finally decided to write down some of her own stories. When she's not writing, she can be found exploring her home state of Oregon, listening to true-crime podcasts, or searching for her next book boyfriend.

Website: catherinecowles.com
Facebook: catherinecowlesauthor
Facebook Reader Group: CatherineCowlesReaderGroup
Instagram: catherinecowlesauthor
Goodreads: catherinecowlesauthor
BookBub: catherine-cowles
Pinterest: catherinecowlesauthor
TikTok: catherinecowlesauthor

Also by Catherine Cowles

The Tattered & Torn Series
Tattered Stars
Falling Embers
Hidden Waters
Shattered Sea
Fractured Sky

Sparrow Falls
Fragile Sanctuary
Delicate Escape
Broken Harbor
Beautiful Exile
Chasing Shelter
Secret Haven

The Lost & Found Series
Whispers of You
Echoes of You
Glimmers of You
Shadows of You
Ashes of You

The Wrecked Series
Reckless Memories
Perfect Wreckage
Wrecked Palace
Reckless Refuge
Beneath the Wreckage

The Sutter Lake Series
Beautifully Broken Pieces
Beautifully Broken Life
Beautifully Broken Spirit
Beautifully Broken Control
Beautifully Broken Redemption

Standalone Novels
Further to Fall
All the Missing Pieces

For a full list of up-to-date Catherine Cowles titles, please visit www.catherinecowles.com.